THE
MAGICIANS
OF MAZDA

ABOUT THE AUTHOR

Ashwin Sanghi is among India's highest-selling English fiction authors. He has written several bestsellers in the Bharat Series (*The Rozabal Line, Chanakya's Chant, The Krishna Key, The Sialkot Saga, Keepers of the Kalachakra, The Vault of Vishnu*) and two *New York Times* bestselling crime thrillers with James Patterson, *Private India* (sold in the US as *City on Fire*) and *Private Delhi* (sold in the US as *Count to Ten*). He has also co-authored several non-fiction titles in the 13 Steps Series on Luck, Wealth, Marks, Health and Parenting.

Ashwin has been included by *Forbes India* in their Celebrity 100 and by *The New Indian Express* in their Culture Power List. He is a winner of the Crossword Popular Choice Award 2012, Atta Galatta Popular Choice Award 2018, WBR Iconic Achievers Award 2018, the Lit-O-Fest Literature Legend Award 2018 and the Kalinga Popular Choice Award 2021.

He was educated at Cathedral and John Connon School, Mumbai, and St Xavier's College, Mumbai. He holds an MBA from Yale University. Ashwin lives in Mumbai with his wife, Anushika, and son, Raghuvir.

You can connect with Ashwin via the following channels:Website www.sanghi.in

Twitter @ashwinsanghi
Instagram @ashwin.sanghi

Koo @ashwinsanghi
Clubhouse @ashwinsanghi
Facebook fb.com/ashwinsanghi
YouTube youtube.com/ashwinsanghi
LinkedIn linkedin.com/in/ashwinsanghi

ACKNOWLEDGEMENTS

IT WOULD BE impossible to write the books that I do without the assistance, input, guidance, love and support of so many. Here are some of those without whom this book may not have happened.

My publishers, HarperCollins Publishers India—in particular, Ananth Padmanabhan and Udayan Mitra, who have ensured that this book reaches my readers quickly and efficiently.

Prita Maitra, my primary editor, who continues to be indispensable in editing the Bharat Series; Ashok Rajani, my perfectly ruthless fact-checker; Swati Daftuar, whose eye for detail has given this story its final shine.

Rupesh Talaskar, my talented illustrator, who meticulously executed the map and illustrations to complete the narrative, and Semy Haitenlo, who provided us with a stunning visual to crown the book.

Ameya Naik, the versatile composer who conceived the haunting track used in the book's trailer, and the team at Oktobuzz for the outstanding video trailer and social media support.

Deepshikha Kumar and Nijansh Verma of SpeakIn for their advice and input on my speaking tours and events. Also, Ashoo Naik and Chirag Nihalani of Collective for their efforts towards bringing my stories to a wider audience through cinema, television and OTT.

My parents, Mahendra and Manju Sanghi, and my siblings, Vidhi and Vaibhav, who have always encouraged me to follow my dreams. My wife, Anushika, and son, Raghuvir, who have been my constant support in my writing endeavours. Had it not been for their unconditional love, none of my books would have been possible. My little rakhi-sister Farah, who has taught me that not everything in life can be explained and that some things are better left unexplained.

Gautam Padmanabhan, my friend, philosopher and guide who gave me my first publishing break and has encouraged me through several stories including this one.

The late Ramprasad and Ramgopal Gupta, my maternal grandfather and maternal granduncle, who inspired me with their stories and books. Their blessings prevent the ink in my pen from running dry.

Previous Titles in the Bharat Series

The Rozabal Line (2008)

'In *The Rozabal Line*, Ashwin Sanghi does a Dan Brown by mixing all the ingredients of a thriller—crusades, action, adventure, suspense—and pulling off, with dexterity and ease, a narrative that careens through cultures and continents, religions and cults.' ~*The Asian Age*

'*The Rozabal Line* by Ashwin Sanghi is a kickass thriller that forces you to re-examine our histories, our faiths.' ~Pritish Nandy

'Sanghi's flair for religion, history and politics is clearly visible as he takes the reader across the world spanning different decades. A mixture of comparative religion, dangerous secrets, and a thrilling plot makes for an esoteric read.' ~*The Statesman*

'Sanghi has got the sure-fire formula right.' ~ *The Times of India*

'A provocative, clever and radiant line of theology, Sanghi suggests that the cult of Mary Magdalene has its true inspiration in the trinity of the Indian sacred feminine, thereby out-thinking and out-conspiring Dan Brown.' ~*The Hindu*

Chanakya's Chant (2010)

'With internal monologues and descriptions as taut as a-held-by-the-thumb sacred thread, we have Ashwin Sanghi's cracker of a page-turner, *Chanakya's Chant*. Two narratives flow like the Ganga and Yamuna ... a brisk technicoloured thriller.' *~Hindustan Times*

'I'm utterly enthralled. A delightfully interesting and gripping read. The historical research is deeply impressive ...' ~Shashi Tharoor

'A gripping, fast-paced read, the novel is a true thriller in the tradition set by Dan Brown.' *~People Magazine*

'Political grooming and conspiracy remain at the core of Ashwin Sanghi's historical thriller. Bloodshed, legal trials, betrayals, murders, assassination attempts and all that which make this into a page-turner.' *~Sakaal Times*

'Released in India to wide acclaim, *Chanakya's Chant* is a political page-turner.' *~Business India*

The Krishna Key (2012)

'Why should racy historical thrillers or meaty fantasy sagas come only from the minds of Western writers? Ashwin Sanghi spins his yarns well and leaves you breathless at every cliff-hanger. No wonder his books are bestsellers!' *~Hindustan Times*

'While the plot is set in today's world, one can expect to travel back and forth in time with generous chunks of history and nail-biting fiction.' ~*The Telegraph*

'An alternative interpretation of the Vedic Age that will be relished by conspiracy buffs and addicts of thrillers alike.' ~*The Hindu*

'Just finished *The Krishna Key* by Ashwin Sanghi. Rocking story and incredible research. Loved it!' ~Amish Tripathi

'Sanghi manages to blur the line between fact and fiction and give a whole new perspective to history and the Vedic Age.' ~*DNA*

The Sialkot Saga (2016)

'*The Sialkot Saga* moves at a breakneck pace hurtling through time and space uncovering ancient secrets and burying modern ones.' ~*The Hindu*

'The book spreads across decades and centuries, till it reaches present day India and will sure have both historic and thriller readers in for a treat.' ~ *The Times of India*

'There are books that take time to develop an interest and then there are books that grip you from the very first page. *The Sialkot Saga* is one such book that hooks you from the start.' ~*Hindustan Times*

'There's never a dull moment in the book. In fact, the story takes on such a pace that the overwhelmed reader is compelled to put the book down and take a deep breath on many an occasion.' ~ *The Financial Express*

'Sanghi weaves a masterpiece building up the readers' involvement in the novel with every turn of the page.' ~ *The Pioneer*

Keepers of the Kalachakra (2018)

'The book can't be put down till all pieces of the jigsaw puzzle are put together.' ~*The Financial Express*

'The author packs a powerful punch … spicy and saucy, a survey of the past and the present … without a dull moment, without a dull page.' ~*The Sunday Standard*

'Science and spirituality collide in Ashwin Sanghi's latest thriller.' ~*India Today*

'Spread over a vast canvas, the novel has an engaging plot laced with mythology, history and legends.' ~*The Hindu*

'Ashwin Sanghi's *Keepers of the Kalachakra* is as explosive as a time bomb ticking in your hand. Every chapter springs an unpredictable surprise.' ~*Deccan Chronicle*

'*Keepers of the Kalachakra* has it all: political characters that remind you of real-life politicians, a racy, complex plot and enough improbable twists to keep you hooked.' *~Hindustan Times Brunch*

The Vault of Vishnu (2020)

'In an enthralling alchemy of myth and science, Ashwin Sanghi gives us the sixth book in his Bharat Series. As with all Ashwin's books, the research is meticulous and the technical(ese) leaves one gasping as *The Vault of Vishnu* takes the reader through the highs and lows of history, myth, physics, warfare technology, AI and biochemistry.' *~The Times of India*

'*The Vault of Vishnu*, like all of Ashwin's books, is a heady mix of history, myth, science and thrills.' *~The Hindu*

'A very interesting and intriguing thriller, thanks to the author's storytelling gift and painstaking research on Hindu metaphysics.' *~The New Indian Express*

'Sanghi's latest work uses his favourite tool—mythology—and blends it with history to deliver some edge-of-the-seat action.' *~Hindustan Times*

ASHWIN SANGHI

THE MAGICIANS OF MAZDA

HarperCollins *Publishers* India

First published in India by HarperCollins *Publishers* 2022
4th Floor, Tower A, Building No. 10, Phase II, DLF Cyber City,
Gurugram, Haryana – 122002
www.harpercollins.co.in

2 4 6 8 10 9 7 5 3 1

Copyright © Ashwin Sanghi 2022

P-ISBN: 978-93-5489-908-9
E-ISBN: 978-93-5489-882-2

This is a work of fiction and all characters and incidents described in this book are the product of the author's imagination. Any resemblance to actual persons, living or dead, is entirely coincidental.

Ashwin Sanghi asserts the moral right to be identified as the author of this work.

Typeset in 11/14.7 Minion Pro at
Manipal Technologies Limited, Manipal

Printed and bound at
Thomson Press (India) Ltd

This book is produced from independently certified FSC® paper to ensure responsible forest management.

Salutations to Maa Shakti, the One who powers my pen.
Thank you, Maa, for your abundant blessings.
I am nothing without you.

Yatha ahu vairyo atha ratush ashat chit hacha
Vangheush dazda manangho shyothananam
angheush mazdai
Kshathrem cha ahurai a yim daregobyo dadat vastarem.

—Yasna 27:13, *Zend Avesta*

DISCLAIMER

This book is a work of fiction. Names, characters, places and events are either the products of the author's imagination or used in a fictitious manner. Any resemblance to actual persons, living or dead, or actual events is purely coincidental. Historical, religious or mythological characters; historical or legendary events; or names of places are always used fictitiously. No claim regarding historical or theological accuracy is either made or implied. Historical, religious or mythological characters, events or places, are always used fictitiously and deviations from the accepted record also occur within the narrative. Images and maps are for illustrative purposes only and are presented without any claim of accuracy.

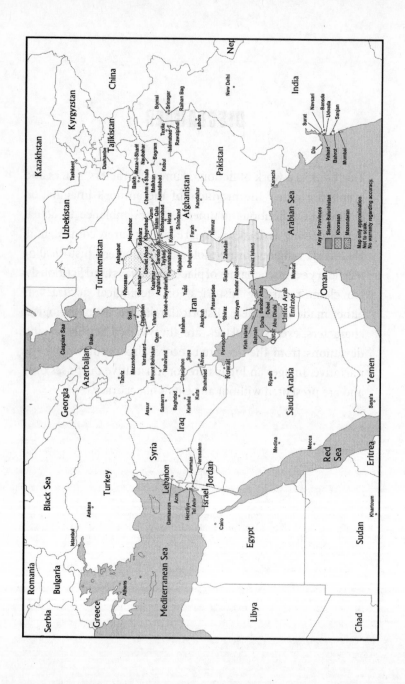

PROLOGUE

THE FIFTY-FIVE-YEAR-OLD MAN made his deliberate way up to the stage. He was dressed in a no-fuss blue blazer and khaki trousers, a deep-red tie matching the scarlet square that peeped from his pocket. The smile on his face was a friendly one, softening any severity of feature and signalling a singular approachability. Quite unlike someone who had won the Kettering Prize just last year. He walked up to the podium slowly and looked at the audience. He swept his gaze over the politicians, academicians, businessmen and bureaucrats who were applauding.

The din subsided the moment he placed his hands on the lectern and leaned into the microphone. In the expectant silence that followed, he began, 'Some four centuries before Christ, the Greek Hippocrates told his pupils, "Declare the past, diagnose the present, foretell the future." But then, he was the *father* of medicine. Had anyone asked *me* to foretell the future when I was a young graduate from Stanford, I'd have been stumped. And had anyone then pointed out to me how inextricably the past is linked to our future, I would have … laughed.'

The hall at Oxford could have been a museum, each wall lined end to end with portraits of renowned monarchs, artists and scientists, each bathed in the light filtering in through exquisite stained-glass windows. The ceiling was a flawless example of a sixteenth-century hammerbeam roof, the timber, untampered by veneer, aglow. It could have been the interior of a vast Gothic cathedral. He took it all in without appearing to look and paused reverently.

'But here we are in the present,' he picked up his theme, 'celebrating a future that has been fashioned from our past. And why? Because, at every point in experience, history, philosophy, science and our lives ahead *do* intersect. I have come to believe, as I hope you will, that it is foolish to describe them as discrete entities. I declare that we have been misled on that. Any scientist worth his lab coat *has* to be a philosopher. Just like the greatest philosophers have thrown their weight behind science.'

'In Japan,' continued the speaker, 'there lived a great Zen master during the Meiji era. One day, a scholar came to him for an explanation of his philosophy. The master poured the visitor a cup of tea from a kettle. He continued to pour even after the cup was full. The scholar saw that the tea was spilling over the cup and said, "Stop, Master. There's no more room for tea in the cup."'

The speaker paused, allowing the image to sink in. Then he continued, 'The Zen master smiled at his guest and said, "The cup has a limited capacity—like you. You have filled yourself with opinions, beliefs, prejudices and attitudes before coming to me. How can I possibly show you Zen, unless you are willing to empty your cup first?" Over the past decade, I have tried my best to be that proverbial empty cup.

'Indian gurus have said that true wisdom lies in knowing that one knows nothing. I am grateful to the universe for having taught me that. I proudly stand before you today as the man who knows nothing. And I raise a toast to my friend Jim Dastoor, who is dead.'

The audience rose to their feet as one, in a long, rapturous ovation. Still clasping the lectern, the Kettering Prize awardee examined the cufflinks on his shirtsleeves. He no longer sensed the public's adulation as his mind travelled back to the friends he had lost in his quest.

1

THE MAN IN uniform had not known that pulling a trigger was so easy.

That rainy evening, he had walked with a group of security guards along Great Russell Street in the fashionable and busy Bloomsbury district of London. They side-stepped the vehicle-distancing bollards and walked through the gate of a black iron fence. Then they cut across a yard to reach a neoclassical building dating from the Georgian era. Over 300 men and women were part of the elite unit that guarded the British Museum at all times.

The museum housed eight million objects within an expanse of 75,000 square metres. On most days, around 17,000 visitors walked into its hallowed halls. Established in 1753, the place was often in the news for all the wrong reasons. After all, most of the exhibits had been sourced from around the world when Britannia reigned. Britain's colonial past had come under severe scrutiny, one reason being the 'looting' of national treasures from conquered lands.

Not that this knowledge dimmed the curiosity of its gawking visitors.

The museum hosted some of the world's most priceless objects. These included the Rosetta Stone, the key to deciphering Egyptian hieroglyphs. There was the colossal granite head of Amenhotep III, the pharaoh who ruled Egypt between 1390 and 1325 BCE. Another precious item was the Sutton Hoo Ship burial helmet worn by an East Anglian king from the seventh century CE. And then there was the most famous item of all, the ancient Cyrus Cylinder. On its clay surface was written, in Akkadian cuneiform, a declaration by the great Achaemenid king, Cyrus, in the sixth century BCE.

This evening, after a quick but thorough inspection, the group of guards crossed the Queen Elizabeth II Great Court with its high steel-and-glass lattice roof. The area had once been open to sky but had been redeveloped as a covered enclosure sheltering the treasures in the surrounding galleries.

One of the guards from the group broke away covertly and headed towards Room 52, one of the several galleries that dotted the museum. Once he was within spitting distance of '52', he hid himself in a supply closet that he had identified some days earlier. He had already obtained the schematics of the museum that showed locations of the security cameras in the area. That had been easy enough, given his access to the security command centre. The entire museum was a high-security zone, integrating cameras, alarms, access control and a digital radio system.

Inside the closet, the man sat and waited.

By 5 pm the security team began escorting visitors out while courteously thanking them for having come. An hour later, caterers entered. By 7 pm, the entire Great Court had been transformed by an elegant arrangement of damask-covered tables, flowers and dinnerware for a corporate event. The wining and dining wrapped up by 10 pm.

By midnight, the relentless hum of life below the beautiful roof of the Great Court stilled. A dense silence permeated the cavernous galleries that circled it, each one bursting with artefacts that represented multiple arcs of human history. Some said that the museum was haunted and that one could hear strange sounds at night. But tonight, even the ghosts had apparently taken time off.

A little after midnight, the door to the supply closet opened. The guard stepped out and made his way towards Case Number Four, Exhibit No. 1880.0617.1941. On his way, he carefully avoided the laser barriers that were scattered across the room. Planning a path that would remain out of view of the cameras and yet dodge the beams had been difficult but the drills to overcome these challenges had been patiently rehearsed days in advance.

Within minutes, he was in front of the glass case that contained what he was after: the Cyrus Cylinder. The words had been inscribed at the behest of Cyrus the Great, who had ruled the vast kingdom of Persia around 2600 years ago.

The guard pressed a sequence of keys on his mobile with gloved fingers. The sequence activated a bug that would freeze the camera that pointed towards the display case, but only for sixty seconds. He fished out a diamond cutter from his bag and applied a suction cup to the area that he planned to cut. He worked quickly and methodically, ensuring that his tool created a circular cut of even depth in the glass. He then used the suction cup to gently prise out the cut portion and reached inside to grasp the cylinder.

'Hey, you!' a voice cried from another part of the hall. The thief froze and cursed under his breath. He had managed to overcome the best of security technology, only to be screwed by human intervention. There should have been no one on rounds in this area at this time. Murphy's law. He forced himself to focus on the job at hand. He delicately lifted out the cylinder that was less than thirty centimetres in length and placed it in his bag. Then he swung around to face the direction of the voice.

'What do you think you're doing?' said the woman as she ran towards him. She was a little startled to see that he was a security guard like herself. Her mad dash towards him quickly tripped the laser beams. A shrill alarm was triggered.

The thief realised that desperate times called for desperate measures. He pulled out the Colt 1911 from his holster and pointed it at the running figure as she approached him. He had never used it before. He paused just momentarily before pulling the trigger. The guard crumpled to the floor as blood spurted from her abdomen.

The thief now ran towards the East Stairs, no longer paying any attention to cameras or beams. He quickly emerged in the Great Court from where he sprinted towards the exit at Montague Place. He knew that perimeter control would get activated within a few moments. In such an eventuality, his electronic pass would no longer function. He made it with just a few seconds to spare.

Quickly mounting the motorbike that had been parked there for him, he zipped away into the dark and misty night of London.

2

SHE WAS BLISSFULLY unaware that four intruders lurked inside her home.

The morning alarm on her iPhone had been set to the ringtone of music from a harp. It started softly, then gradually gathered volume until Linda stirred. She looked at the phone on the dock for the time. It said 6 am.

Surprised to see that Jim's side of the bed had not been slept in, she got out of bed, stretched, sighed and pulled on her tracksuit and sneakers. Then she picked up the book she had been reading at night, Fitzgerald's translation of *The Rubaiyat of Omar Khayyam*, meaning to return to it after her morning routine. Then she made her way out of the master bedroom.

The house was a picturesque five-bedroom structure that overlooked Lake Union, one of the nicest areas of Seattle. From the outside, it looked like a cedar-wood cabin but inside it was minimalist and modern with polished concrete floors and a globular stainless-steel fireplace prominently installed in the centre of the living room. Large plateglass windows provided a breathtaking vista of the lake and the boats that dotted it.

It was Linda's habit to wake up early and put herself through an hour of yoga and thirty minutes of swimming before starting her day. Before she commenced her fitness regime, though, she would always get the coffee started for Jim and herself—Hawaiian Kona. An old habit from their courtship days, that particular routine never varied.

Although in her late forties, Linda maintained the figure of a teen, which was hardly surprising considering the care she took to exercise. This, in addition to the undimmed brightness of her eyes, her dimples and the shining golden hair, was just part of the package Jim Dastoor had fallen in love with on their first date, and what kept him as devoted as a dog even two decades into marriage.

Linda made her way to Jim's study. *Maybe he had worked through the night at his desk?* But the study was empty. She quickly scanned the messages on her phone. Jim had texted her at around midnight when she had been fast asleep. His text said that he was going to be pulling an all-nighter at the laboratory and that he would see her for breakfast at home.

She sighed and made her way to the kitchen to fix the Kona. Omar Khayyam had advised, 'Be happy for this moment. This moment is your life.' Linda immersed herself in the coffee ritual. In Zen Buddhism, a simple tea ceremony was often used by monks as a means to transformation and awakening. It forced one to observe the interdependence of wood, fire, water, tea, metal and earth. To simply *be* in the moment.

Linda remained oblivious to the fact that around thirty minutes before her alarm had gone off, two black Toyota RAV4 vehicles had bypassed the biometric access system at the main gate. The occupants had used a 3D thumbprint embedded on a vinyl glove. The gate had smoothly rolled away to welcome the intruders. The two vehicles had silently glided down the driveway and come to a halt at the porch. Four men dressed in dark blue jeans, black hoodies, soft sneakers, gloves and balaclavas had stepped out from the SUVs.

One of the men had quickly gotten to work on the control panel, the simple computer that armed and disarmed the security system of the house. Over previous days, the team had used high-resolution drones to survey the property and had succeeded in capturing the keystrokes required for access to the main door. There was a soft beep as the control panel allowed them entrance.

Once inside, they quietly fanned out, searching the living room, the study, as well as the bedrooms, omitting only the master bedroom where Linda lay asleep. Just as they were about to enter her bedroom, her alarm rang. The men, who were just outside the master bedroom when Linda walked out, hurriedly hid themselves in the guest bedroom, a room adjacent to and adjoining Jim's study.

In the kitchen, she filled the ground Kona into the filter cup and topped up the water as she perfunctorily scanned through the assorted alerts and news on her phone. Although her attention was on the phone, she discerned a brief movement through the corner of her eye.

But it was too late. The men stormed in before she could react.

Two of them grabbed her, sending her coffee mug crashing to the floor. They pinned her to the kitchen counter, while a third efficiently bound her wrists and sealed her mouth with duct tape. Her eyes rolled around wildly in panic as they brought her under their control. Her phone fell to the ground but did not shatter, its protective case shielding it.

Owing to her fitness and strength, she would have been a handful for any ordinary abductor, but it wasn't a fair fight. She kicked one of the abductors with her unbound legs and caught him in his crotch. He doubled over in pain but recovered smartly, his hoodie getting snagged and torn on the oven grill as he came up. She soon lay on the kitchen floor, struggling but incapacitated. A bloodstain formed on the floor. Linda's right leg was bleeding from a wound inflicted during the scuffle. Luckily, the cut was superficial.

One of the abductors stood by her head, pointing a Glock G19 at her, while another bent down and quickly administered a shot of Propofol into her arm. The other two quickly went about their task of searching the house for something that seemed profoundly important to them. They paid particular attention to Jim's study, scanning his files, drawers, cabinets and desktop.

One of them said, 'It's not here. Just as I suspected. We'll need to take her.' Linda's eyes widened in panic. They were planning to abduct her. *This was no house burglary gone wrong.* But by then the Propofol was having its effect on her. She knew that she was about to pass out.

Linda's phone pinged. The man charged with guarding her picked it up with a gloved hand. It was a message from Jim indicating that he was about to leave the lab. The abductors knew that his office was a ten-minute drive away. They would need to leave quickly.

Two of the men quickly brought the comatose Linda to her feet, half-carried her to the waiting SUV, and pushed her inside. The other two filled a small haversack with papers, files, USB memory sticks and the hard drive from Jim's computer. They would need to examine it all later. They quickly loaded the haversack into the rear of the second RAV4.

They closed the main door behind them and split themselves between the two SUVs, with Linda lying unconscious in the back seat of one. Already bound and gagged, she was now blindfolded. These men took no chances—ever. The black tinted windows were opaque from the outside, and no one would be able to see that the men were transporting a hostage.

The four were determined to get what they wanted. And Linda would provide the means to their end.

3

LESS THAN FORTY kilometres by road from Surat is Navsari, a city inextricably linked to the history of Parsis in India. Parsis are the descendants of the Zoroastrians who fled from Iran to escape Muslim persecution and eventually settled in Gujarat around 720 CE. While many places are associated with this event, Navsari is the place that sheltered the Parsis for several centuries after they were driven out of Sanjan, the place where they had first landed in Gujarat. The birthplace of stalwarts such as Dadabhoy Naoroji, Jamsetji Tata and Jamshedji Jeejeebhoy, Navsari lies just thirteen kilometres away from Dandi where Mahatma Gandhi ended his famous Dandi March, in protest against the tax the British government levied on salt in India.

An aged visitor to Navsari, Pestonji Unwalla, ignored the city's star attraction, the Zoroastrian Fire Temple, and made his way through the predominantly Parsi enclave of Tarota Bazar. Within Tarota Bazar lies the First Dastur Meherji Rana Library. Established in 1872, the library contains more than 45,000 printed books on different subjects, but is famous for its collection of about 630 rare manuscripts written in

Avesta, Gujarati, Pahlavi, Pazend, Persian, Sanskrit and Urdu. The library is named after a Zoroastrian priest, Meherji Rana, who had visited Akbar's court at the command of the Mughal emperor, who wanted to learn the key tenets of the Zoroastrian faith.

The white-bearded octogenarian entered the majestic blue and off-white structure and walked with a little difficulty up the flight of stairs leading to the main reading room. It was afternoon; the room was enveloped in a somnolent silence only punctuated by creaking ancient ceiling fans and the occasional cry of a hawker from the road below. The air was thick with the musty smell of old leather-bound covers, and portraits of the library's patrons hung from the iron grille that ran around the perimeter of the mezzanine. The old man ignored the other patrons, who were leafing through newspapers and magazines in the reading room, and directly ascended a wrought-iron spiral staircase in one corner.

Somewhat winded, he arrived in an area filled with cupboards that were chockful of books. He then began the slow and laborious process of searching for the tome he sought. Thirsty after his climb, he licked his lips in anticipation of the thick gulkand ice cream that he would treat himself to after his task was completed.

The sheer scale of the collection would be daunting to most people, but Pestonji Unwalla had a secret resolve. His quest was for books listed in a 1923 catalogue by an Ervad Bamanji Nasarwanji Dhabar. From that catalogue, Unwalla had been able to eliminate the chaff and draw up a shortlist of the most likely candidates. He worked efficiently, scanning his list, searching for each book, running through its pages and then putting it back religiously in its place. One by one, his list became shorter. He scanned through the nineteenth-century illustrated and lithographed *Shahnameh*, the Persian epic by Firdausi. No luck. *Outlines of Zend Grammar* in Avestan. Nope. When he saw a 400-year-old copy of the *Khordeh Avesta,* his heart lifted briefly as he leafed through it, but it turned out to be one more false lead.

He was about to move on to another cupboard when he saw it. *Kalila wa Dimna* by Abdullah ibn al-Muqaffa. He picked it up and took it over to a reading table. Carefully turning the delicate, tissue-thin pages, he saw the handwritten scribble— and couldn't believe he'd found what he had. It was just six lines, written in the Avestan language using the Pazend script. *Strange to find Pazend jottings in an Arabic book.* Unwalla quickly took a photograph using his mobile phone. Could it be Number 27? He looked at the words once again and mentally translated the text. He couldn't be sure, but his instincts told him that he had found what he was looking for. He eagerly took more pictures.

Unwalla had not yet made a visit to Diu, a town on the coast of the island of the same name. Undoubtedly, Diu had archaeological treasures vested in the remains of two dakhmas and a fire temple, now protected by the Archaeological Survey of India. But Diu had been abandoned by the Parsis within nineteen years of their arrival there. Unwalla remained unconvinced that there would be any records or archives of value there. He had wisely realised that Navsari would be his best bet. And he now knew that his hunch had been a good one. Maybe Diu could be on the itinerary another day.

If he was right, then it would mean that centuries of history and tradition would be upended. It was possible that the guardians themselves were unaware of what lay beneath the religious symbolism. A key piece of their heritage had been entrusted to the safekeeping of an inner group, but it was something that belonged to Zoroastrians everywhere, not just the ones in India.

He realised that the communication he had received from Behrad Soroushpur was justified. He knew he must get back to Udvada to receive his visitor from Iran.

4

THE GEMINI CELLULAR Research Center, more commonly called the GCRC, was quiet at this early hour of the morning. The first few support staff would start coming in by 7 am. But the senior researchers had no fixed hours, often spending days without breaks, then taking a couple of days off to spend in virtual hibernation.

The facility was small and self-contained, situated within the industrial district of Georgetown in Seattle. At any given time, GCRC was home to a maximum of twenty people, including scientists and support staff. It was one of the smaller buildings in the block and resembled a cube, the existing concrete frame of the building having been given a new skin of channel glass and perforated metal. Maple trees, ubiquitous in Seattle, dotted the grounds that surrounded the cube.

Each of the five key researchers of GCRC had their own private labs within the cube. The primary one was used by Jim Dastoor, GCRC's principal research director and founder. The one near his was used by Dan Cohen, his second-in-command and long-time friend.

Within Jim's lab, two extra-long rows of gleaming white laboratory tables stretched wall to wall, their brilliance punctuated only by cutting-edge equipment: microscopes, spectrometers, thermal cyclers, DNA sequencers, incubators, centrifuges and evaporators. Ingenious angling of the windows bathed the lab's interiors in abundant natural light during the day. One wall to the right of the lab contained a massive bookshelf with Jim's research files and reference volumes. The wall to the left contained a bank of LED screens that could be used to magnify microscopic material. Alternatively, the screens could be used for video conferences.

Jim had not left the premises the previous night and there had been many such nights in recent months. Jim often joked that had he and Linda not been so completely in love, she would have suspected that he was having an affair. Luckily Linda understood the importance of what Jim was trying to achieve. After all, she was the one who had suggested his current research project. She had even christened it.

Jim referred to his research notes, then peered again at the microscopic samples under the compound microscope; its eyepieces were personalised, with the optical power of his near vision ground into the lenses. He knew that they were just a few days away from the final breakthrough. The cells under his gaze proved that this particular concentration was working better than expected. The challenge now lay in being able to synthesise the source.

Jim pushed himself back tiredly from the table and gently massaged his eyes. There was something immensely pleasing about his personality. His dense black hair had turned salt-and-pepper only along his sideburns. His aquiline features and high intellectual forehead gave him a regal bearing. But there was a softness about him that was accentuated by the gentle smile that often played on his lips. He picked up the Warwick glasses that lay on the table and placed them back on the bridge of his nose. He got up from the stool, placed his palms on his back and arched it. Sitting hunched over a microscope for hours was painful.

He looked at his watch. Was it too early for a conference call? His concern was only momentary. Working at GCRC usually meant that any time was fine for anyone. Jim pressed a shortcut sequence on his keyboard and waited for the LED screens to come to life. They popped open within a few seconds. Soon all five partners of the GCRC were in video-conference, two of them looking groggy-eyed.

'Sorry to disturb everyone so early,' said Jim, 'but I'm wrapping up a long night at the lab. Just thought that I should let everyone know that our Phase Three experiments have been successful. I am convinced that we have in our hands a formulation that could replace virtually every other medicine on the planet.'

Jim's oldest partner, Dan Cohen, spoke up. 'Are we sure that it can trigger the regeneration process?' Like Jim, he was a Stanford graduate, but he looked a lot older than his collegemate. A nasty divorce a few years ago had seemingly sucked all the optimism out of Dan's life.

Jim nodded. 'We know cells can be easily damaged, but they can nearly as easily repair themselves. It's only a problem when a cell's cytoplasm spills out during a rupture. We need to find a way to stem the loss of cytoplasm and *then* figure out how to regenerate the cell by recreating what has already leaked out. This is precisely what Hamzaa Dura does—under the right conditions and at the right calibration.'

'That's good news,' replied Dan. 'But how will you replicate the source material?'

Jim was on the same page with Dan. 'We've tried to address that question, but our present systems cannot replicate it,' he admitted. 'It seems to be beyond synthesis. Our hope lies in finding another source—or creating new technology to synthesise it. A final option could be to find ways of making it work at homeopathic levels of dilution, so that it would last for a few thousand years.' He added on a note of positivity: '*We are not giving up.*'

'But are we now—in effect—working beyond the known periodic table?' Dan continued to probe.

'Yes,' replied Jim. 'Science has always theorised about chemical elements that could have an atomic number higher than that of Oganesson, but to date we have been unable to synthesise those elements. In the eighth period and beyond, all elements remain undiscovered or—at the worst—merely hypothetical. But our Phase Three findings have given us reason to rejoice—which is why I was in such a hurry to communicate with all four of you—*the constituents of Hamzaa Dura are in that undiscovered zone.*'

'This could be the mother of all cures, Jim,' said Dan softly, breaking the brief astounded silence. Then he swiftly returned to his sceptical self. 'Have you considered moving forward on chemical patents?'

Jim smiled at his old friend. 'All of you know my views on that,' he replied. 'The GCRC has been financed by benefactors who believe in our mission to heal the world. And over the years we have come up with several profitable projects, ventures that have created substantial income streams to finance our not-for-profit work. But Hamzaa Dura is meant to serve humanity, not corporations. I do *not* want the GCRC to apply for any chemical patents. Just as no patents were filed for the discovery of insulin.'

Dan sighed, then attempted a grin. 'We know that, Jim. All of us. You have devoted the better part of a decade trying to figure this one out. None of us will contradict your opinion in this matter. And we are proud of being able to say that we have progressed to the stage that only human trials remain to be done.'

'Thank you, Dan,' said Jim, with a brief nod. 'I agree that we are now at the fag-end of our experiments. If this works consistently, we may have the solution to curing different types of carcinomas. It could also be the answer to Alzheimer's, cystic fibrosis, Hepatitis B and many viral infections that are still thought to be incurable.'

'But it will also have significant ramifications for the pharmaceutical and healthcare industries,' cautioned another partner. 'The pharma giant Asclepius ...'

'I know,' acknowledged Jim, ruefully.

'Asclepius has acquired thirteen drug manufacturers in the last fifteen months,' said the same partner. 'They are out to take us over, Jim. I can feel it. We are dealing with very aggressive adversaries.'

'True,' said Jim, nodding again. 'But our loyalty must be to humanity as a whole, not to vested interests within the industry. Do I have your unconditional support on this?'

All four nodded their assent. 'By when do you wish to make an official announcement?' asked Dan.

'We are still a few weeks away from that,' replied Jim. 'But the world will get to know soon enough once we apply to the Food & Drug Administration for permission to commence human trials. Naturally, we'll keep this matter under wraps until then.'

Jim disconnected the con-call, and exhausted as he was, immediately dialled Linda's number.

There was no answer.

That was quite normal at this time, he told himself—she was probably deep in some yoga pose or swimming energetic laps of the pool—and Jim forgot about the matter. Linda, unconscious and trussed up, was in fact headed from Seattle to Portland.

5

JIM DROVE HIS Subaru Outback along the I-5 to Lakeview Boulevard East, taking exit 168A. It was a journey that took him just little more than ten minutes each day. He was usually happy to listen to a composition by his great-granduncle, Homi Dastoor. But today, he switched to Vivaldi's *Concerto for Two Violins in A-Minor*. He absorbed the duet as he took in the picturesque landscape that he never tired of. And reflected on his wonderful life.

The life he now led was worlds away from his hometown, Mumbai. Growing up in India, he'd never imagined he would one day make his home 12,500 kilometres away in Seattle. That, too, with someone as lovely as Linda.

Jamshed was born to an affluent, traditionally Parsi family, his father being one of India's most respected businessmen. All Jamshed's friends called him Jim, or Jimmy. Jim's father had wisely realised that his son was not cut out for the world of commerce and that his true calling lay in the pursuit of science. He had encouraged Jim to make his way to Stanford. And Stanford was where he had met and merged with his two greatest loves: Linda and the laboratory.

Linda Evans had not been the prettiest girl on campus, nor had she been a star student. But when Jim met her in the students' cafeteria, their first encounter led to an extended conversation. Too shy to ask her out, it was not he but Linda who suggested they meet again over coffee. It was longest cup of Hawaiian Kona he would ever have.

Linda was the daughter of a white liberal Protestant father from San Francisco, and a Hindu mother from Jakarta. She had that perfect combination of looks that hybrids are blessed with, and her mixed parentage had also ensured openness of mind. In no time at all, they began to go steady, and by the time they married, just a few months after Jim had earned his PhD, Hawaiian Kona had become a daily fixture in their lives.

He forced himself back into the present. Upon reaching home, Jim drove through the gate, passing Linda's red Tesla parked at its usual spot up the driveway. He opened the main door and was taken aback by what he saw. Everything had been turned topsy-turvy, every room a shambles. Lamps lay broken on the floor, carpets had been flipped over, tables had been moved or toppled. The house had been ransacked.

'Linda!' he shouted in fear.

He walked briskly towards the poolside, then to the cabana and then ran to the kitchen. There were bloodstains on the kitchen floor and shards of a coffee mug. 'Linda!' he shouted again, hoping that she was in the bedroom upstairs. Noticing her phone lying on the floor, he picked it up to check, but there were no recent calls recorded. The last call had been his own, made from the lab. The last message received was the one he had sent her just before leaving it.

Jim ran up the stairs to check the bedrooms and the study, but a voice inside him told him that his worst nightmare was coming true. In his study, he noticed that his filing cabinet had been forced open, drawers in disarray, the innards of his desktop exposed, the hard disk missing.

Jim returned to the living room and dialled a number. The call was made to the one person who Jim thought could help him: Greg Walters.

Greg was the deputy chief of the Seattle Police Department. The two men often played racquetball together at their club. Greg had been driving to work when Jim called. 'Give me five minutes, Jim,' said Greg reassuringly, executing a perfect U-turn to head to Jim's place instead of the police station. 'In the meantime, I'm asking your home security provider to send me the footage from your surveillance cameras. I should have it by the time I reach you. Don't worry, Jim, we'll find her.'

Although professionally calm, Greg was a worried man. Washington State had the fourth-highest number of open missing-person cases in America. He hoped that Linda would not become part of that grim statistic. He ran his hand through his dark brown hair. He had brown eyes to match, inherited from his mother, a Yazidi immigrant.

Greg called his second-in-command to rush a forensics team over to Jim's house and to get the security agency to transmit the surveillance footage from the house. He then broke a few traffic rules to ensure that he got to Jim's swiftly, making it in less than six minutes.

He quickly took in the chaotic scene in the house. *Burglary gone bad? Home invasion? Abduction? Murder?* He began playing the video of the surveillance camera feed on his phone, drawing Jim's attention to it.

The video feed showed that two Toyota RAV4s had rolled in at 5:30 am. Four men had alighted, overridden the home security system, and emerged thirty minutes later half-carrying a blindfolded Linda whose arms were tied, and mouth taped. There were no cameras inside the house, but the video system of the driveway had remained active throughout. *How did they come by the thumbprint?* wondered Greg when he looked at the main gate footage.

The forensics team arrived a few minutes later. One of them had succeeded in zooming in on the licence plate of one of the RAV4s. Greg immediately put out a 'Be-On-Look-Out' notice—a BOLO—for the licence plate. In the meantime his deputy checked the registration database. The vehicle belonged to a Nevada company, in all probability a shell. The only office-bearers were lawyers and accountants.

The team took photographs, collected blood swabs from the kitchen, dusted for fingerprints and gathered up filaments of fibre; one of the abductors seemed to have torn his garment when it snagged on the oven grille. A recent photograph of Linda was procured and logged into the database with another BOLO for her. In the meantime, Greg tried to plug the gaps with Jim.

'Do you or Linda have any specific enemies you know of?' asked Greg.

'None that would stoop so low,' Jim replied categorically.

'Any debts or business issues?' went on Greg. The answer to this, too, was in the negative.

Given Jim's affluent family background, he had never had to worry about financial security. When his sister Avan had taken over as head of the family business, he had been provided a large sum in lieu of his stake. The money had helped meet GCRC's initial capital requirements. Today, his partnership stake at GCRC alone was worth millions. Linda's abduction could be a simple case of kidnapping for ransom, Greg pondered. But then, why was the house searched or stuff pilfered?

'I'm sorry, Jim, but I must ask you this,' he asked delicately. 'Is everything all right between you and Linda?'

When he saw the flash of annoyance on Jim's face, Greg instantly regretted having asked the question. It was well known in Seattle's social circles that the couple had stayed truly in love, even after twenty years of marriage.

'What could the abductors be looking for?' asked Greg, quickly changing course. 'Why did they take away your hard drive? Or your files and flash drives?'

Jim knew the answer, but his head was reluctant to accept what his heart already knew.

6

THE PHRASE *Daftar-e Magham-e Moazzam-e Rahbari* is quite a mouthful for most people. Translated, it simply means 'the Office of the Supreme Leader of Iran'. It is located in central Tehran at the corner of Palestine Street and Azerbayejan Street. Also known as the Beit Rabari Compound, it serves as the official residence, administration bureau and principal workplace of the Ayatollah. The compound contains about fifty buildings with around 500 employees, virtually all of them on deputation from the military and security services. Within the complex are several offices, meeting rooms and auditoria, entirely surrounded by security barriers and high walls.

The primary resident, the Supreme Leader, was no ordinary man. With an uncanny ability to survive all odds, he was the proverbial cat with nine lives. Consider this: He had been arrested six times during the reign of the Shah of Iran, Mohammad Reza Pahlavi. He had been the target of an assassination attempt, but survived, although an arm had been temporarily paralysed. The previous Ayatollah had planned on naming another as his successor, but a falling-out between the men had propelled the current Ayatollah into his numero uno position. The Ayatollah was nothing if not lucky.

Around eighty-two years old, the Ayatollah had pink cheeks, a cherubic smile and a Gandalf-like white beard. He always wore classic leather shoes with laces, not the coarse sandals usually worn by the ruling clerics. His footwear was perfectly matched with his grey pin-striped robe, and his cloak and turban were also synchronised in inky black. The black turban, of course, was an indication that he was a Sayyid, a descendant of the Prophet Mohammad. A string of small turquoise prayer beads hung from a perfectly manicured hand. This was a man who paid attention to immaculate grooming.

Behind this soft exterior was a tough, uncompromising politician who had once been commander of the Iran Revolutionary Guard Corps—the IRGC—and the principal negotiator during the Iran Hostage Crisis of 1979. He also remained one of the key strategists right through the eight-year-long Iran–Iraq war. Years later, he refused to yield to American sanctions in the face of Iran's nuclear programme. Now, he was 'supreme' in every sense of the word, far more powerful than the Iranian President or Parliament.

The Supreme Leader looked at the single sheet of paper in front of him. He read it quickly and looked up at Amir Khademhosseini, head of Iran's IRGC-Quds Force. One among five branches of the IRGC, the IRGC-Quds Force was responsible for unconventional warfare and military intelligence operations. Khademhosseini stood at attention in front of his desk.

'So, you were wrong?' asked the Ayatollah simply.

Khademhosseini knew better than to make excuses. 'I was wrong, oh *rahbar-e mo'azzam*,' he replied. 'I truly thought that we would find the Athravan Star in the British Museum, much like so many other priceless artefacts that the English stole from our country. But ...'

'But? You chose to use a stupid man from a security agency, who stole an artefact of only nuisance value to us, and killed a guard in the process?'

'My agents have spent the better part of a year bribing officials in England,' said Khademhosseini. 'According to some of our sources, the broken Cyrus Cylinder was an indication that it could have once been hollow. We were working on the assumption that the hollow could contain the Athravan Star. Also, the reference to Marduk ...'

'All that you have succeeded in doing is creating an international incident,' said the Supreme Leader, still not raising his deceptively soft voice. Then he swiftly focussed his hypnotic eyes at the officer. 'Ensure that the perpetrator is not traced back to you. We do not need further problems with the West.'

'Yes, oh rahbar-e mo'azzam,' replied Khademhosseini. 'But what shall we do with the cylinder? After all, it is a most valuable national treasure. Now it is back in our hands.' He desperately wanted to reach for the packet of Farvardin in his pocket but killed the very thought. *Smoking in the presence of the Supreme Leader!*

'Find a way to get it back into the museum,' replied the Ayatollah. 'It was a piece of miserable writing by a non-Islamic king following a false faith, and foolishly honoured many centuries later by that scoundrel, the Shah of Iran. We do not need to be in awe of that wretched object.'

The Cyrus Cylinder had been discovered by archaeologist Hormuzd Rassam in 1879 among the ruins of Babylon. Rassam possessed an official *firman* from the Ottoman Sultan to carry away whatever was discovered. So, Rassam had carted off loads of priceless stuff in full public view. Many years later, the Shah of Iran, Mohammad Reza Pahlavi, had wished to take credit for the universality of Cyrus's message. He grandly referred to the cylinder as the first declaration of universal human rights, a view that was later debunked by scholars. The cylinder, however, continued its hold over the sentiments of the Iranian people, and had been loaned back to the country to exhibit twice: The first time, in 1971, to coincide with the Shah's celebration of 2500 years of the Persian Empire; and once more, in 2010, when it attracted over half a million viewers over a four-month period.

'But the Athravan Star has never been on display,' Khademhosseini sought to convince the Supreme Leader into coming round to his point of view. 'Nor has it ever been referred to officially. Given that the Cyrus Cylinder refers to Marduk, and the Athravan Star may be connected with Ashur—the deity that was assigned Marduk's qualities later—I thought I was on the right track. Now, I'm wondering, how do I acquire it?'

'*That* is the national treasure we need,' said the Supreme Leader. 'Not the damn cylinder you've appropriated for no good reason. Having that cylinder in our midst will only be one more reason for human rights groups to remind us of the perceived want of them in Iran.'

Khademhosseini remained uncomfortably quiet. He did not want to say that the Athravan Star was a Zoroastrian treasure rather than an Iranian one. Hundreds of years of Islamic attacks and rule had also resulted in a huge drain of priceless items into Arab treasuries. Except that the Athravan Star could truly be *anywhere* in the world.

'Have you considered the India connection?' asked the Supreme Leader. 'There are fables that the Persian physician Borzuya brought it with him from India. Then there are tales that it lay hidden in the Peacock Throne that was brought by Nadir Shah from India. Isn't it possible that the Indians want it back?'

'That is possible, o rahbar-e mo'azzam, and you are absolutely right to consider it,' said Khademhosseini, liberally lathering on the soft soap. 'But isn't it possible that it may have been removed from India by the British, just like the Kohinoor diamond?'

'You are looking at this problem from the wrong end of the telescope,' the Supreme Leader reproved him. 'Instead of thinking about *who* could have it, focus on what it *does*. When you switch your gaze to its qualities, your path will get illuminated.'

'Forgive me, o rahbar-e mo'azzam, but I did not understand your words.'

'Folklore tells us that the Athravan Star had the most miraculous properties, almost magical,' replied the Supreme Leader. 'Think carefully about *that*.'

7

JIM'S PHONE STARTLED them with its ringing, although they had been expecting the call. A trace had already been set up on both Jim's and Linda's phones so that incoming callers could be traced. Jim answered the unknown number hesitantly. 'Yes?' he said, sounding unperturbed.

'Listen, Jim,' the voice rasped. 'You know that we have Linda. We have no intention of harming her as long as you cooperate.' The voice was steady. There was no hint of aggression in it.

'I will cooperate to every extent I can,' said Jim. 'Name your price. Just don't hurt her.'

'Touching,' said the voice, taking on a purr. 'My research indicates that you have been married two decades. Most couples are fed up with each other by then.'

Wearing headphones, Greg's techies were working on the computer console that had been set up by them on the dining table. 'He's using VOIP,' one of them whispered to Greg. *Voice Over Internet Protocol.* They shook their heads in disappointment.

'Find the IP address,' Greg whispered back. 'At least it will give us some idea of his location.'

'The guy is way ahead of us,' said the techie unhappily. 'He's using chained VPNs.'

Greg cursed under his breath. Virtual Private Networks—or VPNs—masked the identity of the user. But the abductors had gone a step further. 'Chaining' the VPNs meant that they were using multiple VPN providers, so that each was linked to the other. Getting a court order for each would be impossible and time-consuming. And the place of origin could quite easily turn out to be a country like Ukraine, Sudan or Colombia, where an American warrant would not even work.

Greg signalled to Jim that he should continue talking. Although they could not trace the call, they were recording it so that they would be able to analyse it later for background sounds that could help pinpoint a location.

The voice at the other end emitted a canny laugh. 'Tell those cops sitting on their dumb asses in your house that even if I remain on this line for the next half hour, they will be unable to trace me. So, are you ready to do as I say?'

'Yes,' replied Jim. 'But first I need proof that she is safe.'

There was a rustling sound as the abductor handed over the phone to Linda. Her groggy voice came on. 'Jim, I'm okay sweetheart,' she said feebly. He knew that she wasn't. She was trying to ensure that he did not panic.

'Don't you worry either, honey,' Jim said into the phone. 'I'll have you released soon. I love you, baby …'

The kidnapper snatched the phone away from Linda mid-sentence and spoke into the phone himself. 'You spoke to her,' he said. 'Now do you want to know how you can *save* her?' Jim hastily scribbled notes as the voice gave him instructions and the order in which to follow them.

1. Go to your laboratory and pull out all the Hamzaa Dura from your climate-controlled safe.

2. *Take a data dump of all the research notes on your computer and transfer it to a storage drive.*
3. *Put all the stuff in a bag. Go to Seattle King Street Station, board the 7:25 am Amtrak to Portland.*
4. *Once you reach Portland Union Station at 10:55 am, await further instructions on your phone.*

'Keep your phone charged and free at all times,' said the voice. 'And no law enforcement should be accompanying you. You will be under constant observation. If we notice anything odd, all our commitments regarding your wife's security no longer stand. Understood?'

Jim agreed with alacrity. Hamzaa Dura marked the highest point in his life—but one: Linda.

The line was cut and he looked enquiringly at Greg for further advice. 'While we go about doing everything that is forensically required,' the detective warned him, 'you, Jim, will need to show those bastards that you're serious about following through on their instructions.'

'And how do I show that?' asked Jim.

'Do everything they say,' said Greg. 'We have some time in hand before you reach Portland. Let's see if we can come up with something by then.'

'And should I actually carry the Hamzaa Dura with me?'

'I have no clue what that is, Jim,' Greg owned. 'How about we drive over to your laboratory, and you can fill me in on why this thing is so damned valuable to them.'

'But they may be tracing our movements,' replied Jim.

'All the more reason to go there so that they know you are serious about giving them the genuine stuff.'

8

JIM AND GREG headed back in Greg's car to Georgetown where the GCRC was located. It was a dark morning, but all the lights inside were switched off. Except, that is, those in Dan Cohen's lab, where Dan was already busy on a global research project to start clinical trials on a cancer vaccine. The project was in its final stages, possibly the reason for his early start.

They parked in Jim's VIP spot and walked the short rest of the way. Entering the cube was like gaining access to Fort Knox. At the gate, a retina scan allowed Jim to approach and open the main door. Thereafter, the elevator required an alpha-numeric code to take them in and up. Once they reached the third floor, where Jim's laboratory was located, the door to the lab required Jim's palm print before it obediently slid open. Greg whistled softly. They didn't have stuff like this even in high-security prisons.

As they entered, the laboratory lights came on but at an appropriately dimmed level. 'Brighter,' said Jim addressing the invisible voice command system in the room. The high-tech lab was instantly bathed in whiter light. 'Aircon,' said Jim. Soon, the gentle hum of air conditioning became audible.

'So why don't you tell me what you've been cooking up?' said Greg. 'I'm guessing it's something that has aroused the worst form of greed in our friends on the line a little while ago.'

Jim didn't immediately begin to explain. No one, other than the five partners of GCRC, and Linda, knew about Hamzaa Dura and its remarkable qualities.

Greg picked up Jim's hesitation. 'I know this is difficult, but you need to tell me all, Jim. I can't help you unless I know exactly what motivates the people who have taken Linda.'

The scientist walked over to the far-right corner of the room that was lined with bookshelves and pressed an almost invisible button along its edge. The bookshelf unit slid away with a whoosh, revealing an electronic safe built into the wall. It looked like an ordinary safe but wasn't. Temperature, humidity, air quality and atmospheric pressure could be accurately controlled within it.

Jim punched a sequence of numbers into the safe's keypad. There was a short beep and the door opened. Inside the safe was a single earthen box with a tight lid, which displayed an odd-looking symbol, much like the insignia pilots wore, a sphere supported by wings. Jim took out the box and gently prised off the lid. Inside it was a grainy white powder with the consistency of detergent scrub.

'Is this what they want?' asked Greg with raised eyebrows. As a policeman, he wondered why anyone would go to such lengths to obtain what seemed to be an ordinary lab chemical.

Jim nodded. 'This is the source material that we call the Hamzaa Dura.'

'What does that mean?' asked Greg.

'In Arabic, *Hamzaa* means "to prick or to stimulate". *Dura* is the root of the word "durable". So, Hamzaa Dura implies the ability to stimulate durability. It is possibly the most revolutionary discovery of the twenty-first century.'

'Why?' asked Greg.

'What does it actually mean to be alive, Greg?' asked Jim in return. The question was rhetorical, and Jim went on to answer it. 'One of the extraordinary characteristics of living systems—one that differentiates them from machines—is their capacity to heal themselves,' continued Jim. 'But sometimes that does not happen. At the multi-cellular level, one can spawn new cells to replace dead cells. But sometimes, this process too can malfunction. We have now discovered a way by which we can effectively enable defective cells to heal themselves.'

'Boy!' whistled Greg under his breath. 'And could this whatchamacallit cure a bunch of diseases?'

'Almost all,' replied Jim, with slightly more gravitas. 'It could become the panacea for all ills. Come with me.' Jim picked up the earthen box, closed the safe and restored the bookshelf to its usual deceptive form. He placed the box on a counter and used a remote-control unit to turn on one of the LED screens that occupied the left wall. A video clip came on.

'What are we looking at?' asked Greg, squinching his eyebrows. All he could discern was a blob of jelly.

'It's a human cancer cell that has been magnified many millions of times,' replied Jim. 'Cancer cells are different to normal cells in various ways, the primary difference being that they do not stop growing and dividing themselves to increase their numbers. That's what results in a tumour. A tumour is actually billions of copies of the original cancerous cell. This video shows the development over several weeks, but the footage has been sped up to show the evolution within a minute.'

Greg could see the tumour forming in front of his eyes. 'So, your stuff, this Hamzaa-thingie, can stop this?' he asked.

'A precise if somewhat unusual description, I must say,' Jim said, not exactly laughing. 'Normal cells obey signals that inform them when they have reached a given limit and must die. But something in cancer cells stops those signals from working. Hamzaa Dura is the ultimate failsafe signalling material. It can not only be used to repair diseased cells, but also to signal cancerous cells to stop growing. In effect, it could eliminate some diseases, and extend life spans in general.'

'Why isn't this out in the market?' Greg's question was only to be expected. He had lost his Yazidi mother to lung cancer just a year ago. This stuff could have saved her.

'Because it has taken us a decade to figure out the right balance of ingredients in Hamzaa Dura to treat different ailments,' replied Jim. 'Plus, the original material occurs naturally—unless we can find a way to synthesise it, we cannot go in to mass-production of something with the guarantee to cure.'

'What if you gave the kidnappers something else—a jar filled with dummy material?' asked Greg, catching on quickly to the potential of abuse by chemical pirates. 'How would they know that you're lying?'

'The very fact that they know the name Hamzaa Dura—a name that has only been shared between me, my immediate team and Linda—implies that they would also know if I were bluffing. There has been a leak, Greg. They even had my thumbprint to access the main gate of my house. I can't say who it is, but I cannot take any risks with Linda's life.'

Greg looked like he understood Jim's dilemma. 'I promise,' he said gravely, 'we'll find a way to help you out of this. In the meantime, get the data out from your servers quickly. And then let's head to the train station. I'll drop you off there. But you need to know that one of my men will be tailing you. Just like *they* will be.'

Jim was uncomfortable with the idea. 'They specifically said that they would be keeping a watch. If there are policemen with me, they will no longer guarantee Linda's safety.'

'He's not a policeman,' explained Greg. 'He's a private investigator who does odd jobs for me. He will always remain at a healthy distance from you but will be following a GPS tracker we will place in your shoe.'

Jim agreed wearily as he began downloading the data from his servers. He was close to breaking down but couldn't afford the time for such indulgences. The two most important entities in his life were in danger.

To rescue one, it was possible he'd have to lose the other.

9

THE HOLIEST SITE of India's Parsis is in the Gujarati seaside town of Udvada. Originally known as Unthwada, it had been an area where camels grazed, before the Parsis made it famous. Located in the Pardi taluka, just around twenty-four kilometres away from Valsad, a small fire temple known as the Udvada Atash Behram was what drew the devotion of the community.

The temple hosts the throne of a sacred fire known as the Iranshah. While the enclave is around 265 years old, the fire itself has been burning for almost thirteen centuries. A group of 18,000 followers of the prophet Zarathustra had fled Islamic persecution in Persia in the eighth century and reached—via the small fishing village of Diu—a town called Sanjan on the coast of Gujarat. They were granted refuge by King Vijayaditya of the Western Chalukyas, known as Jadi Rana in Zoroastrian texts.

The Parsis had promised their God, Ahura Mazda, that they would consecrate a sacred fire—an Atash Behram—if they made it safely to their new home. Alas, political intrigue forced them to move the fire's location many times: from Sanjan to Bahrot, then Bansda, then Navsari, then Bulsar and finally to Udvada, where it remained.

Behrad Soroushpur had arrived the previous day from Tehran to Mumbai via Dubai. He had then driven north for four hours to reach Udvada, a quiet, peaceful village dissected by narrow lanes with minimal traffic. Elegant yet crumbling bungalows with cantilevered balconies, carved columns and patterned entablatures dotted the area. The silent lanes and vacant homes, interspersed by some inhabited ones, spoke of the ancient heritage that Udvada boasted. Soroushpur breathed in the sandalwood-infused air and uttered a prayer as he heard the deep gong of the bell. It was easy to get lost in the atmosphere of Udvada. He forced himself into the present.

He checked in directly at the Globe Hotel, thankful to the three generations of Parsis who had kept the 1924 hotel running against all odds. After a night's rest and a hearty breakfast, he set out to meet the man with whom he had been corresponding all these years.

He crossed the Atash Behram on Dastur Street but did not go inside. An imposing piece of architecture, the roofed top floor stood atop Persian column capitals with large scrolling forms and winged bulls. He reckoned he'd visit the temple later. For the moment, the upcoming meeting was far more important.

He walked down the road to a raftered house with a polished wooden *katera*, or railing, around an *otla*, the front porch. On the porch was an easy chair with retractable arms, on which sat a white-bearded octogenarian. Pestonji Unwalla, who had just got back from Navsari, saw Soroushpur from a distance and waved.

The visitor was duly ushered in by Unwalla's chubby wife, dressed in her usual *gawan*—a corruption of 'gown' with a *mathabandhana* around her head. Unwalla was an influential man, having worked for many years in Mumbai for the Bombay Parsi Panchayat. He was no longer active, having retired to his ancestral home in Udvada a couple of years ago.

It was hot and the visitor declined the offer of tea. Instead, a double-lemon soda from Kolhaji's was quickly procured for him by Unwalla's manservant. It came in an antiquated thick-glass bottle and was just the pick-me-up he needed. Five minutes later, a plate of nankhatai biscuits from Bharat Bakery also appeared.

'Thank you for agreeing to see me,' said Soroushpur. 'The need to work together has never been more urgent.'

Unwalla smiled. 'There are only nine families that have had the privilege of tending the Iranshah,' he said. 'Andhyarujina, Unwalla, Bhadha, Katila, Dastoor, Bhaijina, Patel, Mirza and Sidhwa. Some of us have been true to the faith. Others …' He left the sentence unfinished.

The nine families were the descendants of Dastur Nairyosang Dhaval, who had combined sixteen different fires to spark the Iranshah on a beach in Sanjan sometime around 720 CE. The nine families tended the fire in rotation for a month each, on every occasion going through the ritual purification with *baresman*, bundles of sacred twigs, and wearing their white muslin *jama*s and *paghri*s. In addition, they covered their noses and mouths with fine muslin to avoid polluting the sacred flame with human exhudations.

'Do you have it?' asked Soroushpur.

Unwalla nodded. 'It was scribbled at the back of a very old book in the First Dastur Meherji Rana Library. We believe that twenty-six *rivayat*s—or directions—were received by Parsis from our brethren in Iran between 1478 and 1773. It appears that one was not formally written up. It was sent as a mere jotting. On its receival, it was transmitted only orally from generation to generation.'

Unwalla pulled his phone out of a bag beside him. He scrolled through his photos and zoomed in on the one he had taken in Navsari. He handed it to Soroushpur. It was just six lines, written in Avestan, using the Pazend script. Soroushpur tried deciphering what it said but gave up after a few minutes. Unwalla laughed. He took out a slip of paper from his pocket. 'I have translated it for you,' he said.

Across the Jabbar, light dazzles the eyes
As three great fires roar from the skies
Behold, the Athravan in the Daitya prays
And the Anu people to the heavens gaze

They know the fourth that comes from three
Means powerful Yasna for all time to be.

Soroushpur's voice trembled slightly as he read the words aloud. Seeing the word 'athravan' in this text was exciting. It meant that his suppositions regarding the Athravan Star could very well turn out to be true. 'Do you think this could have been part of the *Five Treatises*?' he asked.

'Difficult to say,' replied Unwalla. 'Too many translations have happened along the way. It also depends on whether we believe the Borzuya story or not. But it does not really matter. The meaning is that our ancestors were revealing the source of the Athravan Star to us.'

'What should be my next step?' asked Soroushpur, his voice quavering faintly.

'That is not for me to say,' said Unwalla. 'All I know is that there are some people who have forgotten their duty. It is time to rectify that wrong. And the only way is for likeminded people as us to work together.'

'Do you think I should go to Navsari?' asked Soroushpur.

'I have been there for you. You will find nothing new there,' replied Unwalla. 'I shall also be visiting Diu on your behalf. But remember, the Iranshah was eventually moved out of Navsari and came here to Udvada. Anything associated with it would have also been moved. As I said, the very guardians of our ancient powers have turned against us. But this text is telling you that what you seek *does* exist. For all our sakes, retrieve it.'

'How do you advise my going about it?' asked Soroushpur.

'Maybe you could visit Bandar Abbas?' suggested Unwalla.

10

GREG AND JIM reached Seattle King Street Station. Jim got out of the car, said goodbye to Greg and entered the station concourse. He bought a ticket at the machine for the 7:25 am Amtrak to Portland. His watch showed 7:15 am. Passengers were to board from Platform 6, so he made his way there. In his hands was a leather duffel bag containing what Linda's abductors wanted.

A man dressed in a black leather jacket was maintaining a careful distance from Jim, all the while keeping him in his line of sight. If he lost Jim, he would still have a signal from the GPS tracker installed by Greg in the sole of Jim's right shoe. Jim's tail was a former cop who had been asked to resign from the force following a shootout gone bad. He had handed over his badge and gun but had built up a lucrative investigation business on his own. He helped Greg from time to time. This was one of those times.

Jim boarded the train and settled into his seat. He put on his earphones to listen to a Zoroastrian chant, the *Yatha Ahu Vairyo*, which always brought him peace. This particular version had been performed by one of Jim's great-granduncles, Homi Dastoor, who had migrated from Mumbai to Vienna to pursue a career in music. For the moment though, Jim's thoughts were entirely focused on Linda. He was praying that God would keep her safe and bring her back to him. *Yatha ahu vairyo atha ratush ashat chit hacha …*

Several rows behind Jim, the ex-cop pretended to read a newspaper. He kept one eye on Jim and another on the people around him. A man dressed in a black hoodie had hovered around Jim all the while: in the waiting room, on the platform and now inside the train. The private investigator's gut told him that this man was one of the operatives of the abduction group. The security video from Jim's house had also showed the abductors wearing black hoodies.

Three-and-a-half hours later, the train pulled into Portland Union Station. Jim took his duffel bag and disembarked. Following him was the man in the black hoodie; behind them was Jim's security tail. Jim paused to look at his phone as it pinged. It was a WhatsApp message. *Cross the NW Broadway Bridge and come to the City Center Parking. No tricks. Her life is in our hands.*

As a matter of precaution, Jim forwarded the message to Greg. He then walked out of Portland Union with determination in his step. He was going to get Linda back. Exiting the station, he walked across NW Broadway Bridge which was almost devoid of walkers.

Greg's man maintained some distance between himself and the hoodie, secure in the knowledge that Jim was within sight. But midway across the bridge, the hoodie turned around and came charging towards him. The act caught him completely by surprise. His attacker delivered a blow to his jaw, knocking him to the ground. Before he could recover, he realised that his assailant had his elbow around his neck and was clamping a chloroform-soaked kerchief to his face. The hoodie held him in a vise-like grip until he passed out. The private investigator was left comatose on the walker-biker pathway that ran along the length of the bridge.

By then, Jim had already crossed the bridge, and continued along Broadway Street until it turned right towards Weidler Street. At the corner was the parking facility. He warily made his way inside. The parking area was mostly empty, having been constructed primarily for events held in the Moda sports arena nearby. As he wondered where to go next, his WhatsApp beeped again. *Come to Level 2, Slot B-42.*

Jim made his way to the parking slot. Stationed there was the black Toyota RAV4 that had been captured on the home security video in Jim's driveway. He felt his heart would explode—it was beating so hard and so rapidly.

Nervously approaching the SUV, he discerned that the rear door was partially open. He reached the vehicle and opened the door wide. The sole occupant of the car was Linda, sitting upright, but bound and gagged. Her eyes were terrified, darting towards him and then away from him. Jim, simply grateful that she was alive, did not grasp the warning in her desperate eyes.

Jim reached inside the vehicle to remove her gag and to untie her. It was then that he felt the cold metal of a gun against his head. 'Don't turn around,' said the voice he remembered from the telephone call. 'Did you bring what we asked for?'

Jim wordlessly gestured towards the leather bag that lay on the ground near his feet. Another man in a balaclava appeared, picked up the bag and unzipped it. He took out the earthen box containing the Hamzaa Dura and held it up to their leader. 'Good,' said the man behind the voice. 'Now, bring out Mrs Dastoor.'

The masked man opened the rear door on the other side, used box cutters to free Linda, and roughly pulled her out. She staggered out of the SUV, slightly dazed and also stiff from hours of being tied up. The masked man suddenly pushed her away from the SUV. Simultaneously, the man holding a gun to Jim's head delivered a sharp blow with the butt of his Glock to Jim's neck. Jim felt woozy as he slumped forward into the rear seat of the vehicle. The abductor grabbed Jim's phone and smashed it on the ground.

'No!' cried Linda, who had landed on her hands and knees a short distance away from the SUV. But it was too late. A driver started up the RAV4 while the other two held Jim and his leather bag between them. The driver screeched out of the garage as she watched, sobbing.

The abduction had never been about her. They had wanted Jim's material *in addition to Jim*. Linda had simply been the bait to reel him in.

11

IT WAS GIVEN to me, but little did I know that it could get me killed.

You see, I was born into wealth. My father had inherited it and, had I wanted, it would have been bequeathed to me. Four generations of my family before me had lived in Bombay—now known as Mumbai—as creators and inheritors of wealth.

In 1858, my great-great-grandfather, Shapoor Dastoor, had moved to Mumbai from Udvada, a Zoroastrian pilgrimage town in Gujarat. He passed on the fortune he built to my great-grandfather, Navroze. It then went to my grandfather Rustom, and further on to my father, Baman. My father bequeathed most of it to my sister, Avan. A small, yet significant, portion came to me.

My name is Jamshed, but most people call me Jim. I used my inheritance to found Gemini Cellular Research Center, or GCRC, in Seattle.

The year 1858, which was when Shapoor Dastoor chose to relocate from Udvada to Bombay, witnessed the aftermath of a blood-bathed insurrection. The English had just quelled a rebellion by Indian sepoys in which thousands had died. The English called it the 'Sepoy Mutiny' while Indian history textbooks call it 'The Great Rebellion'. I prefer the latter version. Rebellion is in our Dastoor blood.

It wasn't the ideal time to be making life-changing decisions, but Shapoor had made up his mind. Bombay was a magnet that attracted treasure, trade and talent. Parsis fit the bill perfectly, having worked for many decades with English trading partners in Surat, and built up considerable fortunes.

Of course, today's Mumbai is a thriving metropolitan hub of around twenty million souls. It is the engine of Indian commerce and industry, besides being the heart of India's glamorous cine-world, Bollywood. But that was not how the city started. A millennium ago, Mumbai consisted of seven nondescript islands that lay separated by uninhabitable swamplands.

The fishing communities of Kolis and Aagris were the earliest settlers in these islands. The region then became part of the Mauryan Empire around 2300 years ago and was transformed into a hub of Buddhist learning. After that, successive ruling *dynasties—such as the Satavahanas, Abhiras, Vakatakas, Kalachuris, Chalukyas, Rashtrakutas and Silharas—governed the islands. Then, in 1343, the sultans of Gujarat captured the islands. Around two centuries later, the Portuguese took over the islands following a treaty with the sultans. The Portuguese set up a trading hub there and called it 'Bom Bahia'—the 'good bay'. Not that there was much goodness about it. All that Bom Bahia seemed to yield was mosquitos and pestilence.*

Nevertheless, the Portuguese settlement grew and Bom Bahia became a commercial hub for trade in coir, rice, coconuts, cotton and tobacco. By 1626, the Portuguese had established a substantial warehouse, a few churches, a fort and a shipyard. Soon, Bom Bahia also boasted spacious homes for the wealthy merchants who operated from there. Eventually, trade in other commodities such as silk, onyx and muslin also opened up.

The Portuguese identified their opportunity in Bom Bahia not only as a commercial, but also a divine one. They encouraged their men to marry local women because it fit in nicely with their plans of actively proselytising on behalf of the Catholic Church.

But in 1626, there was a war between the Portuguese and the English. A naval battle took place off the coast of Suvali, near Surat. The result was a decisive win by the English, who were surprised to find that many of the Portuguese vessels had gone missing towards the end of the battle. Only later did the English discover that the Portuguese had a secret refuge that they called Bom Bahia, a safe harbour that they could retreat into for mooring and repairing their ships. The English soon attacked Bom Bahia, razed the manor of the Portuguese governor to the ground and also burnt two Portuguese ships that lay docked in the yard. The Portuguese fled for their lives.

A mere three-and-a-half decades changed everything diametrically. In the summer of 1662, King Charles II of England married Catherine of Braganza, the daughter of the king of Portugal. Catherine's family gave Bom Bahia to Charles as part of his new queen's dowry. But Charles had neither the inclination nor the resources to rule those distant swamps and a few years later, struck a deal with the British East India Company, by then a behemoth that operated twenty-three factories in India. The company agreed to rent the islands from Charles for an annual sum of ten pounds, and Bom Bahia was anglicised to 'Bombay'.

12

I AM TOLD that the East India Company needed Bombay because it was a deep-water port which allowed access to bigger ships with deeper drafts. They set about preparing Bombay for greater things to come. The islands needed a fort and garrison to protect them. Also required were a strong, reliable quayside, a warehouse and a Customs house. The company already had a governor in Surat, a capable fellow called Gerald Aungier. He was packed off to Bombay, where he went about implementing the mammoth Bombay project with the efficiency of a machine.

A stumbling block was Bombay's weather. Hot and muggy for most of the year, the city's heat only dissipated during the heavy and unrelenting monsoon—with ensuing epidemics of cholera, typhoid and malaria. The English used to say that the average lifespan of Europeans in Bombay was 'three monsoons'. We are also told that only one in twenty European children survived infancy in Bombay.

Against such odds, the English ploughed ahead. The directors of the company sent Aungier a copy of the plan that had been drawn up for the city of London after the Great Fire of 1666. It was meant to serve as a guide for developing the new port. Aungier kick-started an ambitious building programme that involved constructing causeways to link the disjointed islands. In addition, the city was upgraded by a hospital, a printing press, a mint and an Anglican church.

Until then, Englishmen settling in Bombay had often married local women, but now the company encouraged English ladies to travel to Bombay to seek matrimonial alliances. The English also urged our Parsi community to come and settle in Bombay. We Parsis are the descendants of the Zoroastrians who fled from Islamic persecution in the old Persia in the eighth century. But it was a full nine centuries later that the first of us arrived in Bombay.

Dorabji Nanabhoy is remembered as the first Parsi who came to Bombay. Originally recruited by the Portuguese to liaise with the local population, he was later employed by the British to collect taxes. Around three decades later, it was Nanabhoy's son who raised a militia to protect the city from Muslim attacks. He was later conferred the title of 'Patel' by the grateful British. Another early Parsi inhabitant was Kharshedji Ponchajee Panday, who supplied materials for building the city's fortifications.

My family's historical records say that Aungier wanted the city to be a magnet to business enterprise. To make that happen, he wisely adopted principles of religious toleration and local self-government, contrary to the Portuguese policy until 1662. Aungier introduced land laws that would enable people to buy land and build houses without hindrance. He backed it by creating a court system and a local police force. As the world now knows, his ideas worked. The population of Bombay had been around 10,000 when Aungier had first arrived. This grew to 80,000 in just eight years.

But the growth of Bombay was not without setbacks. This was a time when ships routinely pirated each other on the high seas. In 1688, the English captured fourteen Mughal ships and brought them to Bombay. A year later, the Mughals retaliated, and hit back hard. They laid siege to the English fort and the company eventually had to sue for peace through reparations. Peace came, but at a terrible cost. Bombay's wealth made its way to Mughal coffers, and the city decayed. Soon, farmland and houses lay abandoned.

It was several decades later that the Bombay we know re-emerged. This time, the company took the precaution of establishing a group of patrol ships—called the Bombay Marine—to protect the coast and harbour. Interestingly, this force eventually morphed into what is now called the Indian Navy!

The East India Company already had dealings with Parsi traders in Surat. Most of the Parsis were concentrated in Gujarat at that time since the initial wave of Zoroastrian refugees from Iran had first settled there. Now the company wished to entice them to Bombay. Parsis were better educated than most natives *and were far more open to Western influence and modernity. So in 1672, the year the English laid the foundation stone of St Thomas' Church, they also wisely provided land for the first Parsi dakhma. You see, whilst Hindus cremate their dead and Muslims and Christians bury them, we Zoroastrians practise what are known as sky-burials. For this we require special towers called dakhmas.*

Aungier claimed, with some justification, that Bombay was the city 'which by God's assistance was intended to be built'. True—Bombay would need God. But, more importantly, it would need the Parsis.

13

FOR REASONS NEVER *delved into, we Parsis have an incredible life-expectancy. Just think about it. Pirojsha Burjorji Godrej, co-founder of the Godrej empire, died at the age of ninety. Sir Cowasji Jehangir Readymoney, philanthropist and industrialist, died at eighty-three. Homi Nusserwanji Sethna, the man behind India's first nuclear test, died at eighty-six. JRD Tata, one of India's most beloved industrialists, died at ninety. Field-Marshal Sam Manekshaw, the hero of the 1971 Bangladesh War, died at ninety-four. India's famous astrologer, Bejan Daruwalla, died at eighty-eight. And they all lived in India—a country where it is a rare person who gets to spend more than sixty-nine years on earth.*

Notwithstanding our longer lifespans, Parsis eventually do die. So, we build circular, flat-topped towers called dakhmas.

Corpses are exposed to the elements on the tops of these towers, and vultures are encouraged to pick our bones clean. It prevents our dead, decaying bodies from polluting water or fire, which are considered in our faith to be symbols of purity, and fulfils a last act of charity—a virtue also binding on Parsis—nourishing the needy. Some of my friends, not all of them Parsis, see in it an early consciousness of man's duty to environment.

Recently, and ironically, vulture populations have declined owing to the overuse of diclofenac, a common anti-inflammatory drug found in both human and animal corpses on which they feed. We Parsis have been forced to set up solar concentrators to accelerate decomposition, breed more vultures, and advise our members to stop using diclofenac.

But that was certainly not an issue in Aungier's time! Providing land to establish a Parsi dakhma was a political masterstroke; Bombay's Tower of Silence was put up in the Malabar Hill area. Around the same time as the dakhma, the first Parsi fire temple of Bombay, the Mody Hirjee Wacha Dar-e-Mehr, was also established. The influx of Parsis from Gujarat to Bombay now began in earnest, and the English had their wish fulfilled.

Soon, Bombay was in full stride. Goldsmiths and diamond-cutters made their way to the city, and it sparkled with their jewellery. Weavers followed and spun fine yarns of silk and cotton in vibrant colours. Gujarati traders, coupled with Parsi ship owners and Marwari moneylenders, transformed Bombay into a commercial hub. Five decades later, shipbuilders even began assembling ships in Bombay. In the next century, textile mills began to appear. Among the first few cotton mills was one established by my great-great-grandfather. These mills marked the beginning of Bombay's industrial revolution.

The swamps were filled in completely and a railway line constructed, connecting the city to distant Thana—today's Thane. In 1818, the English succeeded in capturing Poona, now Pune. With the English having firmly defeated the Marathas, all the land routes to Bombay were now under English control. Newer and newer public buildings, styled along the lines of those in Victorian London, raised their lovely heads in the city. Bombay had arrived.

One particular Parsi gentleman, Lowje Wadia, had been carefully lured by the English to Bombay in 1736. He was a master builder who was given the job of building the city's dockyard. By then, the port in Surat was already silting up and the English wanted the lucrative Indo-Persian marine trade to migrate to Bombay. The Parsis not only brought that profitable business with them to Bombay, they also turned East and initiated the Bombay-China trade.

In 1756, the Parsi merchant who spurred the Indo-Chinese trade to flourish was Hirji Jivanji Readymoney. By 1833, there were thirty-five Englishmen and fifty-two Parsis living in China. Eventually, the Parsi who would dominate the Indo-Chinese trade in future years was Jamsetji Jijibhoy. He made his first visit to China in 1797 and built a dazzling fortune from that journey. He did not know it, but the Chinese authorities were searching for something that had been referred to in a text gifted to Kublai Khan by Marco Polo. But more about that later.

As the nineteenth century approached, Parsis began involving themselves in industrial enterprises. They established Bombay's first English printing press in 1780 and its first

Gujarati printing press in 1812. Many Parsis had already become wealthy owners of fleets. The Banaji family owned over forty ships. The Wadia, Jijibhoy, Dadysett and Readymoney families also had substantial fleets.

There were several reasons why my ancestors flourished in Bombay. Our community was distinct from the high-caste Hindu traders who were reluctant to travel overseas or to mix socially with the English. The Hindus were always paranoid about getting themselves 'polluted' and thus excommunicated by the orthodoxy. We Parsis had no such reservations in regard to travel or the company we broke bread with. In our world, whisky or gin took care of all pollutants! We spoke English fluently in addition to local languages. That made us perfect intermediaries. Over the years, we also built up a reputation for honesty and reliability.

By the time that the Bombay Chamber of Commerce was established in 1836, all ten of its founding Indians were Parsis. We were also at the forefront of banking, with Parsis having established the Bombay Bank, the Oriental Bank, and the Chartered Mercantile Bank. By 1850, Parsis owned around half of Bombay!

One of the many Parsis who would eventually migrate to Bombay was my great-great-grandfather, Shapoor Dastoor. He came to Bombay in 1858 from his hometown of Udvada, having fled from the priestly career that awaited him there. Among the articles he brought with him to Bombay was a little earthen box with a pilot-insignia like emblem that no one besides him was allowed to touch. In addition to that was a memorised text that no one knew the meaning of.

This box, its contents and the memorised test were usually reserved for the most rebellious member of the next generation. Shapoor Dastoor was certainly that, having unceremoniously dumped his Udvada heritage and the prestige accorded a man of God!

14

I T WAS A big move for Shapoor Dastoor in 1858. All his forefathers had been priests. But Shapoor's runaway act didn't cost him dear. The priestly families of Udvada were mostly wealthy landowners, so it may be safely assumed that Shapoor's family resources made his transition to Bombay a huge sight easier. I am told that his father even provided Shapoor—albeit a tad reluctantly—the initial capital for his ventures in Bombay.

I gather that Shapoor possessed gentle, soft-spoken charm. He always dressed neatly and spoke English fluently. He wasn't particularly intelligent but made up for that by being incredibly hard-working and sincere. His affable nature opened many doors for him.

One of his earliest acquaintances in Bombay was an Englishman called Murdoch. Shapoor had been strolling along the stretch of Bombay's docks one evening when he noticed a clearly inebriated Englishman lying in a crumpled heap on the bund. Shapoor had helped him up, procured a mug of sugary tea, coaxed it down his throat, and then accompanied him home. It had been the start of an enduring friendship. Shapoor *always joked that he had found 'a Murdoch on the dock at seven o'clock'.*

Murdoch was what the English called a 'country trader'. Country traders were merchants authorised by the East India Company to carry goods between India and China. Murdoch ran a fairly good business on behalf of the company. He would transport opium from India to China and carry back silver, tea, silks and porcelain into England using the India route. But now the lucrative opium trade was under pressure. You see, Arab traders had first exported opium to China in the sixth century. By the seventeenth century, opium addiction had become such a problem in China that several emperors had passed decrees outlawing it. The trade continued to flourish, of course. First the Portuguese, then the English, made opium the mainstay of their trade with China. It meant millions of impoverished poppy farmers in India—because the company had monopolised the trade—and millions of opium addicts in China, but who cared? Business was too damn good.

The Opium War had already taken place in China two decades before Shapoor's arrival in Bombay, and a second one was now underway. The two wars would only strengthen the commercial privileges of colonial powers in China. Eventually, these wars would unleash forces that toppled the Qing dynasty. Unusually for his time, Murdoch realised the need to diversify his business interests well before the opium trade was strangled.

At that time, raw cotton was shipped to England from India, spun into cloth in England and shipped back to India. There was an opportunity to set up a textile mill right there in Bombay itself. In fact, the first steam-operated cotton mill had already been set up by Cowasji Nanabhai Davar in 1854. The

Petit family were also mill-owners. Murdoch wondered why he couldn't do the same.

He had friends in Manchester—where all the Indian cotton was being spun for sale to India—who were willing to sell him used looms on reasonable terms. Murdoch had become a successful businessman chiefly because he recognised his own limitations. He loved his whisky, and his card games, and his gambling parties. He may have been a bachelor, but a different woman warmed his bed every night. Furthermore, he was intent on making these enjoyments the habits of a lifetime. Sitting in the hot, cramped office of a dusty textile mill, poring over files, was certainly not his idea of enjoyment. That was when he realised that the ideal person for that particular job was Shapoor Dastoor.

The problem was that Shapoor was unwilling to be in anyone's employ. So, Murdoch offered him a simple deal instead. Murdoch would put up the capital and procure the land and machinery. Shapoor would do everything else—in short, the grunt work. In return, Shapoor would have a twenty-five per cent stake in the venture that would increase to fifty per cent if the company showed profits in the first decade. Shapoor was hesitant at first, but then his wife Deena convinced him that it was the opportunity of a lifetime. Shapoor took the challenge and Gemini Mills was born, the name having been chosen by Deena for a very specific reason.

Providence smiled on Shapoor and Murdoch's venture: Just as the mill was about to start production, the American Civil War broke out. America met around eighty per cent of the world's cotton demand, but the war meant that those supplies would be drastically cut. Global cotton prices went through the roof, and Indian farmers ramped up their acreage to meet demand. Shapoor's mill was the beneficiary of those increased local supplies. During the first decade of operation, there wasn't a year when Gemini Mills did not enhance production capacity; nor was there a single year that the company did not pay out a dividend. Shapoor soon found himself becoming an equal partner with Murdoch, having easily surpassed the profit targets that the two partners had initially set for themselves.

Quite unlike the Great Rebellion of 1857, Shapoor's personal act of rebellion had worked.

15

SHAPOOR WAS A perfectionist. Unsatisfied with the coarse cotton cloth that his mill was producing, he experimented with different kinds of the fibre and even convinced Indian farmers to grow softer, finer varieties from Egypt which yielded longer thread. He also kept a very close eye on the mill and made continuous improvements to better production quality and quantity. Emphatic about appointing managers of a very high calibre who understood his vision, he was equally particular about improving conditions for the labour force. He instituted policies that were visionary for the time: paid leave, medical benefits at company cost, a school for employees' children and subsidised housing.

Production and profits skyrocketed but Murdoch, the inveterate womaniser, eventually succumbed to the inevitability of syphilis, better known as the 'pox'. Shapoor was dumbfounded *when Murdoch's solicitors revealed that the Englishman had named Shapoor the sole beneficiary of Murdoch's half of the mill. Shapoor was now its sole owner.*

Incredibly—or perhaps not so incredibly—by 1870, Parsi families owned nine of Bombay's thirteen textile mills. My family was foremost among them, owning the most profitable one: Gemini Mills.

Shapoor soon transformed himself into a pucca Englishman. He moved his family into a spacious manor and maintained a shiny horse-drawn carriage. The house had a grand marble staircase and European furniture. Mosaic tiles on the floors, and electric chandeliers, an innovation for the time, gave the house a grandeur seldom rivalled by other palatial homes. Large marble bathrooms with English plumbing and the priciest American fittings completed each suite. Over the years, Shapoor travelled the world and brought back art and antiques that he lovingly installed around the house. He was one of the earliest owners of a motorcar in Bombay. The house even boasted one of the first elevators and ice-making machines in the city!

Shapoor and Deena were just as rich in generosity. They threw the most lavish parties, and dinner always meant several courses that ended with exotic ice creams, an undreamt-of novelty for those times. Among the guests were Bombay's rich and famous, in addition to the Englishmen who ran the city. It was not surprising that Shapoor was among the first Indians to be knighted and eventually made a baronet of the British Empire. The Dastoors had arrived.

They were blessed with two sons, Homi and Navroze. Although the boys were brought up in luxury, their basic values were never compromised. You must remember, Zoroastrian philosophy emphasised the value of their own trinity: good thoughts, good words and good deeds—humata, hukata *and* huvarastha. *Shapoor and Deena never allowed the boys to forget those. Deena would remind the boys that all that money gave a person was the freedom of not having to worry about it.*

Homi and Navroze were never permitted to slack off on rules because of their father's wealth. They followed strict routines and were reprimanded if their grades fell. Pocket-money was controlled, and they had to finish whatever food was placed on their plates. Staff were on hand to help with chores but were always to be treated with respect.

Homi, a shy and introverted sort, loved Western classical music. It was evident that his heart lay in musical, not currency, notes. Luckily, his mother realised this and encouraged him to excel at the violin. When Shapoor returned home in the evenings, he would hear the strains of Bach, Beethoven and Brahms emerging from Homi's room. It caused him both elation and anxiety. The father was happy to see a maestro in the making ... but he so desperately wanted his elder son to take over the reins of the business!

It required Deena's consummate diplomatic skills to bring Shapoor around to an alternate view. He eventually gave his elder son his blessings to move to Vienna to pursue a career as a violinist. Homi willingly gave up his share in the family enterprise so that his younger brother Navroze could get on with expanding it.

And Homi became famous. He came to be called the 'Vivaldi of the East'! I listen to his compositions with delight to this day. I am very proud that I can claim him as my great-granduncle.

Homi, having eschewed a future in a business he was heir to, was a rebel too, and therefore became the next custodian of the little earthen box and the memorised text that no one knew the meaning of.

16

JIM WOKE AND looked around in a daze. What he registered was that he was inside an aircraft of some kind, the clothes he was wearing were not his own, he had a splitting headache and his mouth felt like paper. As if all that weren't enough to befuddle his senses, his hands were securely bound together with heavy-duty zip ties.

When he recovered somewhat, Jim realised that he was in a private jet. The seats were upholstered in plush napa leather; the table in front of him had a walnut veneer; there were only six seats in the aircraft; and each was generously appointed.

Seated across from him was a neatly dressed man in a pullover and jeans, with an immaculately groomed beard and wearing rimless glasses. 'My apologies for bringing you in like this, Jim,' he said with a smile. He nodded to an assistant, who came forward, cut the zip ties that held Jim's hands together and retreated. Jim rubbed his wrists, happy to be freed. Well, almost.

'You must be thirsty,' said the man. 'Get some water,' he instructed the steward. The steward dutifully placed two small bottles of mineral water in front of Jim, who quickly unscrewed one and gulped it down. Then he looked at the man seated opposite and mentally asked a series of questions in rapid succession. *Who are you? Where am I? Where is Linda? Why have you abducted me?*

'Calm down, Jim,' said the man, a smile hovering on his face. 'You have many questions, and I shall attempt to answer them one by one. But first, eat something. Regain your strength. Would you like a Tylenol for that headache? Sorry about that, but we *had* to knock you out.' Jim tried figuring out the man's accent. It was American, with a hint of the Middle East.

The steward came back and placed a napkin with a tray of food in front of Jim. It contained nuts, assorted cheeses, pickles and breads. At the corner of the tray was a small bottle of Tylenol. Jim swallowed a pill first. Then he realised how hungry he was, not having eaten since the previous night. His host busied himself with his messages while Jim ate. The steward brought Jim coffee after he had eaten. Jim accepted the hot brew gratefully as he looked back at his host.

'Do you mind telling me what this is all about?' asked Jim, feeling slightly better after his reluctant repast. The pounding in his head seemed to have lessened.

'My name is Ali Zamani,' said the man. 'I am in charge of this operation. You see, your Hamzaa Dura is of no use to us without you. We cannot download your mind into our computers, can we? So we had had no alternative but to carry you along with it.'

'Where is Linda?' asked Jim, ignoring everything else he said. 'Is she safe?'

'Absolutely,' assured Ali. 'She is on her way back to Seattle and will be reaching your home in the next thirty minutes.

We had no intention of harming her. But we also knew that the only way to get your cooperation was to use her as bait. Fortunately, our plan worked.'

'And where are we now?' asked Jim, staring out of the window at nothing but an endless blanket of clouds.

'We are on our way to Worcester—Massachusetts—having departed an hour ago from Portland International Airport. Please do not worry. It is my responsibility to ensure that you are well looked after.'

'Why Worcester?' asked Jim, curtly.

'Everything will become absolutely clear as soon as we arrive at our destination,' replied Ali. 'As I've already said, you have my sincerest apologies for having brought you here in this manner. But I would like to make it up to you by treating you as an honoured guest, not as a captive.'

'That's so kind of you,' replied Jim. His sarcasm was not lost on Ali Zamani.

'Where are my clothes?' asked Jim curiously. He had been wearing his work clothes in the morning—a linen shirt, sweater, khaki cotton trousers and brown leather loafers. But now he was in a t-shirt, jacket and chinos. His leather shoes had been replaced by soft sneakers.

'We had to change your clothes and footwear while you were unconscious,' replied Ali. 'We were unsure of which tracking devices might be on your person. As it turns out, we were right in being careful.'

'Who *are* you?' asked Jim. 'And please don't repeat your name. You know what I mean.'

Ali looked amused. 'I represent people who are very interested in you and your discoveries. And we would like to ensure that both you and your research are well-protected.'

Jim realised that he would not be getting any further information from Ali. He massaged his temples with his hands and then stretched. 'I'm stiff,' he said to Ali. 'Mind if I get up and move about a bit?'

'Go ahead,' replied Ali. 'Let me remind you, though, my assistant is just a few seats away from us. He is a retired Navy Seal. If you try anything funny, you will end up increasing your discomfort.'

Jim unclipped the seatbelt that had locked him in place and stood up. The Seal also got up but remained at his spot. Jim walked down the aisle, turned around and walked back to his seat. He repeated this a few times.

In the process he got a look at the wallpaper inside the aircraft. It bore a pale gold logo, repeated at intervals, made up of a name written in Palace Script. The jet was obviously owned by that organisation.

Asclepius.

17

THE PRIVATE JET touched down at Worcester Regional Airport and a haggard Jim was requested to deplane, with Ali Zamani and the others holding him hostage. As he climbed down the stairs of the aircraft, he saw that there was a limousine parked on the tarmac below him.

Jim and Zamani entered it and occupied the rear seats while one of the armed men sat up front next to the driver. The opaque windows made it impossible to see where they were headed. The now-familiar Asclepius logo was present on the headrests of the seats. Ali, who maintained a determined silence throughout the ride, exuded a pleasant smell. Jim tried figuring out the fragrance and settled on Jo Malone. Probably Wood Sage & Sea Salt.

Around thirty minutes later, the car halted. The doors were opened from the outside by a security guard. As Jim stepped out, he saw that they were within an expansive estate with manicured lawns that seemingly stretched till the horizon. At one end was a New England manor; at the other was a huge, modern commercial block. Towards a corner of the plot was a smaller block marked as an on-site hotel. Emblazoned high on the wall of the corporate block was the Asclepius logo.

The guard escorted them to the entrance of the manor. At the main door of shadowed glass, a butler ushered them in. They crossed carpeted corridors, the walls of which bore priceless paintings by Gauguin, Warhol, Rubens and Cézanne. At the far end of the final corridor was a massive oak door.

When the butler opened it, they entered an ornate study that smelled of books, leather and cigar smoke. Seated behind an ornamental desk was a podgy, fair-complexioned man in an expensive suit. 'Welcome to Worcester, Jim,' he said, rising from behind his desk and coming round it to shake hands. He was less than five feet tall even in his elevator shoes. 'My name is Ryan Parker, and it is my honour to host you at my humble abode.'

Jim shook hands as a matter of courtesy before asking, 'Who are you?'—although he already knew the answer. Ryan Parker, sixty-three years old, was the tycoon with a Napoleonic complex who ran Asclepius, one of the world's largest pharmaceutical companies. Jim had seen his picture on the cover of *Forbes*, featured as the man who gobbled companies and formulations for breakfast. He was the vulture that one of the GCRC directors had warned him about. Asclepius employed over 95,000 people around the world and delivered its products to over 150 countries. It was at the cutting edge in areas such as oncology, immunology, infectious diseases, ophthalmology, cardiology and neurology.

Parker's personal life was the stuff of lifestyle magazines. His current wife—his third in three decades—had been a Hollywood star before she married him. Private jets, yachts, penthouse apartments, villas and luxury cars were ubiquitous in his surroundings.

He motioned in the direction of a sofa, inviting Jim to sit. Occupying a chair next to him, he began, matter-of-factly, 'You already know of me, but you probably do not know of the association that I represent.'

'Association?' asked Jim.

'I represent a group of pharmaceutical companies,' explained Parker. 'Together, we account for seventy per cent of the global pharmaceuticals market. I am the president of the association, and we strive to work helping each other.'

'You mean you run a cartel,' said Jim drily.

Parker laughed. 'Call it what you like, Jim,' he said jovially. 'You know better than anyone else that this is a high-stakes game. After taking into consideration the costs of failed trials, the average research and development cost to bring a single new drug to market is almost a billion dollars. No point in replicating those costs across companies. It is also meaningless to kill margins through aggressive competition.'

'Why have you brought me here?' asked Jim. It was a foolish question, because Jim knew the answer this time too.

'We believe that there is a huge opportunity in your Hamzaa Dura,' replied Parker. 'An opportunity for you—and for us. We would be foolish to blow the chance of working together.'

'Potential business partners do not abduct one another,' replied Jim. 'Or their spouses.'

'Sometimes the ends are more important than the means,' said Parker. 'Frankly, I knew that you would be unwilling to discuss Hamzaa Dura as a business proposition without practically carrying you here. Your position on the matter is already known to us.'

'Who told you about my purported position?' asked Jim. His mind raced, trying to connect the dots. The only ones in GCRC who knew about his work were his four other directors. But it seemed impossible that any one of them would have betrayed him.

'We have our ways,' replied Parker. 'We didn't get big without keeping tabs on everyone else. Hamzaa Dura is an opportunity as well as a threat. We would much rather look at it as the former than the latter.'

'And what if I choose not to cooperate?' asked Jim.

'You are here with us,' replied Parker. 'Your research and raw materials are also with us. One option is that we jointly leverage the opportunity. The other option is that I eliminate my perceived threat. The direction that we take will depend on you.' The tiger had bared his teeth—and not in a smile.

'Hamzaa Dura belongs to the whole of humanity,' replied Jim. 'That's why GCRC has not applied for any patent. We want the whole world to be able to reap the benefits from this discovery. I have never been driven by money.' *All that money can give a person is the freedom of not having to worry about it,* as Deena, Shapoor Dastoor's wife, would have said.

Parker laughed. 'I figured that you'd change your mind.'

'And if I don't?' asked Jim warily.

'Let me give you a tour of our premises,' said Parker, airily changing the subject. 'Maybe you will understand what you're up against. I have the power to make most people change their minds.'

18

THE CITY OF Bandar Abbas, capital of Hormuzgan province, is a port located on the southern coast of Iran. Behrad Soroushpur had been here before, but never with the curiosity that characterised this particular trip. He had planned to avoid coming here, but his conversation with Unwalla in Udvada had prompted him to visit.

His desired destination would have been the ancient town of Hormuz, but that was long gone, lost in the sands of time. The closest modern city was Bandar Abbas. And the waterbody that surrounded it—the Straits of Hormuz— preserved the memory of its ancient neighbour. The name also attached itself to a small island off the coast that was still known as Hormuz Island. Surprisingly, the clerics of Iran had not attempted to change the name. Were they not aware that the name 'Hormuz' was a version of 'Ormazd', the short form of the Zoroastrian 'Ahura Mazda'? *God?*

Soroushpur headed straight to the old bazaar, where the jostling crowd of humanity glistened with sweat from the heat and humidity. However, the temperature had done nothing to reduce the bustle in the narrow streets. Tiny shops and improvised stalls sold a little bit of everything, from sweet dates and tobacco leaves to dried seafood, fruits and vegetables. Tucked away in one of the lanes was a bookstore without a signboard. The proprietor sat outside smoking a hookah. Soroushpur stopped at the entrance and greeted him. The old man smiled at him, displaying yellowed teeth, and they went inside the shop together.

'What brings you here today?' asked the proprietor.

'A craving for knowledge of the old Hormuz,' said Soroushpur. 'As you know, most of the land and sea routes radiated from here outwards to Asia, Africa and Europe. A number of Zoroastrians mounted a last stand at Hormuz before they fled by sea to Diu or by land to Sistan.'

'True,' replied the proprietor. 'You want old books about that period?'

'Actually, I was wondering if there were any scrolls or parchments that may have been left behind by the fleeing groups at the time of the eighth century?' Soroushpur defined his quest. 'After all, you have been one of my best channels when searching for old documents.'

'My family has dealt in books and manuscripts for many generations,' said the old proprietor. 'I have not seen it for myself, but I used to hear stories about the time when a group of Zoroastrians had to sail under desperate circumstances. They had with them some very important written material in a book by Borzuya. It appears it was left behind.'

'Any guesses where such material would still be?'

'No need to guess,' replied the proprietor. 'It was passed on thirty years later, by my ancestors, to Ibn al-Muqaffa.'

'Was there no other important Zoroastrian text that would have passed through the hands of your forefathers?' asked Soroushpur avidly.

'I can tell you the most obvious one, but I'm not sure you would believe me,' said the man, still grinning.

'And that would be?' asked Soroushpur.

The old man turned away to search for something. For the next few minutes, he rummaged through his cupboards, pulling out books and putting them back. He opened drawers of an antique chest that sat against the far wall, took out books from inside and mulled over them. He then opened a trunk that lay on the floor; he even stood on a chair to access some of the higher bookshelves. Suddenly, he let out a little yelp of joy as he found what he was looking for.

'Here it is,' he said, opening the book to a particular page. Soroushpur looked at the cover. *The Travels of Marco Polo*, the thirteenth-century travelogue written by Rustichello da Pisa, derived from the narratives of Italian explorer Marco Polo. Soroushpur placed his forefinger at the passage that the proprietor had pointed out.

Merchants come hither to Hormuz from India, with ships loaded with spicery and precious stones, pearls, cloths of silk and gold, elephants' teeth, and many other wares, which they sell to the merchants of Hormuz, and which these in turn carry all over the world to dispose of again. In fact, it is a city of immense trade.

Marco Polo then went on to say that Hormuz sent not only pearls to China, but also ten thousand horses each year to India. 'What does Marco Polo have to do with my question?' asked Soroushpur.

'According to my ancestors, the Zoroastrians who stayed behind in Persia wanted to send certain documents to their cousins in India. This was in the thirteenth century. But all their efforts were in vain. When Marco Polo came here, he amassed many of those documents for himself. So, whatever it was neither remained here nor reached India.'

'What was the book called?'

'*Kalila wa Dimna*, by Abdullah ibn al-Muqaffa,' replied the proprietor with confidence.

19

THE CITY OF Tehran often appears from the sky as a haphazard collection of mismatched jigsaw pieces. And this image is reinforced on land when one approaches Ferdouzi Street, which lies towards the southern end of the capital. Nearby stands one of the few surviving fire temples in the city.

Located a stone's throw away from this temple is an ordinary residential building with a common courtyard. But this residence isn't open to just anybody. All the quarters are occupied by carefully chosen members of a group.

Inside a darkened room of a first-floor apartment stood Behrad Soroushpur, dressed entirely in pristine white. On his head was a crisp, white turban. His oiled moustache and beard matched the rest of his white ensemble. Tall and ruddy-complexioned, he was head of a group that called itself the Gabrabad Action Front, or the GAF. Soroushpur had just returned from an important visit to Udvada and Bandar Abbas.

Maintaining absolute secrecy was of vital importance to the GAF. Ever since the Islamic Revolution of 1979, Zoroastrians in Iran had come under increasing scrutiny. There were barely twenty-five thousand of them left in a country of eighty-four million people. Security forces always viewed them with suspicion. In fact, Iran's primary intelligence agency, VAJA, had special instructions to keep a close watch on them for the slightest sign of 'un-Islamic' behaviour.

Seated on upright chairs in a circle around Soroushpur were a group of men dressed in ordinary clothes. Soroushpur stood apart in his pure white attire, addressing the group softly in a language that was neither Farsi nor Azeri. It had no similarity to any of the other languages spoken in Iran, including Kurdish, Arabic or Balochi. In fact, the words were unlike any other language anywhere in the world. It was a special code that only members of the GAF learnt and used. 'Have you done a sweep of the room and its people for wires or bugs?' asked Soroushpur. A man nodded. Upon his nod,

Soroushpur switched to Dari, a dialect that had been invented by the Zoroastrians during the years of Islamic persecution.

'It is becoming evident that the government, the *Nezam-e-Jomhuri*, is making plans to retrieve the Athravan Star,' said Soroushpur.

'This cannot be allowed to happen,' burst out one of the members fiercely. 'The Muslims took away everything that we Zoroastrians held dear. We cannot allow them to take this away too.'

'It is not ours to give or take,' said Soroushpur. 'It has not been in our hands for 1300 years. We don't even know what it is! Can anyone describe it? All we have are fantastical accounts of its magical properties. Even my meeting with Pestonji Unwalla in Udvada cannot be considered definitive. I am trying my best to get some additional information using my Yazidi researcher, Nasr Tamoyan, at Gundeshapur but these things take time.'

'That does not change the fact that it rightfully belongs to us,' replied another. 'But even if we desire to pre-empt the government, the fact remains that the IRGC has incredible resources, far greater than ours. If they want something, they have the capacity to get it. See how they managed to move forward on the uranium enrichment programme, despite all the hurdles in their way.'

Soroushpur felt that the speaker had made a valid point. Iran's nuclear programme had been initiated in the 1950s, with the US as a partner. After the Islamic Revolution, the Americans had withdrawn, but Iran had managed to continue the programme with cooperation from countries such as France, Argentina and Russia. The programme now consisted of multiple research sites, two substantial uranium mines, a research reactor and three uranium enrichment plants. All this had been achieved at a huge national cost arising from international sanctions estimated at almost a hundred billion dollars in lost oil revenues and foreign investment. When Iran's rulers wanted something, they went after it with a vengeance. Even twenty-four years of rule by Saddam Hussein in neighbouring Iraq had been inadequate to get Iran to yield an iota.

'The bigger question is how do we get our hands on it,' said Soroushpur. 'It's a zero-sum game. If we have it, others do not. If they have it, we do not.'

One of the older members voiced his opinion. 'It should never have been allowed to leave Iran. It is a historical blunder that we need to set right.' Many heads nodded in agreement.

Soroushpur's was not amongst them.

Outsiders did not understand that a hierarchy operated within the Zoroastrian community. The Mobeds were considered to be the highest in that layered structure. After the Arab conquest of Persia, most Mobeds had fled to India, but some had stayed behind, including Soroushpur's ancestors. This was probably why many members looked up to him.

'There is no point in debating the past,' said Soroushpur. 'We have been dealt a set of cards. We need to play intelligently with those we have.'

'Many of our treasures were taken away and we never bothered to ask where,' said another member. 'Where is the Cyrus Cylinder today? Are we even attempting to get it back? There is a buzz that a thief tried stealing it from the British

Museum a few days ago. Heaven knows, it will soon be in a collector's museum rather than rightfully in our hands.'

'But we cannot compare the Cyrus Cylinder with the Athravan Star,' said Soroushpur. 'Even the sacking of Persepolis by Alexander did not take the Athravan Star away from us. And now we find ourselves in this terrible predicament— plotting ways to take back what should never have gone. And what Pestonji Unwalla says is conjecture at this moment.'

'But what if it isn't conjecture?' asked a member. 'Can we afford to take the risk?'

The other men agreed that Soroushpur was right, but they all knew the odds of mounting such an operation. It would require tremendous financial resources and global coordination to make it happen.

Soroushpur stroked his beard thoughtfully. 'We may not need to mount a huge operation if we can find the right man. If the mountain won't come to Mohammad, Mohammad must go to the mountain.' The members of the group wondered what Soroushpur meant by quoting that old adage.

In the Islamic Republic of Iran, even mountains had to bow to Mohammad's will.

20

THE NAKED MAN entered a chamber that was almost entirely draped in red latex and black leather. The lights inside were dimmed and tinted with red. From the walls hung chains, handcuffs, collars, leashes and assorted implements of sexual fetish. He took in the sight, his heartbeat racing faster in excitement.

'Get down on your knees,' came the voice of his mistress. 'Who told you that you can be anything other than a four-legged creature in my presence?' He quickly went down on all fours, his humiliation only increasing by the second. Before he could crawl further, a whip lashed his rear. He winced in pain but knew better than to make a sound. Ignoring the stinging sensation, he allowed himself to sink into the pleasure zone of his deprivation, humiliation and subjugation. Mistress Lucinda was not for the fainthearted. But she was utterly addictive. He did not know whether he loved, hated or feared her more.

After their session was over, she kissed him gently on his lips, her eyes twinkling mischievously. Dan just *knew* that it was love. Sure, the world would call it his fetish or perversion, but it *had* to be love. He simply could not do without the pain and pleasure that Lucinda delivered.

Two hours later, bathed and fresh, as if having showered after an invigorating workout at the gym, Dan Cohen walked to the coffee shop a block away from the GCRC cube. He occupied his usual booth and ordered his customary lunch—a bacon-lettuce-tomato sandwich, salad and coffee. Dan was Jewish and nothing gave him greater pleasure than incorporating bacon into his diet, almost as a snub to the memories of his controlling mother.

Dan was a creature of habit. Just twenty minutes later he would be in his lab, fresh as a daisy, as that twee, tired simile went. His regular waitress was off today, and he wondered whether this one would give him his BLT the way he liked it. She took his order and walked towards the kitchen. Dan's gaze lingered on the swell of her buttocks as she swayed away. His mind was fantasising delicious scenarios around her. He forced himself to ditch the thought. There was simply too much work to do on the vaccine project.

Dan was the same age as Jim, and both had met as freshmen at Stanford. Their paths had diverged for a few years after Stanford, when Jim had pursued his BS with a dual MD-PhD degree, while Dan had gone to work in the pharmaceutical sector after his doctorate. Dan had excelled in jobs with Pfizer and Johnson & Johnson before ditching the big boys to join Jim's venture. Dan's wife, Susan, had been against the idea. But when their marriage broke up, Dan wanted a clean break from his past. His entry into GCRC had been very important for Jim. During those first few years, it was Dan's work that had kept the revenues rolling in.

Dan had barely taken a few sips of his coffee when his phone rang. It was an unknown caller. He took the call hesitantly. 'Mr Dan Cohen?' asked the voice. Dan realised that the voice was not only coming through the phone but also from above him. He looked up and saw a thin pale man with mousy red hair, dressed in a wrinkled grey business suit. The man sat down opposite Dan. 'Glad to see that you picked up my call,' said the man who called himself Luke Miller. 'I was watching to see if you would.'

'What do you want now?' asked Dan. There was irritation in his voice, but also a hint of nervousness.

'Come now, Dan, you already know what we need from you,' said the man. 'Alas, the life that you have been leading has far too many secrets. Your wife realised it a little late. Luckily for you she never talked. But if some of those compromising photographs were to emerge, I shudder to think what would happen to your career.'

Dan stirred his coffee vigorously. Why hadn't he kept his pants zipped up? Why couldn't he have had a simple affair? Why had his personal tastes always been so weird? Had he been 'normal', Susan would never have left him. And what was 'normal' anyway? What made one sexual fantasy more perverted than another? *And why the fuck am I wired so* ab*normally?*

Luke seemed to sense the conflict within Dan. 'I'm your friend, Dan,' he said persuasively. 'Why do you worry? Nothing will ever come out. You have my solemn promise.'

'But I'm not sure I can help you,' said Dan.

'Nonsense,' replied Miller. 'We can both help each other. All that you need to do is to apply your mind to our little problem at hand.'

'I already helped you with his thumbprint,' argued Dan. 'You said it was to gain access to his biometric records.'

'And we are grateful,' replied Miller, carefully omitting to tell Dan what the true purpose had been. 'But we need to cover all bases.'

'Jim Dastoor is my friend,' said Dan. 'We were in Stanford together. We built GCRC together. I would never do anything to harm him or the company.'

'Sometimes we must do things to protect ourselves,' said Miller. He stopped talking when the waitress approached with Dan's order. Even in this stressful situation, Dan seemed pleased to have received his BLT the way he liked it.

'What would you like?' she asked the visitor, after serving Dan.

'Just some coffee, please,' he said. 'Black, no sugar.'

As she left, Miller said with a wink, 'She managed to get your order just right, it seems. Although your usual waitress isn't here today. Do you fantasise about this one too?'

Dan was quiet. *They know everything about me.*

The waitress came back to pour coffee for Miller and left. Miller took an envelope from his jacket's inner pocket and slid it over to Dan. 'This contains detailed instructions,' he said. 'A little bird told me you're in the final shortlist for the Kettering Prize. Don't blow your chances with a tabloid headline about how you like to get blown.' He tittered at his own awful joke.

21

PARKER AND ZAMANI accompanied Jim as they took a well-concealed elevator from Parker's study to a floor below. A walkalator—a moving walkway similar to the ones in airports—inside a temperature-controlled and brightly illuminated tunnel took them from the manor into the corporate block that Jim had observed when they had driven in. When they reached the end of the passage, a retina scan-activated door allowed them into the basement of what was probably the largest-ever research facility that Jim had seen in his life.

A short escalator ride brought them to the first level, to an atrium entirely of gleaming white marble. At the centre of the atrium was a gigantic bronze statue of Asclepius, the Greek God of medicine, the mythological figure from whom the company derived its name. Believed to have been the son of Apollo, Asclepius had several daughters, one of them Hygieia, the Goddess of cleanliness, the other Panacea, the Goddess of universal remedies. The rod of Asclepius, a snake-entwined staff, continues to remain a symbol of medicine, incorporated even into the logo of the World Health Organization.

The block occupied around 24,000 square metres of laboratory space split on eight floors and wrapped around a massive atrium flooded with illumination from an array of LED lights. The roof above the atrium was of curved steel-and-glass, fashioned to resemble the pointed end of a drop of medicine. Around 500 scientists dressed in white lab coats operated from this single location.

More importantly, Parker had housed this facility right next to his mansion so that he could personally supervise the research engine that powered his behemoth. As Asclepius carried on gobbling up competitors, it shut down their labs and relocated them to Worcester. As older products disappeared from Asclepius's list of patent-protected medicines, newer ones emerged—almost magically—to replace them. There was also the minor tweaking of compositions and reengineering of molecules to create almost similar drugs, using new patents when older patents expired. Obviously, these 'new, improved' drugs cost much more, thus adding to the company's bottom line, and lining the pockets of the greedy manufacturers, 'innovative' scientists, 'flexible' lawyers and slimy senators, all with malleable and ductile morals.

But Asclepius was no provider of magic cures. It was a ruthless, well-oiled machine that delivered a massive yet steady stream of pharma-dollars each year to a bunch of hard-nosed shareholders.

'Come,' said Parker, as they took an escalator to the second floor. 'Let me show you our replication lab.' The entire floor was devoted to what Parker casually referred to as 'replication'. Tens of scientists sat hunched over their equipment and counters or scurried about like rats inside a giant maze. 'Any new drug on the market anywhere in the world is immediately brought here for study. It allows us to determine its efficacy, whether we can formulate our own competitor product to it, or whether we need to buy up the company or formulation.'

He paused for effect. 'You're wondering about the other floors,' said Parker. Jim was not. But Parker wanted to share more information. 'We have a portfolio of hundreds of products,' he explained. 'Teams work on improving existing formulations as well as conduct fresh research to discover new cures—just like you do.'

Jim was staring at the high-tech facility that had obviously cost hundreds of millions to construct and outfit. Rows upon rows of biochemical analysers, cell counters, harvesters, freeze dryers, electrophoresis analysers, flow cytometers, gas and liquid chromatography samplers, hyper spectral imagers, and incubators were neatly installed in the perfectly planned interiors.

'Your Hamzaa Dura is already in their hands,' said Parker—quite unnecessarily—as he saw Jim staring. But before Jim could react, Parker said, 'Don't worry, we know that the quantity is limited in supply. We shall have to be careful. But after understanding what you are up against, does it make any sense for you to hold out against us? What is the advantage? We know that you have not yet been able to synthesise it. Why not try again, together with us?'

'So that you may milk it for the next twenty years?' said Jim. 'Hamzaa Dura is for all of humanity, just like insulin!'

'We could discuss terms that may be agreeable to you,' said Parker smoothly. 'For example, if you wish to retain but license it for a period of time, I would be willing to consider such a deal.' He looked for reactions on Jim's face but there were none. He simply shook his head.

'In the meantime,' said Parker, 'I am asking Ali to accompany you to our guest accommodation where you can give it some thought. In the best surroundings. The suites in the guest block are luxurious and are provided with all the facilities of a deluxe hotel.'

'What if I have nothing to consider?' asked Jim. 'What if I wish to leave?'

'Are you a fan of the music group, *The Eagles*, Jim?' asked Parker.

'I can't see how my music preferences are important right now.'

'If you are indeed a fan of that wonderful band, you will know the famous lines from their song *Hotel California*.'

Jim now knew what Parker meant.

We are programmed to receive
You can check out any time you like
But you can never leave

22

THE SEATTLE FIELD Office of the Federal Bureau of Investigation, the FBI, is located in the Abraham Lincoln Building on the corner of Third Avenue and Spring Street, having moved many times before settling in here. The Seattle office boasts of hundreds of agents and millions of dollars' worth of equipment, transport, software and firepower, quite unlike the original 1914 office that had a grand total of nine agents with no guns.

Seated inside a spacious wood-panelled conference hall were Linda Dastoor and Greg Walters. Fred Smith was the FBI special agent handling their case. Fred had been involved in many cases dealing with violent crimes, cybercrime, white-collar fraud and child abduction. His experience in such a wide range of cases owed to the fact that the FBI's authority is the broadest among all law enforcement agencies. It is a misperception that the FBI mostly deals with cases relating to foreigners and terrorism. The truth is that the vast majority of FBI probes have involved American citizens. And a kidnapping across State lines—such as Jim Dastoor's—would fall well within its ambit.

But the path to the FBI's involvement had been convoluted. After Jim's kidnapping at the Portland parking lot, Linda had staggered over to the security office. Based on her plea for help, the attendant had run inside to call the police while Linda had slumped to the asphalt. Five minutes later a patrol car had pulled up. The police had helped Linda into the car and driven her to the Portland Police Bureau, a few minutes away.

The duty sergeant who introduced himself as 'Chuck' had settled her into an interview room and arranged for water and coffee. Linda had explained the situation as calmly as she could. She could see the sergeant's eyes widen as she narrated how she had been kidnapped from her home in Seattle and used as bait to hook her husband along with his research material. In the midst of the interview, Chuck's phone rang. He answered the call. It was Greg Walters from Seattle. The men knew each other from their days at the Academy. 'Listen Chuck,' Greg had said. 'I've got a situation on my hands, and I need your help.'

As he listened to what Greg was saying, Chuck realised that the person sitting in front of him was one of the people Greg was talking about. Chuck had immediately handed the phone to Linda. Greg's voice had come through. 'Hi, Linda. You don't know me—I'm Greg Walters from the Seattle Police Department. Jim and I sometimes play racquetball together at the Seattle Athletic Club. When you were kidnapped, Jim had reached out to me to help find you.'

'And here I am, but Jim's gone,' Linda whispered weakly. She quickly explained to Greg what had transpired at the parking area where Jim was kidnapped and she was released.

'Are you injured?' Greg had asked, his Yazidi eyebrows lifting in concern.

'Thankfully not. Just some minor bruises and a cut from the scuffle in my kitchen. Some more from the binding ropes. But please Greg, find Jim. Please make that your priority!'

Greg had been looking at the pulsating blip on his screen as he spoke to Linda. It indicated the location of the GPS tracker in Jim's shoe. 'I am tracking him as we speak,' Greg had explained. 'They smashed his phone but didn't realise that a GPS tracker had been installed in his shoe. Meantime, I think you should come back to Seattle. I need you here to help with my investigation.'

Linda had thanked Greg and hung up. Still dressed in the tracksuit she had casually pulled on in the morning, she hadn't bathed, her mouth tasted like cardboard and her hair was an absolute mess. She was sure she looked and smelled yucky. But she knew that even if she were home and safe, her mind would not be at peace until she saw Jim again.

In Seattle, Greg had continued staring at the moving blip on his screen as it made its way across the Vietnam Veterans Memorial Highway. Looking at the route, he knew where the blip was headed. Portland International Airport.

'Have you found out where Jim is?' Linda asked Greg the moment she met him back in Seattle, a persistent tic in her cheek revealing her extreme anxiety.

'We lost him at Portland International Airport,' Greg replied. 'He's probably on a flight. We're going to need the FBI.'

Greg felt his phone buzzing and picked up the call. It was his contact at the FBI's Seattle Field Office, Agent Fred Smith. 'Thanks for returning my call, Fred. As I messaged earlier, this is about the Jim Dastoor abduction. I need your help with analysis of the surveillance feed from Portland International Airport. We also need passenger manifests of all flights that left the airport. Frankly, I hope that you feds can take up the case because I'm feeling a little lost here. Jim could be almost anywhere by now—within the US or even outside it. An Interpol Yellow Notice for Jim would help. I can be at your Third Avenue office within the hour.'

Now, inside the FBI conference room, Fred Smith's phone rang. He looked at the number and took the call. 'Are you sure?' he asked. He cut the call and looked at Linda. 'Jim's clothes, including the leather shoes that had the tracker, were found in a dumpster at Portland International Airport. So now we know that he was taken there and that his clothes were discarded. Our team is trying to review the security footage from the airport but that will take some time.'

'Jim could be dead!' Linda said in a defeated whisper.

'I think not,' soothed Fred. 'If they wanted to kill him, they didn't need to abduct him and take him to the airport. No, it's evident that they wanted him and his material. We simply need to figure out where they have taken him. We also need to understand the nature of Jim's research. Whom can we speak to?'

'There's only one person who could brief you on that,' replied Linda. 'Jim's fellow director, Dan Cohen.'

23

THE GUEST BLOCK located on the Asclepius estate contained fifty rooms spread out on five floors. A graceful lobby in oakwood flooring was accented by a Persian rug and a centre table adorned with fresh blue hydrangeas. This led to a bank of three elevators, of which one did not have standard call buttons. Ali Zamani used his ID card to call that particular elevator. Inside, there were no buttons or floor indicators. The elevator doors simply slid shut and took them to the fifth floor.

Unlike the other floors, this floor had only five rooms, each the size of a grand suite. Ali led Jim to room 501, a corner suite elegantly furnished with a kingsize bed and a seating niche, and two floor-to-ceiling walls of plexiglass overlooking the vast gardens of the estate. It had all the usual amenities of a luxury hotel, including a flat-screen television, coffeemaker, minibar, premium linen, soft towels, bottled water, a marble bathroom and central air-conditioning. And yet, examined more closely, the suite had no WiFi signal, the channels on the television screened only in-house movies, the telephone could only connect to Ali's number and none of the windows could be opened. All the furniture was heavy and bolted to the floor; all the linen and towels were of fragile fabric, meaning they could not be used as ropes; no sharp or breakable items were present. So suicide would be difficult or nearly impossible to commit. It was, in effect, a luxury prison.

'The five rooms on this floor are for our "special" guests,' said Ali with a smirk. 'The remaining floors operate like a regular hotel for our corporate visitors. Just pick up the phone if you need to reach me. Meals of your choice can be sent to you round the clock; housekeeping staff and laundry services, too. We aim to keep you comfortable.'

Ali Zamani caught Jim inspecting the room. 'Please do not even think of trying to leave,' he warned. 'The elevator going down needs my access control. The windows are sealed shut and made of unbreakable polycarbonate. You have no means of communication to the outside world. There is no bathtub in which you can drown yourself. The voltage is too low for electrocution. Spend this time wisely and think. Ryan Parker can be a generous business partner to work with.' Ali Zamani left, shutting the door behind him. Jim heard the soft buzzing of an electronic doorlock. He tried the door handle, but the knob did not turn. He was well and truly a prisoner. It was the Hilton from Hell.

Jim slumped into the sofa. He experienced a tumult of feelings but the chief among them was anger. He was angry about the last-minute interruption in his research schedule; angry about Linda being put in harm's way; angry about his inability to prevent the likes of Parker from milking what could be a solution to the many cruel ailments of mankind. The strain was so immense that he lost all sense of time. His body wanted neither food nor water. Just sleep. A wave of exhaustion swept over him, and he dozed off on the couch, dreaming of Linda.

A few hours later he awoke to a sound. It wasn't the main door. No, that would have been a distinctive whirring sound. This seemed to be coming from the bathroom. The lights were switched off and the room was entirely dark. What time was it? Jim sat up on the couch and screwed up his eyes, attempting to discern who it was. The figure stepped out of the bathroom, tiptoed over to the sofa and sat down on the adjacent easy chair. And then Jim caught the fragrance—Jo Malone, Wood Sage & Sea Salt. It was Ali Zamani.

'How did you appear in my bathroom like a bloody djinn?' he snapped.

'You're coming with me,' said Zamani simply, not bothering to answer the question.

'Do I have an option?' asked Jim wryly.

Zamani laughed. He stood up and pulled Jim to his feet. 'Follow me,' he instructed briefly.

Together, they entered the bathroom. Inside it, Jim noticed that the full-length mirror on the wall to the left had been pulled off its clamps. Behind it was a white door, smoothly finished in Corian so that it blended seamlessly into the white tiles. Zamani gave the door a gentle nudge and it swung open on a spring mechanism.

'Get inside,' said Ali. 'A long ladder runs inside the shaft. Follow it to the end. You will eventually reach the basement. I'll be behind you.'

'What's all this secrecy about?' asked Jim. 'Hiding something from your employers?'

'Why do you ask so many questions?' barked Ali in response.

'You already have me inside Asclepius's private prison,' said Jim. 'You have every freedom to take me out through the front door. Yet you choose to make me leave via a bathroom duct. Something is not quite right. And, hey, where's my package?'

'I shall answer all your questions when the time's right,' said Ali. 'But do you want to get out of here or not? This is a limited period offer.'

Jim paused to think. How could he possibly be in a situation worse than his current one? And getting out of here would throw new possibilities his way. It was like getting another chance to toss a coin after an unfavourable outcome.

'Yes,' breathed Jim. 'Let's get out of here.' He clambered into the bathroom duct, gripped the steel ladder and began making his way down the rungs. Above him, the bathroom door swung shut and Ali's footsteps followed him down. The light that had been filtering through the door was now gone. The shaft was entirely dark. Pitch black. Jim ignored the darkness and his own fears. One step at a time. The only way was down. When he was sure that he had completed the descent, he took a deep breath and waited in place.

Until he was knocked out by what hit him next.

24

'YOU REALLY NEED to stop injecting me with strange substances,' complained Jim, as Ali Zamani came into focus. It was evident to him that they were back on an aircraft.

Zamani laughed. 'It was done for your own safety,' he replied. 'Now that we're airborne, please consider yourself my honoured guest.' *I really wish you'd stop honouring me*, thought Jim. Jim noticed that Zamani's appearance had changed. Gone were the pullover and jeans. Those had been replaced by a military-green uniform of the IRGC. Emblazoned on it was a logo of a hand brandishing a machine gun, the insignia of the IRGC-Quds.

Jim looked around him. This was no luxurious corporate jet like the Asclepius one he'd been in before. This was transparently an outdated commercial aircraft. The seats and decor were reminiscent of aircrafts from the '80s. The carpet, wallpaper and upholstery on the seats were as tattered. Jim tried looking at the inflight signage to get an idea of the owner, but there was nothing distinctive to go by. The yellowed safety signs were solely in Arabic.

Jim knew better than to ask futile questions. Zamani would tell him when he felt like it.

That turned out to be sooner than he had imagined. 'You're wondering why I pulled you out of Asclepius and brought you here,' said Zamani. Jim would have nodded, but his neck was too stiff and sore from the jab it had received.

'You are aboard a special aircraft arranged by the IRGC,' said Zamani softly. 'Registration of the flight plan is in the name of Crescent Star Airways, but the few seats sold are entirely to my men. We are headed to Tehran via Doha.'

'I don't understand,' began Jim weakly. Zamani brought a finger to his lips to gesture for silence.

'Yes, it is true that I work for Parker—and Asclepius. Or so they thought until recently. My true employer is the IRGC. It has a division known as the IRGC-Quds Force, a special operations group that reports directly to the Supreme Leader of Iran—the Ayatollah. I am simply fulfilling my commitment to deliver you to the IRGC-Quds. And my name is *not* Ali Zamani. That is an alias. My real name is Javad Mosaffa.'

It was common knowledge that the IRGC had been through troubled times during the nuclear sanctions on Iran. Businesses owned by the IRGC had suffered. Those losses had been partially offset through smuggling, but an overall financial loss remained. Then some important figures within the IRGC had been assassinated, including a key commander of the IRGC-Quds Force. The Supreme Leader had given them a pep talk. The force was now hitting back.

'But what can they possibly want from me?' asked Jim. Mosaffa gestured towards a haversack that lay on the floor next to his feet.

'You brought my stuff?' asked Jim, staring bug-eyed.

'All of it,' Mosaffa assured him. 'Your notes, files, drives—and the Hamzaa Dura.'

'How did you get it out from the Asclepius facility?' asked Jim. 'That place is like a fortress.'

'Simple,' replied Mosaffa. 'I never had to take it out because I never took it in.' Jim stared at him a second time. He had clearly seen his material in the Asclepius laboratories.

'When you were on the Asclepius corporate jet,' Mosaffa explained, 'I switched the bags. The material at Asclepius—including the material inside another similar box—is entirely fake. The flash drives contain junk files. Everything genuine is right here. They will only realise the switch today.'

'But why?' asked Jim. He was still trying to figure out how he had gone from being a captive of Asclepius to being a captive of the IRGC-Quds. He wasn't quite sure which of the two captors he preferred. Scylla or Charybdis? Only time would tell.

'I was planted at Asclepius many years ago by Iranian intelligence,' replied Mosaffa. 'There are hundreds like me who work silently. We're sleeper agents who live within countries and organisations until we are activated for duty.'

'But why Asclepius?' asked Jim.

'The company was developing antidotes to chemical warfare,' replied Mosaffa. 'As you know, Iran and Iraq have fought a very long war. Our dispute with Israel and America is still on. We needed protection from chemicals and nerve agents—some of them our own.'

'But then you turned your attention to me,' said Jim.

'I was the one who suggested to Parker that your abduction be carried out by an Asclepius team headed by me,' said Mosaffa. 'Parker thought that I was grabbing you for his purposes. Little did he realise that Asclepius was a pit stop on your way to Tehran.'

'I thought all angles had been covered by CCTV cameras inside that hotel,' said Jim.

'That's why I came into your room through the bathroom duct and took you out the same way,' replied Mosaffa.

'And how did you get me out of the hotel?' asked Jim. 'Wouldn't someone have noticed?'

'Once you were in the basement, we placed you inside a laundry cart,' replied Mosaffa. 'The cart was wheeled into a laundry truck that brought you to a local airport—Spencer. We did not want to take a chance taking you through Worcester. The rest was easy.'

'But why does the government of Iran need me or my research?' asked Jim.

'You've discovered the reason by now, Jim,' replied Mosaffa. 'Please do not insult my intelligence by faking innocence.'

Jim went quiet. There had been recent instances of Iran mounting domestic and international operations to go after those they considered to be enemies of the regime. An opposition political leader and three dissident writers had been killed within a span of two months. An online activist had been shot dead in Istanbul's Shishli neighbourhood more recently. Of course, the intrigue worked both ways. The Americans had assassinated some of Iran's top nuclear scientists in a bid to slow down the country's nuclear ambitions.

But why was Jim Dastoor suddenly on Iran's radar? What could they possibly want?

And then Jim saw the connection.

25

IN HIS LABORATORY, on the same floor as Jim's, Dan Cohen had concentrated on his work of separating proteins from cancer cells, then immunising patients against those proteins by using them as antigens. Through this process, Dan hoped that he would be able to stimulate the immune system to kill cancer cells. Parallelly, he was also tweaking the herpes simplex virus to selectively replicate within tumour tissue. Hopefully, this would also trigger an immune response. With this cutting-edge research, the Kettering Prize was well within his reach. Unless Jim's Hamzaa Dura got the job done first.

Dan sighed as he pushed away his files. He left his laboratory, letting the door behind him lock securely. But he did not make his way to the elevator. Instead, he crossed the corridor that separated his laboratory from Jim's. Getting inside would require some effort though. He mentally reviewed the steps that he would need to take.

In Dan's hand was a clear plastic square, of sides around twenty centimetres. On its surface was etched a handprint which had been surreptitiously lifted off a can of Diet Coke trashed by Jim in the cafeteria a few days ago. That particular can had also been the source of Jim's thumbprint.

Dan paused a few steps short of Jim's door. Ensuring that he remained outside the vision of the security camera stationed nearby, he pulled out a pair of wire clippers from his pocket and cut the cable that provided the video feed from the camera to the central recorder unit. Satisfied that the feed was disrupted, Dan stepped up to Jim's door, took a deep breath and placed Jim's handprint on the scanner panel. He waited for less than ten seconds before hearing the reassuring whirr of the door opening.

Dan hated himself for conspiring to betray Jim, but he saw no alternative. Dan's work on the cancer vaccine was likely to make him a prime candidate for the Kettering Prize. A single blot on his personal reputation would be enough to ruin any chance of his coming within touching distance of it.

He stepped inside, closed the door and waited for the lights and the aircon to adjust to his presence, then approached the corner at the far right that held Jim's bookshelves. He ran his hand along the edge to find the invisible button that Jim had often used in his presence. A moment later the bookshelf slid away revealing the electronic safe. Dan took a slip of paper out of his pocket. It had the digital combination that Jim had shared with him months ago. It was to be used by Dan only in the most serious emergencies. He punched in the numbers and allowed the door to swing open. Open Sesame.

But there was no treasure within.

Where was the stuff? It had been there until yesterday. And Dan knew that Jim never took any of his research material home. It was a rule that he had followed meticulously. Dan ran his hands along the sides of the safe, almost expecting to locate a secret panel, but met with no such luck.

He shut the safe, slid back the bookshelf and began checking drawers and cabinets in the laboratory. He soon realised that many of the storage units seemed less packed than usual. All he wanted was that *one* earthen box containing the grainy white powder.

A few minutes later, Dan realised that his search was futile. He phoned Luke Miller, the thin and pale man with mousy red hair. He explained his predicament. 'I am inside his lab,' explained Dan. 'I have searched everywhere but it is no longer here. Jim has obviously shifted it entirely. Nothing remains.'

'You know the consequences of lying to us?' asked Miller.

'Trust me,' replied Dan. 'I know. I would not be calling you unless I had tried and failed.'

There was an uncomfortable silence on the phone. 'Make your way downstairs to the corner of Fourth Avenue and Findlay Street,' said the man eventually. 'There is a hotdog stand at the corner. I'll meet you near there in an hour.'

Fifty-five minutes later, Dan was near the stand painted with the sign 'Georgetown Dogs'. Miller approached from the opposite side and proceeded to order a hotdog. When Dan looked at him, Miller nodded towards the gate of a warehouse.

Dan slowly approached its large metal door. It made a screeching sound as it opened. As he walked in alone, large industrial lights came on and the warehouse was bathed in light. And then he saw a sight that made him want to vomit his guts out.

In the centre of the cavernous space was a giant metallic hook suspended from a ceiling crane. The crane and hook had been strategically located for maximum effect. Hanging naked from the hook was Mistress Lucinda, her blonde hair only partially covering her face, which had slumped forward. Her body had been slit open from throat to genitalia. Hanging out from her were her intestines. Underneath her, on the epoxy flooring, was a giant red pool into which blood dripped steadily.

Dan felt his phone buzzing. It was Miller. 'Just thought I'd let you know what we are capable of,' he said softly to Dan. 'We already have her photos in this condition, plus one showing you entering the warehouse and time-stamped. And of course, all of your previous trysts with her are recorded by us. I wonder if you realise that the stakes just got a lot higher.'

Dan attempted to swallow his saliva, but there was none left in his mouth.

'When I told you that we wanted Jim's material, it was not a request,' said Miller. 'It was an order. Do whatever you need to. You have two days.'

26

I AM TOLD *that after his arrival in Vienna, my great-granduncle Homi Dastoor realised that his faith was already globally famous due to a composition by Richard Strauss called* Also Sprach Zarathustra, Op. 30. *Not to be outdone, Homi took a revered Zoroastrian prayer, the* Yatha Ahu Vairyo, *and set it to an operatic score. It is one of the most sacred Zoroastrian prayers.*

Yatha ahu vairyo atha ratush ashat chit hacha
Vangheush dazda manangho shyothananam angheush mazdai;
Kshathrem cha ahurai a yim daregobyo dadat vastarem.

Translated, it means: As the master, so is the judge to be chosen in accord with truth. Establish the power of acts arising from a life lived with good purpose, for Mazda and for the Lord whom they made pastor of the poor.

Needless to say, it was a hit among Zoroastrians all over the world. And it also established Homi as one of the finest musicians of his time. Whenever I am in trouble, I hear this particular rendition of the prayer. I derive immense strength from it.

In the meantime, Homi's younger brother, Navroze, earned a degree in chemical engineering at Oxford, and returned to join the family business. He took to the world of business like a fish to water. Most importantly, he had a head for numbers. Before people twice his age could calculate something with pen and paper, Navroze would already have the answer figured out in his head.

It is said that when Shapoor Dastoor, Homi's and Navroze's father, died in 1901, Bombay turned out in full strength to mourn its hero. They lined the roads leading up to the Tower of Silence where vultures would be given free rein to feast on his remains. Shapoor had not only built a business empire, he had also created institutions that would live on after him.

During his lifetime he had established one of Bombay's finest hospitals, an immensely respected university and a charitable foundation that had helped thousands. His son, Navroze, my great-grandfather, would have a tough legacy to live up to.

When Shapoor's will was read, he had left a substantial cash settlement to his wife Deena and his son Homi—along with that little earthen box. Another chunk of his fortune went to the charitable trust that he had founded. The bulk of his fortune, including his precious shares in the business, went to his younger son, Navroze.

Luckily, Navroze Dastoor was nothing short of a business genius. He could spot trends much before they became trends. He foresaw that it was just a matter of time before a great war would break out in Europe. When World War I started in 1914, the thirty-four-year-old Navroze was perfectly positioned to provide war supplies to England—more than three million tonnes of food rations, uniforms, horses, mules, weaponry and even armoured vehicles et al. There would be no looking back after that. The Dastoor empire would soon encompass cement, power, steel, jute, tea, chemicals and shipping, eventually employing well over a hundred thousand people in its assorted businesses.

Unlike his father, who was an Englishman at heart, Navroze saw himself as a nationalist. He was friends with Gandhi, Nehru and Patel. The Parsis that came before him had been quite happy to maintain their cosy relationship with their English masters. After all, it was the English who had allowed them to make the transition from Surat to Bombay and thus flourish. But Navroze never forgot that it was a Hindu king, Jadi Rana, who had offered refuge to his community in Gujarat as they fled Muslim persecution in Iran. Navroze understood that it was only a matter of time before the English would have to quit India. If and when that happened, the Parsis would need new friends.

Some degree of political awakening had already emerged by then within the Parsis, but it had remained muted on account of the business relationship that they enjoyed with the English. Now, things began to change. The early political organisations in Bombay—the Bombay Association and the Bombay Presidency Association—were both funded and led by Parsis. The Indian National Congress was founded in 1885 in Bombay, and many of its leaders were Parsis, including Dadabhoy Naoroji, Sir Pherozeshah Mehta and Sir Dinshah Wacha. In fact, the only three Indians who succeeded in getting themselves elected to the British Parliament were also Parsis—Dadabhoy Naoroji, Muncherji Bhownagree and Shapurji Saklatwalla.

While competing businessmen made much ado about everything they did, Navroze worked quietly, preferring to stay out of the limelight. He was not keen on joining the social whirl, unlike his father, and preferred spending quiet evenings at home with his family or intimate friends. It also meant that he could squeeze out extra hours each day to work on expanding the business—which did wonders for the enterprise.

27

NAVROZE WAS CONVINCED *that India would need rapid industrialisation. And who better than the Dastoor family to make that happen? The very first sector that caught his fancy was steel. He travelled to America to sign a collaboration agreement with one of the biggest steelmakers of the day.*

Another Parsi, Jamsetji Tata, had already established a steel factory in Jamshedpur—against discouraging odds—so why not Navroze? The English were scornful of Navroze's efforts: 'The only thing his steel will be used in will be the nails in his coffin,' said his English competitors, forgetting that we Parsis require neither coffins nor nails when we die.

But Navroze pulled it off, and how. Just as the first ingots rolled out, he turned his attention to cement, possibly because slag, a waste byproduct of steelmaking, could be used in it. By 1920, Navroze had established a factory in Gujarat to produce what the English called Artificial Portland Cement.

Within another decade Navroze had laid the foundation stone for a thermal power plant. It was a juggernaut of capacity expansion in existing businesses and their diversification into new industries. A time would come when it would be easier to list what Navroze Dastoor did not make. His frenetic pace of production made Navroze one of the wealthiest men in India. But he never forgot one core principle: all that money can give is the freedom of not having to worry about it.

The Dastoor family tree shows that Navroze had three children—two daughters and a son. His wife, Nazneen, was his pillar of strength, bringing up the children almost single-handedly. Navroze was simply too busy nurturing and expanding the business side of things to spare quality time for his offspring. For the most part, Navroze was an absentee father.

But the three children—Persis, Meher and Rustom—were Nazneen's world. No detail was overlooked in their upbringing, and no expense was spared in their education. An English governess ensured that they were always well-spoken and immaculately groomed. A private farm in Poona was created for the kids to practise becoming outstanding equestrians. Tutors for multiple languages were always to be found filing in and out of the house. Each of the children learnt to sing, dance or play a musical instrument. Evenings were devoted to sports at the gymkhana that had been established by the Dastoor Trust. Weekends included mandatory reading hours.

But then tragedy struck. The eldest child, Persis, contracted smallpox. Around thirty per cent of those afflicted with the dreaded pox died. Priests from Udvada and Navsari performed sacred yasnas to pray for her recovery while the finest doctors prescribed the best treatment. Nothing worked.

A pall of gloom descended over the Dastoor home. Nazneen retreated into a shell that she never emerged from again, only to follow her daughter to the Tower of Silence a few years later. The doctors attributed her death to lung cancer, but the cause was more accurately heartbreak.

My grandfather, Rustom, was the youngest of the three children. For the remainder of his youth, his sister Meher was his mother, friend and guide. Rustom was a deep-thinking and introspective child. He attended the Cathedral & John Connon School in Bombay as a matter of course, his interests leaning heavily towards poetry and art. Much against his father's wishes, he refused to pursue a degree in science or business, choosing to follow his true passions at the Sorbonne in Paris.

He returned to India several years later, accompanied by his French bride Cecile, and enthusiastically took up a teaching position at the JJ School of Art, the famous institute founded with a generous donation from Sir Jamshedji Jeejeebhoy in 1857.

Cecile was the sweetest and gentlest woman he could have chosen to marry. Her svelte figure, starlit eyes and unconsciously provocative mouth would have driven any man crazy. But more importantly, she loved Rustom deeply and made it her mission to make him happy; to not only love him as a wife but protect him like a mother.

But the environment the newlyweds found themselves in was far from welcoming. Cecile wanted to be part of Rustom's life, and he applied for her to be accepted into the Zoroastrian faith. There was an instant uproar. The Bombay Parsi Panchayat filed a suit in the High Court to challenge her admittance. Eventually, the court decided against Rustom's suit. India's Parsis were making it clear that they wished to insulate themselves from outsiders.

A community that had prospered by doing business with the English now had a problem with one of their own officially sleeping with the French!

28

THE RUSTOM–CECILE MARRIAGE *was a scandal that was animatedly discussed at all Parsi weddings, and navjotes—the ceremonies in which Parsi children would be formally inducted into the faith. Navjotes marked the time from which a child would begin wearing the customary 'sedreh' and 'kushti'—the sacred vest and thread.*

But none of the horrified whispers around them had much effect on Rustom and Cecile. They knew that they completed one another—and that was what mattered. They had only one child, my father Baman.

But all of this posed a dilemma to my great-grandfather, Navroze, who had been pinning his hopes on Rustom eventually returning to the business. When he realised that it was not to be, he gave charge of only the family's charitable trust to Rustom. It turned out to be the smartest move ever, both for the Dastoors as well as for India.

Rustom genuinely felt for humanity. He loved animals and turned vegetarian early in life, an incredible transformation for a Parsi who had hitherto enjoyed his mutton dhansak and sali boti. Cecile too was exceptionally soft-hearted and could not bear to witness the grinding poverty of India. Both threw themselves into the workings of the trust.

The other strong influence in Rustom's life was his uncle, Homi. Rustom would often visit him in Vienna and was amazed by the respect and adulation that Homi received as one of Europe's finest musicians. Naturally, Homi chose Rustom as the next guardian of the earthen box and memorised text. Shapoor's rebellion had been to leave Udvada and seek his fortunes in Bombay; Homi's rebellion had been to leave India and seek greatness in Vienna's world of music; Rustom's rebellion had been to shun corporate greatness for social responsibility.

The trust had already established a university and a hospital, but Rustom felt that it needed to touch the lives of ordinary people. He established one of the widest village-adoption programmes that would ensure development at grassroot level. The trust's food programme was expanded to ensure that the issue of malnutrition—a key driver of infant mortality—be addressed. Thousands of village schools were upgraded, and a special teachers' training programme was instituted. The trust worked actively towards promoting sustainable agriculture, water conservation, inoculation and financial inclusion for millions of ordinary Indians. It built micro-dams, dug wells and offered micro-credit. In short, it became a saviour to rural India.

Rustom and Cecile had found what they were good at: making other people's lives better. Cecile was also intensely spiritual. She would regularly go on meditation camps in the hills. Her friends—politicians, business magnates, yoga gurus, mendicants—trod all walks of life. She loved reading. Her collection of books at their weekend home in Khandala was on the scale of a well-stocked library.

But the Dastoor empire's dilemma remained. Who would take over the business from Navroze? If left to Rustom, it would be donated away entirely. But Navroze was nothing if not shrewd. He decided that the inheritance could easily skip a generation. He set his sights on his grandson, my father Baman.

When Baman turned twenty, my great-grandfather Navroze quickly pulled him into the business. India had attained independence two years previously and challenges and opportunities abounded. Unfortunately, millions had died in the partition of India and Pakistan occurring at the same time. Knowing that he was the only one who could prepare Baman to engage successfully in the world of business, Navroze lost no time in doing so.

Baman had always been clever, but his education was limited to a BA from Elphinstone College in Bombay. When people commented that Baman was smart in spite of a limited education, Navroze would retort, 'The boy is smart precisely because of his limited education.'

The pressure on Baman to quickly join the enterprise was overwhelming, but he took to the new waters effortlessly. Over the next few years, he worked alongside managers and shop-floor workers to understand the nitty-gritties of each operation. Navroze ensured that Baman was regularly shunted from one company to another and from one post to the next, because he wanted the young man to have as wide, and deep, a perspective as possible. By the time Baman entered the headquarters of the group, he knew something about everything rather than everything about something. It was precisely the sort of macro-vision that was needed to push the boundaries of the Dastoor empire even further.

Baman had always loved Shirin, a girl he had known from his schooldays. When the time for marriage came around, it was a foregone conclusion that the two would be hitched. It was an utterly simple wedding held at the Manekji Sett Agiary. Shirin was dressed in an ornate white 'gara'; Baman was smartly outfitted in a Parsi 'dagli'—a white, high-necked coat—and a 'fetah', the tall, black traditional headgear for men.

They were married on Hormazd Roz, the first day of the Parsi month. The bride and groom sat facing east, with a curtain separating them. They sprinkled each other with rice. Then an egg was broken, followed by a coconut. Finally, water was sprinkled on either side of the couple. The priests removed the curtain, joined the couple's hands together and tied a piece of cloth around them seven times. All the while was recited the Yatha Ahu Vairyo.

And they lived happily ever after.

29

UNDER THE GUIDANCE *of his grandfather, Baman not only consolidated the Dastoor dominion, he also made forays into new sectors: fertilisers, engines, synthetics and banking. Most importantly, he brought about cohesion and clarity in the group. Navroze had been so busy with expansion that he had had little time to focus on systems, processes and management policies. Baman possessed just the right bent of personality to embrace and put into practice those relatively new ideas.*

I was born to Baman and Shirin on the twenty-fifth of May 1968, my sister Avan having arrived a year earlier, in 1967. That year had brought a mixed bag of experiences: the birth of my sister Avan, and the consignment to the sky of my great-grandfather Navroze. The Parsi community mourned his death as though they had collectively lost a father.

But now the Dastoor empire had two vital arms. One arm made money under my father, Baman. The other arm, under my grandfather, Rustom, found ways to give it away. Both were equally important.

The next year, 1968, would not only be remembered for my birth (yes, I'm humble!) but for the wonderful movie, 2001: A Space Odyssey, directed by Stanley Kubrick. I watched the movie many times during my growing years, unaware that the film would be intimately connected to my future.

I attended the Cathedral & John Connon School, while my sister went to the JB Petit High School for Girls, both schools being a short distance away from each other. I always knew that my heart was set on science, not business. I was fascinated by my biology and chemistry lectures, particularly when they involved laboratory experiments. No sooner had I completed my twelfth grade, I began making plans to leave for college in the US. I had been offered a place at Stanford University to earn a degree as a Bachelor of Science. I even had my road ahead of that fully mapped out. I knew, for instance, that I would follow up my BS with a dual MD-PhD.

A week before I was set to leave, my father called me into his study. 'I know that your heart is not in business,' he said to me. 'Your grandfather was much the same.' He gazed thoughtfully at my face before adding, 'I want you to go where your passion takes you. You will always have the safety-net of a trust fund. If you do not get to enjoy the luxury of taking risks, who will? Farrokh Bulsara would never have become Freddie Mercury nor would Homi Bhabha have become the father of India's nuclear programme if they hadn't walked less-trodden paths.' I had a lump in my throat. I did not know what I could say to express gratitude to my father. Then he said, 'In the meantime, I too shall be breaking with another outdated tradition.'

'What is that?' I asked my father.

'There is no reason why the reins of our business should only be in male hands,' he replied. 'Your sister Avan has proved that she is as capable—if not more—than many men I know. I plan on grooming her to take over from me.'

I smiled. What a relief! Sometimes, the burden attached to a business one inherits far outweighs its bounty. I went up to my father and hugged him. He had tears in his eyes. He quickly dabbed at them with his handkerchief. Opening a drawer in his desk, he took out a small earthen box that bore a strange symbol of a sphere supported by wings, almost like a pilot's badge. He handed it to me.

I peered at the strange object. 'What is it?' I asked, mystified.

'Your grandfather, Rustom Dastoor, decided to leave this to you because he knew that you would chart your own course, like he—and others like him in our family—did before you.'

He led me by the hand to a small cocktail cabinet set against the wall I'd never noticed before. 'Let's spend the evening together,' he said, 'so that I may pour whisky for us to drink for the first time together. I have a long story to tell.'

I felt like an adult, a proper 'bawa', at last. My father and I settled down on a couch in the living room. He poured his favourite Johnnie Walker Black Label for both of us. No fancy single malts for Baman Dastoor. Just unfussy scotch and soda with two cubes of ice. He requested the attendant, who was waiting on us, to leave.

'As you know,' he began, after a long swallow of his drink, 'your great-great-grandfather, Shapoor Dastoor, was the first member of the family to move to Bombay. That was in 1858. But before that, all his ancestors had been Zoroastrian priests. Shapoor's own father was a priest in Udvada. Our family name, Dastoor, comes from the word "dastur", which means "priest".'

I already knew that, but I listened intently anyway. For us Parsis, Udvada is our holiest site, because it houses the centre of a sacred fire we call the Iranshah. While the enclave in Udvada is put at 265 years old, the fire itself has been burning for almost thirteen centuries. You see, we Parsis are not only a religious group but also an ethnic one. We are the descendants of Zoroastrians from Iran who formed a settlement in India— Gujarat, actually—around 720 CE.

But Udvada is not the first place our ancestors made a landing. According to the Qissa-i Sanjan, *an account of their early years, the first group of Zoroastrian refugees had come to India from an area that is now described as Greater Khorasan. This area lies north-east of the region now comprising Iran, Iraq, Azerbaijan, Turkmenistan, Tajikistan and Afghanistan. Alas, the term 'Khorasan' is in the news these days for all the wrong reasons, being used by the Islamic State to designate their Central Asian branch. Little did I know that those countries would come back to haunt me in later life.*

30

MY FATHER CONTINUED to ramble on, drink in hand. 'When Islamic persecution had been at its fiercest,' he recounted, going even further back in time, 'a group of devout Zoroastrians had gone into hiding. For a while, they stayed concealed in the mountains of Khorasan, but at length were forced into Hormuz, that lay at the horn of the Persian Gulf. But the Muslim rulers remained hot on their heels. Finally, a wise dastur who could read the stars, announced that the time for a further eastward movement had come. Around 18,000 of them set sail from Hormuz and landed at the fishing town of Diu, along the Saurashtra peninsula.'

I was aware of the Diu story, too. The refugees had remained there for the next nineteen years before another astrological reading prompted them to move further east and they set sail once again. A terrible storm arose when they were mid-sea and it seemed that all would be lost. So the Zoroastrians prayed to their God, Ahura Mazda. They promised Ahura Mazda that they would consecrate their most sacred fire—an Atash Behram—if, and where, they made landfall safely.

My father took another gulp of his whisky. 'The terrified refugees eventually landed at Sanjan, on the western coast of Gujarat,' he said. 'The ruler of Sanjan was someone they called Jadi Rana.' (I remembered reading somewhere that scholars now associated 'Jadi Rana' with Vijayaditya of the Western Chalukyas.) 'The refugees sought his permission to make Sanjan their home,' continued my father. 'Jadi Rana did not have a problem with the refugees staying temporarily, but the idea of a permanent settlement unnerved him.'

Reportedly, Jadi Rana then offered a bowl of milk to the leader of the refugee group, filling it to the brim until it overflowed. It was his way of conveying to the refugees that his kingdom was already full. But the wise Parsi dasturs stirred some sugar into the milk and returned the bowl to the king. It was a subtle message to Jadi Rana that they would only add flavour and sweetness to the land without causing an upheaval.

'Jadi Rana was delighted by the gesture. The more he heard about the Zoroastrian faith, the more he was convinced that it resembled Hinduism. Zoroastrians revered the cow; their deities like Varuna and Mitra were respected not only in the Zoroastrian Gathas but also in the Rigveda; their sacred fire was much like the agni of the Hindus; their yasnas were similar to Hindu yajnas; their Avestan verses sounded like Vedic Sanskrit; and while the Zoroastrians had daevas and ahuras, Hindus had devas and asuras. How could such a similar people pose a threat to his? Jadi Rana agreed to give them sanctuary, allotting

a square plot of three farsangs—or nine square kilometres—for their use.'

None of the stuff that my father was telling me was new. I had learned most of it in school from Mrs Batliwala, our Parsi teacher who taught English. Jadi Rana had apparently set down four conditions for their stay on his land. First, the refugees would adopt the local Gujarati language in favour of Farsi; second, their women would dress as per local custom; third, the men would lay down their weapons and swear never to use them unless ordered by the Rana; and last, their wedding ceremonies would only be conducted in the evenings.

The refugees were happy to agree to those terms. The Muslim invaders in Iran had offered them only three options, all terrible: one, convert to Islam; two, pay an exorbitant Jizya tax and accept the cruelty and humiliation that accompanied it; three, be put to death. In comparison to the invaders, Jadi Rana was benevolence personified.

Having settled in Sanjan, the Parsis remembered the oath that they had taken when confronted by the storm. They approached Jadi Rana to give them his consent to consecrate an Atash Behram there. Jadi Rana gave it some thought. He realised that the new people were not historically alien to India. The Sassanian Empire, the last Persian imperial dynasty before the arrival of Islam, had maintained trading outposts as far as Sindh. The Gujarat coast lay along the maritime routes used by Zoroastrian sailors. Contact between the Zoroastrians of Iran and Indians went back centuries. Even the Puranas and the Mahabharata used the term 'Parasikas' to refer to the 'Parsi' people who inhabited the regions west of the Indus. Jadi Rana gave his consent for the construction of an Atash Behram.

An Atash Behram is the 'highest form of fire' that could be placed in a Zoroastrian temple. Lighting such a flame is a complex task. Sixteen different types of fires have to be collected and combined while maintaining exacting ritual purity: Fires from a brickmaker, blacksmith, goldsmith, potter, baker, armourer, dyer and brewer were collected. These were supplemented by fires from a prince, an ascetic, a soldier, a shepherd, a mint, a cremation pyre and a Zoroastrian priest. The sixteenth was fire produced by atmospheric lightning. This was obviously the toughest to obtain.

The high priest of the Parsis, Dastur Nairyosang Dhaval, prayed for eight days without break. On the ninth day, his prayers were answered. He succeeded in capturing a spark from a bolt of lightning. The sixteen fires were combined, using special implements that they had carried with them from their homeland. Among those tools was a small earthen box.

The rites performed by the Parsi priests did not go in vain. The flame of the Iranshah—a name literally meaning the 'king of Iran' in exile—emerged, burning with the fiery power of a thousand yasnas.

Little did Dastur Nairyosang Dhaval know that there were several people who were out to steal it.

31

'WE HAVE SURVEILLANCE footage that shows Jim being taken out of a private aircraft that landed in Worcester,' said FBI agent Fred Smith on the phone. 'It was a corporate jet that belonged to Asclepius.' Greg, Fred and Linda were on a video call.

'We should immediately obtain a search warrant for Asclepius,' said Greg. 'They are the largest competitor to GCRC. This could be aggressive corporate rivalry.'

'But we have another problem on our hands,' said Fred.

'What other problem?' asked Greg, further alarmed.

'When I heard that Jim was being taken to Worcester, I reached out to the bureau's Boston office. They quickly scanned arrivals and departures through airports in the Boston area. The search radius was for those areas within fifty miles of Boston.'

'And?'

'Jim was recognised by FACE at Spencer Airport several hours later,' said Fred.

'FACE?' asked Greg.

'The bureau has the ability to match surveillance footage against 640 million photos culled from driving licences, passports and mugshots,' replied Fred. 'The system is called Facial Analysis, Comparison and Evaluation—so, FACE.'

Greg had heard about the system but was unaware that the FBI already had it in place. *Photos to the tune of 640 million! Must be driving privacy nuts crazy.*

'Unfortunately,' continued Fred, 'he later boarded a flight to Doha. We know that it is a flight that eventually goes on to Tehran.'

'Tehran as in Iran?' whistled Greg.

'Yes,' replied Fred. 'The airline in question—Crescent Star Airways—is considered to be a front for the IRGC. Although we do not allow direct flights in and out of Iran, we allow this one to operate so that we can keep a check on any suspicious travellers to and from the country. It actually lessens our workload.'

'Was Jim alone?' asked Greg.

'The system picked up Jim being carried onto the flight in a wheelchair,' replied Fred.

'Oh, no!' Linda almost yelped, as if personally wounded. 'What have they done to him?'

'Don't worry, Linda,' soothed Greg. 'He was probably under sedation. The wheelchair would have been a way for his captors to get a supposed invalid aboard the flight with only cursory inspection.'

'Exactly,' said Fred. 'The airline records indicate that special handling was requested because the passenger was a patient suffering from motor-neuron disease.'

'Fred, do you know who accompanied the patient?' asked Greg.

'Yes,' replied Fred. 'An employee of Asclepius. Social security records indicate that his name is Ali Zamani. Immigrated to America six years ago. Worked as a private security contractor before landing a job three years ago at Asclepius. We've had our eye on the security agency for some time now because they seem to have a thing for recruiting refugees from the Middle East.'

'Why is Asclepius kidnapping a scientist, only to dispatch him to Tehran?' wondered Greg.

'We can't be sure that this is an Asclepius plan,' replied Fred. 'Let me see if I can dig up some more gen on Zamani. We need to figure out whom this man actually represents.'

Linda cut in on the conversation. 'Thank you for your help, Fred, but I don't plan to wait for the FBI. I think I'll take my chances and go to Tehran myself. Any delay may mean my losing Jim.'

'I don't think that's a good idea,' said Fred gently. 'America and Iran do not have diplomatic relations. We have no embassy in Tehran. We rely on Switzerland as our protecting power in Iran and the Iranians rely on Pakistan as their protecting power in America. If the Iranians decided to capture you, we wouldn't be able to do anything. In any case, how would you even know where Jim is in that country? What could you possibly achieve by going there?'

'What can I achieve by being here?' shot back Linda. 'At least Jim will have a chance if I put in a personal plea. Let's face it, your diplomatic requests are not going to achieve any results.'

Fred knew she was right. If the Iranians had decided to abduct Jim, nothing would make them give him up. The Americans had understood that in 1979, when fifty-two of their diplomats had been held hostage by the regime. Even now, Iran was known to be holding four other Americans in prison.

'You can't go in without a visa,' pointed out Fred. 'You first need to apply for a travel authorisation number from the Iranian Ministry of Foreign Affairs—the MFA. After you get that, you apply for an Iranian visa to the Pakistan Embassy in Washington, D.C.'

'So?' asked Linda.

'When your name goes to Iran's MFA, don't you think they will already know your connection to Jim?' asked Fred. 'Isn't it possible that you would be walking into a trap? What if this abduction has nothing to do with Asclepius, and has been sponsored by the Iranian government itself?'

There was a pause in the conversation. Linda was digesting what Fred had just said. She would need to reconsider her options.

'Have either you or Jim visited Israel?' asked Fred.

'We went two years ago on tourist visas to Jerusalem,' replied Linda.

'Chances are that Iran would reject a visa application from anyone who has an arrival stamp of Israel on their passport,' said Fred.

'Any way to enter without a visa?' asked Linda in desperation.

Fred paused. 'Kish Island,' he replied after some hesitation.

'What's that?'

'Kish Island is called the "Pearl of the Persian Gulf". It is a small island in the gulf and US citizens do not need a visa to travel there. But getting to Iran's mainland from the island would be a challenge.'

Someone seated next to Linda entered the video frame of the call. 'However, I agree with Linda,' said the fourth participant. 'We cannot afford to lose time.' Fred and Greg looked at the new entrant to the conversation. It was Dan Cohen, Jim's fellow director.

Earlier in the day, Linda had connected them to Dan herself. He had told them about the nature of Jim's research. Fred had picked up a hint of tension in his voice but had been unsure whether to read anything into it. *Probably just shock at the fate of his fellow director,* Fred concluded.

'I am willing to accompany Linda to Tehran,' said Dan. 'It's Jim's life which could be at stake, dammit.'

32

IT WAS STILL dark in the village of Raihan Bag in Kashmir. But it wasn't too early in the day for Baba Malik. He began his mornings at 4 am, with meditation followed by prayers. By 7 am he was ready for a light breakfast consisting of *chhir chot*—a pancake prepared from riceflour and caraway seeds—washed down with hot *kahwa* tea.

He lived alone in the little cottage made of unevenly broken rocks glued together with clay and topped with a sloping roof of native deodar. But any lack of finish to its construction was more than compensated for by the stunning backdrop of lofty mountains, mist-laced forests and brooks clear as glass.

The frugality of his life suited Baba. People who knew of him travelled great distances to meet him, but Baba never accepted payment from anyone. No one really knew Baba Malik's age. He was described merely as 'one of the oldest residents of Raihan Bag'. People called him 'Baba' because he was old and wise, although Baba did not look a day over forty. There was a youthful glow to his fair-skinned face, and he possessed the put-together physique of a much younger, well-exercised man. He dressed entirely in white, a cloth draped like a fakir's over his head. Next to him on a roughly woven carpet where he now sat, was a copper pot exhaling incense. Baba Malik was ready to grant audience to his first visitors of the day.

The first, an elderly lady, knelt before Baba. He acknowledged the genuflection with 'Adaab' and the delicate touching of his forehead with his fingertips. 'What troubles you?' he asked softly.

'Baba, I have a fever that fails to subside,' said the woman. 'My stomach cramps are also terrible. As a result, I am unable to do housework. My husband and my sons refuse to help with any domestic chores. I just wish that I could get back on my feet.'

'Lemon water,' said Baba succinctly.

'What do you mean?' asked the woman. 'I have tried every medicine from the local chemist, and you say that simple lemon water will cure me?'

'Yes, it will,' replied Baba. 'From where do you get your drinking water?'

'The well near Jamia Masjid,' replied the woman.

'Send one of your boys to Wular Lake,' said Baba. 'Ask him to draw a pitcher of water from there. Sip that with lemon juice through the day. Come back to me in a day. You will be fine.'

The woman got up, *salaaming* gratefully. The Baba raised his hand in a gesture of blessing. 'Go in peace, sister,' he said.

The next visitor stepped into place. He was a middle-aged man dressed in a traditional Kashmiri wide tunic, a *phiran,* worn over loose folds of *suthan-shalwar* pajamas. He described an adaab and sat down, grimacing. 'What is your ailment, brother?' asked Baba.

'My gout is killing me,' said the man. 'The pain comes suddenly, with swelling, redness and tenderness in many of my joints. Last night it felt like my big toe was on fire. Even the weight of the bedsheet on it was intolerable.'

'I understand,' replied Baba. 'I am giving you this dry powder. Mix it with a little almond oil and apply it to your joints.'

'That's all I need to do?' asked the man incredulously.

'Do you drink?' asked Baba.

'It is prohibited by Islam,' replied the man piously.

'That's not what I asked,' said Baba. 'Do you drink?'

'Only occasionally,' answered the man, ducking his head.

Baba's face crinkled in mirth. 'No more alcohol for you,' he said. 'And monitor your diet. Reduce meat in your diet and drink more water. Yes, that's all you need to do.'

'Thank you, Baba,' said the man as he accepted a small paper packet of Baba's medicine. 'How much do I owe you?' he asked.

'There is a donation box outside,' said Baba pointing in its direction. 'If you think I have helped you, feel free to put in it an amount you feel is appropriate. My healing is not for sale. I use anything that people give freely for the benefit of others.'

Baba carried on through the morning without a break. It was late afternoon when he got up to have a spartan lunch. He chewed carefully, and with pleasure, as he remembered the number of people he had helped.

For the tiniest moment, a frown crossed his face. He wondered when he would be discovered and his secret laid bare. He shuddered before pushing the thought aside. *Haramukhuk gosain*, he thought. *Better to have a short memory.*

33

THE BOEING 727-100 touched down at Tehran Imam Khomeini International Airport. A blindfolded Jim was whisked away from the aircraft into an unmarked IKCO Samand car, a vehicle that was ubiquitous on Iranian roads. He was then transported to DC1A—Detention Centre 1A—a prison facility that was part of the Sarallah campsite in northeast Tehran.

DC1A was a multi-storeyed construction designed to house political opponents of the regime. The building was fairly new, having been built just a few years ago. There were other locations that the IRGC could just as easily have chosen for Jim. But the advantage of DC1A was that it could be quickly customised for special prisoners. And Jim Dastoor was definitely special.

Amir Khademhosseini, the head of the IRGC-Quds Force, was waiting for his special guest inside DC1A. He had embarrassed himself by going after the Cyrus Cylinder and was therefore keen to redeem himself in the eyes of the Supreme Leader. The cylinder had been returned to the British Museum in an unsigned parcel, but that was mere damage control. Khademhosseini knew that he would have to deliver results soon.

It had been a stroke of luck when one of his sleeper agents had told him about Asclepius and their competition with the Gemini Cellular Research Center. Working on a hunch, Khademhosseini had reached out to agents across the world to find out more about Jim Dastoor and his family. Once he had a complete dossier in hand, he was satisfied that this particular endeavour was not a wild goose chase. He then asked Javad Mosaffa—alias Ali Zamani—to bring him in. It was undoubtedly a bet, but the odds were in his favour.

Jim was unaware of which floor he was taken to. When his blindfold was removed, he realised that he was inside an interrogation room, windowless and sparsely furnished. 'Hope you had a comfortable flight, Mr Dastoor,' said Khademhosseini sardonically, exhaling a puff of smoke from his Farvardin cigarette. 'The remainder of your stay with us will depend upon your cooperation. The more you share with us, the greater the chances of your release.'

'And if I don't share?' asked Jim. He was exhausted and nervous, but his anger was far greater than any other emotion.

'I would hate for your lovely wife Linda to have to mourn your premature death,' replied Khademhosseini. Jim knew that the man was serious. The stay at Asclepius had been a walk in the park in comparison to this. Jim was regretting having left the Hilton from Hell.

'You see, Mr Dastoor, your invention interests us—intensely,' said Khademhosseini. 'Not only because of its potential to generate substantial revenue, but also because of your particular ancestry.' Jim remained quiet.

'Ever since the Glorious Revolution, the world has conspired to put Iran down,' continued Khademhosseini with a slight snarl. 'But they did not succeed in their evil designs. We continue to flourish even in the face of Western and Zionist conspiracies. And now it is time for us to reclaim our position in the world and, Insha'Allah, you are going to help us do that.'

'I don't know what your people have told you,' said Jim, 'but I am a simple researcher and I have nothing that could help you achieve your ambitions'.

Khademhosseini emitted a nasty laugh. 'Do not try to mislead us,' he said. 'We know of the immense potential of your work. But we believe that it is rightfully ours. The Athravan Star should be in Iran, where it belongs.'

Jim mulled over what Khademhosseini was saying. 'I have absolutely no idea what this thing you call the Athravan Star is,' said Jim.

'This is one among many centres run by the IRGC,' continued Khademhosseini, ignoring Jim's reply. 'Former inmates will tell you of the methods we employ to detect lies. Trust me when I say that you do *not* want to get on my wrong side.'

Jim recalled reading an article about Iran's prisons on his news feed. Prisoners were often subjected to long periods of isolation, administered electric shocks, deprived of food, interrogated for hours on end, deprived of sleep, systematically beaten or raped … the list was woefully long.

'You already have my Hamzaa Dura as well as the full body of my research,' argued Jim. 'What more do you need?'

'Medical equipment needs doctors to work them,' said Khademhosseini. 'Just like aircrafts need pilots to fly. Supercomputers need coders. Your research is useless without the scientist behind it—you.'

'I can't help you,' said Jim. 'My work is meant to help all of humanity, not a narrow and vested interest.'

The slap across his face was like no other that Jim had ever experienced, stinging like a burn under the impact of Khademhosseini's vicious swing.

'What you have experienced is only a taste of things to come,' said Khademhosseini silkily into Jim's ear. 'Think about what you want to do from now on very carefully. Once my patience runs out, you will be left in the hands of real specialists in making people suffer—and who mightily enjoy their job.'

Turning to one of the guards, Khademhosseini instructed him, 'Take him to one of our coffin cells. Let him stew in his own juices for a while but do not let him die. Make him wish that he were dead, though.'

34

THE KISH AIR flight from Dubai landed at Kish Island at noon. It was the only convenient choice, the other international connection being from Abu Dhabi. Of course, the greatest number of tourist arrivals at Kish Island were from Iranian cities such as Tehran, Isfahan, Shiraz and Mashhad, but those routes required visas.

Linda and Dan walked into the terminal at Kish International Airport and headed to passport control. The official scanned their passports and asked, 'Hotel reservations?' Dan showed him a confirmation of their reservation at the Dariush Grand Hotel. The official glanced at it, then took their photographs and fingerprints before stamping their passports. They now had travel permits that were valid for fourteen days. In addition, Linda had also thought to bring along Jim's passport, which had been lying in a drawer of his bedside table.

Linda was escorted to a separate room where a securitywoman provided her with a complimentary headscarf. She rapped out, unsmilingly, 'Women are required to wear headscarves in public while in Iran. Please dress appropriately—long skirt, smock or manteau. Enjoy your stay in Kish Island.'

They cleared Customs and got into a Toyota Camry taxi. 'Our taxis are unmetered,' said the driver. 'Fare to your hotel is three dollars.' Dan dipped his head in agreement, and they headed to their hotel. The driver eyed them in his rearview mirror as he drove.

'First time?' he asked in stilted English.

'Yes,' said Dan. 'Which are the interesting places to visit here?' he asked.

'This is free trade zone,' explained the driver. 'You go shopping malls, resorts, beaches ... Coral beach beautiful. You also try Underground City—old, *old* aqueduct. Then, Birds Garden, Dolphin Park, Aquarium. Many many places— you have time? Your hotel best hotel. But too big charge for tourist. I not cheat. You go somewhere you call me. My name Firooz Jamshidi. Number on back seat pocket.'

Kish Island had once been one of the numerous private resorts of the former Shah of Iran for his elite guests. A mere ninety square kilometres in size, it could be whizzed across from its western edge to the eastern in fifteen minutes. They reached their hotel in eight. Built to resemble the architecture of Persepolis, it was named after the Achaemenid emperor, Darius—or Dariush, as the hotel seemed to prefer.

They checked into two comfortable rooms on the second floor, freshened up and met downstairs at the Apadana restaurant. They had both agreed to turn off their mobile phones and remove the batteries. It was a sensible precaution to stay out of earshot of Iranian authorities. After they had ordered lunch, Linda asked, 'Any idea how to trace Jim?'

Dan took a sip of his tonic water and replied, 'We will need the help of Fred Smith. The bigger question is, how do we get to mainland Iran once we know where he is?'

'I'm not sure if Fred Smith can help us,' said Linda. 'American agencies have virtually no human intelligence inside Iran and are dependent on satellite snooping. Impossible to know where Jim was taken once he landed. Tehran is huge. Jim could be anywhere, and that's assuming that he's not been taken outside of Tehran.'

She paused. 'I have been doing some research,' she then said. 'Do you know that Iran is one of the biggest markets for cigarettes in the Middle East?'

'So?' asked Dan curiously.

'The CIA has always had a presence here in Kish. In 2007, one of their agents, a guy called Robert Levinson, disappeared from here. He was reported to have been held in an Iranian prison for more than a decade. It is presumed that he died in Iranian custody.'

Dan was confused. 'You've lost me. What has that to do with cigarettes?'

'I'm coming to that,' said Linda. 'Kish is a free trade zone,' said Linda. 'All the tobacco majors, including British American

Tobacco and R. J. Reynolds, supply huge quantities of their stuff to Kish. But these companies are fully aware that an island of 40,000 residents cannot consume the quantities that they supply. Major portions of their cigarette consignments are smuggled into mainland Iran in small motor launches. Levinson had been in Kish trying to figure out how those routes operated. The agency possibly wanted to understand whether those channels could be leveraged in some way.'

'I'd heard about Levinson,' said Dan. 'It was in all the newspapers. I think he became the longest-held American hostage in history, before dying in custody. You really want to go down that road?'

'Desperate times call for desperate measures,' quoted Linda. 'Did you notice the back seat of the taxi that we came in?'

'I wasn't really looking,' said Dan.

'It had a *faravahar* drawn on the plastic cover,' said Linda.

'A what?'

'A faravahar,' said Linda. 'It's a symbol depicting an elderly winged male holding a ring. It was used by the Achaemenid emperor, Darius, in his inscriptions. But later it became a symbol associated with the Zoroastrian faith. That driver, Jamshidi, was not a Muslim, but a Zoroastrian.'

'And how does that help us?'

'There are only around 25,000 Zoroastrians still in Iran—a country of eighty-four million people,' explained Linda. 'At one time Zoroastrians were in the majority. The Zoroastrians who remain are still victims of prejudice and have no loyalty towards the regime.'

'What's your plan, exactly?'

'It's in two parts,' replied Linda. 'First, we reach out to Jamshidi and see if there is a possibility of his helping us cross the Gulf to the mainland. My gut tells me that he will have a connection.'

'And second?'

'We pray very hard that our plan works,' replied Linda drily.

35

THE DAYS WERE getting shorter in Kashmir. It was five in the evening, but the premature darkness made it feel like nightfall. He sniffed at the scent of apple and cherry orchards nearby. His leather jacket, and the lambswool pullover underneath, were just right to face the icy winds of near winter.

Rajbagh, in the Civil Lines area of Srinagar, was one of the priciest residential areas of the city. Earlier, several Kashmiri Pandit families had their homes here. There had been around 77,000 Pandit families living in 1200 locations, in peace with their Muslim neighbours—that is, until 1989. Then militancy erupted and mosques issued declarations that the Pandits were kafirs, unbelievers. It meant that the Pandits had to leave Kashmir, convert to Islam or submit to death. It was medieval Islamic theology reawakened. Almost all Pandits fled to refugee camps in Jammu and Delhi.

He stopped outside a house that bore no nameplate on the gatepost. This particular resident had chosen to stay. He had been abducted from his home in 1992 by militants.

They had shifted him from one location to the next over two months, but he had survived. Eventually, he returned home and was greeted by his Muslim neighbours with due courtesy and respect. His friends and family in refugee camps wondered what had made Vijay Bhargava special. Why had his abductors let him go? And why had he been welcomed back into the communally charged Srinagar?

The visitor to Bhargava's house rang the bell. It was answered by a manservant who ushered him into the living room where a tall, fair man, with a receding hairline and a hooked nose, was waiting. On the bridge of his nose sat a pair of Bulgari spectacles. He was dressed in kurta-pyjama and soft Gucci loafers. Draped around his shoulders was what must have been an exorbitantly expensive *shahtoosh* shawl—a fabric made from the hair of a threatened species, the Tibetan antelope called chiru. Bhargava was a man who appeared to like his little luxuries.

But his indulgences did not take away from his distinguished career and credentials. He had served as a Cabinet minister in the Indian government, been a member of the Lok Sabha, completed a stint as governor of Himachal Pradesh, and acted as chancellor of Banaras Hindu University. In addition, he had been posted to several countries—Portugal, Iran and Brazil—as ambassador. Also, at eighty-four, Bhargava could pass for someone in his mid-sixties.

'Come in, my friend,' said Bhargava, rising from his chair and proffering his hand. Both men sat down beside a picture window that framed the distant Gopadri Hill, atop which was situated the Shankracharya Temple. Bhargava had been sipping kahwa, garnished with strands of saffron and slivers of almonds. He poured a cup for his guest from the kettle facing him.

'Did you have trouble getting into Kashmir?' asked Bhargava.

'Since when have people such as I had trouble getting in and out of places?' asked his visitor smugly.

That's why I need you to handle this, Bhargava thought. 'I see that the game has begun,' he said aloud. 'The whole world seems to want Jim Dastoor and his magic.' Guest and host exchanged looks of satisfaction.

His visitor took a sip of his kahwa and replaced the cup. 'What would you like me to do?' he asked, getting down swiftly to business.

'You and I have worked together in the past,' said Bhargava. 'You know that I do not like loose ends in anything that we do. Your present role puts you in the unique position of being able to save lives, while ensuring that what belongs in Bhargava hands must return to them.'

'What about Baba Malik?' asked the guest.

'His ancestors are a blot on Kashmiri history,' said Bhargava. 'Even when I was under attack from the Kashmiri separatists, I stood my ground. Have these people forgotten that in the first millennium, Kashmir was Buddhist and Shaivite. Islam arrived only in the thirteenth century, and promptly began on its mission of proselytisation.' He paused, his breath quickening. 'It was our land,' he whispered. '*Our* land—of the most beautiful meadows, rivers, valleys, orchards, lakes and mountains of God's creation. And see what Wahhabi Islam has done to it!'

'I know what you mean,' said the younger man, adding more prosaically, 'I hear that today, the sound of bomb blasts and gunfire are the norm. The problem with Abrahamic faiths is their eagerness to convince those of other faiths of the error of their ways. My country was only one of the many overrun by fundamentalism.'

'I trust there will be no conflict between what I want and what your employers want?' asked Bhargava austerely.

'I don't tell them everything,' replied the guest. 'But I don't think there will be any conflict. As long as I save the lives identified by my employer, I don't see any reason why I cannot deliver to you what you want.' He stroked the stubble on his chin. 'Why *do* you want it? Maybe it's not my place to ask.'

Bhargava's face relaxed. 'Even during my international postings, you and I had an open relationship,' he said. 'Remember that problem in Ardabil that you helped me with? And remember the Chabad House matter that I helped you with? As two men who have helped each other in the past, let me tell you that my objectives have been the result of sometimes emotional, sometimes rational, thinking. Now I wish to think spiritually.'

'I will help you,' said the visitor. 'But I shall not make any compromises on the deliverables to my employer.'

'I appreciate that,' said Bhargava. '*Gol posht o ru nadareh,*' he said in Kashmiri. *Turn your back to me when you need to. After all, a flower has neither front nor back.*

36

THE SMALL FISHING trawler had only a tiny superstructure aft, with a working deck amidship. It was dirty, grimy, greasy and smelly, but perfect for the smuggling runs that it undertook frequently from Kish Island.

The crew knew better than to head directly north—that would bring them into the key port of Bandar Aftab, a high-security area. Instead, they charted their course northwest towards the smaller Chiruyeh. It would be easier to dock there secretly. On board was the taxi driver, Firooz Jamshidi. Accompanying him were his two white-skinned friends.

Linda had taken the bull by the horns at Kish. She had telephoned Jamshidi and asked if he would be willing to be their tour guide for the day. The driver had enthusiastically agreed. Once they were together in the car, Linda had broached the subject cautiously. First, she needed to confirm her conjecture that Jamshidi was indeed Zoroastrian. Then, she had tried to gauge his loyalty to the Iranian regime.

'I am no traitor,' he had replied almost aggressively. 'I love Iran government. You foreigner peoples tell lie about us.'

But then Linda did something quite remarkable. In a low voice she began chanting, *Yatha ahu vairyo atha ratush ashat chit hacha … Vangheush dazda manangho shyothananam angheush mazdai …* It was Jim's go-to prayer, but she knew it better than he did.

Jamshidi brought the cab slowly to a halt. When he turned around, his expression had changed dramatically.

His eyes welled up, their floodgates unlocked. 'They take our lands and houses and say no more fire temples! No pray in schools!' It all came out in a rush. 'Books? Hah! We can no print more than three thousand copies of Zoroastrian book. Parliament has nearly three hundred member. Only one is us! No newspaperman will talk, or Shia Muslim will punish him bad!'

He paused, but only for breath. 'Rashidun Caliphate, bad to us. Umayyads, Abbasids, also bad. Kings—Timurids, Turcomans, Safavids, Afsharids and Qajars—no better. Little, *little* hope under Reza Shah Pahlavi and Mohammad Reza Shah. They tell us, this your home. But then come 1979. Islamic Revolution! All bad work of Ruhollah Khomeini. In your world his name only "The Ayatollah".'

'I feel your pain and your anger,' Linda told him, close to tears herself. 'I am married to a Zoroastrian and have heard many similar stories.' Linda then explained her predicament. 'Jim is somewhere in Iran, probably Tehran. God alone knows how he is being treated by the IRGC. My own government is incapable of helping me inside Iran. I need your help to get to Tehran and to find a way of reaching Jim. I am willing to pay whatever price you ask in return.'

'I not promise,' replied Jamshidi, looking thoughtful. 'But I ask some few people softly, softly. Maybe we find way to go. But big secret it is. No talk on telephone—they listen everything.'

The next day they got out again with Jamshidi for another 'tour'. As they got into his car, he said, 'My friend take cigarettes in boat from Kish to Chiruyeh in mainland. You can go, but secret, secret. From Chiruyeh, eighteen hour on road to Tehran. If there is any check on road, big problem. You are Americans. No proper paper also.' He thought some more for a bit. 'I come with you.'

'You would do that for us?' asked Linda. 'That's incredibly kind of you, Firooz. But I do not wish to put you or your family at risk with the authorities.'

'No family,' said Jamshidi. 'Wife dead ten years. Car accident. No children also. Plus, I want to help Zoroastrian husband of Madam.'

'It still begs the question,' interjected Dan, 'how would we get by without any papers? We only have a fourteen-day travel permit for Kish. No visa for Iran.'

'We will take help from other people. I cannot do on my own.'

'Who would help us?' asked Linda.

'I know one person,' said Jamshidi. 'But I cannot ask before you say yes. Because there is danger. But what can you do without danger?'

'Who is this person?' asked Dan cautiously.

'His name Behrad Soroushpur,' said Jamshidi. 'Live in Tehran. Head of Gabrabad Action Front group. Jee-ay-ef.'

'What is Gabrabad?' asked Dan.

'Name of one ghetto to which Zoroastrians are running from Muslims, when "Two Centuries of Silence" is happening. That is meaning two hundred years of fear and hiding! The people of the GAF want that *never* happen again, so they are making Zoroastrians come awake. If you agree, I ask Soroushpur for help.'

Linda and Dan silently agreed to take the risk. 'Yes, please speak to Mr Soroushpur,' Linda said. She looked over at Dan.

He smiled faintly, but she could make out that he harboured reservations that he wasn't about to share with her.

37

JIM COULD HEAR his own heart inside that hellhole. It was barely two metres long, a metre wide and a metre-and-a-half high. The small space he was in was unlit and unventilated except for an opening towards the front. It was impossible to stand up inside it and any movement entailed crawling on all fours. A small hole in the floor had been provided for relieving himself.

The overpowering smell of human urine and faeces had seeped into the rusting iron walls of the cell over the years, which no amount of soap and antiseptic would ever remove. It was the infamous 'coffin cell' and the IRGC had several of them inside the facility.

Within Iran, people often used the term *nahad-eh movazi*, which translated to 'parallel institutions' and referred to the extra-legal limbs of state coercion. This was one of them. Released prisoners called it *enferadi*, solitary confinement, an infernal form of psychological abuse and torture. A few days in one of these cells could break the resolve of any detainee and ensure that he capitulate, permit being videotaped, sign any confession, and spill all information.

Memories of the humiliation that he had endured before being placed into the coffin cell still played in a loop inside Jim's head. After being sent away by Khademhosseini, he had been taken to a processing room where he had been photographed and fingerprinted. Then he had been asked to remove his shoes, clothes and anything else on his body other than his spectacles. Stark naked, he had been asked to bend down; a prison doctor shoved an unlubricated gloved finger into his anus and performed an entirely unnecessary, painful and humiliating cavity search. It was part of the routine aimed at psychologically chipping away at prisoners. He had then been given a coarse, blue-and-white striped uniform to wear.

They had then led him barefoot to the coffin room. It was vast, with several horizontal cells stacked one upon the other against a wall, much like the body drawers of a morgue. Gaps between the coffins allowed the drainage lines to run. The tiles leading to the coffins were slick with blood, urine and sweat, and he felt his naked toes curl with revulsion.

All sorts of sounds were emerging from the coffins— coughing, screaming, puking and thumping—but when he crawled into his own, those sounds were muffled. Small mercy, since they had, at least, confirmed that he was not alone.

Minutes turned to hours; hours turned to days. He lost track of time. Sunrise, sunset, day or night was all the same inside that black hole. Initially, he had tried counting, but gave up on that idea very quickly. How much time had he been there? He could feel his sweat trickling down his back. And then he felt something else on his thigh. He quickly slapped his hand on the offending area and the sensation subsided. It had probably been an insect of some kind. *This is the kind of place where people lose all hope of ever seeing the sun again. They're doing their best to break you, Jim boy. Don't let them.*

An opening somewhere creaked slightly. A bowl containing a mush of soya beans, lentils and potato was placed on the ledge built into the opening. Along with that was a plastic cup of water. Jim gulped down the water quickly. He could barely discern what was in the food bowl, but he quickly wolfed it down. He felt instantly like throwing up, but fought to keep it down. *I have to live. To see the sun again. You are not going to break me.*

Eating was not as bad as expelling. To position oneself to use the little hole in the floor involved some serious gymnastics. The bastards had ensured that most prisoners would fail and would be forced to lie there in their own excrement. Only Jim's fitness and flexibility ensured that his cell remained relatively clean.

Jim knew that he needed to retain his strength. He began to systematically stretch his limbs, one by one. Right leg, bend, stretch, lift. Left leg, bend, stretch, lift. Rotate shoulders. Flex and rotate arms. Rotate head. A few half way sit-ups. He was not going to allow the bastards to get to him. After he was done with his physical routine, he started doing the deep-breathing meditation that his grandmother Cecile had taught him during one of his visits to Khandala. 'The ancients knew that there was a connection between breath and mind,' she had explained. 'When our minds are agitated, our breath also becomes irregular. So they figured that one could calm the mind by calming one's breath.'

Jim had tried praying. His mind drifted back to Mumbai when his family would chant the *Yatha Ahu Vairyo* together. He remembered the countless times he had heard his great-granduncle Homi Dastoor's version on his AirPods or inside his car. His mind wandered to a memory when he had taught the prayer to Linda who was eager to learn about all such things.

Yatha ahu vairyo atha ratush ashat chit hacha. Vangheush dazda manangho ...

38

RYAN PARKER HAD never been so angry in his life. First, there was the news that Jim Dastoor and Ali Zamani had disappeared. Next, the discovery that 'Ali Zamani' was an alias and that the man's name had actually been Javad Mosaffa. Finally, the revelation that the white powder thought to be Hamzaa Dura was crude washing powder inside a fake earthen box. Sodium carbonate! Parker was a man who prided himself on being a step ahead of everyone else. The present situation was humiliating in the extreme.

He paced up and down the room and then collapsed into the studded leather chair behind his desk. He pressed a key on the sleek platinum keyboard and a video-conference window opened on the monitor.

The face of a thin and pale man with mousy red hair appeared on the screen. Luke Miller had worked as an agent for Parker for many years. There was no such thing as clean business in Parker's world. That was an oxymoron; you could either be clean or be in business. Miller had done almost everything unpalatable in his line of work. He had forged documents, stolen formulations, blackmailed competitors, kidnapped scientists, sabotaged products and bribed regulators. But this was the first time that he had killed. There had absolutely been no other option. Dan Cohen had simply been *too* committed to Jim Dastoor. He had to be shaken up; the only way to do that had been to use Mistress Lucinda.

'That man who called himself Ali Zamani was added by you to my team,' said Parker accusingly. 'Why didn't you look into his background more closely?'

'I did examine it,' protested Miller. 'But the Iranians did a very good job of covering his tracks. All references to anyone called Javad Mosaffa are entirely absent, both in America and Iran. And his IRGC-Quds training was invaluable. He executed the Jim Dastoor abduction flawlessly. I really thought we had an invaluable asset in him.'

'Why can't you admit it when you screw up?' asked Parker. He reached out to pluck a Cohiba Siglo V from his desk humidor. He cut it with a gold-plated cutter that looked like a guillotine and lit up.

'I'm the first to admit when I do,' said Miller, as he watched his boss's cigar-lighting ritual. 'But you will agree that I did not depend solely on Zamani. I opened up the second channel—Dan Cohen—almost simultaneously.'

'And what did that achieve?' asked Parker. 'Besides you getting your jollies by cutting up a dominatrix?'

'I believed Dan Cohen when he said there was no Hamzaa Dura in the laboratory,' replied Miller. 'And that was because I knew he's terrified of me. At this moment he is entirely in my control.'

'How does that help if the stuff's not on him?'

'I didn't get a chance to update you on that,' put in Miller hastily. 'Jim's wife, Linda, has undertaken a trip to Iran with the objective of finding and freeing him. At this stage, I can't say if she has any help from American agencies, but I'm keeping my ears open. I know she has been in touch with the FBI.'

'So?' asked Parker.

'Well, when I heard the news, I told Dan to attach himself to the rescue party,' replied Miller. 'He could easily assume the role of the concerned friend who is willing to put his life at risk to save Jim.'

'Where is he now?'

'He's with Linda on Kish Island, a small tourist destination in Iran,' replied Miller. 'He has so far not asked me for any help.'

'Why should we be helping to retrieve Jim Dastoor?' asked Parker. 'Let him rot there. With him out of the way, my competition is taken care of.'

'The Hamzaa Dura, Jim and the body of research are all with your former employee, Mosaffa,' replied Miller. 'The Iranians have the material, they have Jim, they have the research.'

'Those mullahs can't do anything with it,' said Parker. 'They barely have enough time between praying five times a day. In any case, since when did Iran become interested in pharmaceutical discoveries?'

'That is a country which has an advanced nuclear research programme,' Miller reminded him. 'It would be foolish to dismiss that fact. And there has to be a reason why they want

Jim Dastoor and his Hamzaa Dura. Keep in mind that Jim Dastoor was born and brought up in India as a Parsi.'

'Parsi?' asked Parker. 'What's that?'

'The Zoroastrians who fled from Iran in the eighth century to India to save themselves and their religion from being wiped out by Muslim invasions,' replied Miller. 'Parsis, as they are more generally known now, have hugely depleted in numbers. There are at best around a hundred thousand around the world, mostly in India. There is some connection between the Parsi Jim Dastoor and Iran, other than a fought-over homeland. I just don't know what it is—yet.'

'What's next on the agenda to find out?' asked Parker, blowing out a large ring of Havana smoke.

'If we find Jim Dastoor, we locate Mosaffa. Once we find Mosaffa, we find the Hamzaa Dura,' replied Miller. 'We must pull out all the stops to help Dan Cohen reach Jim Dastoor.'

'How will *you* help?' asked Parker with barely hidden contempt. 'If you had such wonderful connections in Iran, we would not have been hoodwinked by Mosaffa!'

'Valid criticism,' admitted Miller, nonetheless refusing to be insulted. 'But I do have a few Iranian relationships intact. During my days at the CIA, we had cultivated a few high-level relationships in Pakistan. Some of those were men who had considerable access to the corridors of power in Iran.'

'Do you know where in Iran Jim Dastoor actually is?' asked Parker.

'Not yet,' answered Miller. 'But I soon will. And once I do, I will do everything possible to get Dan there. He has the most to lose by not delivering on his commitment to me. Trust me, he'll do everything that we tell him.'

Miller secretly, and with amusement, paraphrased Theodore Roosevelt in his mind. *If you've got a man by the balls, his heart and mind will surely follow.*

39

IT WAS 4 am and the water was calm. The fishing trawler cut its engines and waited a few kilometres away from shore. Linda and Dan tried to visually map the shoreline, but it was too dark. Ten minutes later they heard the splashing of oars. A tiny rowboat drew alongside the trawler. It had only one occupant. 'Sobh bekheyr,' he said to them. *Good morning.* Jamshidi returned the greeting with a smile.

Jim and Linda thanked the captain of the trawler after paying him the agreed amount. Then Jamshidi helped them off and into the boat of Behrad Soroushpur, whose usual white turban and ensemble had been replaced by khaki chinos and a white linen bush shirt. His beard had been trimmed and groomed. No words were exchanged on the boat.

Twenty minutes later the rowing boat hit the sandy shore of Chiruyeh. It was evident that Soroushpur was avoiding the cluster of residential properties, mosques and shops that dotted the coastline. Instead, they landed on a desolate stretch of beach. A green Saipa car was discreetly parked some distance away. Soroushpur and Jamshidi dragged the rowboat to the beach and dumped it next to some others. The four of them walked to the Saipa and entered the car.

Soroushpur and Jamshidi sat in front, while Dan and Linda got into the rear seat.

'*Haleh shoma chetoreh?*' asked Soroushpur, looking at them in the rearview mirror.

Linda replied warmly, 'We're fine. Thank you so much for agreeing to help us.'

'*Khosh amadid*,' replied Soroushpur. 'When Firooz informed me, I knew that I would have to help you. For over thirteen centuries, India has hosted our sons and daughters, the Parsis. This is my way of showing my appreciation of one who is both Indian and Zoroastrian, your husband.' *It's also my way of preserving the Zoroastrian heritage.*

'We have to cover a distance of around 1400 kilometres,' went on Soroushpur as he started the car and headed into Mogham-Bostanu Road. He had covered the route before, but on this occasion, the risk at each checkpoint would increase with two foreigners in the back.

'Let us try not to stop too often along the way,' Soroushpur advised. 'There is a thermos of *chai shirin* at the back along with a bag of *noon-e barbari* bread. Hopefully that will sustain us until lunchtime.'

'Thank you,' whispered Linda, truly overwhelmed by Soroushpur's efforts to minimise all risks.

'Keep your headscarf on at all times,' Soroushpur cautioned Linda. Turning to Dan, he said, 'There is a cap on the rear seat. Wear it whenever we are near a checkpoint. It will make it more difficult to identify your face. I'm going to claim that you are Russians.'

'Any idea on how we're going to go about tracing Jim?' asked Dan.

'I'm making two major assumptions,' replied Soroushpur. 'The first is that the man who abducted your colleague is part of the IRGC-Quds. The second, that your friend is being kept in Tehran, not in some other city.'

'And based on those assumptions, what do you think?' asked Linda.

'The most famous detention centre is Ward 2A of Evin Prison,' said Soroushpur. 'Then there is Detention Center 59 in the Vali Asr Military Base, also Detention Center 66 in the Ghasre Firoozeh Garrison and Detention Center 1A at the Sarallah campsite. He could be in any one of those.'

'How do we figure out which one?' asked Dan.

'Leave that to me,' said Soroushpur. 'Had we not been street-smart, we Zoroastrians would not have survived in Iran. I have my contacts in various places. By the time we reach Tehran, I should have some idea of where he is being held.'

They had just crossed Bandar-e-Mogham when a police barricade loomed ahead. '*Rahvar*,' said Soroushpur as he slowed down.

'What?' asked Dan.

'Rahvar—traffic police,' replied Soroushpur. 'Not a problem, given that my car papers are all in order.' He pulled up to the barrier and lowered his window. 'Sobh bekheyr,' he greeted the official politely.

'Papers,' the man demanded brusquely.

Soroushpur handed the required documents. The policeman went over them and seemed satisfied. Then he noticed the two foreigners in the rear seat. 'Who are they?' he asked.

'Family friends from Russia,' lied Soroushpur. 'They have valid visas.'

'Let me see the passports,' said the officer, scrutinising the rear passengers more closely. Linda could feel her heart racing. This could mean 'game over' even before it had begun.

'Sure, officer,' replied Soroushpur. He handed over his own passport to the policeman. The officer looked at it and then stared hard at Soroushpur. His expression did not indicate anything. He calmly took out the fifty-dollar bill tucked inside the pages of the passport, pocketed it, and returned the passport to Soroushpur. The fifty was more than a sixth of his monthly wage. The fact that it was paid in American dollars rather than Iranian rials made it even more valuable.

'*Khoda hafez*, God speed,' he wished Soroushpur.

'*Be salamat*,' Soroushpur replied with equal courtesy as the policeman pulled away the barrier and allowed the car to pass through.

Soroushpur whooshed a sigh of relief as he drove away. 'The good thing about Iran,' he said with a lighter heart, 'is that everything here has a price.' He looked at his phone. There were missed calls from Nassr Tamoyan at Gundeshapur. He made a mental note to reach him. The Yazidi researcher probably had some news for him.

Linda couldn't bring herself to relax completely. It had been a close call. And they still had 1350 kilometres to go. Then she remembered a piece of wisdom from the Persian philosopher Omar Khayyam. *Be happy for this moment. This moment is your life.*

40

THE CITY OF Ahvaz is located around 800 kilometres from Tehran and is close to the Iraq border. There is not much that is special about Ahvaz, except the Karoun river that splits the city into two—the western and eastern sections. Only one other little fact is worth noting. The western part of Ahvaz is home to the headquarters of the IRGC-Quds Force. Amir Khademhosseini, head of the IRGC-Quds Force, walked around his office as he conversed. During his tenure, Khademhosseini had expanded the IRGC-Quds into a monstrous body specialising in unconventional warfare and military intelligence. The IRGC-Quds was famous for extending support to non-state actors in several countries, including the Hezbollah in Lebanon, Hamas in Gaza, Islamic Jihad in the West Bank and various Shia militias in Iraq, Syria and Afghanistan.

While Jim Dastoor was still languishing in the coffin cell, the team had begun going through all the items that Javad Mosaffa had procured for them. This included an earthen box with a pilot's insignia and containing a white powder known as Hamzaa Dura. In addition, there were a couple of hard drives and several USB sticks.

Mosaffa sat in one of the visitors' chairs facing Khademhosseini's desk as his boss circled the room. 'How can we be sure that this material is linked to the Athravan Star?' asked Khademhosseini. 'All we know is that American pharma giants would love to get their hands on this stuff. And that emblem on the box looks like a stick drawing that a child could do. What the hell is it? A pilot's badge or an airmail sticker? We have absolutely nothing to show that this has anything to do with the Athravan Star.'

'True,' replied Mosaffa. 'But it is also certain that Jim Dastoor's family is descended from a line of Zoroastrian priests—people who left this country to settle in India.'

'But there are many of those, priests and others,' interjected Khademhosseini. 'Almost 18,000 of them settled in Sanjan. Then there were additional waves of refugees from Sari. Today there are around a hundred thousand around the world. What makes Jim Dastoor any different? And we don't even know what the Athravan Star looks like.' He had returned to his old grouch.

'I have done a little digging,' said Mosaffa. 'You see, when the Parsis arrived in Sanjan, they needed to consecrate a sacred fire known as the Iranshah. There was one priest who was responsible for this task. His name was Nairyosang. He had three children who produced nine grandsons. Their nine families are the ones who look after the fire that is now housed in a place called Udvada.'

'And?'

'Jim Dastoor belongs to one such family,' replied Mosaffa, reading from a file. 'But it is also the family that protected the fire on several occasions when it had to be moved from Sanjan to Bahrot, from Bahrot to Bansda, from Bansda to Navsari, and from Navsari to Udvada.'

'I'm still not clear what you are getting at,' said Khademhosseini, picking up a cup of tea, sourced for him from his favourite *chai khaneh*, a tea shop. He slurped at it with relish, then lit one of his Farvardins, taking a deep drag of the smoke into his lungs.

'If there were indeed a relic known as the Athravan Star and if we were to assume that it was carried off by the Zoroastrians from Iran, then the custody of such a valuable relic would be in the hands of the most powerful families among them.'

'But this man is a scientist,' scoffed Khademhosseini. 'What would he have to do with ancient relics and all that poppycock? All we have of importance is the scientist himself, and the bulk of his research. Yes, those could possibly earn us astronomical amounts in any currency or bullion, if we were to take offers from interested parties. But that's it. I'm still unclear what to tell the rahbar-e mo'azzam. Particularly after that British Museum fiasco.'

'It wasn't a complete fiasco,' said Mosaffa. 'The cylinder referenced Marduk. It said that Cyrus was Marduk's beloved. The reference to Marduk is not something that should be taken lightly.'

'Why?'

'Because deliberate attempts were made 2600 years ago to transpose the achievements of the deity Marduk onto the deity Ashur,' said Mosaffa. He had done his research. 'The image of Ashur was used in later years by many rulers. But Cyrus seemed to be underplaying Ashur. Could it have been to divert attention from the Athravan Star?'

Khademhosseini didn't answer. Theological, historical or mythological information never interested him. He lived his life by a simple maxim: *La Ilaha Illallah Mohammad-ur-*

Rasool Allah. There is none worth worshipping except Allah, and Mohammad is his Messenger.

'May I suggest something?' asked Mosaffa.

'Go ahead,' replied Khademhosseini.

'Keeping the man inside a coffin cell is not going to get us anywhere,' said Mosaffa. 'Without his help we have no way of uncovering the truth. Among everyone here, I probably have the best relationship with him. I was with him when we travelled from Portland to Worcester; I was with him during his captivity in Asclepius; I was also with him on the flight from Spencer to Doha and then on to Tehran.'

Khademhosseini looked at Mosaffa suspiciously. 'You consider yourself to be his friend?' he asked.

Mosaffa snorted. 'Not at all,' he replied. 'But I think I could open a dialogue with him. If we were to take him out of that cell, allow him to bathe and shave, eat a decent meal … maybe I could coax some information out of him. Let me go back to Tehran and try a slightly more appropriate technique.'

'The guards at DC1A say that he has been obedient,' said Khademhosseini snidely. 'I guess that resounding slap that I gave him was enough to cow him down for good. Unlike some of the other coffin cell inmates, this one does not scream or stomp. He even eats the stinking food they serve.'

'He will die if we leave him there,' said Mosaffa. 'We will lose any leverage that we have. He may be a Zoroastrian, but he is a valuable US citizen. Given his knowledge, the Americans would pay a hefty ransom for him. And his competitors would pay an arm and a leg to get their hands on his stuff. Let's play this carefully.'

'You think you can get him to cooperate with your method? Fine. Go back to Tehran and try. But your head will roll if your plan produces no results. I have the Ayatollah breathing down my neck.'

'Thank you, sir,' said Mosaffa, getting up from the chair. 'One more request. May I please move him to a safe house instead of a cell at DC1A?'

'You have a place in mind?' asked Khademhosseini sternly.

'You exert control over many strategic industries,' said Mosaffa. 'One of them is Shahid Daru Pharma. If we could move him to the guesthouse on its premises, I could also use the services of their researchers to translate into layspeak what Jim reveals. I am no scientist.'

'Why do I give you the freedom to do these things?' asked Khademhosseini, with a theatrical sigh.

'Because I eventually deliver results?' Mosaffa asked back.

At Shahabad, around two hours from Ahvaz, where Khademhosseini and Mosaffa were deliberating, another man was also digging to discover the truth. Nasr Tamoyan, a Yazidi scholar, was at the ancient site on the orders of Soroushpur.

41

IT WAS LATE in the evening. My father had finished half the bottle of scotch. I had had only two pegs of it, but large ones, and neither of us wanted the session to end. Both had grown more grandiose and sentimental by the sip, and now congratulated ourselves on being born into a community that may have been numerically challenged, but was pretty much at the top of the heap when it came to contributions to mankind.

I had to eventually force my father to turn in for the night. When I'd dragged myself to my own bed, my thoughts turned to my grandmother, Cecile. She had laboured hugely to acquaint herself with Parsi history, in an effort to 'fit in' with her new surroundings. Alas, the Parsi community had proved too insular then, owing, perhaps to a need for self-preservation arising from centuries of foreign aggression. I made a mental note to drive down to Khandala and meet my worthy grandmother before I left for America.

Grandmother used to tell me that there were three hundred years of peace after the arrival of the Parsis in Sanjan. During this period, the Parsis split into five panths or groups: the Sanjanas of Sanjan; the Bhagarias of Navsari; the Godavras of Anklesar; the Bharuchas of Broach; and finally, the Khambattas of Khambat. Each panth was an ecclesiastic group, having its own clergy, laity and council.

But then the Ghaznavid ruler, Sultan Mahmud Begada, vowed that he would conquer Sanjan. Begada was no ordinary man. Over the years since childhood, he had been fed toxic substances in small doses, so that he gradually developed an immunity to poison. The clothes he wore were burned daily lest they contained remnants of the toxins his body was trained to expel. In later manhood, the invincible Begada destroyed the renowned temple of Dwarka, and chopped its chief priest's body into twelve pieces that were displayed singly on each of the dozen gates of Ahmedabad. He even coerced the raja of Junagadh into turning Muslim.

Begada's force of 30,000 horsemen, accompanied by elephantry and soldiers on foot, then headed for Sanjan. The Hindu king summoned his entire army to defend Sanjan. Then he called the Parsi leaders to his court. 'My ancestors extended their patronage to you and bestowed many favours upon you,' he said. 'In this hour of need, gird up your loins in my service.'

The Parsis had not forgotten their oath of fealty to Jadi Rana. They had sworn to renounce their weapons unless commanded to take them up by no other than the king himself. Around 1400 Parsis joined the Hindu forces in defence of Sanjan. History was, typically, repeating itself. Zoroastrians had been attacked by soldiers of Islam in Iran; they were now being attacked by soldiers of Islam in Sanjan.

The sight of Sultan Mahmud's army was terrifying. His battle-hardened elephants wreaked havoc on the combined Hindu–Parsi forces. The fighting raged for days; the battlefield was soon littered with corpses, and awash in the blood of men and animals. What was more, the sides were unevenly matched. Although the Hindu–Parsi alliance put up a brave front, Sultan Mahmud's forces prevailed.

Naturally, the first concern for the Parsis who survived the slaughter was protecting their precious Iranshah—the sacred fire that they had consecrated with so much difficulty. A group of priests fled with it to the hill of Bahrot, located around twenty kilometres south of Sanjan. There, they hid with it inside a cave for twelve years. Among them was one of my family's ancestors, who carried, also, the little earthen box.

After that dreaded decade and two years, when they thought it safe, they took the Atash Behram to Bansda, where three hundred men on horses turned out to escort them to safety with pomp and ceremony. Bansda, just as Sanjan had once been, became a destination, prospering from pilgrim traffic and the attendant revenue.

The first wave of Parsis had departed Iran from Khorasan, and had later been joined by groups from the town of Sari in the province of Mazandaran. Once resettled in Gujarat, they established Nav-Sari, or the 'new Sari'—much like immigrants to America created New York, New Jersey or New Hampshire. It was from Navsari that an individual called Changashah emerged, a man who would alter Parsi history, again. Zoroastrian texts refer to this person as Changa Asa.

Changashah was concerned that the Parsis of India had lost touch with their ancient Zoroastrian roots. He summoned an anjoman, a community meeting. After much deliberation, the Parsis of Navsari collectively agreed that they needed to re-establish contact with their brethren in Iran, the distant cousins that they had lost touch with for seven centuries. But who would undertake as dangerous a task as journeying to a now foreign land, and reawakening history? Any Parsi entering Iran would be putting his life into the sword-wielding hands of the Safavid king, Uzun Hassan.

One brave soul agreed to take up the job. His name was Nariman Hoshang.

42

FINANCED BY CHANGASHAH, *Nariman Hoshang undertook the hazardous journey, sailing from Broach to the Iranian coast.*

From there he secretly trekked overland to Yazd. Many residents of Yazd were fugitives, having narrowly escaped the wrath of the Safavid kings whose overarching goal was the destruction of Zoroastrian temples and the conversion of non-believers to a strictly Shia version of Islam.

In Yazd, Nariman met the Dasturan Dastur—the chief priest—at Turkabad. Nariman was graciously welcomed, but very little conversation took place because he could not speak the Yazd vernacular of Farsi. Nevertheless, Nariman persevered, and it took him only a year to learn the language.

He eventually returned to Navsari in 1478 CE, carrying back directions from two Sharifabadi priests written in the Pazend script. These instructions came to be called the rivayats, although one of the rivayats remained unwritten, only to be passed on by word of mouth. In addition to them, Nariman brought back a book called Kalila wa Dimna by Abdullah ibn al-Muqaffa.

The rivayats began, 'To the priests, leaders and chief men of Hindustan ...' going on to bemoan the terrible hardships that the Iranian Zoroastrians were suffering under constant attack from their Muslim rulers.

According to my father, both Nariman Hoshang and Changashah became heroes to their people. The process of visiting Yazd and seeking religious direction eventually became a continuous one. Around twenty-six rivayats—or twenty-seven, if you include the secret one—were received by the Parsis between 1478 and 1773. The Iranian Zoroastrians vowed to ensure that their brothers in India would never again lose touch with their time-honoured customs. On their part, the Parsis of Navsari meticulously saved and collated all the rivayats.

Most of the directions were answers to queries on observance of worship, customs and rituals. But a couple of them were metaphorical, ambiguous or mystical, and did not lend themselves to being deciphered. For example:

Across the Jabbar, light dazzles the eyes
As three great fires roar from the skies
Behold, the Athravan in the Daitya prays
And the Anu people to the heavens gaze
They know the fourth that comes from three
Means powerful Yasna for all time to be.

As lovely as that was, what did it mean?

The initiative taken by Changashah made Navsari the new cultural hub for Parsis. Although Navsari was pride of place of the first-ever fire temple since 1142 CE, the town came to acquire greater fame as the birthplace of Changashah. In the course of time, the Parsis of Navsari were able to negotiate a settlement to move the Iranshah from Bansda to Navsari. An Atash-ni-Agiary was specially built by Changashah's son to accommodate it.

But relocation of the Iranshah from Sanjan to Bahrot, then Bansda and on to Navsari, did not come without its share of problems. The Sanjanas—my ancestors included—were the priests from Sanjan who had been tending the Iranshah from its inception. As traditional guardians of the flame, it was they who had carried the fire to Navsari. The move resulted in friction with the Bhagarias, the existing priests of Navsari. The dispute lasted many years and the fire had to be moved several times to avert the intense political wrangling that seemed to follow it wherever it went.

The Iranshah survived it all. And so did the material that came in the earthen box, the one that had first been carried to the shores of Sanjan. It was safely in the hands of the Sanjana line of descendants.

The next morning, when I emerged from my room, I saw that my father was already waiting for me at the breakfast table. Breakfast in our home was always king-size; I was handed a plateload of kheema, akoori, cutlets and buttered pav, and expected to finish it. I obeyed, like the good son I was, pushing aside only the fear of a lifelong problem with cholesterol.

My father had in front of him a book that described the travels of the Iranshah. He read aloud from it as I ate.

The fire had been consecrated in Sanjan in 721 CE, the book said, and had stayed there for the next four centuries—until the attack by Sultan Mahmud Begada. It had been carried by the Sanjanas to Bahrot, where it had stayed in a cave for twelve years before it was housed in Bansda. Finally, upon the persuasion of Changashah, the fire was moved to Navsari, where it stayed for almost three centuries—except for a temporary move to Surat on account of a threat of being looted from its rest.

But the tension between the Sanjanas and the Bhagarias remained, each wanting greater control over religious administration. This dispute resulted in a court battle, in which the verdict was that the Sanjanas could continue to tend the fire, but the Bhagarias would handle all other religious activity. This arrangement was deemed unacceptable by the Sanjanas. They left Navsari with the Atash Behram in 1741 CE and took it to Bulsar—modern-day Valsad in Gujarat. A common

Parsi surname, Bulsara, is a reminder of that region. Again, a dispute arose on division of priestly duties and the allocation of pilgrims' donations.

Just a year later, the fire was shifted once more to the coastal fishing village of Udvada. A new fire temple was consecrated there in 1742 CE and the millennium old Atash Behram was at last given a permanent residence. Udvada remains the home of the Iranshah to this day. The flame has been kept alive for thirteen centuries.

43

MY FATHER TAPPED the small earthen box he had given me the previous evening. I had carelessly left it on the coffee table, and my father had picked it up and pushed it towards me. 'Guard it with your life, son. It has remained in our family line for longer than our collective memories.'

'What is it?' I persisted in finding out.

'You will know when the time comes,' replied my father. 'The honour of serving the Atash Behram stayed with the nine families which descended from the priests who consecrated the original fire, the ones who rescued the fire from the battle at Sanjan. They remained wedded to their duty to guard the flame along all its journeys between Sanjan, Bahrot, Bansda, Navsari, Bulsar, Surat and eventually Udvada.'

'Where do I come into the picture?' I asked, somewhat irreverently.

'You'll find out. All you need to know for now is that our family is descended from that line of Sanjanas,' said my father. 'As you know, our surname—Dastoor—comes from the word "dastur", which means "priest". When your great-great-grandfather, Shapoor, broke with priestly tradition by leaving Udvada, his exit did not alter the special role that our family had in keeping this box safe, and passed to the right hands every succeeding generation. And even within the family, it is passed on to only he who exhibits the greatest spine—sometimes even the most rebellious of the lot.'

'I wonder why,' I mused.

'I have no idea but there must be a reason,' said my dad. 'Your grandfather saw in you a rebellious streak and identified you as the next in line to be the guardian of the box.'

Then he handed me a small card containing a few lines of text. 'What is this?' I asked.

'The secret rivayat,' he replied. 'It is the only one you need to remember. Memorise it, then destroy the note. It came to us covertly from the cousins we left behind in Persia. Many attempts were made to convey it to us, before one finally succeeded.'

I wondered what all the cloak-and-dagger routine was about but held my tongue, simply putting the card in my pocket. 'You mentioned a "special role" for our family,' I said. 'What was that special role?' I pushed away my plate and wiped the corners of my mouth with my napkin.

'That special role goes back to our homeland, much before our people came to India,' said my father. 'That story must start with Zarathustra, the founder of our faith.'

I waited as my father lit his first cigarette of the day. He smoked only State Express 555. He inhaled the smoke deeply before he expelled it. 'It is believed that Zarathustra was born sometime around 1500 BCE in a land known as Airyanemvaeja. But there is no clarity about where Airyanemvaeja was specifically located.'

'Why was he named "Zarathustra"? Does it have a meaning?' I interrupted.

'It could mean "the tender of camels", replied my father. 'But in old Persian, the word "zara" also means "gold". Which is how, in India, gold-embroidery came to be known as "zari".'

'Then what would explain the second half of the name, "-thustra" ... what is that?'

'In Sanskrit, "thushtra" implies a binary star—a twin star like Sirius, Gemini, Mizar or Pollima,' said my father. I found that most intriguing. Many centuries after Zarathustra, a twin star had shone to mark the birth of Jesus Christ too.

Going by what my father said, the birth of Zarathustra was heralded by the appearance of a golden twin star in the sky. He was born on Khordad in the month of Fravardin, now celebrated as Khordad Saal by Parsis. Khordad corresponds with Gemini, the passage of the sun from sixty to ninety degrees from the vernal equinox.

As legends go, Zarathustra is said to have laughed rather than cried as a baby. Zarathustra's family were known as the Athravan Spitamas. The Spitamas were priests—also called magi—and their surname signified descent from a white, shining powder. Zarathustra was the son of a wealthy priest, Purushaspa, and his wife, Dughdhova. Purushaspa sired a large family—Zarathustra was the third of five brothers. He became a priest by the age of fifteen but left his home when he was twenty to pray in solitude. He spent the next ten years in prayer and meditation in the mountains, surviving almost solely on milk, herbs and cheese.

'When Zarathustra was around thirty years old, he attended a celebration of the vernal equinox,' said my father, picking up the thread. 'It was the spring festival that we Zoroastrians now celebrate as Nowruz. He had been drawing water from the purest part of the river for the morning ceremony when the angel Vohu Mana appeared before him. The angel asked him some questions; pleased by Zarathustra's replies, Vohu Mana granted him a vision of Ahura Mazda.'

It became clear to Zarathustra that Ahura Mazda—shortened by successive generations of Zoroastrians to Ormazd, Hormazd and Hormuz—is the supreme being, the uncreated spirit. Nothing exists without Ahura Mazda who is peerless, changeless and timeless.

But opposing Ahura Mazda is Ahriman, the destructive spirit, also known as Angra Mainyu. Human beings are given the freedom to choose one path over the other. 'They can take the path to love and righteous living, or fall on the path to greed and mischief,' explained my father.

I recalled my teacher, Mrs Batliwala, telling the class that the root of the English word 'angry' actually lies in 'angra', the first name of the dark, destroying entity.

44

WE MOVED TO the living room, where my father chose a place for himself on the sofa. 'The three great Abrahamic faiths—

Judaism, Christianity and Islam—had not even been born in the times of Zarathustra,' he said. 'But all of them would draw inspiration from Zoroastrianism. The idea of duality: good and evil, heaven and hell, God and Satan, would be borrowed from Zoroastrianism. The ideas of a shining star, messiah, devil's temptation, Judgement Day and resurrection of the dead would also be sourced from the philosophy of Zarathustra.'

Zarathustra began to preach that the worship of multiple deities and offering sacrifices to them was wholly unnecessary. But this was nothing short of rebellion, according to the beliefs of the elders of the community. Zarathustra said humans had free will and the choices they made would determine whether they attained heaven or hell. The world was a theatre of conflict between order and chaos. Choosing righteousness meant that order—or Asha—would prevail over Druj, the lie.

'Zarathustra's ideas upset many existing mores,' continued my father, sounding like he rather applauded the fact. 'The priests, for instance, had derived their wealth from the sacrifices and religious offerings of devotees to deities they worshipped in blind faith. Rulers drew their absolute power from the divine right said to be bestowed on them by various godlike personages. But in Zarathustra's view, Ahura Mazda only wanted humata, hukata and huvarastha—good thoughts, good words and good deeds. This challenged the very basis of the social hierarchy. So the privileged, and previously divided classes, fearing Zarathustra's teachings would upset their tidy little apple cart, united—to attack his views!'

They now had a common enemy: Zarathustra. And soon his life would be in danger. But in Zarathustra's possession was a small earthen box. How he came by it is a story for another *time. Zarathustra did not know that what lay inside it would save his life one day.*

My father gave me a book about Zarathustra that he had borrowed from Cecile's library. I took it to my room and began to read it. Some of what it told me was familiar, but there were accounts and ideas also there that were refreshingly new. In the beginning, I couldn't figure why Dad was making me plod through dense theological stuff like this, but I remembered that there was always a deeper purpose in everything that Baman Dastoor did.

Zarathustra's ideas had few takers. Initially he only had one convert, his cousin Maidhyoimanha. As Zarathustra's views challenged the priestly power structure, his life was soon in danger. Eventually he had to flee. So he wandered through the countryside in search of people who would be more receptive to his thoughts. In the yasnas can be found Zarathustra's desperate plea to Ahura Mazda.

What land should I flee to? Where should I go?
From my family and from my clan they banish me.
The community to which I belong has not satisfied me
Nor have the rulers of the country.
How, Thee, can I satisfy, O Mazda Ahura?

Eventually Zarathustra arrived at the court of King Vishtaspa in Bactria—in the Balkh province of modern-day Afghanistan—where he claimed to have divine authority to spread the message of Ahura Mazda, the one and only true God.

In those days, there were two classes of the power elite in Vishtaspa's court—the kawis and the karpans—each vying for a greater share of power. The kawis were rulers, much like the kshatriyas of India; the karpans interceded with the gods, much like Hindu brahmins. Both classes, unsurprisingly, viewed Zarathustra with dislike. They were content within the power construct of those times and did not need his meddling. Unfortunately for them, Vishtaspa decided to give Zarathustra an opportunity to prove himself.

Zarathustra began by explaining to the king the conflict between the benevolent Ahura Mazda and the malevolent Ahriman. On Ahura Mazda's side were Spenta Mainyu and six other spirits known as the Amesha Spentas that worked to maintain goodness and light. On his side, Ahriman maintained his legions of evil and darkness.

A grand debate was held that lasted three days. Zarathustra decisively won it, but his victory only served to tie his opposition even more closely together. Powerful voices in Vishtaspa's court spread rumours about how Zarathustra practised black magic and sorcery in secret. Eventually, the king ordered that Zarathustra be imprisoned.

That would have been the end of Zarathustra, had fate not intervened.

45

IT WAS A *horse that saved Zarathustra.*

King Vishtaspa had a favourite horse, Aspisiah, which fell inexplicably ill and was unable to stand on its legs. The king's doctors and priests tried every known remedy, with no success. From within the prison walls, Zarathustra sent word to Vishtaspa that he could cure the steed, although he knew that if he were unsuccessful, the king was quite liable to send Zarathustra to an early death. Toting his satchel to the royal stables, he got down to work.

Aspisiah was cured. The king was overjoyed, and also convinced now of the legitimacy of Zarathustra's claims. In gratitude, the king embraced Zoroastrianism. As did his wife Hutaosa and their son Spentodata. Zarathustra's new religion was known as 'Mazdayasna'—translating to 'ritual offerings to Ahura Mazda'.

Zarathustra composed a short prayer, the Yatha Ahu Vairyo, *words of which are taught to Zoroastrian children to this day. A hymn that was set to music by my great-granduncle, Homi.*

Thereafter, many of Vishtaspa's courtiers followed suit, although those who felt left out of the new power structure continued to nurse their grudge against Zarathustra. But Vishtaspa became Zarathustra's patron. Patron and prophet installed the first consecrated fire, the Adur Burzin Meher, in Khorasan. Outside the temple, Zarathustra planted a sacred cypress tree from his homeland. The tree grew so tall that it seemingly reached the heavens. It lived for thousands of years and survived many generations of families.

Some two millennia later, the Abbasid caliph Mutawakkil ordered that the tree be chopped down to be fashioned into beams for his grand palace at Samarra. His Zoroastrian subjects begged him not to, offering to compensate him with gold instead. But the caliph refused. It turned out to be an ill-fated decision. On the very night when the cypress arrived on the banks of the Tigris, the caliph was assassinated by a Turkish soldier.

But I digress. Zarathustra now had a place of honour at Vishtaspa's court. He married Hvovi, niece to the king. By some accounts, they had three sons and three daughters. Several legends grew around his life: about how he survived many threats to his life—raging fires, wild cattle, wolves and demons. There were also stories about his compassion towards the poor and towards stray dogs. And tales about the Ahriman tempting him and Zarathustra driving the devil away. Possibly, that would later be the inspiration behind Christ's forty days and nights in the Judaean Desert.

At the age of seventy-seven, Zarathustra was murdered within a temple he had consecrated; the assassin was a Turanian called Turbaratus. This happened during the storming of Balkh by King Arjasp. Arjasp believed that Zarathustra, as mentor to Vishtaspa, deserved punishment for causing people to desert their old gods. Even as he lay dying, Zarathustra forgave his assassin for the bloody deed.

During his meditations, Zarathustra had often put questions to Ahura Mazda about good and evil. The answers that came to him were memorised and repeated to his followers who did the same. These answers would be passed down from one generation to the next orally. These 'Gathas', put into writing many hundreds of years later, became part of a wider body of religious scriptures called the Avesta.

In later years, Alexander's armies invaded Persia. Alexander's own people, the Macedonians, would find out more about Zarathustra and refer to him in their writings as Zoroaster. But the Western world neglected to recognise that Zoroastrianism had been the inspiration for the monotheistic religions of Judaism, Christianity and Islam. They also obliterated the fact that Zarathustra's philosophical roots were embedded in his homeland, Airyanemvaeja.

Zarathustra may not have known that his ideas would flourish under the Achaemenid kings—Cyrus, Darius and Xerxes. Zoroastrianism would be almost wiped out after the sacking of Persepolis by Alexander the Great, but would rise once again during the Sassanian period, only to later come under vicious attack from Islam. But through each era of tumult, the earthen box with the strange emblem continued to be passed on from one Zoroastrian generation to the next.

After the death of Zarathustra, the box would continue to be protected by an inner circle of Zoroastrian priests. Given that Zarathustra had rebelled against existing power structures, a new tradition was established. The box would move from one rebel to the next, but within the priestly lineage. These men were the ones who really knew what powers lay in it.

They were known as the magi.

46

AROUND TWO HOURS by road away from Ahvaz, where Khademhosseini and Mosaffa were deliberating, lies Shahabad, a village that is home to less than a thousand families.

Very close to Shahabad are some ancient ruins, now identified as the ancient Academy of Gundeshapur. Not many archaeologists had done any significant excavation work there except for the lone Yazidi scholar Nasr Tamoyan. Even he had not received any meaningful financial support—except for a small monthly stipend paid by someone in Tehran. That patron was Behrad Soroushpur from the Gabrabad Action Front.

Given his terribly constrained budget, Tamoyan had relocated to Shahabad from where he undertook daily expeditions into the ruins. Each day he would collect and catalogue as many pottery fragments as he could find without having to dig too deep. He knew it would be foolish to undertake extensive excavations—an area as wide as Gundeshapur would require an entire army of historians, archaeologists and scholars—but Tamoyan dug on, the glutton for punishment that he was.

Gundeshapur had once been the academic seat of the Sassanian Empire. Founded by King Shapur I—hence Gunde-*shapur*—in the third century CE, it comprised not only a university and library but also one of the most advanced hospitals of its time. But Gundeshapur only reached its zenith under King Kusrow I who liberally gave grants to Greek philosophers, Nestorian academics and Persian physicians to relocate there and carry on their academic pursuits.

After endless months of unearthing almost nothing, the last day had been quite exhilarating for Tamoyan. He had found a fragment of a clay tablet that contained exciting information. He had tried contacting Soroushpur on the phone, but the man's connection had been out of reach. Tamoyan was unaware that his patron was busy transporting an American woman in search of her Parsi husband somewhere in Iran.

He finally got through. 'I have been trying to reach you since yesterday,' complained Tamoyan.

'Sorry about that,' replied Soroushpur. 'I have been on the move, and network coverage has been an issue. Tell me what you have found.'

'I've found something that specifically refers to Borzuya!' Tamoyan told him eagerly.

'What does it say?' asked Soroushpur immediately.

'It reconfirms that the Persian physician Borzuya was sent by Kusrow to India in search of an elixir,' replied Tamoyan. 'But more importantly, it refers to a text that he brought back—something that was meant to be used in conjunction with a substance that was no longer in India.'

'Is there any way to identify it?' asked Soroushpur.

'Not at the moment,' replied Tamoyan. 'What we have are just fragments of information. Without many more men and resources, it will be impossible to carry out a full examination of the Gundeshapur site.'

'Our resources at the GAF are limited too,' said Soroushpur more slowly. 'All I want to urgently know is what exactly the Athravan Star is. Give me some way of identifying it. Then tell me what its powers are.'

'I'm trying my best,' said Tamoyan. 'Remember that Gundeshapur fell into decline after the Muslim conquest of Persia. The city surrendered way back in 638 CE. So, it's possible that many important items may have been removed or destroyed.'

'I understand,' said Soroushpur disappointedly.

'One more thing,' said Tamoyan. 'There is reference to something called *The Five Treatises*. Apparently, this was the text that Borzuya translated into Pahlavi upon his return to Gundeshapur.'

'Is there a way to get that text?' asked Soroushpur, his hopes reviving.

'Borzuya's Pahlavi version is lost,' replied Tamoyan. 'Luckily, a translation into Arabic by Ibn al-Muqaffa survives. I should be able to locate that.'

The levers in Soroushpur's head were clanging into motion. Wasn't that the Arabic book that Unwalla had discovered in Navsari? 'Please do try,' he said. 'I am not too hopeful of finding a reference to the Athravan Star in that translation, but we have to cover all bases. We should also keep in mind that Kusrow was known as "Anushiravan."'

'That word must count for something,' agreed Tamoyan. 'Gundeshapur was way ahead of its time in mathematics, philosophy, medicine and astronomy. Shapur's wife was the daughter of the Roman Emperor Aurelian. She brought two Greek physicians to Gundeshapur. In addition, the pagan philosophers who had been banished by the Byzantine emperor Justinian were also allowed to settle there. Even the Nestorian academics from Nisbis were resettled in Gundeshapur after emperor Zeno shut down their institutions. Many doctors from Urfa in Assyria also settled here. This accumulation of knowledge would have peaked by Kusrow's time.'

'Exactly,' said Soroushpur. 'All this knowledge, combined with the powers of the Zoroastrian magi, would have been a treasure chest.'

'Only until the Sassanians were in power,' Tamoyan reminded him. 'After the seventh century, Gundeshapur began to project itself as an Islamic institute of higher learning. Anything that conflicted with the Qur'an became an issue.'

'Keep looking,' urged Soroushpur. 'Find me a link. The Athravan Star belongs to Zoroastrians around the world. We cannot allow it to fall into wrong hands. And if it *is* in wrong hands, we need to retrieve it.'

'Sure,' said Tamoyan. 'Where are you?'

'On my way to Shiraz,' said Soroushpur. 'I was just thinking …'

'Yes?'

'Could you take a flight from Ahwaz to Shiraz? It's only an hour.'

'Why?' asked Tamoyan.

'You could meet me at Persepolis,' said Soroushpur. He was standing some distance away from his car and staring at Linda and Dan as he spoke.

47

THE JOURNEY FROM Chiruyeh to Tehran would take them through the cities of Shiraz, Isfahan and Qom. Soroushpur decided that they would break their trip in Shiraz because it was the approximate halfway mark. The added advantage was that it was a large city. It was far easier to remain hidden in crowds. 'Most people forget that Shiraz is the capital of Fars Province,' said Soroushpur as they drove along Route 65.

'Fars as in Pars?' asked Linda.

'Exactly,' said Soroushpur, impressed by her knowledge. 'We get the word Persia from Pars. It's also why Zoroastrians of India are called Parsis. The remains of the Achaemenid capitals Pasargadae and Persepolis are located in this province. The ruins of Persepolis are just an hour's drive away from Shiraz.'

At any other time, the mention of Persepolis would have sent Linda's heart racing and she would have instantly made a dash to visit the ruins. Persepolis had been the splendid ceremonial centre where people from all over the world came to pay tributes to their Achaemenid king. It was made up of several massive structures, some built by King Darius I and some by King Xerxes. It had been burned down in 330 BCE by Alexander. But today, the mention of Persepolis produced no excitement in Linda. *All I need is Jim,* she thought. *Nothing else matters.* 'Shiraz is also the city of the poet Hafez, if I recollect right,' said Linda absentmindedly.

'Absolutely,' said Soroushpur. 'Shiraz has been called the city of saints and poets. The traveller Ibn Battuta came to Shiraz in the fourteenth century. The two most famous poets of Iran, Hafez and Saadi, are from Shiraz. Their tombs are on the north side of the current city boundaries. Hafez, a Sufi, called himself a lover of the old Zoroastrian magi.' Linda nodded. She had read some of Hafez's translated writings: *In the monastery of the magi, why do they honour us? Maybe the fire that never dies, burns in our hearts.*

Iran's drivers followed no rules, it seemed. Pedestrians and vehicles jostled with one another on the streets, and it was believed that road accidents were the second-highest cause of mortality in the country. On several occasions Soroushpur shouted at other drivers who competed with each other like stampeding wild buffalo. Soroushpur laughed when Linda mentioned it. 'In the jungle, it is the survival of the fittest. On Iranian roads, it is the survival of the fastest!'

They themselves drove carefully through the city until they reached the famous Eram Garden along the northern shore of the River Khoshk. 'It is also the city of flowers,' said Soroushpur. 'Have you noticed the profusion of gardens and orchards? Oh, I forgot to say, before the advent of Islam, this was also the city of wine!'

They turned right from Eram Street to Jomhoori Eslami Boulevard until they pulled up in front of a small hotel called Fars House. 'It's a boutique hotel and the manager here is a Zoroastrian,' explained Soroushpur. 'He will not ask any unnecessary questions.'

They parked and got out of the car. The manager Keikhosrow, a rosy-faced and rotund gentleman, ushered them in hurriedly. He dispensed quickly with all the formalities at the reception and guided them to rooms on the second floor. To Linda it seemed like he was avoiding having them linger in the lobby for a moment longer than necessary.

The rooms were simple and clean. 'I will arrange for dinner to be sent up,' said the manager pre-emptively. 'Better that you do not wander about. There is substantial police presence on the streets owing to the funeral of a local politician.'

Soroushpur thanked him. Turning to Dan and Linda he said, 'Let's try to leave early in the morning. In the meantime, I have established contact with my liaison in Tehran. Within the GAF, we speak only in code on phone calls that are usually monitored. There has been talk that an important prisoner was brought into DC1A. But we're still trying to establish his identity.'

'Is he safe?' asked Linda, in a small voice.

'I really cannot give you more information at this stage,' replied Soroushpur, adding, more kindly, 'but I assure you that you and I are after the same thing.' His words sounded slightly ominous to Linda's ears; she brushed the feeling away.

'There is one thing, though,' warned Soroushpur.

'Yes?' asked Linda.

'There seem to be many more roadblocks,' he said. 'I can't say if it has anything to do with us. But getting out of Shiraz and then travelling a thousand kilometres into Tehran is going to be challenging.' He saw the worried expression on Linda's face and changed his tone quickly. 'Don't worry, we'll find a way to go through safely.'

Once they had retired to their respective rooms, Soroushpur dialled a number from his mobile phone. 'Do we know?' he asked in a language that was not Dari, nor Farsi nor Azeri. The words were unlike any other language anywhere in the world. They constituted the GAF code.

'Yes,' replied the voice. 'We now know that he was taken to DC1A. He was left in one of the coffin cells for some time. But he is likely to be shifted to a private safe house soon. Some directive from the big guns of the IRGC. It will probably be easier to get to him there. But the big question is, what do *you* want *us* to do? I'm not exactly clear what your motivations are.'

Outside Soroushpur's room, the manager Keikhosrow had his ear to the door. Clutching his mobile phone tightly, he was wondering if he needed to dial a particular number.

48

SOROUSHPUR SLUNK OUT of Fars House an hour later. He drove fifty kilometres in a north-eastern direction until he reached the plains of Marvdasht, encircled by the southern Zagros mountains. He parked his car and walked towards the western part of Persepolis.

The distinguishing feature of Persepolis was its massive terrace, supported by a gigantic retaining wall. He walked up the double flight of stairs briskly, without any of the theatrical awe of first-time visitors. His Yazidi friend Nasr Tamoyan from Gundeshapur was waiting at the top.

Soroushpur passed through the *Gate of All Nations*, past the two Lamassu, the mythical winged beings with human heads and bovine bodies, at the eastern doorway. Gift-bearing delegations from around the empire would have had to wait here, seated on black marble benches, before they could pay homage to the reigning Achaemenid king. Not that any of that struck Soroushpur now. He was being propelled by sheer zeal.

Soroushpur and Tamoyan made their way to Hadish Palace, what would have been the living quarters of King Xerxes. The symbol they sought was located there. And sure enough, there it was. The symbol of the faravahar—the winged male figure—holding a ring.

'Most people associate this symbol with Zoroastrianism,' said Tamoyan. 'The Parsis took this symbol with them when they fled from Iran and used it in their iconography. But here in Iran, the symbol was suppressed after the Muslim conquests. It was once again revived during the times of the Pahlavi dynasty as the national emblem of Iran, but the Islamic Revolution of 1979 ended that phase. Surprisingly it has survived in popular culture in Iran and is one of our country's best recognised symbols, although it is not officially sanctioned as one by the government.'

'Thank you for the history lesson,' said an irritated Soroushpur. He had not gone there to be told things he already knew. Nor did he want to hear about modern-day theological interpretations of the symbol: the idea that the three layers of the man's wings represented good thoughts, good words and good deeds, or the notion that the aged male figure represented wisdom, or the view that the ring in the figure's hand represented a covenant. All of these were mere interpretations of a symbol that had been adopted by the Achaemenid kings. 'Is there *anything* you have found that is of help to *me*?'

'I still believe that the answer shall emerge from Gundeshapur,' Tamoyan said, unbudged. 'But if you *do* see the image of a faravahar anywhere, it may not have a connection to the item you seek. None of my findings in Gundeshapur, so far, display this symbol.'

'Why do you think they won't?' asked Soroushpur, shining his flashlight on the faravahar in front.

'Because it was never a Zoroastrian symbol to start with,' explained Tamoyan. 'Earlier forms of the symbol appear in art, architecture, and seals from Egypt, Sumer, Babylonia, Judah and Assyria. By Assyrian times it had become very detailed and elaborate. It was used to represent the Assyrian deity Ashur. How it became a Zoroastrian symbol is a mystery to most.'

'Effectively, what you are telling me is this: I should look for what is *not* there, rather than what *is*!' said Soroushpur, feeling a little put off.

Tamoyan was amused by his annoyance. 'Exactly,' he said. 'Its presence should warn you that it may not be the object you seek.'

'How are your efforts in Gundeshapur proceeding?' asked Soroushpur.

'Very slowly,' replied Tamoyan. 'If your GAF could send me some more money, a few extra hands would really speed things up.'

'We want to do that, but we simply do not have the resources,' replied Soroushpur. 'Remember, Tamoyan, we are not doing this for any commercial gain. This is about preserving our heritage. As a Yazidi who has been hounded by so many communities, you should be able to appreciate what I'm saying.'

'I understand,' said Tamoyan, albeit a tad reluctantly.

'I want to ensure that the Athravan Star is retrieved and given the respect and space it deserves,' said Soroushpur. 'I have Parsi friends in India who think similarly. But please remember that the GAF can barely afford to pay your monthly retainer.'

'Did *you* find anything in Udvada, Diu or Navsari that may help in *my* work?' asked Tamoyan pointedly.

'I've already shared what I found with you,' replied Soroushpur. 'I didn't go to Diu or to Navsari, but my friend Pestonji Unwalla did go to Navsari. He showed me the photograph of what had been scribbled in Avestan in the book *Kalila wa Dimna* by Abdullah ibn al-Muqaffa. You need to find a way to prove its authenticity. For all we know it could just be ancient doodling.'

'I'll try my best,' replied Tamoyan. 'But it's a little like looking for a needle in a haystack.'

'Find me that needle,' said Soroushpur, and turned away.

49

THE MANUFACTURING PLANT of Shahid Daru Pharma was located just twenty-five kilometres west of Tehran in an area known as Vardavard. The company's main manufacturing and research unit sat on a massive plot that stretched along the length of Taleghani Street. While high walls on all four sides isolated the area, inside the perimeter were several industrial buildings in addition to a warehouse, an oxygen plant, two back-up generators, a utility block, a research laboratory, a water treatment plant, an incinerator, an office block, residential quarters, a canteen and a guesthouse. At the main gate was the security office. Neatly quartered by tree-lined internal avenues running north-south and east-west, each zone looked well maintained and was fronted by cypress and walnut trees.

Three vehicles drove through the main gate and stopped outside the guesthouse. Soldiers jumped out from the two Fath Safir utility vehicles that sandwiched a Samand car. They efficiently ensured that the blindfolded and cuffed Jim

Dastoor was transferred unseen to a guestroom on the third floor. Accompanying him was Javad Mosaffa. For the next few days, this would be Jim's prison, surrounded by soldiers, and guarded 24 x 7.

Once his cuffs and blindfold had been removed, Jim asked, 'Where are we?'

'In a guesthouse of Shahid Daru Pharma, Iran's largest pharmaceutical company,' Mosaffa informed him a little grandly.

'And why have we come here?' asked Jim, looking around. It was a medium-sized room with a queensize bed, attached toilet, and all the standard conveniences of a mid-range hotel. But after his stint in hell, this was a veritable paradise.

'I needed a way to get you out of that coffin cell,' replied Mosaffa. 'You are no murderer, political prisoner, spy or terrorist. You are a respected scientist and should be treated accordingly.' Mosaffa had even arranged for simple yet comfortable clothes for Jim. He couldn't be left in prison gear if they wanted his cooperation.

'Why does a private company allow prisoners to be accommodated in its guesthouse?' asked Jim, rubbing his wrists to get his blood circulation going.

'Ah,' said Mosaffa, as if he'd been waiting for a cue. 'Because it has the means. The IRGC is the third-wealthiest organisation in Iran. It receives two-thirds of Iran's annual defence budget of fifteen billion dollars. But more importantly, the IRGC-Quds Force, a division of the IRGC, controls a plethora of strategic industries and commercial operations.' He carefully avoided the term 'black market' which was another huge source of unofficial income for the IRGC.

'What sort of companies are those?' asked Jim.

'*I* am supposed to ask the questions,' Mosaffa smiled to take away the sting of the mild rebuke. 'But I'll indulge you for a moment. The IRGC has ties to over a hundred companies involved in everything from pharmaceuticals to telecommunications to oil and gas pipelines. These companies jointly account for around twenty per cent of Iran's GDP.' Jim, his head still buzzing, took his time to digest the information.

Back at DC1A, Jim had been allowed to exit the coffin cell upon Mosaffa's arrival. He had been allowed to shave, bathe and change into a set of clean clothes provided by Mosaffa. He had then eaten a simple meal of Iranian noodle soup before getting into the car with Mosaffa. Now, at greater ease inside the guesthouse of the Shahid Daru Pharma premises, Mosaffa handed him a cup of coffee. Jim accepted it gratefully. His companion watched him as he silently drank the hot, black liquid. 'You will need to give me something, Jim,' he said. 'I won't be able to protect you from these guys if you do not open a channel of communication with me.'

'So, they're the bad cops and you're the good one,' said Jim. 'The old routine.'

'Take it whichever way you want,' replied Mosaffa, 'but remember you are in Iran. You could get lost in the prison system here if they want. You have to start talking to me if you want to stay out.'

Jim took another gulp of the coffee. It wasn't great but it was hot. And he hadn't had any for the longest time ever. Momentarily, his thoughts went back to Linda and the Hawaiian Kona that they enjoyed every morning together. He had to force himself back to the present. 'What would you like to know?' he asked Mosaffa.

'What exactly is the Hamzaa Dura, for starters,' said Mosaffa. 'What are you hoping to achieve with it? How is it derived or made? What is the source? How is it linked to another object called the Athravan Star?'

'You have the earthen box and my research data?' asked Jim.

'Yes,' said Mosaffa, pointing to the satchel on the coffee table. 'But I am no scientist, so I can make nothing of the contents. If you are willing to give an explanatory overview to a team of scientists from the company, that would be a great start. It would also give the IRGC-Quds Force enough incentive to keep you here.'

'Will they ever release me?' asked Jim as if he was simply curious to know a small detail of his life to come.

'There have been several cases where foreigners were eventually released,' said Mosaffa. 'You are not here as a bargaining chip. You are here because the authorities think that you stole from Iran.'

'That's ridiculous!' exploded Jim, recovering some of his spirit. 'Just because my ancestors went to India from Iran centuries ago, does not mean *I* have any abiding connection to it!'

'Do you deny that your family was a key guardian of the Iranshah flame?' asked Mosaffa.

'No,' replied Jim without hesitation. 'But there were *nine* families that filled that role. In 1858 CE, my great-great-grandfather, Shapoor Dastoor, moved to Mumbai from Udvada. His descendants have had no religious duties since.'

'Even if I take that at face value,' said Mosaffa, 'how do I convince Khademhosseini that you are cooperating with us fully?'

'Because I have nothing to gain by keeping any secrets from you,' reasoned Jim. 'I never planned to derive profits from the Hamzaa Dura. I simply want to complete my research and, yes, *then* make my findings available to everyone. *Free of cost.* There will be no licences or patents. I have no problem in openly sharing my research with the Iranian scientists here. But of what value will it be if I cannot synthesise more Hamzaa Dura for the entire world? The stock is minuscule, and the globe's requirement is huge.'

'Let's start at the beginning, Jim,' said Mosaffa. He turned to the soldier posted at the door. 'Have the video camera set up. Mr Dastoor has decided to cooperate with us.'

50

IT TOOK A while before Linda fell asleep and found herself in the throes of a troubled dream. In it, Jim was inside a tiny room which could be accessed via only a single narrow door which was shut tight against her. She stood outside the door, knocking and pleading for Jim to open it. From underneath the door, there was a flow of blood, much like water seeping from a flooded bathroom. 'Open the door, Jim!' she pleaded, shrieking and banging on the door with her open palm. In a nightmare, to her very real, she could even taste the tears running down her face.

The knocking on the door was loud and persistent. Shaken out of sleep, she looked at her watch. Past 3 am. She staggered out of bed, nauseous with terror, every instinct screaming to her that something was wrong. 'Open door,' a man's voice commanded her from the other side of it. 'If you do not, it will be broken!' Linda unlatched the security chain and undid the double lock with trembling fingers, dreading what she would doubtless confront.

She wasn't wrong. As she opened the door, she saw that the corridor outside contained several soldiers, each one standing at a different door. Other guests who had emerged due to the ruckus, had been rudely told to get back inside and lock themselves in. She quickly realised that this was a late-night raid on four specific rooms—those of Linda, Dan, Soroushpur and Jamshidi. *So this is the end of the long, hopeless road,* she thought in numb despair.

The green uniforms and berets indicated that these were soldiers of the IRGC. The one outside Linda's door was a barrel-chested man with the physique of a boxer. 'Your passport,' he rapped out, like an order issued mid-battle. Linda went back into the room to retrieve it and he followed her. She quickly located it in her handbag and gave it to him. He opened it and checked the first page, comparing Linda to the photograph on the passport. 'You have visa?' he asked, as he flipped through the pages. The travel permit for Kish Island slipped out and fell on the floor. 'What this?' he growled as he picked it up. 'Travel permit for Kish? Then what you doing on mainland?'

A similar routine was happening in the other rooms too. They were all given five minutes to pack up their things and assemble outside in the corridor. Linda could see that the rosy-faced manager, Keikhosrow, was also there. He seemed to be discussing something with one of the soldiers. *Traitor!*

Four travellers, four soldiers and the rotund manager made their way downstairs. Just outside the hotel's entrance stood a grey Neynava military truck with a canvas stretched across the rear cabin. 'Get inside,' said one of the soldiers, his hand on his holster. Linda's group got inside and sat on the bench seats that ran the length of the rear cabin. Two of the soldiers got in with them at the back while the other two occupied the driver's cabin. The truck roared to life and made its way out of the hotel premises and into the streets of Shiraz, the city of saints and poets. *Or the city of hunters and the hunted?*

Linda looked at Soroushpur across from her. She knew he had discerned the panic in her eyes. Next to him was Jamshidi. While Jamshidi seemed nervous, Soroushpur was relatively calm. He seemed to be mumbling a prayer under his breath. Linda turned her head to look at Dan next to her. He looked like a frightened animal in a slaughterhouse. The four exchanged no words.

At that time of night, the roads were deserted. The truck picked up speed as it crossed Jomhoori Eslami Boulevard and then took a sharp left to race along Eram Street and proceed to the Ayatollah Rabbani Boulevard. Passengers and soldiers in the rear were jostled around as the truck sped through the empty potholed streets.

Around thirty minutes later, the truck stopped at a checkpost. The passengers could not see what was going on outside, but they could hear voices. They seemed to be exchanging pleasantries and, possibly, swapping jokes. Their conversation was accompanied by laughter. Five minutes later, they were on their way again.

In the distance, they could hear the muezzin's call to the morning Fajr prayer. Sunrise was still some time away. The soldier at the wheel ignored the call to Fajr and drove on. An hour later they stopped again. The second soldier from the driver's cabin brought bread and tea for them. Linda was in no mood to eat but Soroushpur's eyes urged her to. *Was Soroushpur on their side, too?*

Linda was lost in thought when the barrel-chested driver of the truck, the one who had interrogated her previously, stepped into the rear cabin and asked the other soldiers to leave. He walked up to Soroushpur, causing Linda to wonder what was going on. Then the driver and Soroushpur shook hands with extra vigour, Soroushpur going as far as to stand up and embrace him warmly.

Linda was now certain that they had been betrayed.

51

FBI SPECIAL AGENT Fred Smith went through security check at the high-rise off the Patuxent Freeway. It was one of a drab and boring office block of two buildings skirting Fort Meade, twenty-four kilometres southwest of Baltimore. The buildings are the headquarters of America's chief eavesdropper, the National Security Agency, or NSA. Fred had never been to the NSA before, but the Jim Dastoor case had brought him knocking at the agency's door.

When Jim was kidnapped, Smith had sought the help of the HRFC—the Hostage Recovery Fusion Cell—located at the FBI headquarters in Washington, D.C. The HRFC was comprised of specialists from the FBI, the Department of State, the Department of Defense, and other American agencies that had strong overseas relationships. The HRFC specialised in handling international kidnappings. Ninety million Americans travelled internationally each year, and it was not unreasonable to expect that a few of them would be abducted by the likes of the Islamic State, Al Qaeda or Boko Haram. Then there were the purely ransom-related kidnappings conducted by local criminal groups or drug cartels. The key factor in solving such situations was cooperation with other US agencies that had a global footprint.

In most other cases of kidnapping, the HRFC could rely on the FBI's in-country liaisons and legal attachés. They could also work with the concerned ambassadors and US Embassy teams. Often, they would even request assistance from the country's local law enforcement. The FBI had more than sixty attaché offices around the world that provided coverage for over 180 countries. But they had absolutely nothing in Iran. *Nothing.* Their best hope was the NSA. The HRFC had obtained clearance to seek the help of the NSA in locating Jim. Aware that Linda and Dan had entered Kish Island, they knew that tracing them would be a step closer to finding Jim.

Fred would have found it impossible to navigate the vast ten acres of underground workspace had it not been for a cute redhead who had been deputed to bring him to the meeting room.

Within the labyrinth of the NSA was located one of the world's most powerful supercomputers. The NSA snooped on every piece of communication around the world—regardless of its immediate importance. All that data was eventually funnelled through this supercomputer which daily collected and stored a billion cellphone calls, emails, videos, photos, text files, voice chats, voice-over-IP calls, file transfers and social media messages.

Fred was guided into one of the conference rooms within the Operations Directorate, a division responsible for signals intelligence. He was joined by someone identified only as S31172. Unlike other intelligence agencies, the NSA was famous for never disclosing its internal organisational structure. Only alphanumeric designations were ever shared. In this particular instance, S31172 was the division responsible for crypto-analytic exploitation and discovery within Iran, the Hamas of Palestine, Iraq and Saudi Arabia.

'We have actioned your request twenty-two hours ago,' said S31172. 'We are also liaising with the Special Collection Service that operates listening posts outside of the US.'

'Any luck?' asked Fred.

'Linda's and Dan's own cells are switched off. Iran has two primary mobile phone networks,' said S31172, 'Hamrah-e-Aval and Irancell. Both companies offer SIM card services to foreign visitors and have an extended network coverage in Iran. So, we are working on the assumption that either Linda or Dan could be using one of these.'

'How quickly do you think you could tell me more?' asked Fred.

'You will appreciate that there are 118 million mobile users in Iran,' expanded S31172. 'We have effected a backdoor entry into the networks, but that is only part of what we need to do. After gaining access, we need to eavesdrop for words or names that sound familiar.' *How does one do that on 118 million phone lines?* wondered Fred.

'We will need to feed various terms into PRISM—a complex algorithm created specifically for this task,' said S31172, picking up on Fred's thought. 'And that's why we requested you to drop in today.'

'What can I do?' asked Fred.

'Help us populate the terms that we need to look out for,' replied S31172. 'For example, is Jim a nickname? If so, what is his formal name? We will together have to dredge up all names, surnames, activities, relationships, associates, companies, firms and places that are associated with these individuals. We will then use PRISM to help us identify conversations and messages that may be relevant.'

'What if they are not using mobile phones at all?' asked Fred.

'Then none of us at the NSA can help you,' replied S31172 categorically. 'We snoop on anyone and everyone, but only if there is an electronic footprint. However …

'Yes?' Fred asked quickly.

'Even if someone other than they themselves refers to any of the relevant terms, we may have something to go on.'

52

'I WANT YOU to meet my friend Tariq Heydari from Tehran,' said Soroushpur to Linda. Linda looked fearfully at the muscle-bound Heydari, barely mumbling a half-hearted greeting.

'Don't worry,' said Soroushpur, picking up on her fears. 'Tariq is a secret member of the *Mojahedin-e Khalq*—a group that opposes the existing regime in Iran. He is here to help us. His connections at MMTM may also help.'

Linda saw now that Heydari was a fairly good-looking man except for the bushy moustache. On second thought, though, it balanced the large nose. 'Was what happened in the hotel just a bit of drama?' asked Linda.

'Exactly,' said Heydari, genially, appearing to have perfected his English in a matter of hours on the road. 'Sorry about that, but we had to find a way of getting you out of Shiraz without arousing suspicion. A fake night raid by the IRGC seemed the perfect way.'

Linda exhaled with relief. 'Why do you oppose the government?' she asked.

Heydari laughed. 'Oppose?' he asked sarcastically. 'What opposition? Iran has a democratically elected President and Parliament, but all candidates must first be vetted by the so-called Guardian Council. The Supreme Leader of Iran controls the armed forces, the judicial system, state television, and many other key governmental organisations. The President is a mere secretary to the Ayatollah. Electoral opposition in Iran means nothing—just a secretarial berth.'

'What will be your solution?' asked Linda.

'Forcing open the chokehold that the clergy has on Iran's power,' said Heydari. 'The problem is that anyone who expresses such a view rots in prison.'

Throughout the terrifying journey, Linda had been preparing herself to be thrown in prison. 'These other soldiers with you, the uniforms, weapons, this military truck ... how did you rig this all up?' she asked. She was plain curious by now.

'It was easy enough,' said Heydari. 'There is a military base on the Shiraz-Kazeroun Road. It is presently being relocated to the outskirts under an overall government plan to shift twenty-five such Iranian bases to areas where land prices are lower. No one has a very clear idea of what is lying where. Picking up a truck and uniforms from the new location was a breeze. The security is pathetically inadequate. The best part is that no one will even realise that anything has been stolen.'

'And these men who accompanied you?'

'Part of my political group,' replied Heydari. 'We are alternately outlawed and dismantled by the Supreme Leader. Then we go into hibernation and re-emerge under a new name.'

'And the hotel manager?' asked Linda. 'Keikhosrow?'

'Foolish man,' scoffed Soroushpur. 'He was listening at my door last night. I knew that he had tipped off the authorities of our presence. That's why I needed Tariq to preempt the real soldiers.'

'Thank you,' said Linda to both Heydari and Soroushpur. 'We're truly grateful for your help.' Turning to Jamshidi, she said, 'Thanks, Firooz. Without you we would not have been able to leave Kish. Nor would we have met Behrad. But I think you should consider going back to Kish now. We seem to be in good hands.'

'No,' said Jamshidi, mulishly. 'I told with my own mouth that I go with you. So I go with you.'

'Listen to the lady,' said Heydari to Jamshidi. 'You are of much more value to us in Kish than here,' he added persuasively. 'If this group needs to exit through Kish, you will be there to help them. I can handle it from here. I am also letting go two of our soldiers in disguise.'

Jamshidi looked from face to face, unsure. 'Okay, I go,' he said finally. 'Only, send me message of good health. Also, to get out. Quickly, quickly.'

'Neither Dan nor I know how to thank you,' Linda said warmly.

'Simple to thank,' replied Jamshidi. 'Tell all foreign peoples how good is the peoples of ancient faith in this land.' His large expressive eyes grew wet. 'And how bad we are being.'

Linda smiled. 'You have my promise,' she said as Jamshidi got up and left. Two of Heydari's accomplices also took their leave.

'Now what?' asked Dan. 'We're out of Shiraz. What's the next step?'

'Jim has been shifted out of DC1A,' Soroushpur informed them. 'My agent tells me that he is being held at the plant of Shahid Daru Pharma in Vardavard, near Tehran. We need to figure out how to get him out of there.'

'Why is he being held?' asked Heydari. Linda looked at Soroushpur, then Heydari. *How much information should I share?* she wondered. Then she realised that these were the only people who could help her get Jim out. If she couldn't trust them, why would they trust her? Why would they stick their necks out for her?

'My husband is involved in a breakthrough in medical research,' said Linda. 'He was initially kidnapped by a pharmaceutical competitor in America. But that turned out to be a transit stop. He is now in the hands of the IRGC-Quds.'

Heydari whistled. 'Khademhosseini's goons,' he muttered. 'Very few get out of his clutches alive.' He bit his tongue. Linda did not need to be further agitated.

'What sort of medical breakthrough was this?' asked Soroushpur.

'I'll tell you briefly from the very beginning,' said Linda patiently. 'I must tell you first that Jim's people—Zoroastrians like you—were originally from this country. Centuries ago, they resettled in India, and centuries later, Jim went to America for further studies. Jim and I met in Stanford University where I also studied, and we got married. He went on to create his own research company known as the Gemini Cellular Research Center. Jim believes that he has a formulation that could replace virtually every other medicine on the planet.'

'But the Iranians are rarely after such stuff,' said Soroushpur doubtfully. 'The Chinese would love to get their hands on it; not the Iranians who would rather focus on missiles and nuclear bombs. I wonder why they have gone after your husband.'

'Possibly because they believe that they are the rightful owners of his technology?' said Linda tentatively. 'Frankly, there are too many matters that I am unaware of. But my gut tells me that there are some unresolved issues relating to Jim's Zoroastrian roots.'

'Interesting,' murmured Soroushpur. 'Is his research based on an entirely new formula or is it based on an existing compound?'

Soroushpur knew that he was on the right scent.

53

THE CITY OF Isfahan lies around 400 kilometres south of Tehran and is the third-largest city of Iran. Once upon a time, it was one of the largest and most fabulous cities of the world. Located at the intersection of two cardinal routes, Isfahan is famous for its grand boulevards, exquisitely mosaiced mosques, magnificent palaces and covered bridges. An old Persian says, '*Esfahan nesf-e-jahan ast.*' Isfahan constitutes half the world.

They had made rapid progress from Shiraz to Isfahan, covering the journey of 480 kilometres in around six hours. They were not stopped even once, thanks to the grey Neynava military truck they travelled in. Heydari had been right. No one had reported the stolen vehicle.

Linda sensed that they were skirting the town centre instead of heading there. 'Where are we going?' she asked.

'The *Atashgah-e Esfahan*,' replied Soroushpur.

'Atashgah?' said Linda. 'You mean a Zoroastrian fire temple?'

'Yes,' replied Soroushpur. 'It's almost ten kilometres from the town centre and remains quite deserted. It will probably be the safest place to halt for the night.'

'Is it on a hill?' asked Dan, seeing that the truck was on a sloping road.

'Correct,' said Soroushpur. 'The actual fire temple is around a hundred metres above the surrounding land. But what remains are only ruins, symbolic of the pathetic state that we have been reduced to. I still find it difficult to imagine that Zoroastrianism was the flourishing state religion in Sassanian times.'

They halted the truck some distance away from the hill. Heydari quickly changed into civvies and then took backpacks out of the truck, one for each of them. Soroushpur, Linda and Dan, followed by Heydari, walked up the hill, each with a backpack that marked them as tourists. They left behind Heydari's sole remaining accomplice to guard the truck. It would be needed the next day to reach Tehran.

'Can you see that?' asked Soroushpur, pointing to the circular structure at the top of the hill. 'That was built to protect the eternal fire of the Zoroastrians.'

'An Atash Behram?' asked Linda. Soroushpur was impressed. Then he remembered that Linda was a PhD in history. And being married to Jim had fuelled her interest in the ancient faith of Zoroastrianism. Over time, she knew more about all things Zoroastrian.

'It must have been one,' he replied. 'Only around seven ancient fire temples are left in Iran. Most of them were destroyed or converted into mosques from the seventh century onwards. But fire temples usually had four axial arch openings. Here we see eight, which means that by Islamic times they were using this structure as a lookout tower or citadel. The ones that were not used for military purposes were quite easily turned into mosques.'

'How?' asked Linda.

'By simply adding a prayer niche—known as a *mihrab*—in the arch pointing nearest to Mecca.'

The gentle slope they'd been ascending suddenly became a sheer rockface that had been worn smooth by millions of feet. To make matters worse, crumbled stone lay on the surface, so every step was treacherous. 'This is the reason I chose this place,' explained Soroushpur. 'Very few will have the desire to walk in our footsteps!'

Eventually they reached the top, out of breath. The circular structure was just about five metres in diameter, and built with unbaked bricks, clay and lime. Skirting the primary structure, they made their way to one of the surrounding rooms. Linda figured that it would originally have been a room used by priests or wealthy pilgrims. They sat down on the muddy floor and opened their backpacks. Inside each was a thin roll of mattress, bottled water and packaged snacks.

'We shall spend the night here and get on with the remainder of the journey tomorrow,' announced Soroushpur.

'Any snakes around?' asked Linda. In her experience, ruins were the preferred habitat of reptiles. 'And what does one do for a toilet?'

'The area outside is entirely yours to use—just don't step on the snakes,' joked Heydari. Seeing Linda didn't exactly join in his laughter, he quickly added, 'We'll be digging a fire pit. Once it starts smoking, chances are that snakes will avoid us. We also have this.' He was holding up a canister of liquid.

'What's that?' asked Dan.

'A mixture of sulphur, rock salt, vinegar and lime,' he replied. 'Things that snakes hate. The ideal stuff is ammonia, but that harms humans too. I assume that we are all willing to tolerate the terrible smell?' Linda nodded her head vigorously. Fumes and smells were acceptable; snakes were not.

Just outside their room, a twig snapped. Heydari quickly brought a finger to his lips and trod out softly to investigate, one hand on the pistol inside his jacket pocket. Inside, Soroushpur, Linda and Dan waited with bated breath. He popped back quickly. 'Just a stray dog,' he said.

He went out once again and spoke to someone on his mobile phone, lowering his voice from time to time. Linda tried to listen in but caught only snatches. 'Tomorrow … Shahid Daru … Jim Dastoor … Linda …'

He finished his conversation and came back inside. 'Let's eat something and then turn in for the night,' he said, offering no explanation regarding his call.

'Once we reach Tehran, how do we free Jim?' asked Linda anxiously. 'I mean, even if we are right next to him, won't they be guarding him?'

'You are thinking too far ahead,' said Heydari. 'My contacts in Tehran have already started surveying the factory premises of Shahid Daru Pharma. Hopefully, by the time we get there, we will know where he is being held and how tight the security is.'

Later that night, Linda fell into a deep slumber in spite of her fears—sheer fatigue being the probable cause. Heydari too slept soundly. But Dan did not; pondering Luke Miller's plan kept sleep away.

In that room there was yet another person who was not sleeping: Behrad Soroushpur. He was staring at Linda's sleeping figure and contemplating his next step.

54

CAMP MOSHE DAYAN—ALSO known as Glilot Junction— near Tel Aviv, houses the IDF National Defense College. One of its primary occupants is Unit 8200.

Unit 8200, also known as ISNU—the Israeli SIGINT National Unit—is considered by many to be the premier technical intelligence agency in the world, standing on par with the NSA in all aspects except scale. Most of the staff are coders and hackers in their twenties. Several former ISNU agents go on to found and occupy top positions in IT companies.

The young ISNU agent spoke over an encrypted line to his counterpart designated as S31172 at the NSA. The ISNU maintained a wide-reaching technical and analytic symbiotic relationship with the NSA, often sharing information on access, intercept, targeting, language, analysis and reporting. In fact, the relationship between the NSA and ISNU had played a vital role in expanding the cooperation between the US and Israel. That relationship now encompassed other agencies such as the CIA and Mossad. The most important exchanges between the NSA and ISNU pertained to targets in the Middle East, those that constituted a common strategic threat to the US and Israel. The two agencies often jointly investigated and implemented specific opportunities. Their agreement covered internal governmental, military, civil and diplomatic communications in North Africa, the Middle East, the Persian Gulf, as well as in the Islamic republics of the former Soviet Union.

Both the NSA and the ISNU maintained liaison officers stationed at their respective embassies, but neither the US nor Israel had embassies in Iran, hence the need for S31172 to involve himself directly with an agent at ISNU. 'Any luck?' asked S31172. 'As you know, their lives could be in danger. And in most hostage situations, time is of the essence.'

'There was a conversation yesterday,' replied the ISNU man blandly. 'The name of Jim Dastoor was specifically mentioned. The call was logged from a cellphone in Isfahan. Have sent the coordinates to you already.' S31172 heaved a sigh of relief. It was a pleasure to work with the Israelis. They were professional, efficient—and clinically ruthless.

'Another thing,' said the ISNU man. 'There was repeated reference to Shahid Daru. We've checked. It's a pharmaceutical company located near Tehran.'

'Do you have any resources we could use?' asked S31172.

'Depends on what you want done,' replied the ISNU man strategically. 'My bosses will want something in return.' S31172 knew what he was alluding to. The Israel–USA partnership was not without challenges. The NSA was often reluctant to share information that was not directly related to a specific target. Right now, ISNU needed as many inputs as possible on Iran's nuclear programme. The NSA bosses would have to find a way to sweeten the deal for their Israeli friends.

'Let me see what I can do,' said S31172. 'Meantime, help me get these three Americans, *chaver*.' He consciously used the Hebrew term for 'buddy'. He knew that his only hope for retrieving Jim Dastoor, Linda Dastoor and Dan Cohen was Unit 8200.

'The last location was 32°38'53.7'N 51°34'15.4'E,' said the ISNU man. 'Our Mossad cousins have someone based out of the Elahieh district in Tehran. He is on a cover run in the area that your phone call emerged from. Should we intervene?'

'Thank you,' said S31172. 'That would be great.' He did not bother to ask for details on the agent—only the very best Israeli agents were assigned to operate within Iran. Anyone even slightly off their game would be instantly picked up by the IRGC or 'terminated', to use an Arnold Schwarzeneggerism.

'Do we have no way of establishing contact to tip them off about your resource?' asked S31172.

'No,' replied the ISNU agent. 'That would be risky. Every mobile line in Iran should be considered as an open one. Leave it to our man to establish contact.'

'Fair enough,' said S31172. 'Do you have any surveillance drones in the area that could give us an idea of where they are at?'

'Will do,' said the ISNU man. 'But more importantly, we are already in the process of mapping Shahid Daru. It is very possible that some action may be required there.'

'We have some Kurdish allies in Mahabad,' said S31172. 'If your man needs backup, we could activate them.'

'Not worth the effort,' said the ISNU man. 'Mahabad is almost 900 kilometres away from where they're at. Better that we handle it. We will let you know if any assistance is required in Tehran.'

'Thank you,' said S31172. 'You would have read the file on Jim Dastoor. There seems to be a deeper reason for the involvement of the IRGC. Your man should prepare for the worst.'

'Don't worry,' said the ISNU agent. 'We have our best people working on it. *Be-eyn tachbulot yippol am, u-teshuah be-rov yo'ets.*' S31172 laughed. The ISNU man was reciting the motto of Mossad.

Where there is no guidance, a nation falls, but in an abundance of counsellors there is safety.

55

LINDA, DAN, SOROUSHPUR and Heydari made their way down the hill to the spot where they had left the truck the previous evening. They walked up and down the stretch of road without finding it. Nor did they find Heydari's assistant who had been left in charge of it. Heydari tried calling his man's mobile, but the number was switched off, the phone battery probably drained.

Heydari looked worried. 'It is unlike him,' he said. 'Something's up.'

'What do we do now?' asked Soroushpur.

'See that *chai khaneh*?' asked Heydari, pointing to the teashop that was some distance away. 'It is just opposite the place we'd parked the truck. The shopkeeper may have seen

something. The three of you stay here—I'll go find out what.'
Linda, Dan and Soroushpur waited under a tree, leaning on
their backpacks.

Heydari walked over to the shop and asked for a cup of tea.
Striking up a conversation with the owner of the chai khaneh
in Farsi, Heydari observed, 'I thought that this was a military
depot. The last few times I was here I saw many trucks.'

'No, no depot,' replied the owner. 'Yesterday there *was* a
lone truck, but a bunch of policemen came and took it away.'

'Why did they? Didn't the truck belong to someone?'
asked Heydari, after taking a casual sip of his tea.

'There was *some* sort of a ruckus,' said the old man. 'Later
on, some onlookers said that the vehicle had been stolen, and
that the police had arrested the young man in the driving seat
and impounded the truck. Kids these days! So brazen about
stealing—that, too, from the military!'

Heydari shook his head in mock disbelief. But his mind
was elsewhere. He was not worried about the truck. They
could always find another way to get to Tehran. Instead, he
was anxious about the colleague who had been arrested.
Should he break down under interrogation—as was likely—it
would be just a matter of time before the authorities swooped
down on the rest of them.

He finished his tea, thanked the old man, paid him and
returned to the tree where Linda, Dan and Soroushpur sat.
'We have a problem,' he said to them. 'The truck has been
picked up by the cops. So has my man.'

'Which means that all of us could now be in danger,' said
Soroushpur, echoing his thoughts.

'Pity,' said Heydari. 'The truck would have made it easier to cross this final leg of the journey. But we can always find an alternative.'

'What about your man?' asked Linda sympathetically.

'Can't do much for him,' shrugged Heydari. 'If I spend time on working out his release, chances are that the delay will give the authorities a chance to grab us. No, we must leave this place as quickly as possible. I will try to get him out once we've got Jim out of Shahid Daru.'

As they were confabulating, a white minivan pulled up near them. It was a beat-up Jinbei Haise—a Toyota HiAce produced under licence from Chinese automaker Jinbei. The driver pulled down the front window and asked, 'You need a taxi?' Both Soroushpur and Heydari found it odd that the minivan had pulled up just at that particular moment. Furthermore, it was still early morning. The flow of tourists had not even begun. It just felt a little too much of a coincidence. But they also knew that the minivan was their only bet at the moment.

They got inside, Heydari occupying the seat closest to the driver's cabin. 'Where do you plan on going?' asked the driver. 'I can show you around Isfahan. The Shah Mosque, Khaju Bridge, Ali Qapu Palace or Chehel Sotoun Gardens?'

'How much do you charge for a one-way road trip to Tehran?' asked Heydari.

The driver looked at them quizzically. 'There are regular flights,' he said. 'Only ninety minutes. There are daily buses and trains too. Why do you need a taxi?'

Heydari pointed at Linda. 'She injured her ankle when we were climbing up to the Atashgah,' he lied. 'We're trying to keep her off her feet.'

'It will cost you two hundred dollars,' said the driver. 'Comes to around eight million rials. The journey is four to five hours long, depending on the traffic.'

'That's too much you're asking for,' said Heydari. He knew that *not* negotiating would be considered suspicious. But he also knew that the actual fare should be around half of that. 'I'll give you a hundred dollars,' he said. The driver agreed without protest, or further haggling. *That's strange*, thought Heydari. *A cabbie who is willing to accept half the quoted price without any negotiation?*

He thanked the driver and asked him to proceed, all the while observing the driver closely. He was dressed in an ordinary white bush shirt hanging over beige cotton trousers and a blue blazer outside it. He had salt-and-pepper hair and a trimmed moustache. Then Heydari realised something. The sunglasses he wore were not of the cheap Chinese variety so commonly seen, but swanky Ray-Bans. And his soot-black moustache didn't match his hair. Something was not quite right about this man. Heydari went on full alert.

He peered from his seat into the driver's cabin in front. The glovebox slightly ajar. Inside it, there was a gun—Heydari identified it as a Sig Sauer P228.

56

MRS BATLIWALA, OUR *English teacher in school, had taught us about what happened in Persia after Zarathustra died. I took a chance and looked her up. She lived by herself in a small flat* in Mumbai's Cusrow Baug, a name linked to one of the greatest Sassanian kings ever.

She was delighted to see me and enquired about my admission to Stanford. She quickly pulled out a bottle of Duke's raspberry soda from her refrigerator and placed it before me. I loved the stuff. It was the usual sugary lubricant for easing down mouthfuls of patra ni macchi and lagan nu custard at navjotes.

'So, what brings you here, dikra?' asked Mrs Batliwala. I explained that I wanted to discuss some aspects of our common heritage with her. She was delighted. She quickly pulled out a couple of books from her bookshelves and sat down opposite me, a faravahar pendant dangling from her neck. 'What would you like to discuss?' she asked.

'Well,' I began, 'I'm told that a new class of priests had emerged under Zarathustra, who came to be called the magi. They were said to have enormous powers, particularly in the fields of astrology, alchemy and medicine. In fact, when I did a little digging, I found that the English word "magic" is derived from the word "magi". I was wondering if you could tell me more about them.'

The dear lonely old woman was only too happy to oblige, and launched immediately into her narrative. 'There was a special order of the magi that was also born,' she said. 'The order guarded many secrets passed down from Zarathustra to the generations of kings such as Cyrus, Darius and Xerxes. Some of those secrets were preserved in great scrolls at the library in Persepolis. Some were preserved in potions, chants, implements and mixtures.'

She showed me some pages from one of her books. It had several images of such items. What the book did not seem to reference was a small earthen box that had been passed down from Zarathustra himself. And a few lines that were only recited orally.

'The magi soon became a hereditary priesthood whose members were credited with deep religious knowledge,' continued Mrs Batliwala. 'Particularly during the reign of Darius I, the magi acquired a dual role, both civil and religious. They became the supreme priestly caste, and their power would remain uncontested during the subsequent Seleucid, Parthian and Sassanian times.'

'What did they actually do for a living?' I asked. 'Besides conducting religious ceremonies, that is.'

'The magi occupied powerful positions in the courts of kings,' replied Mrs Batliwala. 'Monarchs would often avoid taking key decisions without the advice of their magi. The magi accompanied soldiers into battle, carrying with them the sacred fire for divine blessings. They were teachers, sages and scholars, preserving and disseminating knowledge from one generation to the next.'

'They had medical knowledge too?' I asked, draining the last few drops of the raspberry soda.

'Sure,' replied my teacher. 'They were also doctors and healers, carrying a "baresman" bundle of chini twigs with them wherever they went. This bundle of twigs could be pulped and combined in various ways into healing potions. In fact, the magi followed a code that required them to put aside their own needs in order to first tend to anyone needing medical attention.'

'What about the magic bit?' I asked, as inquisitive as a child.

'The magi were said to possess immeasurable spiritual powers,' said Mrs Batliwala. 'It was said that they could read thoughts, walk on water and through fire, transform ordinary metals to gold and appear or disappear at will. Then, a time came when three such powerful magi witnessed an astronomical event that heralded the arrival of a saviour on earth. The celestial event was similar to the one that had been observed at the birth of Zarathustra: the appearance of a golden double-star. Knowing this, the three set forth in the direction of Jerusalem, to where the star guided them, to witness the birth of a new messiah. The Bible refers to the three magi as the "Three Wise Men" and Christmas carols call them the "Three Kings of the Orient". They were magi! And the divine infant they travelled miles to see was Jesus!'

I lost myself in Mrs Batliwala's story. In Jerusalem, King Herod, the ruler of Judea, was alarmed by the unusual arrival of the three magi. They radiated power, travelling with oriental pomp and an oversize retinue of cavalry. And Herod loved pomp. The vain Herod was immediately attracted by the grandeur of the magi and invited them into his court.

'Herod's palace in Jerusalem was grand,' she said as she went on to describe it in vivid detail, as though she had been there herself. 'The palace had been built on a massive, elevated platform of around 16,000 square metres and rested on a succession of retaining walls that rose an imposing five metres above ground level. Two grand buildings—each with banquet halls, baths and accommodation chambers—were built around gardens, canals, porticos, groves and bronze fountains. Each massive stone used in the construction was white marble and *the joints between the blocks were so fine that the structure looked like an unbroken monolith.'*

According to Mrs Batliwala, the magi asked Herod, 'Where is the child who has been born as the king of the Jews? For we observed his star at its rising and have come to pay him homage.' Apparently, the request was a calculated insult to Herod. The magi knew that Herod was an insecure man whose powerful position as the 'King of the Jews' had largely been due to his father's excellent standing with Julius Caesar.

Herod's father, Antipater, had become a man of great influence after marrying a princess from Nabataea. When Pompey invaded Palestine in 63 BCE, Antipater threw his weight behind Pompey. Some years later, Herod also became friends with Mark Antony. This particular friendship would remain a lifelong one. Julius Caesar viewed Antipater as a strong ally and appointed him the procurator of Judaea. In parallel, his son Herod was appointed the governor of Galilee. Some years later, the Roman senate finally gave Herod the title of King of Judaea. 'Unlike most monarchs, this one was appointed, not anointed,' Mrs Batliwala reminded me.

'Then Herod consulted his scribes and found that the prophecies of the Tanach—Hebrew scriptures—predicted that the messiah would be born in Bethlehem,' she continued. 'The Gospel of Matthew relates how Herod pried from the magi the exact date on which the star heralding the birth had been observed by them.'

To Herod, this particular date was confirmation of the prophecy. He permitted the magi to proceed to visit the infant Jesus but extracted a commitment that they would return and tell him the exact location of the newborn.

57

'THE MAGI PROCEEDED to Bethlehem,' continued Mrs Batliwala. 'They carried gifts of gold, frankincense and myrrh for the baby Jesus. They were the same gifts that earlier magi had advised King Seleucus II to offer to Apollo at the temple in Miletus two centuries earlier.'

My grandmother, Cecile, had explained the significance of the gifts to me some years ago. Frankincense symbolised divinity. Gold signified kingship. And myrrh—used in funerary rites—symbolised death. But according to Cecile, the magi had not advised Seleucus to offer a fourth gift—one that signified rebirth—to Apollo. In her opinion, it had been a deliberate omission. So, besides gold, frankincense and myrrh, the three magi also secretly carried a small portion of this fourth gift for the infant Jesus. Supposedly, it would only be used once after his crucifixion.

'After seeing the holy infant, the magi had a premonition,' said Mrs Batliwala. 'It was a warning that they should not return to Herod, or else the child's life would be in danger. They left for Persia via an alternative route. When Herod found out that he had been outwitted by the three magi, he was enraged. Given that the magi had observed the heralding star two years ago, he passed orders to kill all male children in Bethlehem who were two years or less in age.'

My father's narrative, Mrs Batliwala's stories and my grandmother Cecile's book were merging together in my head. I tried making sense of it all.

'After Zarathustra's death, a powerful leader emerged,' said my teacher. 'He unified his people into a nation that could defend itself against the Assyrians. His name was Hakhamanish, and he would be known to the Greeks as Achaemenes.'

'You mean Cyrus?' I asked.

'His ancestor, actually,' she replied. 'Many years after Achaemenes, Cyrus burst onto the Persian stage. He was influenced by Zoroastrian values although he never attempted to impose any particular faith on his subjects. He came to be known as Cyrus the Great. Cyrus considered Achaemenes to be the progenitor of his empire. Over a single decade, Cyrus united various tribes in the region to fashion the Achaemenid Empire, the first Persian Empire ever.'

The story she narrated about Cyrus was an amazing one. As the legend goes, Astyages, the king of Media, was the overlord of the Persians. Astyages gave his daughter's hand in marriage to his vassal in Persia, a young prince called Cambyses. Cyrus was born from this union.

Astyages had a dream indicating that the newborn would overthrow him one day. He therefore ordered that Cyrus be killed. 'Notice how this was similar to Herod wanting Jesus to be killed?' asked Mrs Batliwala. I nodded. I didn't tell her that it was an oft-repeated theme in mythology. In Hindu legend, the king Kansa wanted Krishna dead for a similar reason.

'But Astyages's trusted minister, Harpagus, ignored his king's order and surreptitiously gave the baby away to be raised far away by a shepherd,' continued Mrs Batliwala. Much like Nanda and Yashodhara raised Krishna, I thought.

Because of his brilliance and outstanding ability, Cyrus eventually returned to the attention of Astyages. That would *have been the end of him, but surprisingly, Astyages was persuaded by his councillors to allow Cyrus to live. It turned out to be a fateful decision for Astyages. Cyrus rebelled against his maternal grandfather and overthrew him, thus proving the truth of the prophecy in Astyages's dream. A helpless Astyages found that even his army had deserted him and had joined forces with Cyrus.*

'Cyrus undertook several military campaigns against far more powerful kingdoms of the time—Media, Lydia and Babylonia,' related Mrs Batliwala. 'As a result of his victories, he consolidated much of the Middle East under Persian authority while retaining the local rulers as satraps. Thus, he was able to guarantee continuity and expansion.'

'There was something in that account about Cyrus and the Jews, right?' I asked.

'Yes, arising from Cyrus's compassion,' replied my schoolteacher. 'He conquered Babylonia in 539 BCE by defeating the Chaldean kings who had enslaved the Jews. Cyrus released the Jews from captivity and permitted them to return to their homeland. He even provided the necessary resources to help them rebuild their temple, a fact gratefully recorded by the Jews in Psalm 137 of the Bible.' I knew that. The psalm had been adapted by the group Boney M in 1978 as a hit song. It was called By the Rivers of Babylon. My generation had grown up on that song!

'But remember one thing, son,' said Mrs Batliwala, 'Judaism borrowed many ideas from Zoroastrianism during that time of cross-cultural contact. Concepts such as heaven and hell, the coming of a messiah, the devil's temptation, Judgement Day, the good and bad duality, the shining star and resurrection were *inspired from Zoroastrianism. Those ideas eventually found their way into other Abrahamic faiths.'*

'Incredible,' I whispered.

'More than twenty distinct population groups coexisted under Cyrus's government, based in Pasargadae, close to the modern Iranian city of Shiraz,' said Mrs Batliwala. 'The Cyrus Cylinder, one of the greatest artefacts of Persia, reads like a charter of human rights, coming around two millennia before the Magna Carta of England. The inscription bans slavery and oppression; it deems property forfeitures illegal; it provides for the rights of all worshippers to honour their different gods.'

'But the cylinder does not mention Ahura Mazda,' I said. 'Why?'

'Maybe that was Cyrus's wisdom at work,' she replied. 'The region he conquered worshipped a God called Marduk. In later years the attributes of Marduk would be transferred to Ashur. And after that ...'

'To Ahura Mazda?' I asked.

58

I THANKED MRS Batliwala for her time and left. I had brought her a basket of fruit that I left for her in her kitchen on my way out. Once I was home, I sat in the living room, reading a book from Cecile's library that had been passed on to me through my father.

Lying on the couch, I delved into the history of the Achaemenids. Apparently, the next great Achaemenid hero who believed in Ahura Mazda was Darius I, a nephew of Cyrus, who ruled for thirty-six years from 522 BCE. The Persian Empire is said to have reached its zenith under him.

Darius had not been the legal heir to the Achaemenid throne. His father had merely been the Persian governor of Bactria. But there was a power struggle in which an imposter king, Gaumata, was installed on the throne. Gaumata's reign did not last long, because he was soon assassinated by a band of conspirators, a group that included Darius. The question then arose: Who should succeed Gaumata?

The conspirators agreed to participate in a contest for the throne. All would meet the next morning mounted on their horses. The first horse to neigh would result in his master being declared king. The clever Darius arrived at the meeting having rubbed his hands over the genitals of a mare. Once at the venue, he allowed his horse to sniff his hands. His horse neighed almost immediately and—surprise, surprise—Darius was declared king. I laughed. It seemed to me that deceit was fine as long as the hero won.

Darius spent the next few years putting down rebellions and consolidating his rule. Vast military expeditions followed. He even incorporated a large part of Egypt into his empire. The next year he added northern Punjab, in the Asian subcontinent, as the twentieth satrapy of the Persian Empire.

Darius sired at least twelve children, one of whom was Xerxes, his successor. Darius was a staunch Zoroastrian, but all other religions were tolerated by him, provided that their followers remained submissive. In an inscription on a rock relief at Mount Behistun in the Kermanshah Province of Iran, his words proclaimed:

Ahura Mazda is the great God who set in place this earth,
Who set in place yonder sky, who set in place man,
Who set in place peace for man, who made Darius king,
One king over many, one commander of many.

In another inscription Darius said:

When Ahura Mazda saw this earth in turmoil,
He gave it to me and made me king.
I am king by the greatness of Ahura Mazda.

On Darius's inscription was a symbol of a winged male figure holding a ring. It would eventually become a symbol associated with the Zoroastrian faith—the faravahar. The symbol was not new, having been used by the Egyptians and Assyrians previously, but for the Achaemenid kings, the faravahar was a symbol of Fravashi—the guardian angel who protected the monarch and his people. I grew up seeing that symbol everywhere—at our fire temples, on prayer books, even car stickers. I had recently seen it as a pendant around Mrs Batliwala's neck.

It is said that Darius had to face defeat when he dispatched six hundred ships and a great army to conquer Athens. His soldiers occupied the plains of Marathon, awaiting an opportune moment to mount a surprise attack. When the inhabitants of Marathon realised Darius's plans, they sent the runner Pheidippides to warn the Athenians. It was a distance of forty-two kilometres. That run, of course, would be immortalised in marathon races that are held in cities around the world to this day. My wife, Linda, has participated in many of them herself.

Darius's forces had to withdraw. But the king's lauded contribution lay in creating a system of government that could administer such a vast empire. Darius oversaw an empire that extended from the Mediterranean Sea to the Indus River. His laws were a combination of Zarathustra's teachings and the Code of Hammurabi borrowed from the Babylonians. Darius built imperial highways on a scale never seen before and even constructed a canal between the River Nile and the Red Sea. He built hundreds of qanats, horizontal irrigation wells. In Susa, Darius built a massive palace complex that became his favoured residence. He also built the grandest palace at Persepolis, one that would eventually be burnt to ashes by the conquering Alexander two centuries later. It was Darius who introduced a new currency for the empire—the darayaka. This currency, made common to all the lands under him, made it far easier to collect taxes, and thus led to boosted revenues. He even introduced a new standardised system of weights and measures to streamline commerce.

Darius's son, Xerxes, was a tyrannical sort. His official title was 'Shahenshah'—king of kings. I was surprised to read this. I had always thought that the term had an Islamic origin. Turns out, I was wrong. Of course, Xerxes would be remembered for leading his forces against Greece in 480 BCE and defeating the Spartans at the battle of Thermopylae. He proceeded to sack Athens. But before he could consolidate his gains in Greece, he was called away to Babylonia to crush an uprising. The very next year, the Greeks took their revenge at the Battle of Plataea.

But even more ominously, the price for sacking Athens would be the destruction of Persepolis by Alexander a century and a half later.

59

IT WAS AFTER having perused this book passed on to me by my father, that I decided to pay a visit to my grandmother. After my grandfather's death, Cecile had retired to the hills of Khandala. The house that she occupied there had been built as a weekend retreat by my grandfather, Rustom. But Cecile loved the place so much that she had decided to shift there permanently after Rustom's death. Unsurprisingly, Cecile preferred the crisp cool air of the hills to that of polluted Mumbai.

I told my father of my plans and took off in his white Mercedes-Benz. It was an old car, but my father had retained it for sentimental reasons. On the rear windscreen was a golden sticker of the Zoroastrian faravahar. The symbol seemed to follow me everywhere I went!

Father made sure that our old and reliable driver, Abdul, drove. My father gave him strict instructions about not speeding and being extra-cautious on the ghats. I used the time in the car to memorise the few lines of text that my father had given me along with the earthen box. I then tore it into little bits and disposed the litter at the next rest stop. I reached Khandala in the evening by which time it was cold. Cecile's two German Shepherds ran out to greet me and I gave each one of them a doggy treat.

Age had given Cecile even greater elegance. Her blonde hair had turned a silvery grey, but her blue eyes still sparkled. Her once glowing skin had turned pale but was still smooth. She walked straight and erect, and remained illness-free even *though she was just a year short of eighty. I hugged her. 'Wash up and we'll have dinner,' she said. 'I have made the cook to put together your favourite dishes.'*

'My favourite dish is you,' I teased, winking at her. It was an old joke that never grew stale, and never failed to tickle her. I quickly freshened up and joined her in the ornate dining room. A bowl of French onion soup, my very favourite from her kitchen, was already being placed for me. Cecile broke off a large chunk of a baguette and placed it on my side plate along with a generous swirl of softened butter.

'I'm glad you came,' said my grandmother simply. 'I was worried that I would not get to see you before you left for Stanford.'

'That would never have happened,' I said, and meant it. Cecile had been one of the kindest souls to have showered me with love over the years. There would have been no question of proceeding to America without meeting her to say goodbye.

'There's something on your mind,' she said. 'Tell me.'

'I've been digging into Parsi history, and you are a virtual encyclopaedia on it,' I replied. 'For the life of me, I cannot understand why they treated you as an outsider. You were much more into things than those supposed insiders!'

'I didn't care about all that because of Rustom's love for me,' she said without any sign of rancour. 'He remained devoted to me until his dying day. That carried the greatest weight.'

The rest of the dinner was delicious, although vegetarian. Cecile and Rustom had both given up meat early on in their lives, further highlighting the fact that they were cultural oddities in the Parsi world. The plate that was placed before me looked outstanding. A hot quiche of leek, mushroom, onion, spinach and goat cheese. Dinner ended with apple pie and vanilla ice cream. I was absolutely stuffed by the end. At Cecile's place, I always forgot I was a carnivore.

After dinner, I went into my favourite part of Cecile's house, her library. I scanned the books that the couple had amassed over the years. The shelves were groaning with tomes on almost every conceivable subject: science, medicine, religion, spirituality, history, mythology, culture, philosophy and yoga. In addition, there were works of poetry and fiction, including classics and contemporary writing. Their sheer scale explained why this couple had always had such a universal perspective on life.

I picked up Alexander the Great *by Philip Freeman. Much as I wanted to sit with Cecile and chat, I was tired. I took my grandmother's leave, retired to my room and began to read.*

60

THE FIRST FEW *pages of the Freeman book told me that Alexander III was the son of King Philip II of Macedon. Born around 356 BCE, he became king at the young age of twenty upon his father's death. He would go on to become one of the world's greatest conquerors, thus earning the permanent epithet 'the great'.*

In 330 BCE, Alexander conquered the Achaemenid Persian Empire. After his victory over Darius III at the Battle of Gaugamela, Alexander's army marched to the Persian capital of Persepolis and unleashed an orgy of loot and pillage. In Alexander's scheme of things, it was retribution for the sacking of Athens by Xerxes I. The Achaemenid king had attacked Greece 150 years earlier, razing villages, cities and temples, including the famous Parthenon of Athens. That particular attack had neither been forgotten nor forgiven by the Greeks.

Persepolis—or Parsa as it was then known—was a magnificent ceremonial centre where subjects from all over the kingdom came to pay their respects to the king. The complex comprised several massive structures, including assembly halls, throne halls, treasuries, harems, royal archives and religious libraries. Some of these had been built by Darius I and some by Xerxes. The city's isolated geography also kept it hidden from the wider world. Persepolis had soon become one of the safest places to store the royal coffers, treasures and archives. The most powerful secrets of the magi lay there: sacred texts containing divine chants, purity rituals and secrets of astrology, alchemy, numerology and the science of herbs.

Darius I had carefully chosen the site for Persepolis in a remote area, distant from the old capital. It had been his endeavour to markedly distinguish his reign from those of past monarchs who had ruled from Pasargadae. Each building in Persepolis was an architectural wonder created with the specific intent of arousing awe and amazement. Darius's reception hall was intended to humble all visitors and reinforce upon them the might of the Persian Empire. The grand platform terrace alone was 125,000 square metres in size! On it, he built Apadana, the grand audience hall, with seventy-two columns, each towering nineteen metres high. Atop those columns sat a glorious roof made from rich cedar wood sourced from Lebanon.

Persepolis was a fabulously wealthy city. In an expansive mood, Alexander gave his Macedonian soldiers freedom to loot private homes, taking for themselves all the gold, silver and treasures they could get their hands on. But even after spending an entire day in pillage, the Macedonians could not fully satisfy their greed. They summarily killed the men and dragged away the women and children as slaves.

Meanwhile, Alexander took possession of the royal citadel and seized 2500 tons of silver, arranging for 3000 pack camels and mules to cart it off. History records that Alexander set fire to the royal palace in a drunken frenzy. Purportedly, this was at the instigation of a woman called Thais, the Athenian lover of Alexander's commander, Ptolemy.

But history was mistaken.

61

HEYDARI GAVE SOROUSHPUR a look that he recognised. *There's something wrong about this 'driver'.* They were inside the beat-up white Toyota HiAce. The new driver had miraculously appeared out of nowhere. And then Heydari had noticed the Sig Sauer P228 gun in the loose-lidded glovebox.

The driver seemed to be taking them in the right direction though—from the Atashgah Boulevard to the Chamran Expressway and on to the Isfahan Eastern Bypass Freeway. The driver looked at Heydari in his rearview mirror and noticed his worried expression. Much to Heydari's chagrin, he slowed down.

He pulled up to the side of the road and switched on his hazard lights. Then he reached into the glovebox and took hold of his P228. Placing it in his pocket, he got out and opened the door to the passenger cabin. Heydari, Soroushpur, Linda and Dan waited with bated breath. This could very well be the end of the road for all of them.

Leaning inside, the driver took off his sunglasses. 'My name is Kaveh Abbasi,' he said to Heydari. 'Do not do anything foolish. I may be your only chance of surviving.' Heydari was quiet.

'Your conversation on the mobile phone yesterday,' began Abbasi. 'You were talking to an accomplice in Tehran, and you mentioned Jim Dastoor. That conversation was picked up by Unit 8200. That's why I'm here.'

'You're CIA?' asked Soroushpur.

'No, but we're friends of the Americans,' said Abbasi. Heydari and Soroushpur instantly caught on to the 'we', not 'I'. He was an undercover Mossad agent, the only sort of agent that could still find ways to survive within Iran. Most CIA operations inside Iran had died in the years after the exile of Mohammad Reza Pahlavi. The agency now depended increasingly on its Israeli counterpart to execute any operation within Iran.

'Keeping this vehicle on the freeway shoulder is a bad idea,' said Abbasi. 'The police could arrive any moment. Better that we should be on our way. I am going back to my driver's seat. Just thought I should ease your fears so that you do not take any rash decisions. We can talk more on the way.'

Abbasi shut the passenger door and returned to his seat. He leaned over and placed his P228 back in the glovebox, shutting it. The latch was loose, and its cover swung open again. Abbasi took out the gun from the compartment and tucked it into the inside pocket of his blazer. He then pulled the HiAce back on the freeway and they were again in motion.

'Don't worry,' Abbasi reassured them. 'This vehicle has been sanitised. There are no listening devices here, so we can talk freely.'

'How did the NSA know which phone to trace?' asked Heydari. 'My American friends tell me that they switched off their mobiles on the day they arrived in Kish and dumped them overboard when they were on the boat. And my conversation was from a burner phone.'

'They didn't know which one to trace,' said Abbasi. 'Israel's ISNU helped them. They have backdoors into most mobile networks, including the two in Iran. They did several sweeps in the last twenty-four hours, specifically listening for significant words such as 'Jim Dastoor', and associated names, places and companies. Luckily, you used your phone from the Atashgah last evening. That's the one that the PRISM funnel picked up through ISNU. Almost immediately, the agencies began tracking your mobile location.'

There was silence in the passenger cabin. The power of agencies to eavesdrop was known around the world, but to see it in action was another thing entirely. 'We are still no closer to securing freedom for Jim,' said Linda, breaking the silence.

'But we have a better chance if we pool resources,' replied Abbasi. 'Our sources have confirmed that he is being held in the guesthouse of Shahid Daru Pharma. The IRGC-Quds have guards posted almost everywhere. We know because the Americans have satellites that can see inside the factory.'

America's National Reconnaissance Office—or the NRO—operated a cluster of satellites known as Keyhole. The KH-11 satellites used were built by Lockheed Martin and used the same 2.4-metre mirror that had been used on the Hubble Space Telescope. Word was that the Keyhole system could capture objects as small as five centimetres long on Iranian terrain. Those satellites were now feeding them data from inside the factory.

'Two important questions,' said Heydari. 'One. How do we get inside the premises? Two. How do we get Jim out?'

'What about raw material trucks and delivery trucks?' suggested Soroushpur. 'There must be a regular inflow and outflow of transport.'

'All trucks are being examined to the last micro-detail,' Abbasi informed them. 'Every driver must have security clearance. They are taking no chances. Jim Dastoor is a prize catch. Let us think.' Abbasi went silent, but his mind kept whirring.

Several vehicles ahead, a roadblock had been set up. Drivers were being asked for identification papers. 'Shit!' muttered Abbasi. 'Look at the number of policemen. This seems to be related to your military truck. Your accomplice has squealed.'

It was probable. There was silence inside the minivan as Abbasi, Soroushpur, Heydari, Linda and Dan evaluated their options. The roadblock was still around twenty cars away. It would be a while before their turn came.

'Quietly get out of the vehicle,' suggested Abbasi. 'I am still not identified with your group, and it should be possible for me to get through the checkpost. The four of you, cross the fencing at the edge of the shoulder and make your way on foot along the field that borders this stretch. I will pick you up beyond the roadblock.'

Heydari agreed that it was the best possible plan. 'Four of us getting out together from a vehicle in the middle of an expressway will be highly noticeable though,' he said. 'Why don't you pull over to the side and pretend you are changing a tyre? That would give us an opportunity to get out.'

Abbasi approved the advice. 'Here goes,' he said, as he switched on his hazard lights and swerved towards the expressway shoulder.

62

THEY MADE IT to Tehran in a little over five hours. It would have been less had it not been for the roadblock. The police officers had simply looked at Abbasi's papers and waved him through.

The façade employed by Abbasi was very realistic. He ran a legitimate dry fruits processing and packaging business in Iran. His handlers at Mossad ensured that he clocked in business revenues and kept his financial returns squeaky clean. The home address that showed up on all his documents was in Fereshteh Street in the Elahieh district, the most expensive area of Tehran. It was his affluent profile that had ensured that the poorly paid policemen at the roadblock allowed Abbasi to pass without much ado.

By the time Abbasi had picked up the four, he already had an idea. He shared it with them quickly: 'The Shahid Daru factory generates huge quantities of waste water. In addition, there is faecal and septic sludge that the municipal authorities refuse to handle. All of this is treated through composting at a neighbouring plot of land. A primary sewer line transports the sludge from the factory to the aerobic digestion unit a few hundred metres away.'

'How do you know this?' asked Soroushpur.

'It is my job to know many things,' said Abbasi smugly. 'But since you ask, an acquaintance told me that many industries in Vardavard are up in arms because of lack of municipal services, particularly sewerage.'

'What are you thinking?' asked Heydari.

'If the sewer line were to get damaged, the factory would be up shit creek—pun intended,' said Abbasi. 'They would need to call in vacuum trucks to clear out the mess until such time as the sewer line is repaired.'

Heydari caught on to what Abbasi was suggesting. 'The sheer force of the stink would require vacuum trucks and manpower to come through those gates. They would be unable to inspect them thoroughly. The emergency would compel them to permit us through. I have a question though ...'

'Yes?' asked Abbasi.

'Where exactly are we going to get vacuum sewer trucks?' asked Heydari.

'Call to me and I will answer you,' said Abbasi. 'And will tell you great and hidden things that you have not known.' The rest of the group seemed amazed to hear an Iranian follower of Shia Islam quoting verses from the Old Testament.

'I grew up in Tabrizi with an aunt of Jewish extraction,' he grinned. 'Bible study was par for the course.'

'Fascinating information,' said Dan sourly. 'But it doesn't get us the vacuum trucks.'

'The only entity that has them is TPWW,' said Abbasi. 'The Tehran Province Water and Wastewater Company. We will need to "borrow" a couple of their trucks. And seeing how good Tariq is at the art of stealing trucks, this part of the operation will be his responsibility. He shall be accompanied by Behrad in this exercise.' Heydari and Soroushpur laughed.

'What about us?' asked Linda.

'The sewerage trucks will be summoned to Shahid Daru only if we first create the mess,' replied Abbasi. 'I have asked headquarters to locate a map of the sewer lines at the factory. We know the general layout, but we need more specific layouts to do what we need to. Once we have that, you, Dan and I will figure out which part of the line needs to be severed.'

Linda wanted to argue that the plan was riddled with risks, but she also knew that Abbasi, Heydari and Soroushpur were her best chance of getting Jim out. She kept her concerns to herself.

'Assuming that we can get inside with very few questions asked,' said Dan. 'How do we reach Jim once we're in?'

'The guesthouse is located in the north-east corner of the factory plot,' said Abbasi. 'This is also the approximate location of the underground sewer line. We will be operating right there.'

'But we would need to neutralise the guards,' said Soroushpur.

'A cache of Heckler & Koch G36 rifles is stashed away in a secret location in Tehran,' replied Abbasi. 'We can get those into our stolen trucks.'

'Won't they check the trucks?' asked Linda.

'It will be the responsibility of Tariq and Behrad to find us the dirtiest trucks they can,' said Abbasi with a wicked curl of his lips. 'The weapons will be placed just inside the tank, duly wrapped in plastic. None of the guards will ever look inside. I hope none of you have a problem with excrement?'

There was a disgusted silence. 'I'll take that as a yes,' continued Abbasi lightly. 'Time to get our hands dirty.'

63

LINDA LOOKED AT her watch. It was a little after 6 pm. They had dropped off Soroushpur and Heydari near the Modares Highway so that they could make their way to TPWW. Then they had turned west to circle the Shahid Daru factory.

The map had arrived from Mossad via Signal, the preferred choice for end-to-end encrypted messaging. Although Iranian authorities blocked the app from time to time, Mossad ensured that their agents could connect via special proxy servers.

The maps showed that Abbasi's estimate had been right. The sewerage line emerged from the pharmaceutical plant at the north-east corner. Only 200 metres away was the guesthouse, tucked away towards the back of the plot. Mossad had also shared high-resolution aerial photographs of the factory plot taken by Israel's own Ofek-16 satellite. They were stunning in their clarity, even being able to capture the type of guns in the hands of security guards.

They pulled into the lot of a derelict electric substation and parked the minivan there. Before leaving the vehicle, Abbasi pulled out a duffel bag that had been left for him at the 'secret location' he'd talked about, the city's Botanical Gardens. It contained five Heckler & Koch G36 rifles, one each for Abbasi, Heydari, Soroushpur, Linda and Dan. Also included were several thirty-round translucent magazines, intelligently designed to allow the user to see how many rounds remained in them. In addition to the rifles were a dozen hand grenades, gas masks, a floor scanner, concrete drill and a shovel. Finally, there were two large unlabelled blue cans of nearly five kilograms each.

Abbasi gestured to Dan, and he pulled out the two large containers by their handles. 'What is this stuff?' asked Dan. They seemed to weigh a ton.

'Hydraulic cement,' said Abbasi. 'For the sewerage line.'

'I thought we would use the grenades to blow up the line,' said Dan.

Abbasi shook his head. 'If we do that, we will create a sewage and drainage problem *outside* the factory, not inside. No, this is a product that is used to stop water and leaks in concrete and masonry. It's similar to mortar but it sets extremely fast as it mixes with water. Ideal for anything that is submerged. Just dumping this into the sewerage line will eventually cause a massive block.'

Linda and Dan understood why Mossad agents were considered to be among the best in the world. They were trained to think on their feet, particularly when faced with daunting odds in hostile terrain. More importantly, they were taught to plan and execute flawlessly.

They walked along Fifth Farvardin Street, avoiding Taleghani Street that housed the front entrance of the Shahid Daru Pharma. They cut right and headed to Sixty-Third Street which constituted the north-east corner of the Shahid Daru plot. Along the way, they passed two workmen from a neighbouring factory. Abbasi knew that if they were from Shahid Daru they would have the capsule logo on their uniforms. Linda allowed her headscarf to drop lower, covering the top half of her face.

'*As-salaamu alaikum*,' said Abbasi, cornering their attention. If there was to be any conversation, it had to be with him rather than Dan or Linda.

'*Va-alaikum as-salaam*,' replied one of them. He looked at the three of them curiously. He came closer to them, and his stare made Linda feel uncomfortable. Dan was sweating but Abbasi stayed cool. 'We seem to be lost,' he said in Farsi to the inquisitive man. 'This is my team of engineers from Russia,' he continued. 'They are here to plan a factory building at Shahid Daru, but we can't seem to find the gate.'

The nosy worker looked sympathetic. 'You have missed it,' he replied. 'You are on the back street. You can take a right up ahead to get to Taleghani Street. You will see a large green arch. That's the main gate,'

'*Sepas-gozaram*,' said Abbasi, thanking them. They continued walking along the road and took the right that had been recommended by the man. They waited for a few minutes before popping back after the men had disappeared.

The street was deserted as they went to the spot that seemed to coincide with the location shown on the map. The Shahid Daru boundary wall was less than two metres high and had another sixty centimetres of barbed wire above it. Along the top were rotating video cameras that were pointed both inwards at the factory, and periodically outwards. Abbasi took a shot at an outward pointing camera with his P228. The unit exploded and fell off the mounting angle. 'We need to work quickly,' said Abbasi. 'I'm guessing that we have about fifteen minutes before they send guards to check the reason for video feed disruption.'

Abbasi had a Bosch D-Tect Floor Scanner in his hand. It was capable of detecting water-filled pipes, live cables, ferrous and non-ferrous metals, concrete beams, wooden studs and a range of other things. He quickly activated it. On the tiny screen was a little navigation tool that showed the exact location of the signal that was bouncing back from the ground. The unit sent both sound and visual signals to indicate the presence of the underground object. As soon as Abbasi was sure, he handed the shovel to Dan. 'Dig here,' he said.

Soon they had a hole around thirty centimetres in diameter. Just over a metre below, the sewerage pipe lay exposed. Abbasi bent down with his concrete drill and began puncturing a hole in the brittle stoneware. He let out a little grunt when the pipe was punctured. A foul stench that could kill emerged from within. Dark brown sludge began bubbling through. They quickly put on their gas masks and continued with their work. 'Come on,' said Abbasi to Dan, 'help me. I need you to smash that pipe with the shovel.'

Dan delivered a couple of strong whacks which did the job. The three of them then quickly poured the hydraulic cement down the hole that had been created. 'We don't need to add water because the factory effluent will automatically activate the cement. We simply need to wait for a blockage to form.'

Once the cement had been poured in, they repacked the hole with soil, put back all their stuff into the duffel and headed back in the direction from which they had come. They would wait for Heydari and Soroushpur at a rendezvous point near Taleghani Street before entering the factory premises. While waiting, Abbasi would explain the basics of using guns to Linda and Dan.

'Never thought I would say this,' said Abbasi with a grim grin. 'But it seems that a clogged poop chute can actually be quite beneficial for our health.'

64

THE SANITATION TRUCKS were orange coloured. Heydari and Soroushpur had managed to steal not only the vehicles but also the uniforms and caps that TPWW staff wore. They bided their time for signs of commotion inside the Shahid Daru premises. No sooner did they hear the staff yelling to one another, they started up the ignition. It was necessary that they reach there before the real TPWW team did.

Abbasi drove one of the trucks while Heydari drove the other. Dan and Soroushpur sat on the passenger side of each. Linda would have looked out of place, so she crouched down in the driver's cabin by Dan's feet, praying that the guards would be in too much of a hurry to check them closely.

The guards were relieved to see the two vacuum trucks pull up at the gate. They wondered how TPWW had been so quick in their response. 'The main line is choked,' said Abbasi from the lead vehicle. 'We received the news from your neighbour. For the moment we will need to drain the line and vacuum whatever is blocking it.' The guards carried out a cursory check of the trucks, holding kerchiefs to their noses as they did so. Heydari and Soroushpur had done a terrific job of sourcing the dirtiest possible trucks. 'Do you think we need to check the tanks?' asked one of the guards of another.

'Are you crazy?' demanded his colleague. 'The fucking lorries already stink from the outside and you want to peep *inside* them? Let them through!'

The barrier was lifted, and both the trucks rolled in. 'Which way?' asked Abbasi. Dan looked at the plot layout on Abbasi's phone. 'Go straight up and take a sharp right after that office block,' he said. 'Another few hundred yards and we should be coming to the guesthouse.' Within a few minutes the residential block was visible. Several IRGC-Quds uniforms were visible. It was evident that the brass were not taking any chances with Jim Dastoor.

'Don't stop at the guesthouse,' said Dan. 'Better that we drive up ahead to the location of the sewerage pipe and then make our way back on foot.' Abbasi nodded in agreement. Stopping at the guesthouse would have brought them under the direct focus of the IRGC-Quds. An alarm would be raised, and the IRGC-Quds would be joined by the police and security guards. Retaining the element of surprise was essential, and they had to work quickly, because the real TPWW trucks would roll in soon.

They halted approximately two hundred metres away from the guesthouse, near the boundary wall. They could see the shattered camera that hung from a cable. It was the CCTV camera that they had shot down from the outside. Descending from the trucks, they quickly pulled out and unpacked their Heckler & Koch rifles and rounds.

Neither Linda nor Dan spoke. It was obvious that they were uncomfortable about killing anyone. Abbasi understood their dilemma. 'Remember one thing, my friends. The militia that guards Jim will not hesitate for a moment to put a bullet through you. We shall do everything to minimise killing, but some bloodshed may occur.'

'How?' asked Linda, holding her rifle uncomfortably. 'How do we minimise casualties?'

Abbasi had four grenades and a canister clasped on his belt. 'We are going to create explosions in three areas of the factory where there are no humans. First, the waste disposal pit towards the north-west corner. Second, the raw materials depot towards the south-east. Third, in the front lawn just outside the guesthouse area. The explosions will cause panic and allow us to enter Jim's guesthouse.'

He turned to Heydari. 'How good are you with grenades?' he asked. Heydari laughed. 'I've been chucking them all my life. In Iran, opposition politics means war.'

'Good,' said Abbasi, handing over another grenade belt to Heydari to put around his waist.

'Just remember that the explosions won't happen simultaneously because there will be a delay in my getting from one place to another,' responded Heydari.

'I want it that way,' said Abbasi. He turned to Linda and Dan. 'The two of you will take positions at the front, using the staff toilet block as cover. You will create a diversion from the front by attacking with all guns blazing. Do not shoot to kill, simply shoot near the guards. Soroushpur and I shall enter the guesthouse through the rear service entrance. The heat map shows greater presence on the third floor, around the room that looks out towards the central lawns. We shall rush in there and neutralise the guards holding Jim. We meet back at the trucks in ten minutes and ram our way out. Everyone clear on what they have to do?' The group nodded in agreement.

'Then let's get going,' he said. Heydari had already run towards the lawn and lobbed the first grenade. The sound hit them like a hammer on their eardrums. The ground shook and acrid smoke filled the air. Heydari seemed to be laughing maniacally. He was like a child experimenting with matches. He did not wait for even a split second before he dashed towards the waste disposal pit. The rest realised that they had better get on with their own tasks quickly.

An alarm had been sounded within the factory and two fire-tenders from the gatehouse were heading to the blast. The IRGC-Quds guards at the guesthouse looked in the direction of the blast only to discover that they were under fire from machine-guns. They fired back in the direction of the toilet block while Abbasi and Soroushpur made their way through the service entrance of the guest block.

An IRGC-Quds commando blocked their path near the kitchen. Before he could shoot, Abbasi had already fired. The man's head exploded like a watermelon, spattering blood and brain matter on the stainless-steel counters.

The only certainty in life is death, thought Abbasi as he made his way to the third floor.

65

ABBASI AND SOROUSHPUR bolted up the stairs, knocking down guards as they went along. Respecting the word he'd given Linda, Abbasi was not using his fire power indiscriminately. He used his rifle as a battering ram on some guards while he shot at their hands or feet in other cases. They were soon on the third floor. The corridor was dimly lit but, in the distance, Abbasi could see that one of the doors down it was open and a group of men were making their way out. It coincided with the general location shown in the heat map.

The two charged towards the group, firing above their heads as they went. At the core of the group was a man who seemed to be issuing the orders. Neither Abbasi nor Soroushpur knew what Javad Mosaffa looked like except for the grainy video capture from Spencer Airport. But he seemed to fit Linda's description. If Mosaffa was there, it only reconfirmed that Jim Dastoor was also there.

The IRGC-Quds Force men surrounding Jim and Mosaffa fired back. Each shot reverberated inside the narrow corridor, sending shrapnel, wood, plaster and glass flying. 'We need to take care of not hurting Jim,' said Abbasi.

Both men put on their gas masks. Abbasi lobbed a CS gas canister with all his might at the group. The tear gas instantly fogged up the area and the IRGC-Quds group broke up. Lachrymators such as CS were known to cause severe eye pain, temporary blindness, respiratory distress and, on a lesser scale, skin irritation.

Believing the group to be incapacitated, Abbasi and Soroushpur were in for a rude shock. Mosaffa had pulled on a gas mask, thus protecting himself. He was able to pull off a few shots with his Browning semi-automatic—all the while pushing Jim towards the emergency exit at the end of the corridor. A bullet from Mosaffa grazed Abbasi's left cheek. Another few millimetres to the right and he would have been dead. Abbasi ignored the bleeding wound and gestured for Soroushpur to give him protective fire as he tackled Mosaffa.

Soroushpur let loose a volley of shots, carefully avoiding Jim, while Abbasi charged towards the emergency exit that was now open. He could hear the clatter of feet as Mosaffa dragged Jim along with him down the stairs. He could hear Mosaffa's voice gasping threats to Jim. 'You shall do as I say. These dogs will die here today and cannot help you.'

Both Abbasi and Soroushpur leaned over the railing to get a sense of where Mosaffa and Jim were. They were certainly not on the second floor below. Abbasi made his way down unheard. He struck gold on the first-floor landing. Mosaffa and Abbasi saw each other at almost the same moment. Both their guns went off simultaneously, but Abbasi's bullet hit first. It caught Mosaffa on his right shoulder and his Browning clattered to the floor. Soroushpur lunged forward and grabbed it while Abbasi landed a sucker punch on Mosaffa's face. He fell down but recovered quickly and charged at Abbasi with all his might. Abbasi used his rifle butt as a battering ram and landed a direct blow to Mosaffa's chin. Mosaffa staggered for a moment before crumpling to the floor.

Just then Abbasi noticed Jim running back up the stairs. 'Where the fuck are you going?' he shouted after Jim. He gestured for Soroushpur to follow him. Jim went back to the emergency exit on the third floor and got down on his hands and knees. 'We need to get out of here,' said Soroushpur to Jim but nothing seemed to be registering with the man. A few seconds later he let out a little yelp of excitement as he grasped a canvas bag. It was his prized possession, the Hamzaa Dura, that had fallen from his protective clasp.

'C'mon, let's go,' said Soroushpur to Jim, catching him by his wrist to guide him down.

'Who are you?' asked Jim even as he followed Soroushpur's instructions.

'Haven't time to answer,' panted Soroushpur. 'Linda's waiting outside.' Jim couldn't be sure who these men were, nor could he be sure that they were not hoodwinking him. The teargas had made him woozy and his vision blurred. But the mention of Linda's name was enough to make him go along with them. Just as they reached the ground floor exit, two IRGC-Quds commandos appeared. Soroushpur was caught unaware, but he suddenly saw them fall in a bloody heap before him. Abbasi had fired his Heckler & Koch almost by reflex. They got to escape, relatively unscathed, from the emergency exit on the left side of the block.

Outside there was mayhem. Heydari had set off explosions in three critical areas, two of them with inflammable material. Security guards, local police, workmen and firefighters were attempting to control the flames. A whooping and deafening fire alarm was blaring from the speakers everywhere. A full-scale gun battle was raging between the IRGC-Quds men out in front and the unknown combatants—Dan and Linda— behind the toilet block. Just then there was a loud explosion. Heydari had thrown the fourth and final grenade given by Abbasi directly in front of the guesthouse.

Windows shattered and rained shards of glass, while several IRGC vehicles parked outside became fireballs. It had been a foolish action that could have got them all killed, but it was just the lucky break that Abbasi needed. He pulled Jim, running towards their trucks parked a few hundred yards away. The final grenade also gave Dan, Linda and Heydari a much-needed reprieve to make a dash for the vehicles.

Jim saw Linda running and couldn't believe that she was actually there. 'No time for anything besides getting out of here,' shouted Abbasi as they were bundled into the drivers' cabins. 'Get set for a rough ride. The gate will probably have been blocked by the IRGC.'

'What do we do?' yelled Heydari. The two vacuum trucks charged at high speed towards the main gate through which they had entered. And sure enough, not only were there IRGC personnel but also military trucks that had been placed at an angle to block anyone attempting to exit.

'How many grenades do we have left?' asked Abbasi.

'I used only four,' replied Heydari.

'Go and have yourself a blast, my friend,' said Abbasi as he stepped on the gas and his truck hurtled towards the IRGC barrier.

66

'YOU'RE CRAZY!' SHOUTED Abbasi. 'A certifiable lunatic!'

But it was evident to everyone that his words were said in jest. Had it not been for Heydari's madness, they would not have been able to cannon through the main gate. Just a few yards from the main barrier, Heydari had actually got out of the truck, stood directly in the line of fire and hurled some of their remaining grenades at the trucks that were blocking their path. After that, it had been easy riding for the fleeing group.

Now they were racing down the Tehran-Karaj Freeway. They knew that they had to ditch the trucks as soon as possible. There was probably a citywide lookout for them already. 'We'll turn off to the right,' said Abbasi as he manoeuvred a sharp turn at high speed. 'We'll get on the Stone Caravanserai Bridge and dump the trucks under the bypass. Then we'll have to figure out how to make ourselves scarce.'

Fifteen minutes later, the trucks had been abandoned inside a disused warehouse just off the Stone Caravanserai Bridge. Jim was already dressed in the clothes that Mosaffa had provided him, while the others quickly changed out of their uniforms and into civvies. Jim continued to clutch the canvas bag that he had retrieved almost miraculously from the Shahid Daru plant. Linda helped Abbasi place an adhesive medicated patch on his cheek, over a bullet wound.

'You have already done more than enough for this group,' said Soroushpur to Heydari. He was not wrong. Had it not been for Heydari, that military truck would not have pulled them out of Shiraz early that morning and saved them from the IRGC. It was Heydari who had brought them there in Abbasi's minivan. It was Heydari who had helped steal the TPWW trucks. And it was Heydari and his 'lunacy' that had created chaos inside the Shahid Daru plant, enabling them to rescue Jim. 'We cannot endanger you any further,' said Soroushpur. 'You should say goodbye to us here.'

'What about getting Jim, Linda and Dan out of Iran?' asked Heydari. 'It's a matter of time before the citywide alert will become a national lookout notice for them.'

'That is now our concern,' said Linda, holding her husband's hand tight. 'I am immensely grateful that you helped get Jim back to me. But you are already on the radar of the Iranian regime. We should not endanger your life further.'

Heydari pointed with his chin. 'Whatever it is that your husband is holding there with such care is important enough for people to kill or get killed,' he said. '*Khoda hafez* and *safar khosh*.'

Soroushpur and Heydari hugged each other. 'I have a suggestion,' said Heydari. 'Head into the suburbs, possibly Pardis. There are several unfinished buildings there that remain secluded. From there, make your way eastwards.'

'Why?' asked Soroushpur.

'It leaves open the option of making your exit through the border that Iran shares with Afghanistan,' he said. 'Unless Abbasi can figure out a way to get an Israeli aircraft into Iranian territory, the land route into Afghanistan seems to be your best bet.'

Abbasi shrugged. 'I don't think that an aircraft will be possible at the moment,' he said. 'Iran will be on high alert. But we have Turkey and Iraq to our west, Azerbaijan and Turkmenistan to our north, and Afghanistan and Pakistan to our east. Military presence is greater towards the west on account of Iraq.'

'That's it then,' said Soroushpur. 'We try to get you to Herat, in Afghanistan. The Americans still have a substantial military presence in the country, and it would be possible for you to fly out from one of the air bases.'

'How will you travel?' asked Heydari, lingering over his departure. 'I believe Imam Reza Highway and Route 44 would be your best bet. You could do the trip in thirteen hours if you do not stop on the way.'

Abbasi stroked his chin in thought. Getting to the border was a journey of 1000 kilometres. Along the way there would be checkposts and barriers. What were the odds of three Americans being able to make it without getting arrested? And even assuming that Abbasi and Soroushpur stayed with them, how would they get by without being recognised? As he thought about it, the more daunting the task seemed. And then he had it. The solution was quite simple, once he'd come to think of it.

The satisfaction on his face was noticed by Soroushpur. 'What are you thinking?' he asked. Abbasi pulled up the *Tehran Times* on his phone. 'Read this,' he said.

*Exports from Iran to Afghanistan witnessed a 3.5 per
cent rise in tonnage compared to last year's corresponding
period. Major commodities exported to Afghanistan
during the period included fruits and vegetables, other
foodstuff, industrial goods, and construction materials.
Tomatoes topped the list of exports, followed by iron
bars. A third of Afghanistan's domestic demand for goods
from Iran enters the country by road ...*

'What's cooking inside that head?' asked Soroushpur,
looking up from the article.

'What if Jim, Linda and Dan were to travel as cargo instead
of passengers?' asked Abbasi.

67

THE HARDTOP SHIPPING container was a little over twelve
metres long and a little under five metres wide. But inside,
it was only around ten-and-a-half metres long; around one-
and-a-half metres of the container had been cordoned off
with a false wall. It left a special compartment that could be
used to carry contraband or people. Unless border control
or customs officers were especially vigilant, it would be
impossible to detect, more so if the rest of the container were
filled with merchandise. Alas, such containers were also used
to traffic young children and sex slaves across borders.

The hidden compartment was equipped with a padded
bench, electric lights and fans hooked to car batteries. In
addition, it was stocked with a twenty-litre canister of water

and several boxes of Farkhondeh biscuits, a brand popular in Iran. To one corner of the hidden compartment was a 113-litre waste receptacle. On the ceiling, small holes ensured that fresh air could enter. Towards the right, a square trap door with sides of approximately sixty centimetres had been cut into the container. It had been ingeniously hinged from the inside; the outside cracks had been concealed with epoxy and then painted to match the container's exterior. This would allow the occupants to escape in case of an emergency. An intercom connected the driver's cabin with the hidden chamber.

Linda, Jim and Dan sat on the padded bench inside the secret compartment while the rest of the container was full of dry fruits, canned goods and packaged drinks. Abbasi drove the truck and Soroushpur sat next to him. Any official peeking inside the container would not be able to see the deception. The container belonged to the dry fruit trading company that Abbasi fronted. It was mounted on an Iran Khodro truck that belonged to the same outfit. The paperwork indicating export to Afghanistan was impeccable. The truck usually did the route between Turkey and Iran, but trade sanctions imposed by the US had meant a decrease in that particular trade.

They had spent a few hours in Pardis before leaving on the truck. Located about seventeen kilometres north-east of Tehran, almost half the buildings in the area remained unfinished. Iran's government had attempted to build hundreds of affordable but austere flats in towers on barren land near the capital. Most of them remained unoccupied because of faulty water supply, only intermittent electricity and terrible connectivity. The name 'Pardis' meant paradise in Farsi but was anything but. The tower that Abbasi and Soroushpur chose was entirely empty, because parts of it had been destroyed by an earthquake in 2017. Spending even those few hours in Pardis had been difficult owing to the resident population of rats. Now they sat in the hot and muggy container, experiencing what it felt like to be trafficked like slaves in the twenty-first century.

Linda was willing to overlook everything that she had gone through. Just the sheer joy of seeing Jim alive and free was adequate compensation. Even in the hot and stuffy compartment, she refused to let go of his hand. Next to Jim was the canvas bag containing the earthen box of Hamzaa Dura and his research data on flash drives. It represented more than a decade of his efforts.

Linda updated Jim on everything that had happened since the time of his abduction to the present. She told him about how his police friend Greg Walters had helped, about how they had gone to the FBI and Fred Smith had entered the mix, about their visit to Kish Island and the assistance rendered by the cabby Firooz Jamshidi; how they had come into contact with Soroushpur and eventually Heydari and Abbasi. On his part, Jim contributed his own experiences with Javad Mosaffa—alias Ali Zamani, Asclepius, Ryan Parker, Abbas Khademhosseini, inside the IRGC coffin cell, and of his stint at Shahid Daru Pharma.

Dan listened to their conversation, contributing minimally. He knew that getting out of Iran would require a joint effort, but he also knew that he would eventually have to deliver Jim and his breakthrough research to Luke Miller. Ryan Parker was not a man that one could ignore. Mistress Lucinda was only one example of what the Asclepius gang were capable of doing to people who let them down.

The sound of his name being spoken broke Dan's reverie. 'Dan has been my pillar of strength,' Linda was telling Jim. 'When I decided to come to Iran to find you, he did not hesitate for even a moment in deciding to accompany me,' she said, directing a look of gratitude at Dan, who felt like however frauds feel. 'I would never have allowed you to come here on your own,' he said, keeping up the charade.

'I hadn't known so many people were after the same thing, ' said Jim. 'Thank you, my darling Linda for not giving up.' Turning to Dan, he said, 'You are my closest friend and confidant. I am so damned grateful to have you in my life, Dan.'

'I still don't understand why the Iranian government is after you,' said Linda, going off on another tack.

'They think that I have something they call the Athravan Star,' said Jim.

'What is that?' asked Linda.

'No idea,' said Jim. 'But they seem to think that my possession of the Hamzaa Dura somehow implies I have knowledge of it.'

'But if it is Zoroastrian, then how can the Iranian regime lay claim to it?' asked Linda.

'I can't be certain,' replied Jim. 'The Zoroastrians were systematically killed or converted over several centuries of Islamic rule. If something belonged to that persecuted community, would you say that today's regime should be entitled to it? Once, the whole of Iran belonged to the Zoroastrians. Today, the regime owns even those people and their religious artefacts and symbols.'

'But today's surviving Zoroastrians may feel entitled to it, right?' asked Linda.

Jim nodded. 'But Zarathustra taught us about humata, hukata and huvarastha. Good thoughts, good words and good deeds for all. Anything that can save the world must be for all of humanity, not just a select group.'

The container made its way across Iran's highways. Dan looked at the canvas bag in Jim's lap. He wondered how Jim would feel if he knew his best friend was about to betray him for the Kettering Prize. Until he recalled the earliest piece of advice he'd been doled out when he was really young. *There are two traps to avoid in life. One. Caring what they think. Two. Thinking that they care.*

68

'YOU ALLOWED HIM to escape,' said the Supreme Leader, glaring at Mosaffa. Mosaffa's right shoulder and arm were in plaster. The bullet had been removed from his shoulder, but his face was still swollen from the battering it had received from Abbasi.

'It is an unacceptable lapse,' chimed in Khademhosseini, sucking up to the Supreme Leader.

'Don't try playing that game with me,' said the Ayatollah whirling on him. 'You are the one who put Mosaffa in charge of this mission. You are the one who decided to pull out Jim Dastoor from DC1A and shift him into the premises of Shahid Daru. You are also the one who slipped up on security arrangements at Shahid Daru. Do not attempt to deflect the blame to your subordinate.'

Duly chastened, Khademhosseini shifted uncomfortably in his chair. 'We have had a chance to review the security video from the working cameras at Shahid Daru,' he said. 'One of the people who was involved in getting Jim Dastoor out was Heydari—Tariq Heydari.'

The Supreme Leader's frown deepened. Iran's system permitted elections, but political parties were necessarily required to operate within non-negotiable boundaries of the theological state. In most elections, almost half the candidates would be disqualified by Iran's Guardian Council, which vetted them for their suitability and their commitment to Iran's theological foundation. And Heydari was one of those troublemakers who remained entirely and permanently disqualified. This was the last straw.

Disillusioned with Iranian politics, Heydari had become part of the Mojahedin-e-Khalq—the MEK. The MEK had been founded in 1965 by leftist Iranian students who were opposed to the monarchy of Shah Mohammad Reza Pahlavi. They had allied with the pro-Khomeini forces during the Islamic Revolution. But the group was driven into exile after they mounted a failed attack on the Khomeini regime itself in 1981. Heydari had spent most of his life in and out of Iranian prisons, working unsuccessfully towards dislodging the very regime that he had earlier helped to instal.

'Find the scoundrel and ask the *Dadgah-ha-e Enqelab* to deal with him in the usual way,' commanded the Ayatollah.

'I'm already close to getting him,' replied Khademhosseini. 'His accomplice, a driver, was captured by us from Isfahan. He will break soon.'

'What about the other two Americans?' asked the Ayatollah.

'Jim Dastoor's wife Linda and his fellow director Dan Cohen,' Khademhosseini named them. 'Both came through Kish Island.'

'If they came through Kish, then someone in Kish must have helped them cross the Gulf,' said the cleric. 'Find out who that was. Who is this man with Heydari in the photograph?' he asked abruptly, looking at the photos taken by the surveillance cameras at Shahid Daru.

'Kaveh Abbasi, a dry fruits trader,' replied Khademhosseini. 'Lives in Fereshteh Street in the Elahieh district. Expensive part of town. We're digging into his business now to find out if he could be a front. So far, all his records seem to be in order.'

'He is no trader,' said Mosaffa. 'He is a trained commando. He would never have been able to overpower me had that not been the case.'

'He could be one of America's dogs who do their bidding for a bone tossed towards them,' said the Ayatollah. 'Dig deep and hard. This Abbasi could be their ticket out of Iran.'

'More surprising though is the presence of *this* man,' said Khademhosseini, showing an image of Soroushpur.

'Who is he?' barked the Supreme Leader.

'His name is Behrad Soroushpur,' replied Khademhosseini. 'We've had our eyes and ears on him for a while, but never considered him important enough. He operates from Ferdouzi Street in Tehran and runs a Zoroastrian charity group.'

'The Zoroastrians of this country already know their place,' said the Ayatollah. 'They are not even a speck on the Iranian landscape. Over centuries, Islam has shown them their place as subservient minorities that could be wiped off the face of Iran if we so wished.'

'Yes, rahbar-e mo'azzam,' replied Khademhosseini. 'But this charity also has an activist group associated with it. It is called the Gabrabad Action Front—or GAF.'

'Gabrabad?'

'The ghetto near Isfahan to which many Zoroastrians were deported in the sixteenth century,' said Khademhosseini. 'This group wishes to refresh memories of those perceived injustices.'

'Why have I never heard of this GAF group before?' asked the Supreme Leader, accusingly.

'Because we have never taken them seriously,' replied Khademhosseini. 'They neither have the will nor the resources to pose any danger to our system.'

'And yet this man Soroushpur is seen practically in cahoots with Jim Dastoor and his wife,' said the Ayatollah. 'In addition he is actively helping Heydari and this foreign agent Abbasi.'

'Which leads me to believe that Soroushpur could be after the same thing we are,' said Khademhosseini. 'The Athravan Star.'

'Why should he want it?' asked the rahbar-e mo'azzam.

'The Zoroastrians of Iran see it as their property rather than something that belongs to the Iranian state,' replied Khademhosseini. 'While we do not know exactly what it is or what it does, we do know that there are some references to it in Zoroastrian literature.'

'Really?' asked the Supreme Leader. 'Where?'

'It seems the Zoroastrians of Iran sent several religious directions to their Parsi cousins in India,' said Khademhosseini.

'These were known as rivayats. Apparently, one of these rivayats, an informal one that is not recorded, refers to it.'

The Ayatollah paused in thought, stroking his beard with one hand, while telling the turquoise prayer beads with the other. The other two men knew better than to say anything at such times. After what seemed like an interminable silence, Iran's imam spoke.

'Put out a notice at all airports, ports, railway stations, border posts, bus stations and toll booths,' he said. 'At the same time, find out if Abbasi has any connection to foreign intelligence agencies. Come back to me within twenty-four hours.'

'What about Soroushpur?' asked Khademhosseini.

'Don't act against any of his group right now,' said the Ayatollah. 'We should wait.'

'Why?'

'If you don't succeed in obtaining the Athravan Star, it is possible that he may,' said the Ayatollah, his eyes alight. 'In that event, we may not have to make too much of an effort to get it.'

69

ABBASI DROVE, WATCHING the road carefully. But after a few hours, his mind wandered. Being a Mossad agent based in Iran usually ended only one way. He wondered why he had accepted such a riskbound post. Was it a secret death wish?

He had been born in 1986 in post-revolution Iran as Bahram Amini in the city of Tabriz. His father had been a journalist with a reformist newspaper called *Salam*. The publication had a reputation for investigative pieces that often ruffled feathers in the establishment. His wife brought up Bahram and his younger brother with a mother's typical combination of strictness and indulgence. Bahram had to come up with good grades in school, because only then would his mother serve him his favourite *sholeh zard*—saffron rice pudding that he could savour on his tongue long after he'd licked the large bowl clean.

But then in 1999, pro-democracy demonstrations took place in Tehran University. This followed the closure of the *Salam* newspaper. Clashes with security forces led to six days of rioting and the arrest of more than a thousand students. Bahram's father was also rounded up and accused of having published a secret ministry report that had led to the demonstrations. He was interrogated for over a month before being released. But he came out of that interrogation a broken man. The family tried to rally around him, but it was of no use. He was physically, mentally and emotionally finished. He died from a heart attack at forty.

Bahram's mother kept the family afloat by taking on tailoring projects for women in the neighbourhood. She was good with the sewing machine and her skill ensured that the boys attended school and returned to food on the table. Little did Bahram know that she was bearing the burden of a terrible secret.

The skeleton in her cupboard was that her grandmother had been a Jewess. That particular ancestry was a liability in Iran, as indeed it was in many other parts of the Islamic world. The great Achaemenid king, Cyrus, had conquered Babylonia in 539 BCE defeating the Chaldean kings who had enslaved the Jews. Cyrus had released the Jews from captivity and permitted them to return to their homeland. But some of those Jews had settled in parts of Persia instead of returning to Judea. Their population grew during Sassanian times, but the arrival of Islam changed everything. Like the Zoroastrians, the Jews of Persia would only be oppressed and persecuted thereafter.

Their position improved under Reza Shah Pahlavi. The Shah's emancipated Jews played a vital role in reviving the Iranian economy. On the eve of the Islamic Revolution of 1979, around 80,000 Jews lived in Iran. After the revolution, tens of thousands fled, leaving behind their fabulous properties and possessions. The Jewish population dwindled to a tenth of that number soon after that.

Bahram's family were practising Shiites, notwithstanding the Jewish connection. Over the years, his mother built on her reputation as a quality seamstress. Alas, one of her customers was a Jewish woman whose husband was accused of conspiring with 'Zionists'. Virtually everyone the couple had been in touch with was rounded up by the authorities. This was in spite of the Ayatollah having claimed that 'we recognise our Jews as separate from those godless, bloodsucking Zionists of Israel'. Bahram's mother was also held. She was released a few days later, but the consequences of her arrest were severe on her business. Regular customers now shied away from her services.

Still in his teens, Bahram had been forced to abandon all hope of college. He needed to support not only himself but also his mother and younger brother. He took to selling falafel sandwiches from a cart in Tabriz. The takings weren't much but just sufficient to support his family. His maternal aunt, who also had Jewish antecedents, had foolishly decided to marry a Jewish carpet trader in Tehran. This brought her own ancestry into focus, quite unnecessarily. But she loved her nephew, cocooning Bahram in her love. She did it carefully though, aware of the risks that her proximity would pose for Bahram and his immediate family.

One day, when he was hard at work assembling chickpea dumplings on a bed of cabbage, vegetables and pickles, an elderly customer stopped by. He tried the sandwich and conveyed his appreciation to Bahram. Thereafter, he became a regular at Bahram's stall. Not a day went by when he would not drop in for a sandwich and leave him a generous tip. Young Bahram did not know it at the time, but his customer was one of the oldest recruiters for Mossad inside Iran. Bahram was unaware that the Israeli agency had an entire dossier on him. The circumstances of his father's arrest and death coupled with his mother's partially Jewish ancestry made him a prime target for recruitment.

'How would you like to earn a few hundred times of what you presently make?' his patron asked him one day. 'I'm listening,' said Bahram. They had sipped tea together and the old man had explained how the Islamic regime was systematically targeting everyone who did not fit in with their plans, including Sunni Muslims, Zoroastrians and Jews.

'I should turn you in to the police,' Bahram told the man, but for some inexplicable reason he did not do it. That day when he returned home, he heard the news that his mother and younger brother had been in a road accident. A truck had missed the stop sign and run them over. His mother had died instantly, and his brother was battling for his life in Sina University Hospital. He gave up the fight three days later.

With nothing left to lose, Bahram was waiting when his Mossad recruiter showed up again. He was whisked off to the Israeli town of Herzliya via Turkey. In Herzliya, he was taken to an academy called the Midrasha. Here, he was subjected to various psychological and aptitude tests. Then he was taught the science of intelligence gathering, self-defence, cultivating sources, clandestine communication, recruiting other agents, technology hacks, languages—and assassination. His training culminated with a stint at Camp Moshe Dayan near Tel Aviv.

Several years later, he was a fully trained *katsa*—field intelligence officer—of the Mossad. Just as quietly as he had left Iran, he entered the country in the dead of the night. Provided to him was an entirely new persona. Bahram Amini was dead. And Kaveh Abbasi was born.

One of his first assignments had been called Operation Stanza. Under Abbasi's command, Iran's Natanz nuclear power plant was hit by a sophisticated cyber-attack. An operation that required close cooperation between several countries, it involved introducing a Stuxnet worm which would impede the working of the plant's centrifuges and impair them over time. Alas, there was a leak from one of the American operatives. It resulted in Abbasi's deputy being shot dead in Frankfurt. The operation was successful, but Abbasi never forgave himself for an error that was not his.

From that day on, Abbasi decided to never trust anyone.

70

A STRANGE SILENCE pervaded even as a crowd of three hundred gathered that Sunday morning a little before sunrise in Honarmandan Park in Tehran. Originally a garden and mansion of one of the Qajar princes, the park was now home to the Iranian Artists Forum, Iranshahr Theater, a library, a vegetarian restaurant, a football field and basketball court. Honarmandan Park symbolised leisure in a carefree environment. But today, the atmosphere and the setting were remarkably different from the usual scenes at the park.

Early in the morning a few police cars had pulled up. These were followed by a massive Atlas construction crane that rolled into position behind the police vehicles. A while later, a camera crew had set up their equipment. Policemen had begun erecting temporary barriers using scaffolding. Then the crowds had begun to arrive. The main attraction arrived a half-hour later, surrounded by a posse of policemen. By then the crowd at Honarmandan had been anxiously waiting for over an hour.

Today Honarmandan was not going to be celebrating art or sports, or any of the joyous aspects of life it was devoted to. Instead, in a macabre spectacle, it was going to enjoy death. A condemned man stood motionless in front of two police trucks. Just above him hovered a noose from the arm of an extendable crane. The execution team, clad in black bomber jackets and balaclavas, were intently checking the remote controls they would use to hang the man. From behind the makeshift barrier, the gathering jostled for vantage. 'Let's cross over to the other end,' one spectator whispered to his wife excitedly, drawing her attention to the spot where cameras of the Islamic Republic of Iran Broadcasting had been set up. 'I think that our view will be better from there.' There were several children in the crowd too, eagerly tripping after their parents.

The previous day, the convict's trial had lasted for barely a few minutes in the Dadgah-ha-e-Enqelab, the Islamic Revolutionary Court. The proceedings had been held behind closed doors and a single judge had decided his fate. The 'convict' had been tough to break. It had taken electric shocks, floggings, waterboarding and sodomising to extract a confession from him and his accomplice. The collaborator had been let off for assisting in the capture of their target. Death by hanging was the verdict and there was no appeal mechanism. Iran carried out around 250 executions each year. A death sentence could be handed down not only for crimes as major as murder or kidnapping, but also for adultery, apostasy, homosexuality, drinking alcohol, consuming drugs, or for political opposition. For petty theft, convicts could have their fingers amputated, leaving only the thumb and palm intact. Iran had the distinction of being the second-highest executioner in the world after China.

Hanging was the most common method of capital punishment in Iran. But this was not done with a simple drop, where death could come quickly from a snapped neck. Instead, a construction crane was put to use. The condemned individual would be hoisted up by a crane which would swing him off the ground, allowing him to be strangled in a laborious and agonising way by his restraining noose. Crowds were always encouraged to watch, and some executions were televised to serve as an example to others. Usually, the families of the convicts were forced to attend. Often, they even had to bear the costs of the exercise.

As the sun rose in the east of Tehran, the executioners led the convict, wearing a highly visible red T-shirt, to the crane. His head had been shaved in prison and he was blindfolded and handcuffed. The prisoner stayed quiet, neither crying, nor begging for his life. A representative of Iran's judiciary described the crime and read out the verdict for all the spectators present and on television. The noose was placed around his neck, and he was lifted by the crane. His struggle was evident for all to see as his body swung high above the crowd while his legs flapped about; his sphincter muscles relaxed, and his bowels voided, as seen in his wet and stained shalwar. He died silently, even as some in the crowd shouted in protest, some jeered and laughed, while others used phone cameras to record the scene.

On a separate monitor located in Ahvaz, Khademhosseini watched the hanging as he lit up his first Farvardin of the day. He exhaled with a sigh of satisfaction, not only from the smoke but also from the fact that another troublemaker had been brought to book. Hopefully, the hanging would make the Supreme Leader happy. It had required a massive dragnet to capture the convict in the first place, and liberal use of torture to get him to open his mouth.

Tariq Heydari deserved to die. Khademhosseini stubbed out his cigarette just as the life was snuffed out of Heydari.

71

I WAS SO glad to be in Khandala with Cecile. The next morning, I woke early and enjoyed my morning tea in the pleasant chill of the front lawns of her house. A gentle mist that had rolled in through the hills had covered the grass in a blanket of cottonwool. I checked with the staff and was told that Cecile had woken much earlier to take her dogs for a morning walk. When she returned, we chatted over breakfast in the dining room. I brought up the matter of Alexander having set fire to Persepolis.

'History was mistaken,' replied Cecile. 'Alexander loved Persian culture. In fact, Alexander admired Cyrus, having read Xenophon's Cyropaedia, *which narrated the story of Cyrus's fearlessness in war and his outstanding administrative capacity as king.'*

Cecile went on to tell me that the tomb of Cyrus lay in the city of Pasargadae. Its epitaph read, 'O man, whoever you are and wherever you come from, I am Cyrus who won the Persians their empire. Do not therefore begrudge me this bit of earth that covers my bones.' Unfortunately, Cyrus's tomb had been looted by the time Alexander reached there. Alexander was furious and put the magi guardians of the tomb on trial. He even ordered its restoration at state cost.

There was simply no reason for Alexander to burn the fabulous Persepolis, a city that now belonged to him. After all, it was a city that symbolised the culture of Cyrus, someone whom Alexander respected tremendously. And Thais, the courtesan from Athens credited as the instigator of the inferno, was a mere hetaira, the equivalent of a sophisticated courtesan whose talents included singing, poetry, storytelling, and the erotic arts. While it is true that Alexander enjoyed her company, there was nothing to suggest that he would be influenced by her to that extent. She was Ptolemy's mistress, not Alexander's. In addition, Alexander's trusted Macedonian general, Parmenion, vociferously argued against the idea of destroying Persepolis.

Alexander had held lavish games to mark his victory over the Persians. He offered up splendid sacrifices to the gods and entertained his allies generously. It is also true that during the feasts, intoxication had taken on the proportions of mass hysteria. So it is more likely that the great fire caught the Macedonians by surprise.

'The Persepolis archives contained secrets that had been passed down over generations from Zarathustra to his magi,' explained Cecile. 'The magi could not allow these secrets to pass into the hands of the invader Alexander. After all, many portions of the original Gathas composed by Zarathustra were also stored in special scrolls of the archives. The choice was a difficult one.'

Apparently, the magi lit a sacred fire to perform a yasna and kept pouring butter until the flames leapt to the woodwork and set the entire library ablaze. From there, the fire spread to the rest of the complex. Alexander and his army were forced to abandon the magnificent Persepolis. It was a pyrrhic victory.

Alexander was angry. The most valuable secrets of Persepolis—those of the Zoroastrian magi—had burned to ashes. But the men that guarded those secrets, the magi themselves, had survived. And so also had an earthen box that had been entrusted to the magi by Zarathustra. And a sacred text that was only conveyed orally.

This was a gigantic loss of the amassed knowledge and culture of Zoroastrian Persia. Theological texts of early Zoroastrianism, inscribed on goatskin parchment, were obliterated. Countless jars containing potions and potent remedies had smashed to fragments. So had priceless tapestries, furniture, paintings and artefacts. Most of the cuneiform tablets of clay that contained the secrets of the magi were also destroyed. Some of the tablets buried under the rubble were found later, but turned out to contain mere administrative records of the city.

'Alexander died young, at age thirty-three. He had married a Bactrian princess called Roxanne,' said Cecile. 'In Afghanistan lies a place called Cheshm-e-Shafa or the City of Infidels. That is purportedly the place where Alexander married Roxanne.'

Cecile told me that after Alexander's death there was a struggle for supremacy between his generals. The Achaemenid territories fell into the hands of Seleucus I Nicator. For a brief period, Persia became a Hellenistic state called the Seleucid Empire. At its zenith, the Seleucid Empire spanned Persia, Anatolia, the Levant, Mesopotamia, and the regions that are now represented by Kuwait, Afghanistan and parts of Turkmenistan. It was one of the successors of Seleucus I who would offer three gifts—not four—of gold, frankincense and myrrh to Apollo at the temple in Miletus.

In the meantime, back in India, the great Chandragupta Maurya had consolidated his hold on the Mauryan Empire and wrested the Punjab back from the Greek satraps of the region. When Seleucus marched towards the Indus, he was challenged by Chandragupta's mighty force of 600,000 men and 9000 war elephants. Eventually Seleucus offered his daughter in marriage to Chandragupta and a treaty was formalised through which Chandragupta gained control of the lands to the west of the Indus, including the Hindu Kush, Afghanistan and Baluchistan.

But then a tribe from the north-east overthrew the Graeco-Macedonian rulers and established an empire that was as vast as that of Cyrus. They were known as the Parthians and were a stepping-stone in the creation of a Zoroastrian empire.

72

'THE PARTHIANS WERE Zoroastrians, but they permitted their subjects freedom of worship,' said Cecile. 'They were constantly at war with the Romans who never really took to Zoroastrianism. The Romans were quite happy to worship Mitra, one of the Rigvedic gods, instead of Ahura Mazda. Under the Parthians, a written record of the conversations between Zarathustra and Ahura Mazda was initiated, but it would only come to fruition during the Sassanian epoch, five centuries later.'

'And that was the zenith of Zoroastrianism?' I asked.

'As it turned out, the Sassanian Empire would be the last pre-Islamic Persian Empire,' replied Cecile. 'It was established in 224 CE by Ardeshir I and lasted until 651 CE, when it was overthrown by the Arabs of the Rashidun Caliphate. But the four centuries of the Sassanian Empire undoubtedly constituted the zenith of Zoroastrian culture in Persia.'

The Sassanians were conservative Zoroastrians and undertook codification of the religion. A hierarchy of priestly power was established. Zoroastrianism was declared the state religion and conversions to the faith were undertaken to neutralise Christian proselytising. 'Unlike the Parsis of India, the Sassanians of Persia considered Zoroastrianism to be a religion that one could be converted to without necessarily being born into it,' related Cecile, to my surprised edification.

She allowed herself a moment of wistfulness. 'I wish the Parsis had taken this into account when considering Rustom's application for me to join the faith.' It was evident that the issue secretly rankled with her.

'What about minorities?' I asked, to deflect her sadness.

'Oh, Sassanian rulers tolerated religious minorities such as Jews, Christians and Manichaeans. It was nothing like the theological state based on Islam that would follow.'

'What about the Romans?' I asked. 'Wouldn't they have tried to topple the Sassanians?'

'The Sassanian Empire was the only counterweight to the Roman Empire,' said Cecile. 'They not only maintained good relations with China's Tang dynasty but also with several Indian kingdoms where their exports were highly valued. This was the reason why Jadi Rana was familiar with Zoroastrian merchants even before they arrived seeking sanctuary in Gujarat. It was *also the reason why the port of Hormuz was familiar to Indian and Chinese traders.'*

The first Sassanian king, Ardeshir I, paid particular attention to two key issues: centralising state power and adopting Zoroastrianism as a state religion. His successor, Shapur I, would be remembered for neutralising the Roman Empire by capturing their emperor, Valerian. He also established the Academy of Gundeshapur, that contained his name. And it was under the next great Sassanian king, Shapur II, that Zoroastrian scriptures would eventually be committed to written text.

'But it was undoubtedly Kusrow I, the king who ruled for five decades of the sixth century CE, *who would go down in history as the ideal king,' said Cecile. The Persian tax reforms undertaken under Kusrow enriched the state's treasury and diluted the power of local chieftains and lords. Under him, the Persian military was also reorganised. The forces were now divided into four groups, each with a commanding general so that the reaction time to border threats could be reduced. This was deemed necessary owing to the fact that the Sassanians were threatened by Romans to the west, Huns to the east and Arabs to the south.*

The crowning glory of Kusrow's achievements was the Academy of Gundeshapur which he supported more than any other monarch. It became one of the world's most important centres of learning. Kusrow liberally gave sanctuary to Greek philosophers and Nestorian Christians who were fleeing persecution by the Byzantine Romans. Many of these refugees undertook the translation of Greek and Syriac texts to Pahlavi. 'Kusrow even sent the Persian physician Borzuya to invite Indian and Chinese scholars to Gundeshapur,' said Cecile.

'Borzuya?' I asked. 'Why does that name sound familiar?'

'Borzuya was a Persian physician who travelled from Kusrow's court to Kashmir in search of an elixir that could revive the dead,' replied Cecile. 'Upon reaching Kashmir, he searched for the elixir, but was unsuccessful. It was then that he was directed to a sage called Bhargava. The sage set Borzuya straight. Apparently, the sage asked Borzuya, "When the ignorant can be made wise, of what use is it to bring the dead to life?" He presented Borzuya with a Sanskrit book called the Five Treatises. Borzuya returned to Persia and translated the book into Pahlavi in the sixth century. His Pahlavi version is sadly lost, but a translation into Arabic by Ibn al-Muqaffa survives. Thus, the academy at Gundeshapur soon became a repository of translated works on astronomy, philosophy, mathematics and medicine.'

It was during Sassanian times that the Zoroastrian written texts appeared, many previous versions having been lost during the fire of Persepolis. These texts in aggregate were known as the Avesta. The Avesta consisted of four books or volumes: the Yasna, the book of hymns; the Yashta, the book of prayers; the Visparatu, the book of righteousness; and the Vidaevadata, or the book of laws. The most important of these books was the Yasna which is composed of seventy-two chapters. Of these, seventeen had been sung by Zarathustra himself and were known as the Gathas. The Gathas were thus embedded in the Yasna, much like the Bhagavad Gita is embedded in the Mahabharata. During Sassanian times, the Avesta was also translated into Pahlavi.

But all that was about to change.

73

CECILE AND I walked out of the dining room to stroll in the garden. The mist had cleared, and the distinctive shape of Duke's Nose was visible in the distance. Cecile's dogs were basking in the winter sun, oblivious to our wanderings.

'Did you know that it was during Parthian and Sassanian times that covered fire temples came into being?' asked Cecile, looking at the oddly shaped mountain in the distance. I had trekked up Duke's Nose on an earlier trip. 'Until then, Zoroastrian priests had always considered fire and water as agents of ritual purity and had performed their yasnas in raised areas open to the sky. They usually climbed steps to light their fires in the open courtyards of hilltop temples. Of course, this tradition was a continuation of what were known as the "Three Great Fires", although no one knew exactly where they were.'

From what I could gather, much of the information about these three great fires had been lost down the ages, but it was believed that they were located at places known as Adur Burzen-Mihr, Adur Farnbag and Adur Gushnasp. In fact, the three fires went so far back in antiquity that no one really knew if they had existed at all. In modern times, scholars had attempted to identify the locations of these three great fires. Various places in Khorasan, Balkh, Khwarezm and Azerbaijan were hypothesised to be the sites. But it was unclear whether these fires had come from somewhere else.

Everything great about the Sassanian Empire would soon collapse. But the magi and their secrets would remain.

'I was reading about the Sassanian Empire last night,' I told my grandmother. 'I found it ironic that the very kings who codified the texts, and made Zoroastrianism into a powerful state religion, also presided over its downfall.'

'True,' replied Cecile, 'but the empire had become weak from within. Constant wars with Roman Byzantium had become a huge drain on the treasury. The last Sassanian king, Yazdgerd III, was barely a child of eight when he ascended the throne in 632 CE. That was the same year that Mohammad, Islam's prophet, died. Yazdgerd simply did not have the maturity to control many of the governors who had already declared their independence.'

'And the Arabs saw that as an opportunity?' I asked. The idea of an eight-year-old monarch managing a vast empire seemed ludicrous.

Cecile nodded. 'Even before the ascension of Yazdgerd, Mohammad had sent several letters to rulers far and wide, urging them to convert to Islam and to bow to the word of Allah. These letters were delivered by his emissaries to Persia, Byzantium, Ethiopia, Egypt and Yemen.'

'And they submitted to his will?' I asked.

'Some did,' replied Cecile. 'The letter that Mohammad sent to Persia arrived during the reign of Kusrow II, Yazdgerd's grandfather.'

She walked through the french windows into the library from the garden. I followed her. Cecile made her way to a bookcase and pulled out a volume. It was an English translation of a book called Tabaqat-i-Kubra. 'Read this passage,' she said, pointing to the open page and paragraph. I did and was surprised at my own angry reaction.

In the name of Allah, the Beneficent, the Merciful,

From Mohammad, the Messenger of Allah, to the great Kusrow of Iran.

Peace be upon him, who seeks truth and expresses belief in Allah and in His Prophet

And testifies that there is no God but Allah and that He has no partner

And who believes that Mohammad is His servant and Prophet.

Under the Command of Allah, I invite you to Him.

He has sent me for the guidance of all people so that I may warn them of His wrath

And may present the unbelievers with an ultimatum.

Embrace Islam so that you may remain safe.

And if you refuse to accept Islam, you will be responsible for the sins of the magi.

'The sins of the magi,' Cecile almost spat out the words. 'Of course, Kusrow destroyed the letter. The Persian Empire was too large and powerful to take the message seriously. Mohammad was seen as an upstart by the mighty Persians in those days.' Cecile explained that the rise of Islamic power in the Arabian Peninsula coincided with immense social, political, military and economic weaknesses in the Sassanian Empire. The empire had waged war for years against Byzantium. Both human and capital resources had been depleted substantially. Taxes had become so heavy, most commoners were unable to pay. Wars had destroyed the viability of otherwise vibrant trade routes.

After Kusrow, ten new claimants to the throne were anointed in turn within a matter of just four years. Chaos prevailed.

To make matters worse for the Persians, Mohammad had just concluded a treaty with his tribal archenemies in Mecca. Relative peace within Arabia meant that he could turn his attention to his neighbourhood.

The Sassanian Empire had actually been a coalition made by the Sassanian monarch and Parthian kings. Now the Parthian satraps were openly declaring their independence. Some of the more influential ones even made peace with the Arabs. After Mecca fell to Mohammad in 630 CE, the Persian governor at Sanaa converted to Islam. In return, Mohammad appointed him as his proxy in Yemen. Similarly, the Marzaban in Bahrain also adopted Islam, as did the Sassanian chief in Oman.

'What happened then?' I asked.

'Mohammad died in 632 CE and Abu Bakr became the first caliph,' replied Cecile. 'His first year was spent in consolidating his hold over the Arabian Peninsula. Then he turned his attention to Persia. A few years later, Abu Bakr attacked. He sent his best general, Khalid ibn Walid, to conquer Mesopotamia, which is present-day Iraq.'

Islam was about to change everything in Persia.

74

'OVER THE NEXT decade, most of the key urban centres of Persia were brought under Muslim rule,' said Cecile. 'When Arab militia made their first forays into Sassanian lands, Yazdgerd did not see them as the sinister threat that they were. In fact, the Persian army was not even dispatched, because Yazdgerd *was convinced by his councillors that these were minor attacks by nomadic tribesmen. Without speedy and effective resistance, the Arab forces had ample time to consolidate.'*

As history records, in 637 CE, in the plains of al-Qadisiyyah, a Muslim army under the next caliph, Umar, vanquished a bigger Persian force commanded by their general, Rostam Farrokhzad. The Persian army faced fundamental problems. Their heavy cavalry had proved successful when battling the legions of Byzantium, but it was too sluggish to effectively respond to the agility of Arab cavalry and archers. The Persians were routed.

The Arabs then attacked the Sassanian capital, Ctesiphon, near present-day Baghdad, and Yazdgerd fled. 'Unfortunately, he also left behind a vast cache of the empire's treasury,' said Cecile. 'As a result, the Arabs not only captured the Persian capital city but also seized control over the financial resources of the Sassanian Empire.'

'What happened to Yazdgerd?' I asked.

'He was eventually assassinated,' replied Cecile. 'A coalition of Sassanian governors tried to stop the Arab advance, but they were defeated at the Battle of Nahavand, and the Sassanian Empire fell to the Arabs. Ironically, the Battle of Nahavand set in motion a series of events that would eventually take Caliph Umar's life.'

'How?' I asked her. 'Umar was master of the empire!'

'That story started with someone called Piruz Nahavandi,' said Cecile. 'Piruz had been born into Zoroastrian royal lineage. After the Battle of Nahavand, the people of Nahavand and the nearby city of Hamadan were massacred by the attacking Muslims. Women were raped and countless taken *captive as slaves. Piruz too was captured and became a slave.' I visualised hundreds of shackled slaves being dragged away by the marauding Muslim armies.*

'The new name given to Piruz by his Muslim masters was Abu Lulu,' said Cecile. 'Lulu felt humiliated by the injustices perpetrated by the Arabs on his Persian brethren. He was angry about the exorbitant taxes being charged by the Muslim rulers in conquered territories. He made several representations, but his requests fell on deaf years. That's when he decided to take matters into his own hands.'

'What could a slave do?' I asked.

'Quite a lot, as it happened,' retorted Cecile with spirit. 'His first task was to get inside Medina. Muslims did not allow non-Arabs to reside in Medina, so Lulu offered his services as a carpenter and paid two dirhams a day to an Arab to act as his owner. The Arab then "sold" Lulu to Caliph Umar. This gave Lulu access to his target.'

'And then?'

'Lulu hid a two-headed dagger in his robe,' said Cecile. 'This was a special dagger, the grip of which was in the middle of two outward pointing blades. He then holed up in a corner of the Al-Masjid al-Nabawi, the primary mosque of Medina, waiting for the right moment. Attacking Umar while he was leading the morning prayers, Lulu managed to stab him six times in the stomach.'

'Umar died?' I asked, a little foolishly.

'Three days later,' she said, with satisfaction. 'Lulu tried to flee, but he was surrounded by Umar's followers. He wounded several others before eventually killing himself. Caliph Umar had won Persia, and then lost his life to it. That is the nature of

Persia. It propels rulers to dizzying heights—before smashing them to the ground.'

Cecile looked at me a little ruefully. 'Some Persian cities rose in rebellion by assassinating their newly appointed Arab governors or mounting surprise attacks on Arab garrisons, but these were brutally put down,' she said. 'The remaining chiefs fought vigorously against the invading Arabs, but it was a lost battle. By 651 CE, most of the cities and towns had come under Arab rule.'

As Cecile explained, the Muslim invasion of Persia not only destroyed Zoroastrianism but also fractured Islam itself. A permanent rupture in Islam resulted in a bitter Sunni-Shia rivalry over the next thirteen centuries. In Persia, the Safavid dynasty eventually transformed the land from a Sunni dominion to a Shia stronghold.

'I have never really understood this rivalry between Sunnis and Shias,' I said.

Cecile knew the answer to that one. 'When Mohammad died, most of his followers felt that the inner circle of Islam's adherents should get to choose his successor,' replied Cecile. 'But a minority felt that someone from Mohammad's family should succeed him. This minority group advocated that Ali—Mohammad's cousin and son-in-law—should be the rightful heir. This group came to be known as "Shiat Ali" or the followers of Ali—in short, "Shia".'

'I believe there was a battle over the succession,' I prompted her.

'Yes,' replied Cecile. 'As the story played out, the majority who believed in tradition—or sunna—won. They came to be known as the Sunnis and they installed Mohammad's close friend and confidant Abu Bakr, as caliph. But the Shias were unhappy with this.'

'What happened to Ali?'

'Eventually, he did become the fourth caliph, but only after two before him had been assassinated,' said Cecile. 'But Ali too was killed at the Great Mosque of Kufa—in today's Iraq—in 661 CE, as the vicious power tussle between the Sunni and Shia factions continued. The tussle was not about Mohammad's religious legacy alone. Conquered lands under Muslim domination now provided a rich in-flow of taxes and tributes.'

At its core, this was a battle over inheritance of wealth, not faith.

75

CECILE WENT TO the terrace, ringed with potted plants, which had been one of my grandfather Rustom's favourite spots. He used to love to sit on the swing there, staring out at the hills. Cecile and I sat on its wide, wrought-iron seat, gently rocking ourselves. Neither of us wanted to break away from the subject of our extended conversation—although it was my grandmother, of course, who was qualified to do all the talking, with me as the avid listener.

'The Shias mark Muharram, which has some connection to Persia,' I said. 'What is that?'

'In 681 CE, Ali's son Hussein commandeered a band of seventy-two followers to the Persian city of Karbala,' replied Cecile. 'It was a bid to escape the assassins sent to kill him by

Caliph Yazid of the Umayyad dynasty. Hussein was attacked on the way, a ten-day battle ensued, and eventually, he was decapitated. His head was carried to Damascus as a tribute to Yazid. Thereafter, his martyrdom would be marked each year by the Shias on the tenth day of Muharram, the first month in the Islamic calendar.'

'Tenth day?' I asked.

'It's also called Ashura,' said Cecile. 'The tenth day is very important in many contexts. But that's a discussion for another time.'

But whatever may have been the internecine battles within Islam, apparently they did not affect the Arab stranglehold over Persia. I remarked, 'There are scholars who say that the process of Islamisation was gradual, that most Zoroastrians continued to live under their new masters by simply paying the jizya, tax.'

'Nonsense!' scoffed Cecile. 'The Arabs not only desired Persia's wealth, they also wanted to add thousands of converts to Islam. To impose the new religion, the old one had first to be destroyed. The obvious targets were libraries, schools and centres of learning. The Sassanian capital, Ctesiphon, contained the largest Zoroastrian library. When the Arab commander saw it, he asked for instructions from the caliph. His master wrote back, "If the books contradict the Qur'an, they are blasphemous. And if they are in agreement with the Qur'an, then they are unnecessary." The library was destroyed, and generations of writings were burned.'

'No books survived?' I asked.

'The books that survived the fire were eventually dumped in the Euphrates,' replied Cecile. 'Similar treatment was meted out at the Academy of Gundeshapur that had been so lovingly nurtured by Kusrow I. Some of the most powerful chants and potions were lost. The beautiful Pahlavi translation by Borzuya of the Five Treatises was also lost. Other libraries in Ray and Khorasan met the same fate.'

'Burning books is not the same as killing people,' I countered.

There was an unusual flash of anger in Cecile's eyes. 'Learned people—scholars, historians, writers and magi—were massacred so that there would be little chance for Zoroastrian teachings to survive, Jimmy! Muhallab, governor of Khorasan, vowed that if he triumphed over the Persians, he would run the flourmills with the blood of his victims so that they could feast on that bloody bread. He fulfilled that promise. Then on the way to Mazandaran ...'

'That sounds familiar, too,' I interjected.

'Mazandaran is an Iranian province located along the southern coast of the Caspian Sea,' Cecile jogged my memory—poor as it was—of geography. 'One of the towns there is Sari. Some of the Zoroastrians who fled to India were from Sari and they called a city in Gujarat Navsari, or the new Sari.'

'Ah, yes, I remember the connection now,' I said. 'You were talking about Muhallab on his way to Mazandaran?'

'Muhallab ordered 12,000 captives to be hanged along the sides of the road so that the corpses would provide a befitting welcome to his army,' said Cecile.

'But all wars are brutal,' I argued, playing devil's advocate to the hilt.

'Oh, Jimmy,' sighed Cecile, catching on to what I was really upto—as she did to my pranks as a child. 'One of the battles,' she carried on, after a reproving glare, 'is called the Battle of Jelovala. The word "jelovala" means "covered". The reason *for choosing that name is because 100,000 bodies of the dead eventually "covered" the desert. Over 130,000 women and children were enslaved and sold in the markets of Mecca and Medina. The city of Estakhr fought valiantly against the Arab invaders, but eventually, all its residents were slaughtered. After the Battle of Alis, the commander Khalid ibn Walid oversaw the decapitation of 40,000 prisoners of war. Hundreds of fire temples were redeployed as mosques … I could go on and on … The brutalities that were, and are, committed in the name of religion!'*

'Redeployment of fire temples?' I asked. 'How did that work?'

'Fire temples usually had, and have, four axial arch openings,' replied Cecile. 'These temples could quite easily be turned into mosques by simply adding a prayer niche—known as a mihrab—to the arch nearest to the direction of Mecca.'

Grandmother's pale face had flushed red, and it was evident that my parrying her arguments had reawaken old resentments. She took a deep breath. 'It is fashionable these days to ignore history in order to preserve the peace between faiths,' she said. 'And I am all for peace and interfaith understanding. But that process must start with recognising what happened, not whitewashing it. Forced conversions did happen; destruction of Zoroastrian places of worship did happen. Redeployment of fire temples as mosques did happen. Identification of Zoroastrians as polluted beings, najis, did happen. Transformation of Zoroastrians into beggars by snatching away inheritance rights did happen. The burning of Zoroastrian scriptures did happen. Compulsory humiliation of those paying jizya did happen.' She ran out of breath.

Just like what followed thousands of years ago: Two Centuries of Silence.

76

UP IN FRONT, in the driver's cabin, Abbasi looked at his watch. They had been on the road for about seven hours. He knew that it would be another six before they reached Islam Qala, the border post that facilitated trade between Iran and Afghanistan.

Some 250 trucks crossed the Iran–Afghanistan border through the checkpost at Islam Qala each day. It was one of the busiest border crossings that generated almost a hundred million dollars each year for the Afghan exchequer. The sheer number of trucks passing through would make Abbasi's vehicle ubiquitous. Quite obviously, it was the safest option.

'Which is the next town on our route?' asked Soroushpur.

'Sabzevar,' replied Abbasi. Then he cursed under his breath as he pressed the intercom button to communicate with Linda at the back. 'There's a roadblock up ahead before Sabzevar,' he said. 'I can deal with trade checkpoints, but I fear that this barrier may be in your honour.'

'What should we do?' asked Linda, surprisingly calm. She had been hoping that they would take the Sabzevar route because that would mean passing through Neyshabur, the birthplace of her favourite poet, Omar Khayyam. *Be happy for this moment. This moment is your life.*

'We have the option of bypassing Sabzevar and turning right into Route 87,' said Abbasi.

'Let me think,' said Linda. 'You mentioned Islam Qala as the primary border crossing. That means that there are other crossings too, right?'

'The other two crossings from Iran into Afghanistan are Nimruz and Farah, but both these would bring us square into Taliban territory,' replied Abbasi. 'Not a good idea given that we have three Americans on board.'

'Is Islam Qala safe?' asked Linda.

'Safer than the others,' replied Abbasi. 'It's the easiest crossing point given the sheer volume of vehicles. Also, Shindand Airbase—controlled jointly by America and NATO—is located just 120 kilometres from the border. It is our best bet.'

'But how do we get to Islam Qala if Route 44 is closed?' asked Linda.

'We turn right into Route 87, bypassing Sabzevar, travel south towards Kashmar and then drive north-east towards Islam Qala. It will add a few hours to our travel time, but it can be done.'

'Kashmar,' repeated Linda. 'I wonder why that name rings a bell.' She paused in thought. 'Got it ... the Cypress of Kashmar!'

'What's that?' asked Dan.

'It was an ancient cypress tree,' replied Linda. 'It is believed that the tree was planted by Zarathustra outside the very first fire temple consecrated there by his patron, King Vishtaspa. Although the tree lived for over two thousand years, it was eventually chopped down by an Abbasid caliph for his palace at Samarra.'

'You must be referring to Abarkuh,' countered Jim. 'The Cypress of Abarkuh is said to be around four thousand years old. Supposedly, it was planted by Zarathustra.'

'No,' argued Linda, her scholarly work determining itself. 'The one in Kashmar was chopped down so there's no question of seeing it again. The species of that tree was *Cupressus cashmeriana*. The one in Abarkuh survives but is a type of *Cupressus sempervirens*.'

Soroushpur heard the discussion on the intercom. The expression on his face was unchanged, but a multitude of conflicting thoughts were running through his head. *If Dastoor's ancestors fled Iran to settle in India, then who are the real Zoroastrian patriots—the ones who fled or the ones who stayed on? Is Jim in possession of the Athravan Star? Or does he know what and where it is? How is the box in his custody related to the Athravan Star? Could other treasures have also been spirited away? What is so important about the substance Jim is protecting so fiercely that everyone seems eager to get at it?*

His thoughts were broken by Abbasi's voice. 'We won't stop at Kashmar,' Abbasi was saying over the intercom to Linda. 'We'll just pass through it. I would like us to reach Islam Qala as soon as possible. The three of you at the back will remain hidden, but Soroushpur and I will have to show our route pass. In most circumstances, that should be sufficient to get us through without any additional visa requirements.'

There were a few hundred vehicles waiting in line ahead of their truck. He quickly took the exit towards Kashmar. He was hoping that there would not be another checkpost before Islam Qala. And if that were the case, he hoped that the container deception would be enough to see them through.

'Wasn't there a fire temple in Kashmar?' asked Jim.

'Yes,' replied Linda. 'But neither that particular fire temple nor the tree exist. The temple built by Vishtaspa was called Adur Burzen-Mihr. But we do not know the spot. There is another fire temple close by called Atashgah Castle, but that was built much later.'

'There was something called the *Three Great Fires*, right?' asked Jim.

'There was,' confirmed Linda. 'Their individual names were Adur Burzen-Mihr, Adur Farnbag and Adur Gushnasp. But no one knows the exact locations. Various places nearby— we're in Khorasan now, right?—as well as Khwarezm, Balkh and Azerbaijan have been suggested as possible sites, but no one truly knows. In fact, one wonders whether they even existed.'

Abbasi interrupted over the intercom. 'This discussion is absolutely fascinating, but we have a problem on our hands,' he said.

'What?' asked Jim.

'A photograph of each of our faces has been circulated at key places by the IRGC,' replied Abbasi. 'I had assumed that if the three of you remained hidden, that would be adequate. Now it seems that both Soroushpur and I are also on the radar.'

'So if we do reach Islam Qala, how do we cross the borderpost?' Linda echoed everyone's thoughts.

'Exactly my concern,' said Abbasi, as he sped towards Kashmar.

77

FIROOZ JAMSHIDI, THE taxi driver, had made it back to Kish Island and was thankful that the authorities seemed no wiser. Next day, he awoke early and made his own tea. Packing a *noon-e-taftoon* bread, he quickly started out on his day's business.

He soon picked up a passenger at Damoon Shopping Centre. Dressed in ordinary shirt and trousers, the passenger also wore his arm in a sling. 'The Toranj Marine Hotel,' requested the passenger, climbing into the cab. But halfway through the ride, the injured passenger pulled out a gun and held it to Jamshidi's head. '*Bebakhshid*, but you are coming with me.'

'Who are you?' asked Jamshidi, but in his heart he already knew what this was about.

Fifteen minutes later, Jamshidi was at the eleventh Enghelab Police Station. Seated in one of the interrogation cells that smelled typically of sweat and urine, Jamshidi awaited the arrival of the cop who had arrested him. He could feel the sweat trickling down his back as he sat in the hot, humid and squalid cell, nervously drumming his fingers on the table in front of him. Momentarily, the cell door opened and Mosaffa walked in, holding a file that had Jamshidi's name on it. Mosaffa was an injured soldier, but quite capable of handling a small fry like Jamshidi.

'We already know that you were part of the group that assisted Linda Dastoor,' said Mosaffa. 'At this moment your life hangs in the balance—in public, in your case. A crane will be used to lift you slowly off the ground while you struggle for air. Your friend, Heydari, has already met that fate.' He waited for the profusely sweating Jamshidi's reaction.

'I did not know ...' Jamshidi began hesitantly in Farsi.

'Yes?' urged Mosaffa. 'What didn't you know?'

'I ... I ... I did not know that Jim Dastoor was wanted by the IRGC,' stammered Jamshidi. 'I thought he was hostage. When his wife ask for help, I help her out of the goodness of my heart. Our prophet teaches us about good thoughts, good words and good deeds.'

Thwack! The sound of Mosaffa's left hand against Jamshidi's cheek told him exactly what his interrogator thought of Jamshidi's prophet. 'You may not have known it in the beginning, but you knew it by the time you reached Shiraz. And don't forget, you illegally helped Linda Dastoor and Dan Cohen cross from Kish to Chiruyeh. I have enough evidence to hang you, but death would be too kind a punishment.'

Jamshidi sat still, attempting to focus on his breathing. Mosaffa brought his face near his. 'Have you ever heard of the white room?' Jamshidi nodded. Most Iranians spoke in fear about those rooms at Evin Prison.

'The room is entirely white—walls, floor, ceiling—and you are visually deprived of all colour,' whispered Mosaffa. 'Your clothes are white, and your plain boiled rice is white. Neons above you prevent even your own shadow from creating another colour. The cell is soundproofed. All you can hear is yourself. For days. Days will become weeks; weeks will become months and months will become years. You will eventually go mad, without sleep, experiencing psychotic breaks and hallucinations. You will wish that you'd died on the crane with people around you instead.'

Jamshidi did not respond, so Mosaffa continued. 'While you are stewing in Evin Prison, we will be rounding up everyone who is close to you. We know you have no wife or children, but there are others you love or care for—family, friends—all of them will be raped, beaten, humiliated and broken. For *your* mistake. And we shall be telling you all about it while you are in the white room. How will that feel, do you think?'

Tears ran down Jamshidi's cheeks, mingling with his sweat. He couldn't bear the thought of people in his miserable but small and close-knit community suffering any more than they already did. He did not want to do anything to cause problems for Jim, Linda, Dan or Soroushpur. Especially when he thought of what they would do to the pretty lady, Linda, who could have been his mother, from the kind way she spoke to him.

'I tell you whatever you want to know,' said Jamshidi, choking on his words.

Mosaffa pushed a box of tissues in front of Jamshidi. Then he opened a small bottle of Damavand water and offered it to his prisoner. 'See, what a little cooperation can do?' he egged Jamshidi on. 'Make yourself comfortable and answer my questions.' Jamshidi took a gulp of the water and mopped his face with the tissues.

'Now, think carefully,' said Mosaffa. 'How and why did Behrad Soroushpur join your group?'

'I reached out to him,' said Jamshidi. 'I know that he runs the Gabrabad Action Front—the GAF. Since Jim Dastoor is Zoroastrian, I thought that Soroushpur would be willing to stick his neck out for him. As it turns out, I was right.'

'And Tariq Heydari?'

'I know nothing about him until he picked us up from the Fars House Hotel in a military truck,' replied Jamshidi. 'And once he join the group in Shiraz, I encouraged to leave.'

'What about Kaveh Abbasi?'

'Who is that?' asked Jamshidi.

'Hmm …' said Mosaffa. 'Are you saying that you left the group before Abbasi came into the picture?'

'I have no clue who this man could be,' said Jamshidi.

Mosaffa believed him. 'Was anything said about their exit plan after they had rescued Jim Dastoor?' he proceeded to find out. 'Any possible routes that they would take? Any allies that could assist them?'

'No,' Jamshidi shook his spinning head. 'But Heydari keep mentioning his friends at MMTM.'

Bingo! Mosaffa nearly slapped his own thighs. MMTM. *Mossad le-Modiin ule-Tafkidim Meyuhadim.*

Known to the world by a shorter name. Mossad.

78

THEY STOPPED BRIEFLY at Kashmar. Soroushpur looked in on the three secret occupants at the back of the container. They were tired but otherwise well. Then Soroushpur again noticed Jim clutching at his satchel. *What is this precious substance that you are unwilling to let go of?* He wondered for the nth time.

Soroushpur had a conflict within himself, one that raged more strongly after meeting Jim. His mind switched swiftly from one member of his group to another. He liked Jim. And Linda. They seemed like genuinely good people, although he didn't care for the shifty-looking Dan Cohen. But then, liking Jim increased his dilemma. After all, Jim's ancestors had run away from Iran centuries ago. *Who was braver—the one who stayed or the one who fled?* And if the material in Jim's possession was something that was taken away by his forefathers from Iran, who were its true owners? The Parsis of India? The remaining Zoroastrians in Iran? The Iranian regime? The Indian government? American laboratories that had conducted intense research on it? Or all of humanity?

Soroushpur had been born in 1980, just a year after the Islamic Revolution of Iran. It was an uprising in which the Pahlavi dynasty under Shah Mohammad Reza Pahlavi had been overthrown and replaced by an Islamic republic under the rule of Ayatollah Ruhollah Khomeini. The Shah's dictatorship had repressed dissent and restricted political freedoms, but it had also dragged Iran kicking and screaming into an era of secularism, industrialisation and modernity. Reza Pahlavi's Iran was characterised by women discarding their veils, wearing skirts and short-sleeved tops, window-shopping in Tehran's boutiques, and girls being encouraged to attend university. All that abruptly changed after the revolution.

In the Tehran suburb of Ray, Soroushpur's family home had overlooked a fire temple. But the IRGC conducted their training activities—on purpose—in the open grounds of the temple. Even prayer meetings would be disturbed by intermittent explosions and gunfire. His father, a senior civil servant, would tell him how a fierce mob of fundamentalist Shiites had stormed the temple following the revolution and smashed the image of Zarathustra that adorned its walls. It had been promptly replaced by one of Ayatollah Ruhollah Khomeini. Soon, every Zoroastrian temple and classroom had a portrait of Khomeini prominently displayed. Soroushpur's father, who had held high positions in the bureaucracy of the Shah, found himself barred from such posts, now reserved only for Muslims.

Soroushpur avoided politics and went into academia. He began teaching advanced mathematics at the Sharif University of Technology. When he was just twenty-five, he heard Ayatollah Ahmed Jannati, chairman of the Council of Guardians of the Constitution, ridicule Zoroastrians as 'sinful animals who roam the earth and engage in corruption'. The Zoroastrians had a single representative in Parliament, and he had protested. He had been promptly dragged before a revolutionary tribunal. The tribunal's clerics warned him of possible execution if he ever defied their declarations again.

The tiny Zoroastrian community had been so terrorised by the event that they had avoided re-electing him.

And yet, the community had survived against all odds, even tolerating fundamentalist authorities who routinely monitored their festivals, prayers, weddings and funerals, alleging that Zoroastrianism 'threatened national security and subverted the Islamic Revolution'. Continued humiliation and suppression of his endangered community had eventually spurred Soroushpur to establish the Gabrabad Action Front. He knew it was a risk, but also knew that someone had to speak up for his people and their faith. As a result of his efforts, thousands had recently celebrated Nowruz, also known as the Persian New Year, near the tomb of Cyrus the Great.

Every step had been a struggle for Soroushpur and his family. The appearance of Jim Dastoor in Iran had brought many of those conflicting emotions to the fore. Soroushpur remembered the stories that his parents would tell him of the fabulous power and wealth that Persia had enjoyed during Achaemenid and Sassanian times. He would listen in amazement to the descriptions of the magnificently wealthy Persepolis and that storehouse of knowledge, Gundeshapur. Little Behrad would insist on his father repeating the stories of Zarathustra and the wondrous order of magi who followed him. He never tired of hearing of the incredible powers that these men possessed. In particular, he was fascinated by the story of the Athravan Star.

No one knew exactly what the Athravan Star was, its origins lost in antiquity. Much like with the Holy Grail, each succeeding generation gave it their own spin. Some people considered the Holy Grail, for instance, to be a vessel used during the Last Supper; some thought that it was a magical healing stone; others viewed it as a chalice that held the blood of Christ. Similarly, the Athravan Star was described in various ways—as a rock, gemstone, box, sword, goblet, hammer, crown and tens of other objects. The only element that never varied was the fact that it had been handed down from Zarathustra to his special followers, and that magical properties were associated with it. Another fable around it was that it was passed on to the ones who showed signs of independence and courage.

As Soroushpur gazed at the bag in Jim's hold, he realised that he had an opportunity to correct a historical wrong. Hadn't there been rumours of the IRGC wishing to retrieve the Athravan Star? Wasn't it widely rumoured that the recent theft of the Cyrus Cylinder had been part of that quest? And wasn't the IRGC after Jim Dastoor? Wasn't it possible that Jim Dastoor's appearance in Iran was a sign from Ahura Mazda?

At that moment Soroushpur knew exactly what he needed to do.

79

THE ROAD FROM Kashmar to Islam Qala should have taken only four hours longer. Along the way, they would pass Azghand, Torbat-e Heydarieh, Dowlatabad, Bakharz and Taybad. But today seemed different. Abbasi could see that there were many more vehicles on the road. More worrying was the fact that there seemed to be an increased presence of military vehicles. 'What do you think?' he asked Soroushpur who seemed to be lost in his own world. Not receiving a response, Abbasi asked once again, 'What do you think we should do?'

'Huh?' responded Soroushpur. 'Apologies, I was daydreaming.' Before he could provide an adequate response, the answer became clear. A massive blockade of military trucks, jeeps and soldiers had been set up at Taybad.

Damn, thought Abbasi. *We were just half an hour away from Islam Qala!* This time there was no diversion available to them. They were stuck. He cautiously inched the truck forward. There were around fifty vehicles in front of him, but he could discern the rising excitement among the soldiers. 'Shit!' he exclaimed as he looked up at the sky. It was a whirring sound that had caught his attention. *Drones!* He could only see two small Yasir drones, their designs having been copied by the Iranians from the American Scan Eagle. It became evident to him that it was *they* who were being watched from above. He would have to take a call soon.

He switched on the intercom and spoke to his passengers at the rear of the container. 'We may have to dump the truck,' he said, explaining the situation. Up ahead he could see that the soldiers were dispersing the other vehicles rather quickly. *The bastards are waiting for us,* thought Abbasi. *They know that we're in this truck. Only thirty vehicles ahead of us now.*

'How much time do we have to decide?' asked Jim. *Twenty vehicles ahead.*

'No time at all,' replied Abbasi. 'On your right is a square trapdoor, bolted and hinged. Just slide open the bolt, slam the door hard with your fist, and it will spring open outward and flat against the side. Because of the narrowness of this road, there are no vehicles on either side of us. Now, run.'

'What about the two of you in front?' asked Linda. *Fifteen vehicles ahead.*

'We will abandon the truck at the same time as you,' replied Abbasi. 'The fact that they are clearing vehicles so quickly means that they already know who I am. They've been able to figure out that this container belongs to a trading front.'

'Where do we go once we're out?' asked Linda. *Only ten vehicles up ahead.*

'Head south on foot,' said Abbasi. 'There is a small village called Farmanabad about five kilometres from here. If we are not together, we shall meet there.' *Five vehicles.*

Dan rose from his bench, found the trapdoor and hit it violently. Abbasi had been right. The panel was only held in place by a bolt and a thin layer of paint and epoxy from the outside. The panel fell open with a clatter, revealing a square opening approximately sixty centimetres on each side. Linda went first, followed by Jim, then Dan. Jim was clutching his bag while Dan was holding his Heckler & Koch G36 rifle from the Shahid Daru raid. The passengers in the vehicle behind them were startled by their emergence from the side of the truck.

Jim, Linda and Dan quickly ran off the road and into the desert scrub that bordered it. 'They're following us,' Jim shouted. One of the drones had left the truck and was hovering above them. Dan paused, allowing Jim and Linda to run ahead. He fell to his knees and took aim at the drone that was about six metres above him. He initially missed but eventually succeeded in bringing it down. Then he got up and ran after Jim and Linda.

On the main road, Abbasi and Soroushpur too stepped out of the truck. *Two vehicles ahead.* But unlike Jim's group, both men came under fire almost immediately. There was yelling at the roadblock and soldiers ran into the road, all guns blazing.

'Take cover of the truck,' yelled Abbasi to Soroushpur as they used the vehicle as a shield to protect themselves. Drivers and passengers from the vehicles behind them also got out in a desperate attempt to avoid getting caught in the crossfire. That suited Abbasi just fine. The more people on the road, the more difficult it would be for the IRGC to get a clear shot at them.

Upon Abbasi's signal, Soroushpur made a dash for the desert scrub in the direction that Jim's party had gone. Abbasi kept up his gunfire to keep the soldiers occupied. Then, sensing an opportunity, he too made a dash for it. He felt a bullet whizz by his ear and another graze his ankle, but neither slowed him down. The second military drone followed him but was suddenly brought down by Soroushpur's bullet. Both men quickly raced southwards in the general direction of Jim, Linda and Dan.

The IRGC men fanned out along the road and followed them into the scrub. Abbasi took stock of the situation. Most of the soldiers seemed to be clustered towards the southeast. He pulled out a grenade from his belt and tossed it in the direction of the cluster. It blasted the roof off a military jeep but, more importantly, it gave him and Soroushpur just enough time to commandeer an abandoned ATV. 'Get in,' said Abbasi, twisting the throttle. They took off like a rocket in the direction of Jim's group, sending up huge clouds of desert sand.

The IRGC was unwilling to let go. They mounted the remaining ATVs and took off after them. 'I need you to take them out one at a time while I drive on,' shouted Abbasi at Soroushpur. His accomplice was already on the job. He took aim at the closest ATV and fired. The vehicle spun out of control, the driver hit. Men in another ATV that was catching up with them from their right fired. Soroushpur swung around and aimed at its driver. He saw the man's head explode as his bullet met its mark. The vehicle turned turtle on its occupants.

They caught up with Jim, Linda and Dan, who were on foot. 'Come on,' said Abbasi breathlessly to them all. The two men ditched the vehicle and rejoined the other three, running on foot towards Farmanabad.

80

THE TINY VILLAGE of Farmanabad in the Khorasan province of Iran is home to just 432 families. Jim, Linda, Dan, Abbasi and Soroushpur arrived there late at night, exhausted, carrying no food, water or personal belongings. Just a few rifles and Jim's all-important satchel.

The village was nothing more than a cluster of brick and plaster houses. Although a vast improvement from the time when Iranian rural houses were clayey mud bricks roughly stacked together, and roads were narrow and unpaved,

Farmanabad was still unplanned. Only two buildings were prominent—a white mosque with a few glazed tiles on its fascia, and a dreary school building. Nestled between houses were open-air plots hemmed in by mud and straw walls to hold in livestock.

Soroushpur led them towards the mosque. 'How will going to the mosque help us cross the border?' asked Linda, by now forgivably tetchy.

'An old caretaker of my Tehran property is from this village,' replied Soroushpur, unmoved. 'I have been of some little use to him and his family. I'm sure he will agree to help us. He's been living at the mosque since his wife died.'

'But wouldn't all the villagers be afraid of helping those who are running from the IRGC-Quds?' asked Jim.

'Valid concern,' acknowledged Soroushpur. 'But we are now less than half an hour away from the Iran–Afghanistan border. National identities mean little in these areas. There is also something else about him that may reassure you.'

'What?' asked Jim.

'He is Baloch,' replied Soroushpur. 'The Baloch people are spread across three countries—Pakistan, Afghanistan and Iran. They speak their own language, Balochi. For them, national borders mean nothing. They are ethnically and linguistically one people who happen to be in three separate countries.'

'But this is not Baloch territory,' argued Abbasi.

'Exactly,' replied Soroushpur. 'One would have to travel further south towards Zahedan to be in Baloch territory. But there are Baloch people scattered *all* over Iran. This man is one of them.'

They reached the mosque and, avoiding the front entrance, made their way to the back of the structure and waited behind a utility shed. It was another twenty minutes before a tall figure emerged from the mosque. Soroushpur squinted his eyes to examine the man's face and looked relieved. It *was* Mazaar Askani.

Signalling to the rest of the group to remain out of sight, he went up to the caretaker. 'How are you, my friend?' asked Soroushpur of the startled man. Askani was an old and wiry man wearing a green pathan suit and skull cap. His grey beard trailed down to the middle of his chest. It took him a minute before he recognised Soroushpur and hugged him heartily.

'What brings you here?' he asked Soroushpur.

'I need your help,' replied Soroushpur as he gave him a quick rundown of his situation. The old Baloch's eyes widened as he heard Soroushpur's tale. He remained quiet for a few minutes as he thought things through, stroking his beard as he did.

'Where are your friends?' enquired Askani eventually. When Soroushpur signalled, they came out from their positions from behind the shed. Askani looked at them carefully as Soroushpur introduced each one—Jim, Linda, Dan and Abbasi.

Askani greeted them courteously and then said, 'If I keep you inside the mosque, there is every chance that you will be seen. There is a small cottage for my personal use at the back. Although it is tiny, please use it to rest. In the meantime, I'll arrange some food and water.'

'How do we get across to Afghanistan?' asked Abbasi, wasting no time on preliminaries.

'It won't be easy,' replied Askani. 'The Iranian regime deploys around 3000 troops of the conscript army as border guards.'

'But the border is so long,' argued Abbasi.

'Of the 900-odd kilometres between Iran and Afghanistan, there are 400 kilometres of embankments, 800 kilometres of deep canals, forty kilometres of concrete walls and 140 kilometres of barbed wire fencing. All this has been done to curb the nuisance of traffic in narcotics. Trust me, I may be an old man, but I know.'

'What is the way forward for us, then?' asked Soroushpur.

'Rest for a few hours,' repeated Askani. 'Let me get you something to eat. In the meantime, I shall locate a man that you would prefer not to know. But under the present circumstances, he is your best bet.'

'Who?' asked Soroushpur, warily.

'He calls himself Buhaadur al-Baluchi and he runs a racket in opium, heroin, hash and morphine,' replied Askani. 'If there is someone who can take you into Afghanistan unofficially, it is him.'

'Can we trust him?' asked Dan.

'You have had to trust me also,' replied Askani. 'I am, after all, inviting danger in sheltering you from the soldiers of the IRGC,' he pointed out. 'If it were discovered that I helped you, I would rot inside a stinking prison for the rest of my life. But I have old debts to pay Soroushpur's family, and I cannot forget their kindness to me. Plus, at my age, I may as well do some last thing to make my Baloch ancestors proud.'

He paused to look benevolently on Dan. 'Al-Baluchi will not do anything remotely charitable. He will have to be paid a price—that's something for you to negotiate with him. But I have found people like Al-Baluchi to be remarkably trustworthy so long as you keep your end of the bargain.'

Askani ushered his guests into his small cottage, bare except for a thin mattress that covered most of the floor. He left them for a few minutes to bring water in an earthen pot. A few minutes later he brought some loaves of *khaak*, a hard Balochi bread baked from flour, dry yeast, sugar, salt, milk, water and sesame seeds. 'I'm sorry I have no meat,' said Askani apologetically, as he put the food down along with a wedge of *kadchgall*, a hard cheese made from sheep's milk.

'You have already gone beyond the call of hospitality,' said Jim. 'We don't know how to thank you.'

Askani smiled. '*Huda-e-mayaar bahoote*,' he said. God bless you. But Askani's brain was brimming with ideas. He wondered what his next step should be.

81

THE IRGC-QUDS MEN spread out in every direction from Taybad, where Jim's group had given them the slip. Jeeps, trucks, ATVs and soldiers accompanied by drones searched for the fugitives in all towns and villages located within a radius of fifty kilometres, the distance they calculated the escapees could have covered on foot in that time.

Trailer cabins were parked in an open plot of land in the heart of Taybad where the top members of the IRGC-Quds had stationed themselves. One of them also served as a makeshift office for Amir Khademhosseini. The IRGC-Quds chief was under intense pressure from the office of the Supreme Leader to nab and then make an example out of these 'dogs' and 'enemy agents'.

Khademhosseini was talking on the phone, a Farvardin between his lips. His office was hazy with smoke when Mosaffa knocked on the door. 'Come in,' said Khademhosseini, and waved him to an empty chair. 'What is the latest update?' he asked Mosaffa, disconnecting the call.

'We know they initially ran southwards,' said Mosaffa. 'But we have sent search parties in all directions—to Qumi, Hajabad, Kheyrabad, Sardab, Dehqarown and Mohsenabad. For the moment we are looking at a radius of fifty kilometres from Taybad. If we don't see any results by the afternoon, we may widen the area under search.'

'Do so,' said Khademhosseini. 'But also pause to think. In the present circumstances, what would be their best bet? Go east to Afghanistan? Run south-east to Pakistan? Or north-east to Turkmenistan?'

'We can rule out the western border—to Iraq, Turkey and Azerbaijan,' said Mosaffa. 'They would not have travelled a thousand kilometres east of Tehran if their exit plan was through the western route. So, you are right, their options are Pakistan, Afghanistan and Turkmenistan.'

'Which of those routes would you take?' asked Khademhosseini.

'The Mirjaveh crossing into Pakistan is 900 kilometres away,' replied Mosaffa. 'I do not think they would take that risk given that we are on their trail.'

'Okay,' said Khademhosseini. 'So, we focus on the other two—Turkmenistan and Afghanistan.'

'They are closest to the Afghanistan border,' replied Mosaffa. 'But given that there are three Americans in the group, it could prove hazardous going into Taliban territory. Turkmenistan would be the best option, but President Gurbanguly is an unpredictable sort. Over eighty per cent of his revenue comes from export of natural gas to China. He may play games.'

Mosaffa's phone rang. 'Yes?' he said into it. Then he listened carefully. He raised his eyebrows as he heard the information. 'Keep him there,' he said. 'I'm coming.'

'What is it?' asked Khademhosseini.

'There is a man called Mazaar Askani here at Taybad,' explained Mosaffa. 'He says that he has information about our fugitives.'

'What information?'

'We don't know,' replied Mosaffa. 'He says that he will only speak to you.'

'Who does he think he is?' said Khademhosseini irritably. 'The Supreme Leader?'

'Shall I go to him?' asked Mosaffa.

'No,' replied Khademhosseini. 'Bring him here. You stay with me. Let's jointly hear what he has to say.'

Ten minutes later an old man in a green pathan suit and skull cap was ushered into Khademhosseini's makeshift office. He looked at both the IRGC-Quds men with fear in his eyes. His lips quivered as he opened his mouth to speak. Mosaffa made him sit down and opened a bottle of Damavand for him. The old man took a grateful sip. 'Relax, uncle,' said Mosaffa.

'Tell us whatever you know. We shall protect you, so no need to worry.'

'I am the caretaker of the mosque at Farmanabad,' Askani said. 'Although I am Baloch, I am loyal to my nation of Iran which has given me so much. I have come to you because I have vital information that will be of use to you.'

'Do go on,' said Mosaffa gently.

'You are searching for three Americans accompanied by two Iranians,' said Askani. 'They came to Farmanabad.'

'Are they there now?' asked Khademhosseini.

'No,' replied Askani. 'They are in Qumi, preparing to cross the border into Afghanistan.'

'Any idea where they are in Qumi?' asked Mosaffa.

'There is an abandoned shed off Route 36,' replied Askani. 'They are holed up there. They seem to be waiting for backup.'

'Can you take us to the exact spot?' asked Khademhosseini.

'I can take you there, but I need you to give me your word that you will not start your operation until I've come away,' he said. 'I am worried that they may see my face and hunt me down later.'

'Don't worry, old man,' said Khademhosseini. 'The only ones you need to fear are us. And we're on the same side as you. Unless ...'

'Unless?'

'Unless you're trying to doublecross us.' Khademhosseini stared hard at the man. 'Tell me truthfully, are you trying to divert our attention?'

'I swear on the lives of my children,' said Askani. 'May the wrath of Allah descend upon me if I am deceiving you.'

'The wrath of Allah is nothing compared to that of the IRGC-Quds,' said Khademhosseini quietly.

82

ASKANI LAY BACK in the cot provided to him in the IRGC tent. His thoughts drifted to what had happened earlier that day, before he had showed up at the makeshift office of Khademhosseini and Mosaffa. More specifically, he thought about the meeting he had arranged for the fugitives with Buhaadur al-Baluchi early in the morning.

Al-Baluchi did not really care about nationality. He was Baloch even though three countries did not recognise that particular identity. Baluchistan was spread over the region where three nations—Iran, Afghanistan and Pakistan—met. They had inhabited this land for millennia and no country was going to tell them that they were anything but Baloch. The largest part of Baloch territory lay in Pakistan, containing around seven million people of Baloch descent, followed by Iran with around two million. In Pakistan, Baloch separatism had resulted in several insurgencies, whereas in Iran the rift had taken on sectarian Shia–Sunni overtones.

Al-Baluchi's lair, a cave near Farmanabad, was accessed via a rugged mountain trail, through which Askani had led the group. The interior of the cave was in contrast to its approach. It was furnished with carpets made from wool and goat hair and illuminated by kerosene lamps.

Al-Baluchi was a heavyset man who wore a white pathan suit, and a white turban whose tail looped around his chest.

His black moustache and beard were oiled, and his long black hair fell down in generous curls to his shoulders. Around his wrists were thick gold bracelets. An AK-47 machine-gun sat almost as an afterthought by his side. Al-Baluchi was a wonderful specimen of rugged masculinity, but it was commonly known that his sexual preference leaned towards young men. He was lounging against a leather-skin pillow, smoking a hookah as Askani ushered them into his presence.

'So, you're the people who wish to get out of Iran,' said Al-Baluchi, blowing thick smoke through his nostrils. 'Don't bother introducing yourselves. For me, you are mere commodities that are to be smuggled into Afghanistan. Let's discuss the price. Then we can discuss how we can make it happen.' His English was surprisingly good. Few knew that he had been radicalized in England while pursuing a college degree.

Abbasi stepped up. He would have to bear the costs. Jim had no valuables on his person ever since his exit from Asclepius. Linda and Dan had come as tourists, relying on their credit cards—and Al-Baluchi was unlikely to accept Visa or Mastercard. Soroushpur had some money, but it would be a fraction of what Al-Baluchi would want. Abbasi, as a Mossad operative, was the only one among them who had immediate access to significant resources. 'Let's talk,' he said. 'There are five of us. Explain how you can help us and then we can agree to a price.'

Linda broke in to tell Soroushpur, 'You have already done so much for us,' she said. 'Your home is here in Iran. Why are you planning to cross with us?'

'Because, believe it or not,' Soroushpur disclosed, 'I'm better off with you. By now, my photo will have been circulated among all police and military personnel. My home will have been searched—probably turned upside down. I may as well accompany you to safety and then evaluate my options.' *I also need to find a way to stay with you and ensure that what belongs to the Zoroastrians of Iran is safely returned. Even if it means allying with orthodox Parsis. Or even with the IRGC.*

'This is all very touching,' said Al-Baluchi. 'But may we talk business? So, here's the thing. Barbed wire, embankments and concrete walls are today's devices for demarcating national boundaries. But man has lived in these regions for thousands of years. There are many wondrous feats of engineering that our ancestors achieved. We simply need to rely on them.'

'What do you mean?' asked Abbasi.

'I carry out a roaring business across the border,' said Al-Baluchi. 'In addition, I assist the Jondollah. The Iranian regime hates me for that. Why should I take on the added headache of helping you cross and draw even greater ire from the Ayatollah's thugs?'

'Jondollah?' asked Dan, thoroughly out of his depth.

'The Army of God,' replied Abbasi. 'A Baloch militant group that has carried out many attacks on Iranian soldiers and government officials. I cannot run my operation without their support.'

'Are they a terror group?' asked Dan.

'Iran's Shia clergy has ensured that we Sunnis do not get a voice,' replied Al-Baluchi. 'Jondollah is fighting for the rights of Sunnis. Personally, I don't give a damn. All I want is for my business to operate smoothly.'

'I can make it worth your while,' said Abbasi. 'And I don't just mean money.'

'Go on,' said Al-Baluchi. 'I'm listening.'

'All of us are wanted by the IRGC-Quds,' explained Abbasi. 'Their chief is Amir Khademhosseini. Working directly under him is a key operative, Javad Mosaffa. Both men are hot on our trail even as we speak.'

'So?' asked Al-Baluchi, taking a deep puff from his hookah, the water bubbling gently.

'Suppose we lure them to a location based on a tip-off by our friend Askani,' said Abbasi. 'Once they are there, you ambush them and hold them captive. How embarrassing would that be for the Supreme Leader? And how satisfying for you!'

'I'm not interested in scoring political victories,' sneered Al-Baluchi. But Abbasi could see that he was considering the offer, puffing thoughtfully.

'Are you sure you want to be part of this?' asked Soroushpur of Askani. 'You could get captured or killed by the IRGC-Quds if anything goes wrong.'

Askani smiled. 'I have spent my life finding ways to teach the Iranians a lesson,' he said. 'Don't worry about me.'

Finally, Al-Baluchi spoke. 'You give me Khademhosseini and Mosaffa,' he said. 'My men will be waiting to ambush them at Qumi.' He handed over a slip of paper to Abbasi. 'In addition, you arrange for my agent in Istanbul to be paid this amount—non-negotiable. I will then utilise my special resources to get you and your friends into Afghanistan.'

Abbasi looked at the figure and said, 'Half now and half once we've crossed over.' Al-Baluchi acquiesced without further fuss.

'I will need your satellite phone to contact my man in Dubai,' said Abbasi. 'He will arrange for cash payment to your agent in Istanbul.' Abbasi looked at Jim. *You will need to reimburse me,* he was saying. Jim nodded slightly, picking up on Abbasi's look.

Al-Baluchi rose from his seat and went up to Askani. 'You are my brother in the Baloch struggle,' he said. 'Please accept this blanket as a tribute from me. May you stay safe.' He handed over a parcel wrapped in thick brown paper to Askani that the old man accepted gratefully. '*Baloch samasachar zindabad,*' he said quietly.

83

'CONCRETE BARRIERS AND barbed wire—that's all I can see,' said Jim as he looked at the barren landscape that defined the region between Iran and Afghanistan. They were standing on a hill just a few kilometres away from Islam Qala. Several trucks were standing at the checkposts, the drivers waiting impatiently to be let through. It all seemed ill-organised, with many of the trucks standing still for hours. Most of the infrastructure of Islam Qala had been destroyed a year earlier when a few hundred tankers transporting fuel had caught fire, causing millions of dollars of damage in the process.

'Who do you think caused the fire?' asked Al-Baluchi with a wicked grin.

'You?' asked Jim in shock. 'But why would you do something like that?'

'Besides drug-smuggling along this border, the other big business is smuggling fuel,' revealed Al-Baluchi. 'Fuel in Iran is much cheaper than in neighbouring Afghanistan or Pakistan. The Taliban enlisted my help to create the inferno so that fuel could not reach the foreign troops stationed in Afghanistan. I don't like the Taliban, but they're good to do business with.'

Everyone in the group—Jim, Linda, Dan, Soroushpur and Abbasi—was dressed in Afghan clothes. The men were wearing *khet* and *partug* made of linen. On their heads were turbans. Linda was now wearing a *chador*—a billowing cover-all that fell from head to foot and masked even her face.

'Are you ever going to tell us *how* we'll make the crossing?' asked Linda somewhat irritably, possibly from having had to regress into medieval 'womanly' clothes and see out of eyeholes.

'Follow me,' said Al-Baluchi as they made their way down the hill. He stopped midway at a little alcove which looked like nothing more than an indentation in the hillface. Al-Baluchi went inside and gestured the rest of the group to follow. Once they were in, he used his hands to clear away a thick layer of sand from the floor. Now, a trapdoor became visible.

'You made a tunnel?' asked Dan incredulously.

'I didn't have to,' said Al-Baluchi, handing out flashlights, rubber boots and pickaxes to everyone. 'What did I tell you about my forefathers?' Dan tried to remember. Ah, yes. *Man has lived in these regions for thousands of years. There are many wondrous feats of engineering that our ancestors achieved. We simply need to rely on our forefathers.*

Al-Baluchi opened the trapdoor to reveal a narrow wooden ladder. 'Climb down one at a time, I'll be following.' He ordered his lieutenant to shut the trapdoor behind him. Once they had all reached the tunnel, they could hear the faint sound of flowing water. 'We're inside a *qanat*!' exclaimed Linda, happy to be wearing rubber boots.

'What do you mean?' asked Soroushpur.

'The lands of Persia as well as Bactria—now called Afghanistan—were irrigated by qanats, or horizontal wells.'

'How did they make them?' asked Dan.

'Qanats are slightly sloping tunnels dug nearly horizontally on sloping ground until the water table is pierced,' explained Linda. 'Once pierced, ground water filters into the channel, runs down its gentle slope and emerges at the surface as a stream.'

'I could not have explained it better,' said Al-Baluchi approvingly. 'The qanats have existed since the times of Cyrus and Darius. Afghanistan is famous for its figs, apricots, grapes, melons, cherries, almonds, mulberries, pomegranates, walnuts, dates and saffron. How would any of these grow if man had not watered the desert? Come let's head towards the border.'

'These horizontal tunnels are connected to the surface with vertical shafts every few hundred metres—like the one we descended through,' Linda rambled on excitedly. Until today, she had only read about qanats. 'The ingenious thing about this system is that gravity does the job of moving water over substantial distances with minimal loss to evaporation. But,' she turned to Al-Baluchi for explanation, 'I thought that most qanats were short?'

'This is an unusually long one,' he replied. 'It runs almost a hundred kilometres in an east-west direction. We shall not be traversing the entire stretch. There is a vertical shaft near Herat through which we shall ascend. Above us, the trucks, barriers and chaos will continue. But these qanats do not respect national boundaries, much like the Baloch people, who are one, although spread across countries.'

The group advanced, avoiding the middle of the pathway, which still had a trickle of water running through it. The beams from their flashlights bounced off the smooth glistening walls as they made their way through the ancient irrigation system, amazed at the ingenuity of the Achaemenid, Parthian and Sassanian rulers and their engineers. It was no wonder that kings like Darius could have pulled off marvels like the Royal Road, which ran 2500 kilometres from Iran to Turkey, or the wondrous canal between the Nile and the Red Sea.

The group walked on silently, their boots sloshing in the water from time to time. Their progress was hampered by silt deposits and crumbled rock that blocked their access in some portions. But their pickaxes took care of the problem.

'Relax,' Al-Baluchi reassured them gruffly. 'You shall reach your destination safely.' *What happens to you after that is not my responsibility.*

84

IT WAS 4 pm. Khademhosseini and Mosaffa led the way in their jeep while a military truck followed close behind. Seated behind the two men was Mazaar Askani. 'Don't you think you need more soldiers?' enquired Askani. The two men looked at each other and laughed. 'We don't need machine-guns to kill mosquitoes. If the three Americans and their Iranian accomplices are here, just the ten soldiers behind us will be adequate to neutralise them.'

They silently drove along Route 36 and then turned off the road towards Qumi. In the distance they could see a rundown shed on an equally decrepit plot of land. They stopped a few metres away from the shed and got out of their vehicles. 'Fan out,' Mosaffa instructed the men. 'Surround the shed quietly but do not go in. The entrance may be booby-trapped. Only go in upon my signal.' The soldiers made their way to the perimeter of the plot and took up their positions.

Khademhosseini, Mosaffa and Askani walked from their jeep to the plot. Both IRGC men had their guns drawn as they crept up on the crumbling structure located in an abandoned field. Mosaffa raised his hand in a clenched fist. It was a signal for the soldiers: *Hold your positions.* Mosaffa peered through one of the many cracks. The shed's corrugated roof was entirely rusted and had fallen through, creating gaping holes. Through those holes, the wooden beams that supported the sheets were visible, some of them having fallen down altogether. The walls had collapsed into heaps of rubble; the only thing holding up the structure seemed to be temporary bamboo scaffolding. 'They're there,' he whispered.

He signalled for two of the soldiers to come over and knock down the door. The two soldiers obeyed quickly. Mosaffa shouted, 'Attack!' and they poured inside the shed with Askani following.

But the sight that greeted Askani was not what he expected. In the middle of the empty barn, a group of commandos of Al-Baluchi sat on the floor with their hands and feet tied. A contingent of IRGC soldiers was already present to keep guard over them. Askani took only a few seconds to size up the situation. The trap laid for Khademhosseini and Mosaffa had gone entirely wrong. The IRGC-Quds knew that he had been trying to doublecross them. The entire operation so far had been a ruse for his benefit.

Khademhosseini laughed. 'You really think that we would trust you—a Baloch—to deliver the Americans to us?' he asked. 'We did our own sweep here earlier and found that you and Al-Baluchi had set the whole thing up.'

'H-he threatened me,' stammered Askani. 'I had no option b-but to go along with his plan. Al-Baluchi would have killed me if I hadn't done what he commanded. P-please believe me, sirs!'

'Tragic tale,' Mosaffa clicked his tongue in exaggerated sympathy. 'Now you shall experience our wrath, as I had promised. And remember, there is only one way to lessen your misery. Tell us the exact route by which Al-Baluchi is taking those devils.'

'I have no idea,' said Askani with a terror-stricken look. 'They were talking about crossing at Nimruz into Afghanistan, but that was by no means final.'

'Restrain him,' said Khademhosseini to his soldiers. They sprang forward and cuffed Askani's hands and feet, walking him back to the jeep. This time, a soldier sat at the back of the vehicle, guarding him. Al-Baluchi's men were led to another vehicle.

Askani sat mute as the jeep bumped along the feeder road to reach the highway. He thought of all the atrocities that the Iranian regime had inflicted upon the Baloch people: Arbitrary arrests, fabricated evidence, televised confessions, torture and ill-treatment of prisoners. Their women were routinely trafficked like cattle, and youngsters were left with nothing but crime to live by.

He remembered how he had fled from Tehran after managing Soroushpur's property for years. When someone had accused him of theft, he knew that he would be rounded up by the police. His manufactured confession would then be used to nail him. This was the plight of the Baloch people. Soroushpur had been kind. He had given Askani adequate money to flee and establish himself in Farmanabad, far away from Tehran.

The soldier sitting next to Askani watched his prisoner with the eyes of a hawk. He saw that Askani was praying softly, the blanket wrapped tightly around his shoulders. For some reason the captive kept rubbing his back against the seat, almost like a dog attempting to rid himself of an itch. The soldier looked at the pattern on his blanket—ordinary checks, but bright yellow. As he looked more closely, he realised that the yellow fibres were thicker than usual. He reached out with his free hand to feel the blanket. By the time the realisation hit him it was too late. The fibres were extruded, plastic-bonded explosives—unstable and easily triggered by friction.

The jeep containing Khademhosseini, Mosaffa, Askani and the poor soldier blew up into smithereens. The speed at which energy was released was indicative of a very high binder, not the usual stuff used by terror outfits. The vehicle exploded into a ball of fire and flames engulfed its contents. None of the four passengers uttered a cry because they were already in pieces.

Baloch samasachar zindabad.

85

THEY HAD BEEN walking for several hours inside the damp and dark qanat. The protective clothes they were wearing made the journey even more tedious. Nonetheless, they plodded on. When Al-Baluchi finally stopped to inform them it was time to ascend one of the vertical shafts, there was a collective sigh of relief from the group.

Al-Baluchi ascended the ladder first. Once he reached the top, he pushed with all his might to lift the trapdoor above. A gust of wind came through—dusty but nonetheless welcome. Al-Baluchi climbed out of the qanat and the rest followed: Linda, then Jim, then Dan, followed by Abbasi and Soroushpur.

They looked around as Al-Baluchi shut the trapdoor. 'Where are we?' asked Linda. They seemed to be in the middle of a vast stretch of desert. Only sand dunes were visible in the dim light of the fast-dissipating sunset. 'We're in the outskirts of Kohsan, Afghanistan, around a hundred kilometres east of Herat,' Al-Balochi acquainted them. 'Our aim is to get you to Shindand, the American airbase. That's about three hours south-east from here.'

'How do we get there?' asked Linda.

'Patience,' said Al-Baluchi. He took out his satellite phone and punched in a number.

'*Salam doost*,' he said. *Hello, my friend.* The conversation lasted less than twenty seconds.

'Now what?' asked Dan.

'Now we wait,' said Al-Baluchi, as he sat down on his haunches.

Around thirty minutes later, an armoured Humvee pulled up in the dark. A swarthy driver dressed in a camouflage jacket stepped out. Around his head and the lower half of his face was the checked *keffiyeh* favoured by Arab men.

'*As-salaamu alaikum*,' he said to Al-Baluchi, who responded with the traditional '*Va-alaikum as-salaam*'.

'These are my friends, Akhtar,' he said. 'They need to be transported safely to Shindand. May I depend on you?'

'You need not worry brother,' replied Akhtar. 'They shall be safe with me.'

Jim nudged Al-Baluchi. They stepped away from earshot and Jim asked, 'Who is this man and why should we trust him?' Al-Baluchi put his hand on Jim's shoulder reassuringly.

'His name is Akhtar, and he is part of a breakaway faction of the Afghan Taliban.'

'And you want us to go with a Taliban fighter?' asked Jim incredulously.

'Everyone here is Taliban,' explained Al-Baluchi. 'But there are two major factions. First, there is the Haqqani group which is an ally of Pakistan and Al Qaeda. The second is the Yaqoob group that favours an independent style of working. This man, Akhtar, is from the latter group.'

Jim shrugged his shoulders in resignation. Al-Baluchi bowed slightly in farewell. 'I shall take your leave here. I cannot be away from my base for too long,' he said. Jim thanked Al-Baluchi in return.

Al-Baluchi winked at Abbasi. *Has my money been paid?* The Mossad agent confirmed in his own way that the remaining cash had been disbursed. 'I'll be off then,' said Al-Baluchi, making his way to the trapdoor.

Akhtar opened the doors of the Humvee to the group. All the vehicles used by various Taliban factions were automobiles they had seized from the US army. The interior was a mess of ammunition, jerry cans of fuel, communication equipment, guns, ropes, packaged food and water. There was barely space for three people, but the five of them squashed in somehow, Jim continuing to hold firmly on to his precious satchel.

'*Khosh amadid,* friends,' said Akhtar. 'Welcome to Afghanistan.' He started the engine of the monster 4-CT Armoured Humvee. It roared to life and lurched forward. The group tried looking out of the dirt-streaked windows to get a sense of their location, but all they saw was a vast and dark expanse of nothingness.

About an hour after leaving Al-Baluchi, they noticed another pair of headlights in the distance. As they came closer, they realised that the headlights belonged to two vehicles— both mud-caked Ford Rangers. The two vehicles pulled up by their side. Akhtar cut off his engine and for a minute there was complete silence. Then some words were exchanged in Pashto, the most common language among the Taliban.

Jim looked at Linda. Her eyes had widened in fear. Jim was trying to control the thumping of his own heart, but he too was afraid. They heard the men from the other vehicles laughing along with Akhtar. All around them were the desert sands and darkness. 'Where are we, Akhtar?' asked Abbasi. 'How far away are we from Shindand?'

'*Bebakhshid doost,*' said Akhtar. *Sorry, my friend.* 'We are still a long way from there. At least another couple of hours.'

'Then why have we stopped here?' asked Abbasi. 'Who are these men in the Ford Rangers?'

'They have been sent by my bosses to give us additional security,' replied Akhtar, but he sounded unconvincing. 'They will be accompanying us for the rest of the way. It's not safe for us to be driving through this empty stretch at night.'

He started up the Humvee's engine once again, as did the other two vehicles at the same time. One of them went ahead of them while the other trailed behind. Abbasi looked out from the rear windscreen. The vehicle that was following contained three or four men, all holding machine-guns. He estimated that the composition of the other vehicle would be similar. *If these men are not who they say they are, we're finished,* he thought to himself.

Abbasi looked up at the sky. He could discern the arrangement of stars that made up Orion and his cortege across the southern part of the sky. Then he saw Sirius, the brightest among all the stars, shining with a distinct bluish tinge. Something did not add up.

If Sirius was visible up ahead, then it would mean they were travelling south rather than south-east. His doubts were confirmed thirty minutes later. All three vehicles stopped at a camp. The men from the other two vehicles jumped out and surrounded their Humvee. Their driver, Akhtar, turned around and said, 'You are now guests of the Haqqani Taliban. Do as we say and you'll be fine.'

Abbasi swore under his breath. He should never have trusted that bastard Al-Baluchi. *The swine would sell his own mother for a coin.*

86

MY STAY IN Khandala with Cecile turned out to be the education of a lifetime. I learned more about Persia, Zoroastrianism and the Islamisation of Persia during that trip than I had in my entire lifetime of reading.

One afternoon while we were playing rummy, Cecile said, 'You know how poorly I was treated by the Parsi community here in Bombay. There is no reason why I should hold a brief for them. But why should history always suit the victor's narrative?' I chose to stay silent as I did not want to interrupt her flow. Sometimes, history can be more engaging than cards.

'The Rashidun Caliphate and then the Umayyads succeeded in converting Persian populations to Islam,' my grandmother resumed her narrative with obvious relish, 'but they could not metamorph the Persians into Arabs. The Persians remained distinctly Persian in their language, manners and customs.'

'Even those who converted to Islam?' I asked, putting down my cards.

'For the most part,' replied Cecile. 'But once a Zoroastrian family was forcibly converted, the children were compulsorily sent to an Islamic seminary to learn Arabic and the Qur'an so

that future generations would have no traces of Zoroastrianism left in them.'

'But weren't Zoroastrians treated as dhimmi—or people of the book?' I asked.

'The Abbasids who followed the Umayyads demoted Zoroastrians from the status of dhimmi to the status of kafir, or non-believers,' answered Cecile. 'Dynasty after dynasty found ways to coerce Zoroastrians away from their faith. By the sixteenth century, when the Safavids were in power, forced conversions became the norm.'

Safavid kings, staunch adherents of Shia Islam, persecuted both Zoroastrians and Sunni Muslims to convert to Shia Islam. Fearing desecration, the surviving Zoroastrian magi hid their sacred fires, and totems and spoke in an invented dialect called Dari so that they would not be easily understood. Preserved among their religious relics was an earthen jar with a spherical insignia that had been handed down for generations. Also preserved was a text that was only orally conveyed between them.

'When the Qajar dynasty emerged, any inheritance by Zoroastrians was outlawed,' Cecile further revealed. 'Zoroastrians could be beaten on the streets. Zoroastrian girls were kidnapped and forcefully married to Muslims. Today there are less than 25,000 Zoroastrians in Iran—in a country of eighty-four million people!'

There was no stopping Cecile now. 'One of the Umayyad caliphs instructed, "Milk the Persians and once their milk dries, suck their blood!" The Arabs exploited yet despised the Zoroastrians. They named them ajam, a word that meant "mute". Even the name given to converted Zoroastrians was no better—they were called mavali. Modern India uses the word to indicate an uncouth person, but actually in those times mavali was used for what the Muslims considered "liberated slaves". The word liberated did not mean that they were free, only converted, thus liberated from Zoroastrianism. They continued to remain slaves who could be bought, sold and given away as gifts.'

'Why didn't the Zoroastrians rebel?' I asked, with outrage. After all, they were in the majority.

'Over 130 rebellions took place, but all of them were put down brutally,' said Cecile. 'On each occasion, the Arabs confiscated land and forced the defeated to provide them with gold, silver and young slaves. Many Zoroastrians were deported to a ghetto near Isfahan—Gabrabad—where they eked out an existence in utter poverty.' When Cecile mentioned the name of the place, I did not know then that it would feature so significantly in my life many years later.

According to Cecile, Zoroastrians were regarded as impure and untouchable by Muslims. The walls of Zoroastrian houses had to necessarily be lower than those of Muslim-owned ones. The main door to a Zoroastrian house had to be secured by a single hinge as per law, so that forced entry was easy. Zoroastrians were not permitted to ride camels or horses—only donkeys—and even then, they were required by law to dismount upon passing any Muslim on the way. During rainy weather, Zoroastrians were prohibited from being outdoors, ostensibly because water running off their bodies could pollute those of Muslims. While jizya was compulsory, corrupt officials would extort double or triple the official tax from them. If one did not pay up, the children were beaten in front of their parents.

If a male member of a Zoroastrian family converted to Islam, he was automatically made the sole heir to the family's inheritance, regardless of where he actually stood in the line of succession. Zoroastrians were prohibited from taking up lucrative occupations. Public places were barred from serving them. When shopping, they were forbidden from touching any food items. They were routinely attacked and whipped in the streets. Regulations required Zoroastrians to wear a patch so that they could be easily identified, much like what Hitler did with the Jews many centuries later.

'Even the smallest local fracas could escalate into a major riot that would eventually lead to a massacre of Zoroastrians,' Cecile said, warming to her theme. 'A group of Muslims once destroyed the wall of a mosque in Khorasan and blamed the local Zoroastrians. Under the orders of Sultan Ahmed Sanjar, hundreds of Zoroastrians of the city were rounded up and killed in supposed retribution.'

The Iranian scholar Abdolhossein Zarrinkoob would later write that Arab rule was like a dark night of silence, interrupted only by the hoot of owls and the crash of thunder. And the Iranian writer and historian Shojaeddin Shafa wondered, 'Why did so many have to die or suffer? Because one side was determined to impose his religion upon the other—which could not even understand the reason for the imposition.'

87

THE ARABS WERE eventually driven out by a commoner from Sistan, someone called Yaghoub Saffar. Although he emerged victorious, he fell terribly ill by the banks of the River Tigris. The *caliph's emissaries offered him governorship as well as untold riches, but Yaghoub discarded these offers. 'Tell your ruler that I have lived all my life on unleavened bread and onions. If I survive, only the sword will rule between the two of us,' he said making it clear there would be no peace between them so long as he lived.*

'Thus, the Umayyad Caliphate's rule in Persia ended and Abbasid rule started,' related Cecile. 'But the sufferings of the Zoroastrians only increased. In fact, it was during Abbasid times that Zoroastrians became a minority in Persia. By this time many Persians had been "Arab-ised" and had changed their names and their religion. The newly converted Muslims were even more hostile towards the Zoroastrians than the Arabs had been. Persian scholars who read and wrote in Arabic were valued more than the ones who used Persian. An Iranian vizier, Sahib ibn Abbad, refused to look at himself in the mirror lest he see a Persian reflection in it. Imagine what lengths a man must be driven to, to arrive at that extent of self-loathing!'

According to Cecile, the governor of Khorasan, Abdallah ibn Tahir, refused to respond to any language but Arabic. He banned Persian writings and mandated that Zoroastrians bring forth their religious books to be burned. Anyone found disobeying the diktat was put to death. As Muslim rulers destroyed non-Arabic and Pahlavi texts, Persian scholars resorted to translating those works into Arabic as the sole means to save them. Centuries later, these translations would be held up as examples of original Arab knowledge. It was during these times that a book in Pahlavi by Borzuya was discovered in Hormuz. It was then translated by Ibn al-Muqaffa into a title called Kalila wa Dimna.

'Zoroastrians were not permitted to wear shoes, only slippers,' said Cecile. 'Their trousers had to necessarily be short so that if stones were hurled at them, the stones would hit exposed skin. They were not to wear new garments, only old and tattered ones. Any Zoroastrian entering a Muslim house was required to carry a thick shawl that he could sit on, to preserve the host's floor from contamination by direct contact with Zoroastrian flesh. What do you think, Jimmy? Wouldn't living in Iran have been a veritable hell for a Zoroastrian?' Cecile's lips curled in disapproval.

But it only got worse.

'The Abbasids were followed by the Safavids,' said Cecile. 'This was undoubtedly the blackest age for the Zoroastrians. Texts penned by Islamic clerics were used to instigate animosity toward them. They were even blamed for natural disasters such as floods and earthquakes.'

Cecile angrily pulled out a book from a shelf above the library desk. It was a translation from French. In it was the text of a letter written by a French priest in seventeenth-century Iran. It read, 'Islam is not the only religion of the Iranians, there are many Iranians who have preserved their old religion. But they have none of their ancestral knowledge and science. They live in a state of slavery and absolute misery.'

'Couldn't they just pay the jizya and get on with their lives?' I asked.

'Even those who paid jizya were forced to face public humiliation as part of the taxation ceremony,' replied Cecile. She scrabbled among her photocopied papers and pulled up a stapled bunch. 'These are leaves from a book called Al-Kashshaf, by Al-Zamakhshari, a medieval Muslim scholar of Persian origin,' replied Cecile. 'See this translated passage?' She handed over the papers to me, pointing to a particular paragraph:

The Jizya shall be taken from them with belittlement and humiliation. The dhimmi shall come in person, walking, not riding. When he pays, he shall stand, while the tax collector sits. The collector shall seize him by the scruff of the neck, shake him, and say, 'Pay the Jizya!' and when he pays it, he shall be slapped on the nape of the neck.

'The collector would often mock the Zoroastrian taxpayer for wearing a kushti or sadreh and would rip them off,' said Cecile as I handed back the sheaf to her. 'All this while an invited, sniggering public looked on.' There was a lull in our conversation. I was trying to internalise the enormity of what had happened in Persia.

'Iranian rulers used yet another trick to speed up proselytising,' said Cecile. 'They fabricated a legend, which made Shia Islam appear Iranian in origin. A story was spun that Hussein, the son of the fourth caliph, Ali, had married a captive Sassanian princess by the name of Shahrbanu. This union had supposedly produced a son. Persians were thus meant to be supportive of Shia Islam.'

'Did the ploy work?' I asked.

Cecile sniffed with derision. 'If it had worked, those massacres would have ceased. The worst massacre of the Zoroastrian population took place under the orders of the last Safavid king, Shah Sultan Hussein. Soon after starting his reign, he ordered that all Zoroastrians must necessarily convert to Islam or face harsh penalties. By some estimates, around 100,000 Zoroastrian families lived in Persia at the time. Almost all were either forcibly converted or slaughtered.'

'What happened to Gabrabad?' I asked, returning to the fateful name.

'The population of the slum quarter of Gabrabad was almost entirely wiped out and many bodies were tossed into the river Zayanderud. A French estimate held that around 80,000 Zoroastrians died while some Zoroastrian sources peg the number at even higher.'

Count de Gobineau, the French Ambassador to Iran in the nineteenth century, wrote, 'Only 7000 of them remain and just a miracle may save them from extinction. These are the descendants of the people who one day ruled the world.'

88

AFTERNOON TEA AT Cecile's was always delightful. A trolley with tea, scones, cake and finely cut sandwiches would be rolled into the living room. Each item on the trolley would have been meticulously prepared and elegantly served in silver and china surrounded by frothy muslin and lace. Cecile cut me a slice of soft spongy mawa cake herself. I took a bite and allowed the sweetness to explode in my mouth. What a change it was from our dredged-up history!

'The Safavids were overthrown by an Afghan rebellion under the command of Mahmoud Mir Oveis,' said Cecile, taking a refreshing sip of tea. 'But the victorious Afghans were themselves subdued by a strong military commander, the

Persian Nader Shah, who later invaded India and carried away the famous Peacock Throne.' I would recall this many years later when one of the conspiracy theories floating about said a relic called the Athravan Star had been embedded inside the Peacock Throne. Of course, that was nonsense.

'But Nader Shah employed Zoroastrians,' I argued.

'Indeed, but in senile old age, his dementia drove him to mass murder,' replied Cecile. 'Even though 12,000 Zoroastrians had served in his army, Nader Shah carried out a systematic massacre of Zoroastrians in Khorasan and Sistan. A very small number of survivors crossed the desert on foot and sought shelter in Kerman and Yazd.'

'Why did so many Zoroastrians flee to the port of Hormuz?' I asked.

'Because,' replied Cecile, 'located as it was in the north of the narrow Straits of Hormuz, the city was strategically positioned at the entrance to the Persian Gulf. Up to the medieval ages, Hormuz was a key port for world travellers such as the Italian Marco Polo, the Moroccan Ibn Battuta and the Chinese Zheng He. Zoroastrian merchants built up a very strong base in Hormuz, and this is where they put up a final show of resistance.'

Cecile showed me the translation of an Arabic book, Futuh-ul-Buldan, by Ahmad ibn Yahya ibn Jabir Al Biladuri, a ninth-century writer. He described the Zoroastrians who fought against the advancing Muslim armies at Hormuz. When defeat became inevitable, those who could escape scattered by land and sea. Some fled by land to Sistan, others by ship to the Markan coast of Baluchistan. Yet others—my ancestors—embarked on a harrowing sea voyage to Sanjan, via Diu.

Many centuries later, the Parsis of India despatched an emissary, Maneckji Limji Hataria, to Iran in 1854. He stayed in Iran for a year, studying the condition of the Zoroastrian minority. Upon his return, he filed a report before the Parsi Panchayat. It read:

> This noble group has suffered in the hands of cruel and evil people so much that they are totally alien to knowledge and science. As slaves they receive no payment. Despite their poverty, heavy taxes under the pretexts of land, space, pasture, inheritance and religious tax are imposed on them.
>
> The local rulers have been cruel and have plundered their possessions. They have forced the men to do menial construction work for them. Vagrants have kidnapped their women and daughters.

The final line of his report was the most telling:

> I found the Zoroastrians to be exhausted and trampled, so much that no one in this world can be more miserable than them.

'What were the Zoroastrian magi doing?' I wondered.

'Many of them were put to death and their texts burned,' replied Cecile. 'While general Zoroastrian laity could be converted, the magi could not. They knew that the duty of preserving ancient secrets was entirely theirs. Some of them even killed themselves, preferring suicide over a life of dishonour. Others hid in the remote hills. Yet others took shelter in Hormuz and sailed on to Diu from there, eventually reaching Sanjan. Most of those who went to India were Mobeds—high-caste priests.'

There was a lull in our conversation. On a wall behind the sofa were old sepia-toned pictures of family members—every wall and surface in a typically Parsi home is lined with portraits and photographs. One of them showed my grandfather, Rustom, with Reza Shah Pahlavi, the Shah of Iran. The Shah and his son had tried pulling Iran into the modern era, only to be ousted by Ayatollah Ruhollah Khomeini in 1979.

Standing at the centre of the group was the Nobel Prize–winning Bengali poet Rabindranath Tagore. With my cup still in hand, I stood up to study the photo more carefully. 'When was this taken?' I asked.

'In 1932,' replied Cecile. 'Rustom's passion for art overlapped that of Rabindranath Tagore. The poet was invited to Iran by the Shah, and Rustom was part of his delegation. Tagore thanked the Iranian minister of education and culture for financing an academic chair at Santiniketan. You know what the minister replied?'

'I'd love to know,' I said.

'The minister said, "You do not need to thank us. For one thousand years your nation has hosted our sons and daughters known as Parsis. They left Iran under distressful conditions, but we never thanked you for it. Please accept this chair of Iranian studies as a small token of our appreciation."'

89

'ZOROASTRIANS SAW THEIR *fortunes improve under the Pahlavis, who openly embraced Persia's Zoroastrian roots,'*

Cecile leapt back into her pet subject as soon as the tea things had been cleared. 'Alas, it was short-lived.'

I was aware of this part of Iranian history. Mrs Batliwala had made it sound like a golden age. Reza Shah Pahlavi had deposed Ahmad Shah Qajar, the last king of the Qajar dynasty, and amended Iran's 1906 Constitution to permit his selection as monarch. He founded the Pahlavi dynasty that lasted until his son, Mohammad Reza Pahlavi—commonly called the Shah of Iran—was overthrown in 1979 during the Islamic Revolution.

'Reza Shah Pahlavi and his son Mohammad Reza Pahlavi undertook a massive transformation of Iran and drew attention to its ancient history and Zoroastrian heritage,' said Cecile. 'They even renamed the months according to the Zoroastrian calendar and legislated a number of economic and social reforms aimed at improving the status of Iran's Zoroastrians.'

'But by then most Zoroastrians would have fled, died or been converted,' I reasoned.

Cecile nodded sadly. 'Iran would not have been called by that name had it not been for the Pahlavis and their respect for Persia's Zoroastrian heritage.' I did not press further. 'The Pahlavis encouraged Parsis from around the world to come back and settle down in Iran,' explained Cecile. 'The first World Zoroastrian Congress was held in Tehran in 1960. It was during this time that the two related communities—one in India and the other in Iran—sought reform in their ancient doctrines. Iranian and Indian researchers created a new awakening among Zoroastrians through translations of Avestan texts into modern Persian and English. By then, the West had already been familiarised with Zarathustra through a book by German philosopher Friedrich Nietzsche. That space movie by Stanley Kubrick that you love—dig into its background and you will see what I mean.'

'So how were Zoroastrians treated under the new Iranian regime?' I asked.

'The brief reprieve that the Zoroastrians experienced under the Pahlavis was shortlived,' Cecile said again. 'When the Islamic Revolution took place in 1979, radicalised Shiites attacked the fire temple at Tehran. The portrait of Zoroaster was trampled upon and a photograph of Ayatollah Ruhollah Khomeini was installed in its place. The congregation was warned not to remove the portrait of Iran's new theocratic leader. Zoroastrian schools and classrooms were soon covered with pictures of Khomeini and with verses of the Qur'an that denounced non-Muslims. During the bloody Iran–Iraq War that raged from 1980 to 1988, young Zoroastrians were forcibly drafted for suicide missions. Failing to offer oneself for such missions meant execution for treason.'

It was almost as though Surah 9.29 of the Qur'an had been made the state's mission:

Fight those who believe not in Allah nor the Last Day, nor hold that forbidden which hath been forbidden by Allah and His Messenger, nor acknowledge the Religion of Truth, from among the People of the Book, until they pay the jizya with willing submission, and feel themselves subdued.

'The Islamic Revolution once again relegated religious minorities to the status of second-class citizens, prompting significant immigration of the remaining Zoroastrians,' said Cecile. 'In addition to those who'd come to India, the remaining Zoroastrians also found their way to USA, Canada and UK, which became new homes for the ancient flames.'

A beautiful fragrance of jasmine wafted in from the garden. Cecile smiled beatifically. 'The Persians loved their gardens,' she said. 'Music, drama, art, poetry, literature, architecture and science ... all of it coalesced and flourished in Persia. But the fertile soil of those gardens was soaked in Zoroastrian blood.'

She looked into the distance wistfully. 'Zoroastrian poets Daghighi and Zardosht—and the Sufi Persian poets such as Ferdowsi, Hafez and Khayyam—tried to keep the metaphysical philosophy alive,' she said. 'Hafez, a mystic poet from Shiraz, speaks of his admiration of the Zoroastrian faith in his poetry by referring to himself as a follower of the old magi. In a poem Hafez reminds readers: In the monastery of the magi, why do they honour us; maybe the fire that never dies, burns in our hearts.'

The extended discussions with my father and my grandmother had left me reeling with the weight of information I'd gained. I returned to Bombay from Khandala, and the next few weeks went by in a whirl as I prepared to leave for Stanford.

Although I had known that my ancestors were Zoroastrians who had fled from Iran, I had not fully appreciated the fact that Zoroastrianism had had such a huge impact on the Achaemenid, Parthian and Sassanian kings. I had been oblivious to the might of the Persian Empire and the power that the magi had wielded. I had been clueless about the inspiration that Zoroastrianism had provided to Abrahamic faiths. And I had not fully believed the extent of Islamic persecution in Iran over several centuries.

Most importantly, I had little idea about the vital role that my family had played in preserving the Iranshah flame and that little box with the pilot's insignia. And the text that was now memorised by me.

90

SOME WEEKS LATER, I boarded the flight to America and spent the next few months there getting settled. Thoughts of Zarathustra and his ancient people were far from my mind as I focused on the humdrum present: my living arrangements, classes, assignments and new friendships. I had carried with me the little earthen box that my father had given me, but it remained locked away in a drawer, out of sight and mind. The words I'd memorised meant nothing. They were just words.

Several years went by in pursuits both trivial and life-changing. And then Linda happened.

I met her in one of the campus restaurants when I was pursuing my doctorate. She had collected her order at the self-service counter but had forgotten to include a bottle of water. Picking it up would have meant standing in queue once again. I had offered to buy it for her instead. Her grateful smile had me there and then.

I had been too shy to ask her out, so she did the honours. I found her to be wise, warm and witty. Just a few years younger than me, she was working towards a master's degree in the history of religions. A few months later we found ourselves going steady.

Linda had grown up in California, the daughter of a white liberal Protestant father from San Francisco and a Hindu mother from Jakarta, Indonesia. Her mixed roots and upbringing made her open to all sorts of philosophical and spiritual ideas. She was no ordinary master's programme student; probably far, far *ahead of her class, she kept her professors on their toes. She was inquisitive about my faith and we had many discussions about Zoroastrianism. She would even go to the library and borrow books to fill the many gaps in my explanations.*

One day we were watching my favourite movie together—Stanley Kubrick's 1968 film 2001: A Space Odyssey. *When the overture came on, I was as usual mesmerised. I had heard it a million times, but it never ceased to enthral me. Linda looked mysteriously pleased during the opening strains. I wondered why she was amused. She informed me that the soundtrack was to a score of Richard Strauss's composition.*

When I asked what was significant about that, Linda told me that Strauss had been heavily influenced by German philosopher Friedrich Nietzsche's book, Thus Spake Zarathustra. *The book had prompted him to compose the* Also Sprach Zarathustra, Op. 30. *It was this composition that had been used in the opening of the movie. I was amazed that there was a Zoroastrian connection to the film.*

I also realised that my great-granduncle Homi's own composition based on the Yatha Ahu Vairyo *had probably been influenced by Strauss! That launched Linda and me into a discussion on Zarathustra—and then there was no letting up on that subject for the rest of my life.*

Some months later, we had been lounging in my apartment when my open desk drawer caught Linda's eye. She eyed the earthen box inside it curiously and asked me about the unusual design on the lid. I could only tell her that the object's origin was unknown, but what I knew of it was that it had been handed down over many generations of my family. Although I could no longer be the business head of the Dastoor family, I would still be the designated custodian of the box, partly on account of my having strayed from the ordinary path.

Until that moment, I had never bothered to open the box and peer inside. But Linda's curiosity prompted me to do so. Inside was a white powder of sorts, almost like fine sand. There was nothing distinctive about its smell. I closed the box and forgot about it. Little did I realise that it would change the course of my life forever.

Linda eventually made Zoroastrian history her passion. Over the next several years, while I was working towards my multiple degrees, Linda earned not only her master's but also a PhD in history. In fact, she became far more knowledgeable than me in matters of Zoroastrian history, theology, philosophy and culture.

In my mind, Linda became the younger equivalent of my grandmother, Cecile, an outsider drawn to Zoroastrianism, a mysterious religion as irresistible as a magnet. Once you touched it, there was no coming away.

91

JIM, LINDA, DAN, Soroushpur and Abbasi left the Humvee and were led to a large tent of foam-insulated canvas—US Army issue—with sandbags holding up the arch of the entrance. Evidently, the Taliban depended for a large chunk of their supplies on stuff stolen from the Americans.

The group sat on two adjacent bunk beds and waited. 'If we are in Haqqani's hands, we will be used as bait for the

Americans,' said Abbasi. 'I am still unable to understand why Al-Baluchi delivered us to the Haqqani faction rather than the Yaqoob faction. He had a commercial understanding with us.'

'Maybe something happened to Askani and Al-Baluchi's men,' suggested Soroushpur. 'Al-Baluchi could be pissed off. Of course, simple greed could also be a reason.'

Two men entered the tent. One was Akhtar, the one who had driven them there. The second seemed older and higher in rank. He too was wearing a camouflage jacket and *keffiyeh*, but his beard was bushy. It resembled the one favoured by Mullah Omar, the Afghan mujahideen commander who had led the Taliban during its early days.

'I am Hamidullah Rasul,' he said to the group. 'We are not interested in keeping you captive, nor do we intend to harm you,' he said. 'You shall have use of this tent during your stay here, and access to food, water, toilets and medicines.'

'Why have you brought us here?' asked Abbasi.

'Because each one of you is valuable to us,' replied Hamidullah. 'You three Americans would attract a suitable ransom from Washington, D.C. And you two Iranians are wanted men. I am sure that those Shia devils of the IRGC would love to get their hands on you.'

Hamidullah ran an eye over each one in the group. 'If you try to escape, you will be shot by my guards. Even if you do escape, there is nowhere to run for long distances in any direction. The chances of your survival are next to nothing. I suggest that you go along with us without trouble. Akhtar here will be looking after all your needs.' He turned around and left the tent along with Akhtar.

'We've gone from the frying pan into the fire,' murmured Linda glumly. Jim opened his satchel and looked inside. The box containing the Hamzaa Dura was intact. So were his flash drives. His worry was that the lack of temperature and humidity control would cause the Hamzaa Dura to deteriorate. Soroushpur watched him carefully as Jim scrabbled through the contents.

Akhtar came back with a large earthen pot of water hanging from a wooden stick. He placed the pot on a small table near the entrance along with some paper cups. He popped out again and came back with a large vessel containing mutton curry. On its lid were several naan breads. 'Eat,' he said, as he left them alone. None of them was in the mood, but Abbasi forced them to. 'We need to nourish our energy and our wits,' he said. 'Drink water, eat food, get some sleep and exercise. I need each of you to be in good shape if we are ever to get out of here.'

The group ate and then fell asleep, only occasionally disturbed by the calls to prayer. It did not matter which faction of the Taliban it was, all of them were deeply conservative. From 1996 to 2001, the Taliban had held power over seventy-five per cent of Afghanistan, most of them having received traditional Islamic seminary education. Having been displaced by the American-backed Karzai government, the Taliban were now an insurgency movement, and their writ ran large over vast tracts of Afghan land beyond Kabul. But they were now poised to take over the country entirely as the American forces packed up to leave Afghanistan.

The Taliban combined Islamic Sharia law with Pashtun social values to create a cruelly repressive society wherever they ruled. Women could be caned for not wearing their chador properly and men administered corporal punishment for failing to maintain an appropriate length of beard. Girls were actively discouraged from attending school and modern conveniences such as television or smartphones were banned. The Taliban leaders were famous for prolonged arbitrary detention and summary punishments, including executions. Pakistan's Inter-Services Intelligence—the ISI—and its military had provided wholehearted support to the Taliban forces.

At around 2 am, there was a movement in the tent. While everyone else was asleep, Soroushpur was wide awake. He sat up on his cot and put on his shoes very quietly. Getting up, he tiptoed over to the bed where Jim lay. His satchel was on the small table beside him. Soroushpur looked around furtively. *Am I doing the right thing? What if this has nothing to do with the Athravan Star?* he wondered. But he also knew that this was his only chance. *I can't live my life being scared. What belongs to the Zoroastrians must be returned to them, irrespective of whether they live in Iran, India or anywhere else. How dare Jim Dastoor use a hereditary relic as laboratory specimen! And if the Taliban or the IRGC get me, so be it!*

He gently lifted the satchel off the table and crawled towards the left side of the tent. The thick canvas of the tent was stretched over a wooden platform that constituted the floor base. He would have to cut the canvas to create a flap that he could crawl through. He searched for something that he could use. In a corner he saw the sharpened stick that Akhtar had used to hang the water pot on. He used it to puncture a hole in the canvas, ripping it with care not to awaken any of the group.

Minutes later he crawled through the tent and into the open air, Jim's satchel around his neck. His best bet would be to commandeer one of the Taliban vehicles and drive it directly to the Islam Qala border. Undoubtedly, the Iranian authorities would arrest him. But that was a concern for another day. At least the collective heirloom of the Zoroastrians would be back in their homeland and could become a rallying point for the weary community. For centuries, his Zoroastrian brothers and sisters had been trampled upon. Every misery had been heaped on them. It was time for the Zoroastrian spirit to be rekindled in Iran. And he had to be brave. If Heydari could die for his cause, so could Soroushpur.

He remained in a crouching position outside the tent and looked around. There were only two guards at the entrance of the prisoners' tent. The Taliban's vehicles lay parked on the right. He would need to get from the left of the tent to the right and then figure out which vehicle to use. Then, he would need to ram it through the wooden security barrier at the gate and be prepared for a desert race. On the other hand, if he could get his hands on a vehicle *outside* the camp's perimeter, he would be able to leave quietly, giving himself a head start.

He made up his mind and prayed under his breath. *Yatha ahu vairyo atha ratush ashat chit hacha. Vangheush dazda manangho …*

92

ENSCONCED BETWEEN CALICUT Road and Cochin Street in Mumbai's Ballard Estate, lies a French-inspired structure built by Sir George Gilbert Scott, the man who also built the University of Mumbai. It had been commissioned by Shapoor Dastoor but completed by his son Navroze almost a decade later. Known as Dastoor Centre, it was the headquarters of the Dastoor Group, India's largest business conglomerate. The Dastoors had revenues of over 125 billion dollars and accounted for 8.3 per cent of the total market capitalisation of the Bombay Stock Exchange.

The corner office abutting at the Mumbai Port Trust Building was done up tastefully with Burma teak flooring, hand-woven Kashmiri carpets, a highly polished Edwardian desk and paintings by Indian masters like Raza and Gaitonde. Avan Dastoor sat behind the desk on a well-worn leather swivel chair that had once been occupied by her grandfather. She was in conversation with a very old Parsi gentleman. *Why do we Parsis live so bloody long?* she wondered as she looked at him. *Is it something in our genes, our food or our drink that keeps us going on, and on, and on?*

Avan was a striking-looking woman, always impeccably draped in a crisp Banarsi cotton sari, with just a pair of solitaire diamond studs as accessories. She epitomised elegance in simplicity. Her face was much like her brother Jim's—with an aquiline nose and prominent forehead—but the similarity was accentuated by the short crop of salt-and-pepper hair that she refused to colour.

Avan was an accomplished woman, too, and had taken over the reins of the business from her father Baman in 1999. The Indian government had awarded her the Padma Bhushan in 2005 and the Padma Vibhushan in 2014, two of India's highest civilian awards, for her contribution to the country's development. Under her, the group now straddled multiple sectors including cement, power, steel, jute, tea, chemicals, shipping, fertilisers, engines, synthetics, banking, insurance, real estate and information technology. What was more, the group was a leader in every one of those vertical segments.

'What seems to be the problem, Mr Unwalla?' asked Avan. 'I am wondering why my brother's business activities are of any concern to the Bombay Parsi Panchayat. It has been many years since Jim left India and established himself in America.'

Unwalla was an influential man, having worked tirelessly in the panchayat for many decades. Of course, now he was retired and spent his time in Udvada. But the issue of the Athravan Star and his conversation with Soroushpur was on top of his mind. It had taken him several visits to Dastoor House to finally get an audience with Avan.

'I did not wish to bring this up,' shrilled Unwalla, his nasal voice striking a discordant note. 'But your family is not only a business enterprise, it is the guardian of a tradition. That tradition, I am here to tell you, is in danger on account of your brother.'

'The business enterprise you refer to has donated crores to the panchayat,' Avan briskly reminded him. 'Had it not been for the Dastoor family, your coffers would be empty.'

'Oh, we appreciate what the Dastoor family have done for the Parsi community,' replied Unwalla. 'And we know that when Shapoor Dastoor arrived in this city in 1858, the initial capital came from money that had been collected by your family in Udvada. But when matters concerning our traditions are involved, we must all speak in one voice.'

'In the same way that you all banded together to prevent my grandfather Rustom's wife Cecile from adopting the Zoroastrian faith?' asked Avan.

'You are changing the topic,' fought back Unwalla in his irritating voice. 'Your family—like mine—were part of the original nine families entrusted with tending the Iranshah. But among the nine, yours in particular had an even greater responsibility. Your great-great-grandfather Shapoor chose Homi, and Homi chose Rustom, to be the guardian of that extremely precious relic. Rustom passed it on to Jim. So yes, whatever Jim does is indeed a matter of concern to all of us. *All* of us.'

'There was a reason why it was passed on to the most rebellious,' said Avan. 'Possibly Jim's rebellion lies in using it to advance science, not community feeling.'

'That is unacceptable,' said Unwalla.

'Do you even *know* that my brother has been missing for several days now?' interrupted Avan, her pale face flushing pink. It was the first sign of her pent-up anxiety. 'Instead of coming here to express your support, you show up to lecture me on what you consider Jim's misdoings.'

'You do not seem to understand,' persisted Unwalla. 'Dastur Nairyosang Dhaval could not have consecrated the Iranshah without it. And your brother …'

'And you seem to forget that successive generations dealt with different challenges in different ways,' said Avan. 'There were many things that happened between the life of Zarathustra and the advent of the magi; from Persepolis to Borzuya; from Islamic rule to the stand at Hormuz; from Ibn al-Muqaffa to Marco Polo; from the Rivayats to Navsari; and from Udvada to Bombay. When will you and your colleagues update yourselves?' *Even the vultures have disappeared from our dakhmas, now replaced by solar concentrators. But no chance of an original thought from any of you, God forbid!*

'Even our cousins in Iran are worried,' went on Unwalla, unfazed. 'That should tell you something about how serious this matter is.'

The phone on Avan's desk rang. She had instructed her secretary to interrupt fifteen minutes into the meeting. She listened to her assistant for a moment, put down the receiver and then looked at Unwalla apologetically. 'I'm so sorry but we'll have to carry on this conversation another time,' she said. 'I am needed at an audit committee meeting right now.' Unwalla exited Dastoor House, grumbling to himself. He vowed he would teach the snotty Dastoor family how to respect tradition.

He was unaware that someone had been tailing him for days. That someone now fished out his phone to call Luke Miller. 'Unwalla has been to Jim Dastoor's sister's office several times,' he said. 'I wonder if he knows something about the whereabouts of Dastoor and the Hamzaa Dura.'

Miller listened intently to the call from India, then called Ryan Parker at Asclepius.

93

THEY WERE ROUSED by shouting from outside their tent. Before they could react, several Taliban fighters poured into their tent, guns pointed at them. 'Stay exactly where you are,' shouted Hamidullah. 'Don't even think about following him.'

Jim, Linda, Dan and Abbasi blinked awake, and tried to make sense of what was happening. Then they realised that Soroushpur was not among them. Linda looked at her watch. It was 2:10 am.

'Where is Soroushpur?' Abbasi asked Hamidullah loudly. 'Where have you taken him?'

'Don't play games,' Hamidullah yelled back. 'He's escaped from the camp, probably in connivance with you. But don't worry. He won't get too far. Akhtar and his people are after him.'

'None of us knew of his plans,' Jim told Hamidullah quietly. 'We are as shocked as …' He suddenly realised that his satchel was missing. He looked around the tent anxiously, then got down to his knees and looked under the cot.

'Don't move,' shouted Hamidullah. 'Stay still, or I'll shoot.'

Jim put his hands up in the air and sat down on the bed once again. 'My bag is missing,' he said. 'I was simply looking for it.'

'What was inside it that was so important?' asked Hamidullah.

'Just my papers,' said Jim. He knew that it would not be wise to get into detailed explanations with Hamidullah.

'Any idea where Soroushpur has gone?' asked Abbasi of the latter.

'He cut a hole in this tent and crawled out,' replied Hamidullah. 'Then he made his way to the perimeter where a motorcycle lay parked. He is doubtless headed for Islam Qala.'

Jim was dazed by the information. *Why had Soroushpur decided to jump ship after having helped them thus far? Why did he take Jim's bag and the Hamzaa Dura? Why was he headed back in the direction of the Iran border?* Nothing was making any sense to him.

'The actions of your friend have put all of you at risk,' said Hamidullah. 'Until now, we have treated you with respect. But his escape may change all that.' The noises from outside the tent indicated that several instructions were being issued. Running footsteps seemed to be pointing at full mobilisation of the camp. The sound of vehicle engines revving up confirmed that the chase was on.

'We shall cooperate with you entirely,' said Jim. 'But please help me get my bag back. It contains my life's work.'

'We cannot promise anything,' replied Hamidullah. 'At this point of time our priority is to get him, dead or alive. Everything else is secondary.'

'You are mistaken.' Dan spoke for the first time. 'Your priorities are misplaced.'

'What do you mean?' asked Hamidullah.

'Soroushpur is of no value on his own,' said Dan. 'On the other hand, if you are able to retrieve what he has stolen, there would be people willing to pay you unimaginable sums for it.'

Jim looked crossly at Dan. The direction of this conversation was not helping at all. What on earth was Dan trying to achieve? Hamidullah was looking at Dan and Jim alternately, attempting to determine whom to believe.

'Of how much value is the stolen property?' asked Hamidullah.

'Several thousand dollars,' replied Dan. 'My friend Abbasi here, alone would be willing to pay you fifty thousand dollars for retrieving it.'

Abbasi was taken aback. He had already paid Al-Baluchi for transporting all of them. Now he was being asked to cough up cash for retrieving new material. He looked at Jim and read the subtle nod. *I will reimburse you for everything, my friend. Just go along with it.*

'Recreational drugs in the bag?' asked Hamidullah.

'No,' replied Dan. 'Jim is a doctor, and his bag contains important medicines. If your men can get it back, Abbasi will arrange payment.'

'What about your escaped friend?' asked Hamidullah.

'He isn't a friend,' replied Dan. 'Just an acquaintance.' He felt guilty saying it because since their boat crossing from Kish Island to Chiruyeh, it was Soroushpur who had been helping them. But this latest action on the part of Soroushpur was difficult to understand. *Why steal the Hamzaa Dura? Why head back to Iran?* Then Dan remembered that Soroushpur was part of an organisation called the Gabrabad Action Front. *Could that be the reason that Soroushpur had tagged along, on a personal errand—just like Dan himself?*

Abbasi spoke. 'Verse 5:38 in the Qur'an says, "As to the thief, male or female, cut off his or her hands: a punishment by way of example, from Allah, for their crime. And Allah is exalted in power."'

'I will get it back for you if you are willing to pay a hundred thousand dollars,' said Hamidullah. His finger was on the button of his two-way radio, waiting to issue instructions. Jim sighed. Then he nodded his assent.

Hamidullah spoke on his radio in Pashto. 'Avoid using grenades,' he said. 'Shoot if required but get the bag back intact. We do not want an explosion.'

Jim looked gratefully at Abbasi for having quoted the Qur'an at just the right time. Then a look was exchanged between Jim and Dan. It was a silent acknowledgment by Jim of Dan's quick thinking. And then another idea struck him. *If they could pay their way to getting back the Hamzaa Dura, then why not pay their way out of captivity?*

'Instead of negotiating a ransom with others for us, we are also willing to arrive at a figure for our freedom,' said Jim to Hamidullah, noticing the slight smile on the Taliban's face. For these Taliban thugs, nothing mattered more than additional dollars.

And the occasional word of Allah—when it suited them.

94

THE INDIAN NATIONAL Security Advisor—the NSA—got out of his car at the gate of 7, Lok Kalyan Marg, the official residence of the Indian Prime Minister. There was only one gate to the twelve-acre complex and only those prelisted on the visitors' roster were allowed in. Even the NSA's vehicle was stopped at the gate and he walked in on foot through the arjuna- and gulmohar-lined alley.

B. K. Singh—known as BK to his friends—went towards Number Five, the Prime Minister's residence. BK was a tall man, much taller than the average Indian. His extra-long stride allowed him to cover distances much faster than anyone walking alongside. He was fair and entirely bald, with a thick pair of glasses permanently perched on his nose.

The complex contained five bungalows comprising the PM's residence, a venue for casual meetings, a conference facility, a guesthouse and the last, housing the Special Protection Group. BK entered a doorway flanked by two cabins allocated to the PM's private secretaries. He was met by the senior secretary, who led him across the small corridor adorned with paintings from the National Gallery of Modern Art, and opened the door for him to the PM's meeting chamber, where the man himself was waiting. He smiled at BK and asked without pleasantries, 'So what exactly do we know?'

'Not much more than what we did a couple of days ago, sir,' said the NSA. 'Jim Dastoor was kidnapped in Portland a week ago and has been missing since. My contact at the FBI has indicated that the abduction could have been carried out by Iran. But he too seems genuinely clueless about the motive. Chatter from our friends in Tel Aviv indicate that he may have left Iran and gone—or been taken—to Afghanistan.'

'Any information from sources within Tehran?' asked the PM.

'Ever since the Americans applied pressure on us to reduce our oil imports from Iran, our relationship is no longer as warm,' replied BK. 'That is also reflected in the Iranian attitude towards our involvement in the Farzad-B oilfield and the Chabahar port project. May I ask, sir, does Jim Dastoor really matter to us? He is an American citizen now.'

'We should not forget that Jim Dastoor is the son of India's foremost business leader, Baman Dastoor,' replied the PM.

'Starting with Shapoor Dastoor, successive generations of that family—including Navroze, Rustum, Baman and now Avan—have played a very important role in our country's economic progress.' *Let's also not forget that Jim's sister, Avan, who now runs the Dastoor empire, is a generous contributor to my party's coffers.*

The PM looked out of his window at the peacocks in the garden. 'You know that the Americans are also searching for him?' he eventually asked.

'There has been a communication to that effect, sir, from Fred Smith, an FBI Special Agent handling the Jim Dastoor disappearance,' replied BK. 'The Hostage Recovery Fusion Cell of the FBI has also been in touch. But more importantly, the National Security Agency and Mossad are cooperating to find him.'

There was a pause in the conversation. 'There is something that you are not telling me, sir,' said BK. He was probably the only man who could be so frank with the PM. The PM stared at the NSA through his rimless spectacles. Then he gave in. He would have to take BK into confidence.

'In 1932, Rustom Dastoor visited Iran as part of a delegation led by Rabindranath Tagore,' said the PM. 'Most people thought that he was simply included in the delegation because of his love for art.'

'But?'

'But he was there for a secret reason,' said the PM. 'The Parsis were holding on to something that Iran could claim. In fact, the Shah wanted key Zoroastrian treasures brought back, including the Cyrus Cylinder. Rustom was there to convince Reza Shah Pahlavi to ensure that no such claim was made.'

'What was the claim related to?' asked BK, his curiosity piqued further.

'We do not know,' said the PM. 'Stories say that it was something of immeasurable if esoteric value, and that its properties had been referred to in a work by the Persian physician Borzuya. That text was based on an older Indian work.'

'So you think that Jim Dastoor was kidnapped because this particular object is in his possession?' asked BK.

'The fact that it is Jim Dastoor who was kidnapped, and the fact that he has been taken to Iran, leads to that suspicion,' said the PM.

'What would you like me to do?' asked BK.

'First, find out where he is now,' said the PM. 'Second, find a way to get him back.'

The NSA signalled that he understood. 'I shall activate my sources within the IRGC and find out more. Informally, of course,' he said. 'Anything else, sir?'

'Do you still have your do-gooders in Afghanistan?' asked the PM.

The PM was referring to the teams of doctors, engineers and architects who were working inside Afghanistan in an effort to help the country rebuild itself. But what was it worth? It was all about to come to naught with the impending exit of the Americans.

India had constructed a new Parliament building in Kabul, it had rebuilt the Salma dam and erected several transmission lines. All this was in addition to the Chimtala power station, the Zaranj-Delaram highway and countless schools, hospitals, warehouses, reservoirs and tubewells.

'Yes, sir,' replied BK. 'We have several hundred of them still in place. But most of them will have to be pulled out soon.'

'Any operatives among them?'

'A few,' said the NSA. 'I can speak to Subramaniam.' The massive work being executed in Afghanistan had meant that several intelligence operatives from India's Research & Analysis Wing—or R&AW—could be placed there to keep tabs on the activities of Pakistan's Inter-Services Intelligence.

'When did you last speak to Vijay Bhargava in Srinagar?' asked the PM, pouring hot water for himself from a thermos. Lemon and honey water was his staple drink through the day. He gestured for BK to help himself. The NSA politely declined. Milky filter coffee was his preferred pick-me-up.

'It's been a while,' said the NSA. 'I think that he is somewhat miffed with our administration for not having given him a post.'

The PM laughed. 'By administration, you mean me.' The NSA didn't argue. 'Keep a watch on him,' said the PM. 'Something smells funny in Kashmir and whenever that happens, the scent usually leads to him.'

95

THE MIDDLE-AGED, POT-BELLIED man got out of the taxi at the Al-Fahidi district. It hardly felt like Dubai here. This was a world away from the Burj Khalifa, Dubai Mall, Atlantis and the Palm Jumeirah. Old buildings from Dubai's earlier avatar dotted the district. The people here were mostly

Indians and Pakistanis, not the usual Arabs and Europeans visible at the malls. The district felt more like a location in India, Pakistan or Bangladesh, with travel agencies, tea shops, Indian clothing stores, and mom-and-pop groceries jostling for space.

Visitors to Dubai only saw the glitz and glamour of the tourist spots. They rarely saw how the hidden minions lived— the migrant workers that powered the city. These were usually labour camps packed with shabby dormitories containing metal bunk beds. Communal kitchens and blocks of common toilets completed the arrangement in these unsavoury surroundings. The vast majority of these blue-collar workers saved nothing, remitting virtually everything they earned to their families back home.

The visitor passed the Souk Al-Kabeer—the Old Town— and reached the Dubai Creek where many traditional boats packed with workers were parked. On the waterfront, he walked into an Indian clothing store that was brimming with bolts of fabric, saris and shalwar kameez materials. He crossed the sales area and entered the small office at the back. The Pakistani owner, who looked as old as his environment, was sipping his chai. He looked up at the visitor and offered him a chair.

The visitor placed a leather bag on the desk. 'You want to count it?' he asked. The shopkeeper nodded, got up and pulled down the blinds of the window that otherwise allowed him to look into the sales area. He unzipped the bag and took out the bundles of American dollars. He examined a few notes for authenticity. In particular, he looked for the presence of the security thread, and then held the bills up against the harsh ceiling light to check the watermark. He then efficiently fed the bundles into his counting machine. The process was methodical yet quick. This was a man who had been through the routine many times.

After about ten minutes, the shopkeeper looked satisfied with his count. 'All there,' he said. 'I'll inform Hamidullah Rasul in due course.' When his visitor showed no signs of leaving, the shopkeeper looked at him quizzically, then understood. Picking up his phone, he dialled a number. '*As-salaamu alaikum*,' he said. 'Total amount for four people and one parcel has been received, *janaab*.' The voice at the other end spoke briefly. The shopkeeper disconnected the line and looked at the man expectantly.

The visitor got up, exited the store and walked back to the creek. He boarded one of the rickety wooden *abra*s, the trip costing exactly one dirham. The trusted abra was still the most convenient way to travel along the creek, and more than 15,000 passengers used it each day. The reliable system had remained a fixture from the early days of Dubai. He enjoyed the breeze in his face as the boat made its way down the creek to a point opposite the American Consulate.

He got off the boat and walked into the lobby of the First Islamic National Bank that stood on the north bank of the creek. A secretary was waiting for him downstairs. She quickly escorted him via a private elevator to the third floor where he was met by his relationship manager. They crossed a passage and entered a small conference room. 'We withdrew a large amount from the reserve account this morning,' said the man to his manager. 'Have we received an equivalent from the Gemini Cellular Research Center?'

'We're not sure who the ultimate remitter is,' replied the manager. 'But yes, an equivalent amount was transferred into the reserve account in the afternoon. The transfer came in from Bank of America's Seattle branch.'

The man picked up his phone, using an app called Botim to make a VOIP call to a number in London. The call was automatically diverted to Ukraine, which then bounced to a user in Camp Moshe Dayan near Tel Aviv. 'Just to confirm that we have paid out on account and have also been reimbursed on account,' said the man in Dubai. 'Any further instructions for us?'

96

THE AIRCRAFT THAT waited on the open stretch of road was a Cessna 208 Caravan. The original colour was indistinguishable owing to the thick layer of grime that covered it. It had originally belonged to the Afghan Air Force, but a Taliban attack on an airbase at Mazar-i-Sharif had resulted in several aircraft getting captured and grounded.

The Taliban had been quick to kidnap pilots as well, and get them to train their own men. All this at a time when the Americans were busy pulling out of Afghanistan. The pull-out also meant that further investments in the Afghan Air Force had ground to a halt. The one key advantage that the Afghanistan government had had in fighting the Taliban—air power—had now been diluted.

Their pilot was a young man barely into his twenties. He had taken a few hours of flying lessons from an Afghan pilot who had been held captive for several months. The young Taliban pilot had crashed his first aircraft but had managed to bail out a few moments before the machine exploded in the rugged landscape. When they heard this, Jim, Linda, Dan and Abbasi looked at one another, wondering whether there would be a repeat performance on his part. Jim clutched his bag more tightly than ever.

Soroushpur had been traced to Asmadabad and neutralised during a gunfight. The Taliban fighters had pulled him off the stolen Lithuanian motorbike just before it exploded. They had tried to revive him, but the bullet wound to his right atrium had been impossible to plug. They had dumped his body in a shallow grave and then made off with the satchel. This had been presented to Jim after Abbasi had arranged for all the relevant payments through Dubai. The amounts paid out from GCRC to the Mossad courier in Dubai had been a small price to pay for their freedom and the recovery of the prized Hamzaa Dura.

'What is our exit plan?' asked Jim. The question was directed at Hamidullah, who was now their ally after having been bought for dollars.

'My pilot will fly you to the outskirts of Kabul,' replied Hamidullah. 'From there, Bagram Airbase is just a short distance away. The Americans will be happy to arrange for your safe passage out of Afghanistan.' Jim wondered whether the young man who was being referred to as the 'pilot' actually had the ability to fly the dubious machine but realised they would have to go along with the plan.

The group boarded the aircraft. The Cessna had a sanctioned capacity of nine but there were only five passenger seats in addition to the seats in the cockpit. Of these, only three had seat belts. Since there were four passengers—Jim, Linda, Dan and Abbasi—Abbasi offered to sit in the seat that did not have a belt. 'I am quite used to it,' he joked. 'I've spent most of my life without safety belts.'

Hamidullah provided each one of them with a parachute pack. 'Just in case,' he said. It was not a reassuring statement at all.

A strong gust of wind hit the aircraft and it felt like it would topple over. Oblivious to the weather, the young pilot quickly ran through his version of the startup procedures—fuel mixture, brakes, throttle—'We're ready,' he said, a tad too quickly for comfort. '*Khoda hafez*,' said Hamidullah as he disembarked. '*Khair bebeenee.*'

The pilot turned the key and reached for the starter handle. The propellor swung into action, slowly to start with. Then it blurred as the engine sputtered to life. The plane taxied slowly towards the stretch of open land that was to be their runway. The battered machine rumbled down the open stretch, gathering speed, the three tyres conveying every bump and pothole to the occupants. The pilot pulled back on the yoke and, miraculously, the frazzled bird lifted skyward. The pilot banked the wings steeply, turning east, in the general direction of Kabul. He levelled off at 300 metres above the sandy terrain and his passengers collectively heaved a sigh of relief. *The young man seemed to know what he was doing.*

'See? That's the River Harirud below you,' bellowed the pilot as the sputtering Cessna lurched. Linda was ready to throw up her breakfast of tea and bread. She cursed under her breath. 'Can you see those buildings in the distance? That's Herat. It used to have American aircraft stationed there, but those have been pulled out recently,' yelled the pilot, oblivious to the discomfort of his passengers. Dan peered nervously outside to see what the pilot was pointing out. Afghanistan looked just as devastated from the air as it did from the ground.

The pilot turned the noisy machine to follow the river, which would be his best navigation tool for the first half of the journey. 'In how much time should we reach our destination?' shouted Linda, ignoring the sensation of her breakfast sloshing around inside her belly.

'Assuming that we have no problems, the total flying time is three hours,' said the pilot. Dan muttered some obscenities under his breath, thankful that the din of the engine would prevent the pilot from picking up on them.

After the initial assault on their nerves on take-off, and the relief from being airborne, the passengers settled into the noisy rhythm of the aircraft. Linda ditched her chador. *How do women remain under these heavy tents?* The drone of the engine was hypnotic. Dan and Abbasi drifted off into slumber.

They were rudely jolted from their sleep around ninety minutes later. "We're going down!' screamed the pilot as the Cessna lost altitude rapidly. For a moment Abbasi thought that the crazy pilot was playing a vicious joke on them but within a few seconds he realised the warning was horribly real. The junkheap was plunging downwards. 'We must bail out!' cried the pilot. Below them lay the ruins of Balkh, several miles north of their destination. The damned pilot was way off course.

Linda's head swam as the plane shuddered and went into a tailspin. 'Jump! Now!' shrieked the pilot as he let go of the controls, leapt out himself and pulled the ripcord of his parachute. His passengers followed blindly. Jim was almost beyond caring. He'd ceased to wonder if the parachute opened or not—his head told him he was about to die anyway. Considering the state of the Taliban plane, it was very possible that there would be no parachute in the backpack at all. Nevertheless, Jim held onto his satchel tightly.

97

Linda was now floating with the clouds. Her parachute had successfully deployed, and she felt the wind in her face as she floated towards good old mother earth. Thud! The impact was anything but gentle. But there was no time to ponder over the harshness of her collision with the ground. Less than a hundred metres away, the groaning mass of the Cessna had fallen, shrieking, on terra firma and exploded into a fireball. She braced herself and rolled away to escape from the blast of heat from the resultant wreck.

Finally getting to her feet, she looked for Jim. He had landed just fifteen metres away from her but was struggling to extricate himself from his parachute. Then she saw Abbasi and Dan approaching. There was no sign of the young pilot. 'Where the fuck has he landed us?' asked Abbasi, his face covered in soot. All around them were thick walls encircling a vast area. By his own estimation, the circular enclosure encompassed at least a thousand acres.

'Balkh,' replied Linda. 'I can recognise it from hundreds of photographs that I have seen of this place. But if this is Balkh, then we are way off course. We've come north instead of east.' Linda had bruises and cuts on her arms from her fall but, awestruck by her surroundings, ignored them.

'And where is our pilot?' asked Jim, making a bundle out of his parachute.

'He ran off,' replied Abbasi. 'I saw him making off towards one of the squatter colonies bordering this area. He must be worried about what Hamidullah will do to him when he hears that another of his precious birds has been killed.'

'But the long and the short of it is that we are still in Afghanistan,' said Dan. 'And given our dramatic entrance here, it is just a matter of time before we are again in the hands of some militia or the other.'

The ground had caved in at the crash site. Black acrid smoke was pouring out from the Cessna, which had landed nose down, making a gigantic crater. The aircraft had split into two, and assorted debris lay across a radius of at least a hundred metres. Mercifully, no one among them had been seriously wounded. And Jim's precious cargo was intact.

'You seem mesmerised by this place,' he observed to Linda.

'Oh Jim,' she replied ecstatically, 'this is where it all began! Providence has brought us to Balkh!'

'What's so great about this dump?' asked Dan sourly.

'Zarathustra is said to have left his home in Airyanemvaeja and travelled to Balkh—what the Greeks referred to as Bactria.

It was ruled by King Vishtaspa,' said Linda. 'We are right here at the heart of that region. These ruins were probably the mother of all cities!'

'What made Zarathustra come here?' wondered Jim aloud. With the exception of the massive circular enclosure, there was nothing there but barren land.

'He was fleeing from those who violently opposed his religious views,' replied Linda. 'Vishtaspa became his follower after Zarathustra was able to cure the king's horse Aspisiah. There is a wealth of archaeological treasure underneath us. Alas, no archaeological teams have been able to undertake any major digs here owing to the unstable political situation.' *Better that the treasures remain buried,* thought Linda. *If they are discovered, no telling whether they'd be blown up by the Taliban—as the Bamiyan Buddhas.*

Some of the surrounding walls now encompassed villages while some had been taken over by squatters. In the distance, Linda could see people amassing towards the planewreck. Some of them ran in their direction, shouting. But then she saw clouds of dust as a vehicle raced towards the spot where they stood. It was déjà vu. *How many times will we be captured and released, only to be captured again?* she despaired.

The battered Toyota Corolla screeched to a halt beside them and two men holding machine-guns got out. They were followed by a third man who seemed to be their boss. Perfumed and in a black turban, he spoke, 'I am Haji Wasiq, the shadow mayor of this city.'

Linda shot a quizzical look at Abbasi. *Shadow mayor? What the hell is that?* 'The Afghan government's writ does not operate in most areas outside Kabul,' he whispered to her.

'This region—Balkh—is Taliban-controlled. The government forces are unable to leave their bases. This is mujahideen territory and they appoint shadow officials for every position. Their people are the real power centres.'

By then, a few more vehicles had pulled up alongside. More fighters emerged, one carrying a rocket-propelled grenade launcher, another an M4 assault rifle patently seized from US forces. Haji Wasiq sized up the four of them. 'You shall come with me,' he said. 'Your lives could be in danger given that you are outsiders. The people here do not trust outsiders.' *The people seem fine. You seem to be the problem,* thought Linda.

They were bundled into two decrepit sedans that shot off before anyone else could reach the crash site. On the roads, Linda could see large craters left by roadside bombs. Lined up on either side of the roads were heavily armed men. The Taliban militants asserted their authority through sporadic checkpoints along key routes. They would frequently stop and question drivers of passing vehicles to weed out stooges of the Kabul government. But this was Haji Wasiq's motorcade. They only received salutes.

With the impending withdrawal of American forces from Afghanistan, the writing on the wall was clear: The Taliban would have a free run. And along with them, their friends— the Pakistani ISI—too would celebrate. The Taliban remained ultra-conservative. They were prone to slapping villagers for shaving their beards, smashing the stereos of people listening to music, preventing girls from attending school and enforcing a strict Sharia code of conduct.

'Where are we headed?' asked Linda. There was no reply from Wasiq. They could only wait and see.

98

THEIR CARS CAME to a halt around thirty kilometres from where they had crashed. This area too looked like a cluster of ruins. But among those ruins was a group of newly constructed brick and plaster houses. Several turbaned men, armed to the teeth, guarded the perimeter. The group realised that they were inside Haji Wasiq's lair.

They got out of the cars and followed Wasiq into the largest house, where they entered a large hall, whose walls were painted green and floor covered with a deep red floral Afghan carpet. Along all four sides were mattresses and pillows for people to recline. A tall, dark man with white hair and wearing thick spectacles was waiting for them. He was dressed in a simple pathan suit but looked like he would have preferred trousers and a shirt. He stepped forward and stuck out his hand. 'I am Subramaniam,' he said. 'Chief engineer for the power substation in Balkh.'

'You are wondering who this man is,' said Wasiq. 'Subramaniam is from Hindustan. He's part of the delegation that is involved in rebuilding Afghanistan. He is also my friend.'

There was a tiny little pause before the word 'friend'. Abbasi caught on immediately. Subramaniam was India's R&AW operative in Afghanistan. While most of the Taliban were pro-Pakistan, there had long been rumours of a quiet effort on the part of India to win some of the warlords over. Usually, money was the easiest way. There was no such thing as a unified Taliban. Towards the north, the Taliban were under the influence of Tajikistan; towards the east and south, the Taliban were friends with Pakistan; towards the west, the Taliban worked quietly with Iran. Other countries like Russia, India and China worked silently behind the scenes to win over friends in discrete pockets.

'Where exactly are we?' asked Linda.

'This area is known as *Cheshm-e-Shafa* or the City of Infidels,' Subramaniam supplied. Linda was stunned. She had read reams about Cheshm-e-Shafa but had never imagined that it would house the headquarters of a Taliban chief.

'You know about this place?' asked Subramaniam, noticing her expression.

'Yes, as a matter of fact. For many years, villagers have dug here at Cheshm-e-Shafa for pottery and coins to sell to antique smugglers. That's why this place is scarred by craters. This was once an important Zoroastrian city. I am still unclear why the Taliban are staying here.'

'Because they know that they are sitting on treasure,' replied Subramaniam. 'According to all accounts, there are gold and gems underneath us. Haji Wasiq has located his office and residence right here so that any new discoveries are instantly known to him. It is said that Alexander the Great married a princess of Balkh, Roxanne, right here in 327 BCE.' Jim recalled Cecile having talked about this place.

'Why are *you* here?' Dan asked Subramaniam.

'I have received instructions from the Indian Prime Minister's office to ensure your safe passage,' explained Subramaniam. 'Mr Jim Dastoor is a proud son of India, and it is our duty to protect him and his family and friends.' The group was not convinced.

'Don't worry,' said Wasiq. 'Having committed almost three billion dollars, Hindustan is one of the largest donors to Afghanistan. But without friends like me, Subramaniam here cannot move a millimetre. That's why we're together. It's a mutually beneficial relationship. A couple of years ago, a few Indians were kidnapped. I helped Subramaniam save them.'

'How can we get out of here?' asked Abbasi, getting down to tacks.

'We need to get you to the American airbase at Bagram,' replied Subramaniam. 'Although the Americans are withdrawing, presently Bagram still has US personnel and aircraft there. It's an eight-hour drive to Bagram but with Wasiq's protection, we should be able to get you there safely.'

'When can we leave?' asked Linda, impatient to be done with things.

'Rest for a while,' replied Subramaniam. 'Eat something. The *qabili murg pulao* at Wasiq's place is quite good. We can leave in a few hours.' Linda's nose picked up a whiff of the chicken pilaff cooking and she realised she was starving. They sat on the floor soon enough and ate off a massive, shared platter, each one carving out a little portion for themselves.

'Is it possible to have a look at the ruins of Cheshm-e-Shafa?' asked Linda, calmer, after they had eaten.

'Certainly,' replied Subramaniam. 'Come with me, I'll take you there myself.' Linda, Jim and Dan stepped out of Wasiq's house with Subramaniam.

When they were out of the earshot of Wasiq, Linda asked, 'Why has Wasiq allowed us to be alone?'

'Because he is on R&AW's payroll,' replied Subramaniam simply.

'What will happen to non-Muslims in Afghanistan if the Taliban takes over?' asked Linda.

'I'm afraid that it's more a question of when, not if,' replied Subramaniam. 'The Taliban already controls around eighty per cent of Afghanistan. Only Kabul and its surrounding regions are still under control of the Afghanistan government. The Americans are about to pull out any day now.'

'What will happen then?' asked Linda, as they walked out of Wasiq's house and headed into the rubble. Some of the soldiers stared at Linda, dressed in jeans and tee. They were unused to seeing civilian Western women, that too in clothes that did not obliterate them.

'Leave, convert or perish, will be the order of the day,' replied Subramaniam. 'We are living in the twenty-first century, but the Taliban's version of Islam is not very different to that of the eighth.' Subramaniam led the way. 'I am taking you to the anvil,' he said, changing the depressing topic.

'Anvil?' asked Linda.

'The Muslims called this place Cheshm-e-Shafa because they knew that it was a city of infidels—Zoroastrians,' replied Subramaniam. He pointed into the distance. 'See the mountains around us? They would have had lookout towers. So, this place would have been well defended. Ah, we're here.'

It was an anvil-like stone almost two metres high. 'There is a bowl-like indentation at the top, probably used to store oil to feed the Zoroastrian's sacred fire. This may have possibly been the very place where Zarathustra was assassinated.'

'I see trenches,' said Linda. 'Is there an archaeological dig in progress here?'

'Well,' replied Subramaniam, 'in 2008, a team of French and Afghan archaeologists announced the discovery of these ruins. Since then, looters have had free run of the place. Now, it is Wasiq who has employed his own looters. They get paid around five dollars a day to dig. Generally, looters make the best diggers, since they already know the lie of the land.'

'What happens to any discoveries?' asked Jim.

'Proceeds go into the coffers of the Taliban,' replied Subramaniam. He shrugged. 'I know, I know,' he said shamefacedly. 'It's not a solution. But it's better than having them smash valuable statues and figurines. Anything that is not of obvious value, Wasiq diligently passes on to us. We've had to look the other way because we need to be on the right side of the Taliban. They will be Afghanistan's rulers once the Americans withdraw.'

Linda took in the majestic expanse of Cheshm-e-Shafa. Subramaniam picked up on her feelings. 'This is nothing compared to the Naubahar ruins just south of here. The temple there was originally Zoroastrian and then Buddhist.' Linda knew of the place. The priests of Naubahar were known as Barmaks. They had originally been magi who converted in later years to Islam, while retaining many Zoroastrian customs.

Just then, they were rocked on their heels by a massive explosion. 'Take cover,' shouted Subramaniam to the group. They quickly ducked under the stone arches that led to the anvil.

'What's happening?' asked Dan, the nervousness in his voice evident.

'Drone attack,' replied Subramaniam. 'The Americans are trying to weed out Taliban strongholds. They don't know that you are here.'

99

RYAN PARKER STARED at his phone for a while before picking it up and dialling. The call was picked up on the fourth ring. 'Good morning, Huang Xiansheng,' he said, keeping in mind that Beijing was twelve hours ahead of his time. He used the honorific 'Xiansheng' for Huang. After all, Huang was no ordinary Chinese businessman. It was well known that he was the front for a plethora of businesses that were directly or indirectly controlled by China's Ministry for State Security—the MSS.

The MSS was China's behemoth spy agency. While it was headed by the Minister of State Security, who reported to the Central Committee, its divisions were manned by Bureau Chiefs, all veterans and all powerful in their own right. The MSS was meant to keep tabs not only on countries that were militarily, politically, or economically relevant to China—including the US, Taiwan, South Korea and Japan—but also on regional powers with which China shared borders—including Russia, India and Vietnam.

Huang had no designation at all. He was merely a businessman, and one of the most globally recognised ones.

Using him as their international face, the MSS was able to strike global alliances that looked perfectly innocent: academic collaborations, business partnerships, philanthropic ventures and scientific alliances.

Born in Hangzhou, Zhejiang, Huang had begun learning English at a young age by conversing with English-speaking tourists at a local hotel. For almost a decade, Huang would ride thirteen kilometres on his bicycle to give tours of the area to international visitors. He had then tried to get admitted to the Hangzhou Teachers College but had failed to. Eventually, he had been recruited by the MSS to be their liaison with the outside business world, on account of his language skills.

'Ah, Mr Parker,' said Huang in perfect, unaccented English. 'How nice to hear from you. I assume that you are calling in regard to the matter of Jim Dastoor?'

'I need your help,' Parker went straight to the point. 'Dastoor and his Hamzaa Dura could be game-changers in my world.'

'Not only in your world, Mr Parker,' said Huang.

'What do you mean?' asked Parker, mystified.

'As it turns out, we too have some history regarding this material,' replied Huang. 'That history dates back to 1275 CE.'

'I don't understand,' said Parker.

'You see, in that year, the great traveller Marco Polo arrived at the palace of Kublai Khan in Shangdu—now in Mongolia. He brought with him several gifts for the Khan, some of them from Venice and Constantinople, others from locations he had passed through.'

'And this has something to do with Jim Dastoor's research material?' asked Parker.

'Allow me to explain, Mr Parker. Around 1271 CE, Marco Polo, his father and his uncle had set off for Asia. They sailed to Acre—a city in present-day Israel. From there, they rode their camels to a great Persian port city.'

'Which city was that?' asked Parker.

'Hormuz,' replied Huang. 'The very city from which Persia's Zoroastrians had fled to Diu and then on to Sanjan in the eighth century.'

'Did Marco Polo give something from Hormuz to Kublai Khan?' asked Parker.

'Yes,' said Huang. 'Some of the Zoroastrians left behind in Persia had tried sending some items to their Indian counterparts. These included a book. They entrusted Marco Polo with these items. But Marco Polo reached Kublai Khan first, who insisted on the book being given to him. The book spoke of a wondrous object called the Athravan Star, fabled to have immensely powerful properties. Alas, the object itself was not discovered by Marco Polo.'

'Did Marco Polo or the Khan try to find it?' asked Parker.

'Sure,' replied Huang. 'The Khan appointed Marco Polo as his foreign emissary and sent him on diplomatic missions to India, Burma, Indonesia, Sri Lanka and Vietnam. The agency was a mere cover—Marco Polo's appointed quest was the Athravan Star. When he had no luck finding it, he expressed his desire to return home, but the Khan refused. Finally, he granted him permission to leave in 1291, but not without extracting a commitment.'

'Tell me what it was,' said Parker.

'He asked Marco Polo to escort the Mongol princess, Kokochin, to Persia. There, she was to be wedded to Arghun

Khan. Again, that was the cover. The primary purpose was to send Marco Polo back to Persia to try and find the Athravan Star.'

'Given that we are on the same side of this issue, would it be too difficult for you to speak to some of your contacts in the Pakistani establishment?' asked Parker.

100

THE SKY LIT up and explosions rocked the ground beneath them. The force of the initial blast threw them backwards, and even before they recovered, more explosions followed. They remained glued to the ground as the air became thick with dust and black smoke. 'How long will they continue the bombing?' asked Linda plaintively.

'Not more than a few minutes,' replied Subramaniam calmly. 'They are usually quite precise and know exactly what they are after.'

'This is an archaeological site!' hissed Linda furiously.

'Yes,' replied Subramaniam. 'But that is also one of the reasons why Wasiq chooses to operate from here—knowing that the Americans would be wary of bombing such a site. I guess their impending pullout is making them more aggressive and less particular.'

The group got to their feet unsteadily. They were covered in mud and soot, but unhurt. Just then, another explosion ripped through the anvil. The blast was so strong that it completely tore a crater into the gigantic rock. A few Taliban vehicles in the area were engulfed in flames, sending dense smoke into the air.

After several anxious moments of remaining frozen to their spots, the group moved once again. Each one knew how lucky they were to have survived such a massive attack. Subramaniam's white pathan suit had turned the colour of *khak*, dust. What the world called khaki. They cautiously made their way to Wasiq's house, wondering whether it still existed. In Linda's hand was a fragment of rock that had landed near her.

Wasiq's house was rubble.

Immediately after 9/11, American Predator drones had detected Osama bin Laden, the Al Qaeda leader, from the skies. But the first targeted strike in October 2001 had missed its intended mark of the Taliban leader Mullah Omar, although a few of his bodyguards had been killed in a vehicle outside his hideout. The Americans, undeterred by the botched operation, had continued to arm and deploy both Predator and Reaper drones in Afghanistan, Pakistan, Iraq, Somalia, Yemen, Libya and Syria, their accuracy improving with each strike.

The house where the group had eaten lunch was no longer there. Several of the men guarding it lay dead or wounded on the ground. Cries and wails from people in the neighbourhood filled the air. 'Do you think Wasiq is alive?' asked Jim. Subramaniam wordlessly gestured for the group to follow him.

They made their pockmarked way to a spot where a huge block of stone had been moved amidst the wreckage. Next to it was a trapdoor. Subramaniam used his hands to brush away the thick layer of soot before grasping the handle to lift the door and peer inside. He then made his way gingerly down the steps, asking the group to follow.

Inside the basement they found themselves in, battery-operated emergency lights had taken over. The walls were of thick reinforced concrete, typical of bomb shelters. A calm and collected Wasiq sat inside with a gun in his hand and surrounded by bodyguards. He looked victorious as they walked in. 'Those bastards can keep trying, but they will never get to me,' he sneered.

Even more surprising were the walls behind Wasiq. They were lined with American assault rifles, lasers, night-vision goggles, rocket-launchers, handguns and grenades. 'All gifts from our American friends,' said Wasiq with a wide sweep of his arms. 'They come to battle often—and lose their equipment as frequently,' he chuckled. 'That's why they're pulling out of Afghanistan. They can't even hold on to their weapons!' Afghanistan had always been a notoriously difficult region to govern. Empires and nations had utterly failed in taming the warrior people, earning their homeland a nickname—the 'Graveyard of Empires'.

Linda, Jim and Abbasi sat down on the floor next to Wasiq. Subramaniam joined them. 'We shall have to wait a while before we start our journey to Bagram,' he said.

None of the group seemed to realise that one of their members was missing.

Dan Cohen would have been the last in line down the stairs, but something had earlier caught his eye. Near the main entrance to Wasiq's collapsed house lay one of Wasiq's dead comrades. Next to him was something valuable: a

Thuraya satellite phone. Dan had picked it up quickly and run to the rear end of the house, far from possible earshot of his group or any of the surviving guards. He dialled 00, the outbound prefix and then punched in a mobile number with the US country code prefix. He breathed a sigh of relief as the call went through.

'Yes?' asked the voice at the other end. It was Luke Miller's.

'We're in Afghanistan,' Dan breathed. 'Heading to Bagram later today. Once Jim and his material are in American hands, I don't know what I'll be able to do.'

'Good you called me,' replied Luke. 'You're learning fast,' he added.

'What's my next step?' asked Dan.

'Find a way to delay the group's departure,' replied Luke. 'It will give me time to activate my contacts in the region.'

'Even if I do manage that, what next?' quavered Dan, looking around to ensure no one was listening.

'You guys will be travelling along the AH76 to reach Bagram,' said Luke. 'Just before you reach Bagram is a village called Malkhan. My men will be waiting there.'

'Who are they?' asked Dan. 'I hope they will not hurt any of us?' Memories of Mistress Lucinda came flooding back.

'None of your business,' replied Luke peremptorily. 'You simply need to be aware that your party will be ambushed at Malkhan. Leave the rest to Ryan Parker and me.'

'I'm kind of uncomfortable with this,' Dan whined.

'Not as uncomfortable as you will be when the tabloids publish your photos,' replied Luke. 'Remember the Kettering Prize. Are you going to give up so easily?'

Dan took a deep breath. 'I'll try my hardest not to,' he replied.

'You'd better,' snarled Luke.

101

LINDA AND I *moved in together while we were still students at Stanford. It seemed just the obvious solution to our inability to do without each other.*

One day, over a mug of our even newer addiction—Hawaiian Kona coffee—she said, 'You know a lot about Zarathustra and his teachings, also a fair deal about what happened after *he died. But you seem to know very little about the period before he came on the scene.'*

'Are you talking about when dinosaurs roamed the earth?' I asked lightheartedly. Everything was a bubble of fun so long as she was around to toss it back to me.

'Seriously, Jim,' she forced me back to gravity, 'what was the religion of his people before he introduced his ideas?' asked Linda. 'They must have believed in something. *Coming from somewhere.'*

'Scholars say Zarathustra was born around 1500 BCE, in a land called Airyanemvaeja,' I replied, sobering up reluctantly.

'But there is no clarity on where Airyanemvaeja was,' she said.

I mulled over Linda's words. 'I take it you have a theory,' I deduced from her expression.

'Well,' she replied, on cue, 'in the Western world, "Persia" had been the name for Iran. It was only in 1935 that Reza Shah Pahlavi asked the global community to use the term "Iran" when referring to his country. But where did the word "Iran" come from?'

'Where?' I echoed dutifully.

'The name was first used in the Avesta as Airyanemvaeja,' replied Linda. 'The name can actually be broken down into two words, "airyanem" and "vaeja". "Airyanem" implies Aryan—or noble. And "vaeja" comes to us from the Vedic Sanskrit term "vej", meaning the region of a fast-flowing river. And "Iran" is simply a derivative of the word "Aryan".'

'So, put together, what do all those funny noises add up to?' I asked, still aiming for levity.

'They add up to, as you quaintly put it, "the Aryan land of the fast-flowing river".' Until then, I had never thought about the etymological roots of the word 'Iran'. I listened to Linda with greater attention now, wondering where she was going with her theory.

'Airyanemvaeja provides us two important clues,' said Linda. 'One, that this was a land of Aryans. Two, it was a land that contained a rapidly flowing river.'

'But there are so many rivers in the world,' I argued. 'It could be anywhere.'

'True,' replied Linda, 'but for the moment, let's focus on the fact that Zarathustra established his first congregation in the court of Vishtaspa. That was in Bactria—today's Balkh region, in Afghanistan.'

'So, we should consider the rivers in Afghanistan,' I put in.

'We should,' advised Linda. 'In fact, there is a river called the Haraxvati mentioned in the Avesta.'

'Where is that river located?' I asked.

'Western scholars associate it with the River Helmand or the River Arghandab in Afghanistan,' replied Linda.

'That's it, then,' I said. 'Airyanemvaeja would have been in Afghanistan.'

Linda had on her scholarly face. 'But just think, Jim. What if "Haraxvati" is actually a corruption of the word "Sarasvati"?' That did set me thinking. Could Linda be right?

'The Persians commonly replaced the "s" sound of Sanskrit with the "h" sound,' Linda pursued her line of thought. 'Sindhu became Hindu; soma became haoma; asura became ahura … So, isn't it possible that Sarasvati became Haraxvati?'

'But the Sarasvati does not exist,' I argued. I remembered this from my history classes in school. Our teachers had declared that the river was pure myth!

'It no longer exists,' Linda corrected me. 'But it was the mightiest of the Indian rivers until around five thousand years ago. In fact, satellite imaging has identified the path of the lost river.' Linda looked up something on her computer. Then she began reading from a web page that popped up.

May the divine Sarasvati, rich in her wealth,
Protect us well, furthering all our thoughts with might.
Whose limitless unbroken flood,
Swift-moving with a rapid rush,
Comes onward with tempestuous roar.
Seven-sistered, sprung from threefold source,
Marked out by majesty among the Mighty Ones,

In glory swifter than the other rapid streams,
Created vast for victory like a chariot,
Sarasvati must be extolled by every sage.
Guide us, Sarasvati, to glorious treasure.

'Where is that text taken from?' I asked.

'Mandala six, hymn 69 from the Rigveda,*' she replied. 'The Vedic heartland was traversed by the Sarasvati, which was part of the seven sisters, a family of rivers. Hence the term "Sapta Sindhu" or the "land of the seven rivers".'*

Linda quickly switched the open tabs on her computer. 'There is a hymn in the Rigveda *that starts with the Ganges and describes the rivers as one that travels west towards Afghanistan,' she explained.*

O Ganga, Yamuna, Sarasvati, Shutudri (Sutlej), Parushni (Ravi), hear my praise!
Hear my call, O Asikni (Chenab), Marudvridha (Maruvardhvan), Vitasta (Jhelum) with Arjikiya and Sushoma.
First you flow united with Trishtama, with Susartu and Rasa, and with Svetya,
O Sindhu (Indus) with Kubha (Kabul) to Gomati (Gomal), with Mehatnu to Krumu (Kurram), with whom you proceed together.

'In the Manusmriti *it is recounted that the sage Manu, after escaping from a giant flood, founded the Vedic civilisation,' explained Linda. 'And where did he establish this Vedic—or Aryan—civilisation? In the land east of the river Sarasvati!*

Thus, the Sarasvati was part of Aryan lands. The coincidence is simply too great to dismiss, Jim. Airyanemvaeja would most probably have been the Aryan land of the seven sisters.'

I was confused. What Linda was saying went against everything that I had learnt so far. I had been told that the original home of the Zoroastrians was Greater Khorasan— an area consisting of the north-eastern parts of the land now occupied by Iran, Iraq, Azerbaijan, Turkmenistan, Tajikistan and Afghanistan. India had never figured in that collection. The general belief was that my ancestors had come to India from Khorasan.

Now Linda was telling me that we Parsis had simply returned to our original home!

102

'THERE IS YET *another clue to Zarathustra's origin,' continued Linda. 'One that could pinpoint the region of his birth with even greater accuracy.'*

'And that is?' I asked. After her last exciting revelation, I was determined to keep my mind open to hers.

'Remember the story about the sacred cypress tree that Zarathustra planted outside the first fire temple? The one established by King Vishtaspa?' asked Linda.

'Yes,' I replied. 'It is said to have survived for thousands of years and was only cut down on the orders of the Abbasid caliph Mutawakkil. As per legend, the caliph was assassinated

by a Turkish soldier on the very night the cut cypress arrived on the banks of the Tigris.'

'Full marks,' said Linda snidely. 'That fire temple and tree were in a town in Khorasan. Zarathustra planted that cypress tree there because it represented his home. The species of the tree was Cupressus cashmeriana.'

'So?'

'That species is called Cupressus *"cashmeriana" precisely because it is the* Kashmiri *cypress,' Linda emphasised. 'The Khorasan town that contained the fire temple eventually began to be called "Kashmar" because of that particular tree! Zarathustra's original home was Kashmir!'*

'But that's impossible,' I spluttered. 'Zarathustra's first refuge was Bactria. And his ideas took root in Iran.'

'You are looking at today's political boundaries,' replied Linda. 'They are confusing you. In ancient times, all those countries were part of a gigantic Vedic civilisation that included Kashmir. The Avesta also talks of "Anu-varshte daenya" or the "religion of the land of the Anu people". The Anu tribe, often referred to as the Anavas, lived in Kashmir.' After a brief pause to let her words sink in, she asked, 'In Afghanistan you have a city called Kandahar. Where do you suppose that name come from?'

'It comes from "Gandhara",' she answered her own question, 'the ancient Hindu—and later Buddhist—kingdom located along the Kabul and Swat rivers of northern Afghanistan.'

'Ah!' I said, grateful she'd saved me the trouble of responding to her inquisition. But before I could relax, Linda attacked me with yet another question.

'And who was the most famous character from Gandhara in Hindu mythology?' asked Linda. I shrugged helplessly.

'Gandhari,' replied Linda triumphantly. 'She was the wife of Dhritharashtra—in the epic, the Mahabharata.'

'Oh!' I exclaimed, remembering the stories that abounded around the blind king and his blindfolded queen.

'So, you see, Jim, today's modern political boundaries obfuscate our origins. Aryan culture was not limited to what is now called India. The expanse of Airyanemvaeja would have included many countries stretching from India to Syria. Possibly even beyond.'

'Beyond?' I asked.

'Give it a thought,' suggested Linda. 'Way back in 1380 BCE, there was a treaty between two kingdoms—the Hittites and the Mittani.'

'Where are they on the map today?' I wanted to know.

'They are roughly portions of today's Turkey and Syria,' replied Linda. 'But what's amazing is that the ancient treaty invoked Vedic deities such as Mitra, Varuna, Indra and Nasatya. In essence, Vedic civilisation stretched from India into Europe.'

'As far afield as Europe?'

'Sure,' said Linda. 'Let's go even further west. Ireland owes its name to the word "eire" in their language. But what does that word "eire" actually mean? Noble! How is that different to "arya" or "airyanem", which also mean noble?'

'And then, let's proceed to another interesting connection,' she said next. 'The entire Assyrian Empire, the very cradle of Mesopotamia, had a capital city called Assur. In fact, the name of the empire—Assyria—is derived from Assur. Isn't that strange?'

'Why is that strange? It only follows logic,' I said.

'Because in today's Hinduism, asuras are malevolent forces, and the devas are benevolent ones. In Zoroastrianism we have the ahuras and daevas but with their characteristics reversed.'

'What explains that?' I asked.

'In the Rigveda, the term asura was used to describe a mighty one,' explained Linda. 'The word was more of an adjective than a noun. The term not only applied to gods, but also to powerful humans. Asura was thus a title of the highest honour. It was often used to describe devas too, simply to emphasise their power.'

'So, the use of the word asura to symbolise a malevolent force came much later in Hinduism?' I asked.

'Exactly,' said Linda with confidence in her conclusions. 'The Assyrians called their city Assur, to indicate that it was the capital of a mighty kingdom. The city even had a presiding deity known as Ashur.'

I was attempting to absorb all this new information when Linda dropped her bombshell. 'But even the Muslims and the Jews are connected to Ashur,' she said.

'Now, that's taking things too far,' I said lamely. Because, deep down, I knew that Linda would have cogent reasons for claiming something as outrageous as that.

'The Rigveda describes an ancient war known as "Dasarajna" or the "battle of the ten kings",' cited Linda. 'In this war, a confederation of ten asura kings were pitted against the Bharata clan—the lineage from which India derives its name "Bharat".'

'Where did this battle take place?' I asked.

'Near the River Ravi,' replied Linda. 'The Ravi is one of the seven sisters of the Sapta Sindhu. This battle marked the Vedic *schism, with the asuras being pushed westwards of the Sapta Sindhu.'*

'Resulting in ... ?' I prompted.

'The word "asura" coming to be associated with the number ten because ten kings had allied against the Bharata clan,' said Linda. 'West of the Sarasvati, in Semitic languages, asura came to mean "the tenth".'

'But how does that relate to Jews or Muslims?' I asked.

'The Jews celebrate Yom Kippur—the day of atonement— on the tenth day of the seventh month. Centuries later, Mohammad encouraged his flock to also fast on the same day and this became Ashura, the tenth day of the first month of the Islamic calendar, Muharram.'

'But Ashura is a date that is important to only Shia Muslims,' I argued. 'It had something to do with the grandson of the Prophet Mohammad.' I was trying to recall what Cecile had told me about that years ago.

'That was years later,' said Linda. 'Hussein, the grandson of the Prophet Mohammad, was martyred in the Battle of Karbala. Given that it happened on the Day of Ashura, this also became a day of mourning for the Shia community who supported his line of ascendancy to the Prophet's position.'

'So, the Islamic observance of "Ashura", the Mesopotamian city of "Assur", the Assyrian deity "Ashur", the Rigvedic "asura", and the Avestan "ahura" are all connected?' I asked, amazed by what seemed so starkly obvious now.

'Certainly, they are,' Linda endorsed my understanding of her statement. 'The entire expanse of Airyanemvaeja would have associated the word asura with power. But in later years, there was a division between those who lived to the west and those who lived to the east.'

'You're talking about the division caused by the war of ten kings?' I asked. I was feeling proud that I had remembered that nugget of information.

'I am,' agreed Linda. 'But the divide was best exemplified by two individuals: Bhrigu and Brihaspati.'

'Who were Bhrigu and Brihaspati?' I asked, a tad exasperated. How much further was she going to drag me back till I became a dried-up relic of history myself?

'Bhrigu was the teacher of the asuras, and Brihaspati was the teacher of the devas. The two sages were rivals.'

'How does that have anything to do with Zoroastrianism?' I asked.

'It has everything to do with Zarathustra,' Linda came back strongly. 'Before Bhrigu and Brihaspati, both terms—asuras and devas—were considered terms of respect. The only difference between them was that asuras were considered formless, whereas devas were visible.'

'Hmm, so what does the word "deva" actually mean?'

'Deva means "the shining one". Now, it's impossible for something to shine if it isn't visible, right? So, devas were the visible ones and asuras were the formless or invisible ones.'

'And a sect developed around each?' I asked.

'Yes,' replied Linda. 'The schism resulted in two streams of worship—pitrayana and devayana. The former paid obeisance to the asuras and the latter worshipped the devas.'

'Let's go along with that for the moment,' I said. I wanted to hear out Linda's arguments fully.

'One of the famous descendants of Bhrigu was Vashishtha,' explained Linda. 'He was a devotee of Varuna, the greatest asura of them all. But there was a second great devotee of Varuna. In the Rigveda his name is Jarutha.'

'Jarutha?' I asked.

'Sounds suspiciously like Zarathustra, doesn't it?' asked Linda, with a Mona Lisa smile.

103

'NONSENSE,' I TOLD her. But my tone lacked certainty.

'Jarutha and Vashishtha were on the same side, Jim,' said Linda. 'They were both worshippers of Varuna. But it seems that Jarutha had new ideas that did not sit well with Vashishtha. Jarutha had to leave his home in order to have those ideas accepted. He was the first rebel in a line of rebels.'

This story seemed to be stretching matters too far. Linda picked up the scepticism in my expression. 'Just because it doesn't fit with a version you have heard doesn't make it less plausible,' she said, and continued. 'Jarutha—or Zarathustra as we know him—travelled to Bactria. He went to the court of Vishtaspa—and you know the rest of the story.'

Linda was scrutinising my face to pick up any expression of disbelief. Apparently satisfied that there was none, she continued with yet another exercise in rhetoric. 'Do you know what Varuna was called in the Rigveda?'

'No idea,' I said, as she knew I would.

'He was called Asura Maya,' replied Linda. 'That's because Varuna's supernatural power was "maya" through which he could carry out such tasks as providing rain and creating rivers. It was this Asura Maya who became Zarathustra's Ahura Mazda in the new faith!'

'Why should I believe anything sourced from a Veda, a book of another's religion?' I asked, at last, defiantly.

'Well, for one thing,' said Linda, 'because Vashishtha is not only referred to in the Rigveda but also in the Avesta. The only difference is that the name "Vashishtha" becomes "Vahishta" in the Avesta. I'd described to you earlier, Jim, how "h" replaced "s" sounds west of the Sapta Sindhu.'

'Even if I believe your theory that Ahura Mazda was actually Asura Maya—or Varuna—in Zarathustra's theological construct, there was also an Angra Mainyu—or Ahriman—in opposition to Ahura Mazda.'

'Correct,' said Linda. 'But by the time of Zarathustra, there was an asura-deva divide. Remember that Bhrigu was the guru of the asuras, and Brihaspati of the devas?'

'So?'

'The followers of Bhrigu, including Zarathustra, did not care for Brihaspati,' replied Linda. 'Another name for Brihaspati is Angirasa. In Zarathustra's world, Angirasa took on the persona of Angra Mainyu or Ahriman.' My head was reeling from the onslaught of words that curled and twisted before my very eyes. Linda took a calm sip of her now cold coffee as she observed me.

Finding me still receptive despite my reservations, she went on. 'In Zarathustra's construct, the devas and their teacher Angirasa became negative forces. And you don't have to be told, Jim, that power can be positive or negative. The word "deva" is the root for words like "divine" and "deity". But it is also the root for words like "devil" and "demon". Think about that one!'

There was a pause in our conversation. 'Zarathustra's own family was a priestly one, you do know that, right?' asked Linda.

'Yes,' I replied, like a good student. 'They were called "magi" from which we get the word "magic".' I felt almost virtuous for knowing the answer to at least one of her posers.

'Like the "Three Wise Kings of the Orient" in the Bible,' concurred Linda. 'But where does the word "magi" come from?' Luckily, this turned out to be a rhetorical question as well, and Linda went on to provide the answer before I could open my mouth.

'Magi, of course, is the plural form of the word "magus",' spelt out my in-house thesaurus and encyclopaedia a little too didactically. 'And magus denotes many things: a wizard, clairvoyant, seer, soothsayer, priest or occultist.' Of course, I knew that!

'But the root of magic, magi, and magus lies in the word "maga",' continued Linda. 'In the Rigveda, the word maga implies mastery or command. It denotes greatness and loftiness. Indra is often called a "magavan" or one possessing great power. All the great rishis of Vedic civilisation were magas. Bhrigu, Brihaspati, Vashishtha, Zarathustra and many others were magas! That made all of them magi!'

'But none of this gives us certainty regarding Kashmir being the birthplace of Zarathustra,' I argued.

'The Avesta says "Airyanemvaeja vanghuydo daityayo",' countered Linda. 'That roughly translates to "land of the Aryans by the River Daitya".'

'So?' I challenged.

'Kashmir has a river named Diti which flows into the Jhelum. The entire Jhelum is referred to as the Daitya in the Avesta.'

'How can we be sure of that?' I asked, determinedly sceptical, despite my earlier resolve.

'There is another Zoroastrian work of cosmology, the Bundahishn. It calls the river Daitya "the chief of all streams". It is interesting that the Jhelum has more streams—tributaries— than most other river systems.'

I ceased to prolong the debate, proven out of depth in her ocean of research. 'One final thought for you to consider,' said Linda, unrelenting.

I waited for her to tell me.

'It is said that when Zarathustra was around thirty years old, he attended a celebration of the vernal equinox,' said Linda. 'It was the spring festival that Zoroastrians now celebrate as Nowruz.'

'Oh, yes,' I said. 'I'm told he had been drawing water from the purest part of the River Daitya when an angel granted him a vision of Ahura Mazda.'

Linda appeared unsure whether she really wanted me to play teacher's pet. Then she touched my hand companionably. 'But Jim, were you aware that Kashmiri Pandits celebrate the exact same date? Only, they call it Navreh instead of Nowruz!'

'Also, did you know that all Brahmins, including Kashmiri Pandits, had to encase their upper bodies with a vest called the sadr? The magi were similarly required to wear an undervest called the sadreh. And of course, both social groups required the wearing of a sacred thread. It's probably the reason why Parsi children continue to receive these sacraments to this day during their Navjote ceremonies.' I remembered my own Navjote. Both my sister Avan and I had been given the sacred kushti and sadreh to wear in a grand ceremony at the Seth Jeejeebhoy

Dadabhoy Agiary in Colaba. We had then eaten at a veritable banquet punctuated by gulps of raspberry soda—that elixir Mrs Batliwala treated me to over at her house.

I had always known that my ancestors came to India from Iran. Now Linda was telling me that Zarathustra himself went westwards from India. It was like turning the entire story upside-down in my head. 'The connections between Zoroastrianism and the Vedic religion are just too many to ignore,' said Linda.

'How many more are there?' I asked.

'For example, outside Zoroastrian fire temples you find Lamassu, the mythical winged bulls. And outside Hindu temples you will find Nandi the bull. Don't you wonder why? But,' she said, keeping the best for the last, 'the connection most talked about is the one between the two languages—Sanskrit and Avestan. Look at this ...' Linda pulled up a page on her computer.

Rigveda 10.87.21:
Mahaantaa mitraa varunaa samraajaa devaav asuraaha sakhe ...

Gatha 17.4 Yasna 53.4:
Mahaantaa mitraa varunaa devaav ahuraaha sakhe ...

Even I couldn't suggest it was coincidence.

'There are countless examples like that, where the sentences are almost identical,' said Linda. 'Take, for instance, the words "tam amavantam yajatam" in Sanskrit. In Avestan, they are rendered as "tem amavantem yazatem". Both phrases mean the same thing—"the powerful God".'

'*Take another simple sentence,*' Linda added, *more and more excited about sharing, at last, the precious knowledge she'd hugged all this time to herself, fearing a lack of interest in her fellow students.* '*The sentence reads: "To which God should I sacrifice?"* In the Atharvaveda, *it is "kasmai devaaya vidhema".* In the Zend Avesta, *the words are "kamhai devaaya vidhema". Virtually indistinguishable!*'

'*But mere language does not establish one's birthplace,*' I *bravely picked up the gauntlet yet again.* '*Indians and Iranians could have had a common origin—in some place in central Asia, or the Eurasian steppes.*'

'*In Sanskrit, the land of the seven rivers is Sapta Sindhu,*' Linda *reminded me, stopping just short of rapping my knuckles, I thought with secret amusement.* '*In Avestan it is called the Hapta Hindu. In the* Vendidad, *Ahura Mazda describes sixteen "perfect lands". The penultimate one on that list is the Hapta Hindu. So, this land was not alien to Zarathustra. Add to that what I told you about the cypress tree and the town of Kashmar. And to that, the Avestan reference to the "Anu-varshte daenya" or the "religion of the land of the Anu people". Then factor in the River Daitya. We have to take in all the evidence, Jimmy, not just parts of it!*'

104

SOME IMP—OR, AS *Linda would say,* jinni—*in me, wanted to disbelieve everything she was telling me, but I could not shrug off the facts. Sensing the conflict in my head, she struggled to*

*convince me of her own certitude. 'Even the very word "Gathas",
hymns by Zarathustra, is similar to the word "katha"—which
means a story or poem. Both words stem from the Sanskrit root
"gai"—to sing.'*

'Or chant.'

*'Quite right,' approved Linda. 'The Vedas, like the Avesta, are
chanted. The very word "chant" comes to us from the Sanskrit
word "chhanda" that denotes the metre to which recitations are
made. Go forward in time, and "chhanda" becomes "zend", as
in the Zend Avesta.'*

*'And "avesta"?' the query naturally followed. 'What does
that word mean?'*

*'The Sanskrit word "apistika", denoting a book, became
"avesta",' replied Linda. 'The Vedic "yajna" became "yasna"
in Zoroastrianism. Entire paragraphs from the Gathas can
be converted into pure Sanskrit through sheer phonetic
transference.'*

Linda's every revelation chipped away at the construct in
my head. *'Both faiths include common deities such as Varuna,
Mitra, Yama, Vayu and Aryaman,'* she reaffirmed. *'The
similarities are there for everyone to see—and for some of us
to marvel at.'*

*'Just as Hindus include the word "namo" in their mantras,
Zoroastrians too use the term in phrases such as "Namo Ahurai
Mazdai",' said Linda. 'Then "Nemasete" is another term used
by Zoroastrians which is the equivalent of the Sanskritic
"Namaste". Muslims use the word "namaz" for prayer. Most are
unaware that the word comes from the very same root!'*

Linda jogged my mind. *'Do you remember the story of the
king's horse that Zarathustra cured?'*

'Sure,' I replied. 'King Vishtaspa had a horse called Aspisiah which fell sick.'

'In Sanskrit,' expanded Linda. 'The word for "horse" is "ashva". In Avestan it became "aspa". We've learnt that Zarathustra's benefactor had a beloved horse call Asp-isiah. And the king himself, who was also a great equestrian, earned the title Visht-aspa.'

'That's just linguistics all over again,' I groaned.

'Hindus and Zoroastrians offer prayers to their ancestors,' Linda went on undeterred. 'Both use fire in their ceremonies. Their deities are common. That's not linguistics. The Baresman bundle is not linguistics. It's knowledge derived by tireless research, Jimmy! Just as science is to you.'

'The Baresman bundle?' I asked, latching onto the half-familiar phrase. Then I recalled that it was the bundle of twigs that the magi carried around with them for medicinal purposes.

'They were twigs that could be juiced and combined in various ways into healing potions,' replied Linda. 'Scholars now say that the twigs were from the "chini" tree. Do you realise that the chini tree is actually the chinar, a tree that is ubiquitous in Kashmir? It's also interesting that the Vedic description for the specially woven grass mat in front of an altar is "barhish". The Avestan "baresman" is a cognate of that word.'

'Fire was of supreme importance in Iranian rituals,' continued Linda. 'In ancient Iran, fire was deified as "Athar". Because burnt offerings were never made to God, Athar's role was mainly that of an intermediary between heaven and earth—and between humans and gods. This is similar to Athar's Vedic counterpart Agni. Hindus even have an Atharvaveda!'

She poured on the evidence till I found myself floundering in it. 'The precious nature of fire was acknowledged even outside yasnas,' said Linda. 'Whether in households, or later, in fire temples, fire was maintained with proper fuel, protected from polluting agents and, most importantly—never extinguished.' That explains the trouble that Parsis took to protect the Iranshah through all the travails they were put through.

'What about the "Spenta Mainyus"? Zoroastrian texts revere them as holy spirits. Where are they in Hinduism?'

'Oh, they're there all right. "Spenta" means "energy"; she said. 'The Sanskrit equivalent is "spanda", which is also energy, or motion. But you know what's really interesting?'

'Now what?' I asked, not for the first time.

'In Kashmiri literature the term "spanda" has been used more recurrently than anywhere else. The people of Kashmir composed works of which at least two were called the Spanda Sutra and the Spanda Nirnaya.'

She paused. 'Besides that, we know that Cyrus the Great had overthrown his grandfather Astyages, the king of Media who was the reigning overlord of the Persians. But do most people know why his kingdom was called Media?'

'I doubt it,' I said.

'Because it lay in the centre of the Mesopotamian region,' replied Linda. 'And the Sanskrit word for centre is "madhya". Like the Indian state of Madhya Pradesh. Media was a derivative of Madhya. This was one vast expanse, Jim. One of the great Vedic rishis Kashyapa was married to a woman called Danu. The word "danu" is the word for "river" in both the Avesta and the Rigveda. There is even a theory that the Caspian Sea was named after Kashyapa and that the River Danube was named after Danu.'

'Seriously?' I asked.

'Here's another clue,' offered Linda. 'When Varuna was worshipped, so was his "friend". In Sanskrit, the word "friend" is "mitr". So, the Varuna–Mitra duo began to be recognised in Vedic lands. And then, the Romans liked Mitra even better than Varuna. So, Mitra began to be worshipped on his own by them.'

'Now, you're joking,' I protested.

Linda looked censorious. 'There are many more connections, Jim—and none of them a laughing matter. Around Zarathustra's time there was a kingdom in Mesopotamia whose monarch took the name Tursaratta upon ascending the throne.'

I tried hard, but I couldn't see the connection. 'He probably took that name in honour of the great King Dasharatha of Ayodhya,' explained Linda. 'One of Dasharatha's wives, Kaikeyi, was from Kekaya, a kingdom in today's Caucasus region.'

Linda never ceased to astonish me. 'And examine the word Shahenshah—king of kings. We all think the word is of Islamic origin.'

'Naturally,' I responded. 'Mughal kings in India often took that title.'

'But in the famous Behistun inscription, King Darius calls himself "Kshaetiya Kshaete" or king of kings,' Linda informed me. 'This term became Shahenshah in later ages. But in the original phrase, Darius was calling himself the Kshatriya of Kshatriyas!'

'It's incredible that—' I began, but but Linda cut in, impatient to have it all come out before our private talk was interrupted by life.

'In the Rigveda, *there is a verse: "O Agni, may these three presiding deities—Bharati, Ila and Sarasvati—take their seats here on the grass, along with the sages thereof."'*

'What does that mean?' I asked.

'The word "Bharati" means India; "Ila" is the word for Iran; and "Sarasvati" is the land between India and Iran. All these regions shared a single contiguous culture, Jim.'

'And to think that it extended even further west,' I said in some awe.

'Absolutely,' said Linda. 'Varuna was not only worshipped by the Iranians but even by the Greeks who adopted him as Uranus, the king of Graeco-Roman deities.'

She closed the laptop before her. I took that as a sign of an interval. 'Let me get us another coffee,' I volunteered. 'A really strong one this time.'

Linda whipped around. 'Why, were you dozing off?' she asked icily and with a finality that chilled my heart. 'Honestly, Jim, have you listened to a single word I said?'

'No, no, no—I mean yes, yes,' I burbled hastily. 'It's you I was thinking of—you must be ready to drop after all that.'

And then I said, seriously, 'Thank you, my darling Linda. You've given me a lot to think about.'

105

WE HAD BOTH lost track of time in our back-and-forth. I realised I was hungry. Linda quickly realised that the need for coffee was a disguise for something else.

'*That filet mignon you love?*' *she asked.*

'*Oh, yes!*' *I said with anticipation, thinking of the outstanding steak we'd had a few days ago at Fleming's Steakhouse. It had been served with baked potato, creamed spinach and cauliflower mash on the side. My mouth was watering.*

'*Read this translation of the Avesta,*' *said Linda, wickedly, as she opened her laptop once again. I looked, my hungry spirits a little dampened, at the screen.*

Avesta, Gatha Yasna 16.4
Yea, we worship the Creator Ahura Mazda and the Fire, Ahura Mazda's son, and the good waters which are Mazda-made and holy, and the resplendent sun of the swift horses, and the moon with the seed of cattle ... and we worship the soul of the cow of blessed endowment.

Linda laughed as she saw my raised eyebrows. 'Exactly,' she said. 'Just like the Hindus revere the cow, so do the Zoroastrians. The Sanskrit "gau" or "cow" is the Avestan "geush". In the ninth chapter of the Vendidad *of the* Avesta, *even the purifying power of cow urine is described.'*

Before I could protest, Linda quickly added, 'And no, I'm not asking you to drink it, nor am I suggesting that you stop eating your filet mignon. I'm still pointing out some similarities that have been staring us in the face for ages. Remember the king that Darius overthrew? What was his name?'

'*Gaumata!*' *I burst out, realising that one of the names from Zoroastrian history was based on the Hindu 'mother cow'. I searched my mind, for the sake of argument, for a stark difference in religious practices of the two religions. I found it. 'The Hindus consign their dead to fire,' I said. 'Zoroastrians resort to sky burials.'*

'Sky burials were not unknown in the Sapta Sindhu,' Linda promptly replied. 'In the Mahabharata, *King Astaka outlines three different types of funerals—dahyate, nikhanyate and nighrsyate. Cremation, burial and decay. King Virata had his corpse offered to vultures by Dronacharya. Even Vidura talks of two methods—cremation and being disposed of by birds of prey. When the Greek historian, Aristobulus of Cassandreia, visited Taxila, he found that the dead were often placed in the open air to be devoured by vultures and other scavenging animals.'*

'One final lesson in history,' said Linda, wagging her finger at me. 'What is that Zoroastrian prayer your great-granduncle set to a symphony? The one that you listen to constantly?'

'Yatha Ahu Vairyo,' I said instantly. I knew the words by heart.

'Now let me recite the second line from the Gayatri Mantra, *the holiest chant from the* Rigveda,' *said Linda. '"Tat savitur varenyam". Both "vairyo" and "varenyam" mean the same thing—the universe.'*

Linda and my sometimes-heated discussions continued throughout our lives. It's probably why we got on so well—we always had stuff to chat about. We finished our respective programmes at Stanford, got married and settled in Seattle.

My biotech research company, GCRC, had not yet been born. It was Linda who had suggested the name. We had been sitting in our garden sipping wine and Linda had said, 'Your own name is testament to that fact that the Vedic expanse was one geographical entity.'

'What about my name?' I had asked. 'What's special about Jim?'

'Not Jim, silly,' Linda had admonished me. 'Your original name—Jamshed.'

'Jamshed?' I asked. 'Whatever does that name have to do with any of this?'

'According to legend, Yama was the son of the Sun God, Surya,' said Linda. 'His brother was Manu from whom the Sanskrit word "manushya" and the English word "man" is derived. From Yama descended the kings of the west; and from Manu descended the kings of the east. But both west and east were the same geographical land mass.'

'That still does not explain what it has to do with my name,' I said.

'In the western lands, Yama was called Yima,' replied Linda. 'His full title was "Yima Kshaeta". As you now know, the word "kshaeta" was derived from the term "kshatriya" meaning "ruler". Thus, Yima Kshaeta meant "Yama the ruler". Centuries later, the term Yima Kshaeta got compressed into your name— Jamshed.'

I tried to look unimpressed, but Linda knew that she had me stumped. 'Your birthday is on the twenty-fifth of May,' said Linda.

'Right,' I replied.

'You are a Gemini,' said Linda. 'Have you considered why your parents chose the name Jamshed for you in the context of your zodiac sign?'

'We Parsis have a fetish for using the same names over and over again,' I joked. 'Most of us are Jamshed, Cyrus, Darius,

Pheroze, Zubin, Homi, Nusli or Rustom. There isn't too much thinking involved!'

Linda laughed. 'Jokes apart,' she said. 'Yama had a twin sister called Yamini. So, these twins, Yama and Yamini, provided the concept of the Graeco-Latin twin stars—Gemini. Since you were born a Gemini, it made sense to give you a name based on Yama.'

'That's interesting,' I said. 'The textile mill established by my great-great-grandfather was also named Gemini Mills.'

'Probably because it had two partners—Shapoor and Murdoch,' said Linda. This sort of stuff came so instinctively to her.

'And that brings me to the company that you plan to establish,' said Linda. 'Why not call it GCRC—the Gemini Cellular Research Center?'

It was a wonderful idea. But Linda had more to offer. *'And I even have an idea for your first project,' she said.* For the past few years, I had been working on research into nanorobots that could carry out cellular repair.

'Tell me?'

'That earthen box,' said Linda. 'There is a reason it got passed down to you. Why not start with a hypothesis?'

'That hypothesis being?'

'That the material inside could be connected to the longevity of Parsis,' replied Linda. 'I recall reading that the average lifespan of an Indian is sixty-nine, while that of an Indian Parsi is seventy-five.'

'How would I test the hypothesis?' I wondered.

'You're the scientist, not me,' retorted Linda. 'But if that theory proves right, I have a suggestion regarding what you could call it.'

'What? Stop making me ask!'

'Well, in Arabic, Hamzaa means "to prick or to goad". Dura is the root of the word "durable". So, Hamzaa Dura implies the ability to stimulate durability. There's your name for the stuff.'

She paused. 'You want one more reason for calling it that? Because I am goading you to do it.'

106

IN A VAST campus called 'Zero Point', situated in the heart of the busy Aabpara market area of Islamabad, lie several low-rise structures divided by extensive lawns and fountains. The entrance to the complex is discreet and appropriately anonymous. The overall look of the compound is that of a respectable university with well-maintained buildings, manicured lawns and classical fountains. The only jarring note is the presence of plainclothes officers at the gate, who cautiously direct visitors to their destinations through a maze of barricades manned by military personnel and sniffer dogs.

The directorate for Inter-Services Intelligence—or ISI as it is commonly known—is the very heart of the Pakistani military establishment. Some call it a rogue agency; others call it a state within a state. But no one denies that it is incredibly powerful. In the course of its controversial seventy-three-year history, the ISI had been charged with arming and propelling the Taliban to power in Afghanistan, supporting Islamist terror groups in Kashmir, assassinating leaders in Baluchistan, and interfering in the domestic politics of Pakistan. The institution's precise size and budget always remained a topic of speculation among international intelligence experts.

Adjacent to the ISI headquarters sits a famous mosque, Lal Masjid, or the Red Mosque. It came as a shock when heavily armed hardline seminary students staged a bloody showdown with Pakistani authorities there in 2007. It had ended with Pakistan military forces storming the mosque and more than a hundred people dying. It was the single occasion when the ISI was left with egg on its face for not detecting the presence of a massive arsenal right under its nose. But that had been many years ago, and politics is known to bring together strange bedfellows.

The central building of ISI, which housed the director-general's office on the top floor, was a modern structure with a round, echoing lobby. Unlike many other visitors, the man from Lal Masjid was ushered in smoothly. He was dressed in a beige shalwar-kameez paired with a brown waistcoat. On his feet were Peshawari sandals, polished to perfection. He briskly entered the director-general's chambers and sat down on one of the upholstered chairs in front of the desk. The director-general welcomed him courteously. Behind the DG was a portrait of Mohammad Ali Jinnah, Pakistan's founder. Next to it stood a flagpole with the customary green and white flag of Pakistan. The Lal Masjid man was an ISI operative with a deep network inside Afghanistan, but he spoke perfect English, acquired from his student days at Karachi Grammar School.

'I need your help in a small matter,' said the director-general. 'I had a call from our Chinese friends.' Sino-Pakistani relations were rated highly because China had regularly provided economic, military and technical assistance to Pakistan. Moreover, the two countries had a common foe: India.

'Regarding?' asked the Lal Masjid man.

'Our Chinese friends are the biggest foreign investors in an American company called Asclepius,' explained the DG. 'They control over seventy per cent of the global pharmaceuticals market. Their CEO is well-known: Ryan Parker.'

'Yes, I recall hearing his name,' said the man from Lal Masjid.

'Well, it seems that someone from their company has stolen a critical formulation and run off to Iran with it,' said the DG. There was a scowl on the operative's face. Relations between Shia-majority Iran and Sunni-majority Pakistan were complicated.

'Subsequently, the thief seems to have left Iran and entered Afghanistan.'

'And you want him bumped off?'

'No,' replied the ISI chief hastily. 'Not bumped off. It is vital that he be captured along with his materials.'

'What is his name?' asked the man from the Red Mosque.

'Jim Dastoor,' replied the chief. 'Born in India, settled in America.'

'Indian bastard,' said the operative predictably. 'We'll get him. Any idea where he is?'

'Last sighted in Balkh province,' said the DG. 'Apparently under the protection of Haji Wasiq.'

'I always mistrusted that scoundrel,' replied the masjid man. 'He has this nasty habit of running with the hares and hunting with the hounds.'

The director-general nodded. 'I am given to understand that he and his companions are trying to get to Bagram,' he said.

'Why the worry if the destination is Bagram?' asked the operative. 'Bagram is still controlled by the Americans. If Ryan Parker wants, he can have Dastoor captured there quite easily.'

'It's not quite that simple,' replied the chief. 'Apparently, Dastoor has friends in American intelligence. He could be trying to flee Afghanistan and reach a country that has no extradition treaty with the US.'

'What do you want done?'

'Locate him for me before he reaches Bagram,' replied the chief. 'Ambush his party when they reach Malkhan, around a hundred kilometres short of Bagram. Dump him in a Mi-35M3 chopper and bring him here.'

'How much time do I have?' asked the operative.

'You will need to action this immediately,' said the chief. 'Sound out your Taliban friends in that area if they can intercept his group on your behalf. But please, I need Dastoor alive. Also, we need the materials he stole untouched.'

'Why not pack him off to America?'

'Because I never do anything without extracting an appropriate price,' replied the chief with a grin. 'Osama bin Laden spent years in Abbottabad before the Americans got him. We extracted our price first.'

107

THE TRUCK WAS ubiquitous in these parts. The joke went that a truck driver usually spent more time with his truck than his wife. That was the reason why he wished to have his ten-ton six-wheeler dressed up like a new bride. They were known as jingle trucks because of the metal bells that dangled from the chassis. The truck that Jim, Linda, Dan and Abbasi occupied was painted in a riot of colours from top to bottom. The exterior had painted images of birds, flowers and landscapes. The interior of the cabin was decorated with plastic flowers, beads, tiny flashing lights, mirrors, ribbons and velvet.

Abbasi sat with Wasiq's driver in the cabin while the rest of the group—along with two of Wasiq's men—sat at the back amidst plastic sacks of fertiliser. Wasiq had considerably provided food and water for their journey. Bagram was 400 kilometres away and would ordinarily have taken around eight hours to get to, but this jingle truck would probably add a couple of hours to their journey.

Linda was intently examining a rock fragment in her hand. 'What is that in your hand?' asked Jim.

'It landed near me when the anvil exploded,' said Linda. 'It seems to have some characters engraved on it. Possibly from an ancient sign near the fire temple?'

'What script is it?' asked Jim. 'Cuneiform?'

'No,' replied Linda. 'It's not like what's on the Cyrus Cylinder. Nor is it in the script used by King Darius in his inscription at Mount Behistun. This seems to be writing of a much later age. Probably a script developed in Sassanian times for reciting the *Avesta*.'

'Looks like Arabic to me,' said Dan.

'That's because of the angles and flowing curves, and the right-to-left writing,' replied Linda. 'This seems to be Pazend, the language and script that Zoroastrian priests used for recording their religious scriptures, including the rivayats sent by them to India.'

'Any clue to what it says?' asked Jim. He knew that Linda had studied these language systems as part of her PhD. He always acknowledged the superiority of Linda's learning over his on Zoroastrian history.

'There's only one word that is clear in this fragment,' replied Linda. 'It's "vairyo".'

'Where have I heard that before?' asked Jim, smiling. It featured in his go-to prayer.

'*Yatha Ahu Vairyo*,' Linda intoned. 'Matches with the Sanskrit "varenyam". The famous prayer was written when Vishtaspa embraced Zarathustra's ideas. Many centuries later it was set to an operatic score by Homi Dastoor.'

Jim got up from his seated position and peeked out from underneath the canvas flap to get a sense of where they were. The road behind them was pitch-dark, so if there were any signs of habitation there, they were not visible. 'Any idea how much time we've been on the road?' he asked.

'A little over four hours,' said Linda. Dan, listening quietly, quickly estimated that the journey from Bagram to Malkhan would be a five-hour one, meaning that they would be reaching Malkhan in less than an hour. He wondered what arrangements had been made there for them by Luke Miller and Ryan Parker.

'You're very quiet, Dan,' observed Linda, in a concerned manner. 'Anything the matter? Other than having to go around in circles with no end in sight?' she said to lighten his mood.

'Oh, nothing,' said Dan. 'Just tired. I guess my engine is now running on fumes.' He smiled weakly, burdened by the terrible secret he was carrying. There were moments when he wondered why he had allowed himself to get sucked into all this. Why had he allowed himself to be blackmailed? Why had he been so greedy about the Kettering Prize? It was too late now. There was no going back.

The truck came to a screeching halt as gunshots rang out.

The two Taliban at the back of the truck gestured for the group to remain seated while they themselves leapt out; guns ready to fire. They pulled the flap down after they exited the truck. A crescendo of noise echoed across the barren landscape as a fierce gun battle broke out between them and the attackers. The two guards crumpled to the ground. Seated inside the truck with the rear flap down, Jim and Linda could only imagine what was happening outside.

Suddenly, the flap opened once again. Two strangers, their heads and faces covered in black keffiyehs, pointed their guns at the passengers inside. They shone a flashlight in, first on Linda, then on Jim, and finally on Dan.

'Which one of you is Jim Dastoor?' asked one of the men. Jim brought his hand to his chest in response. Before he could even bring his hand down, a deafening shot rang out in close proximity. Linda screamed.

She looked up trembling in the aftermath of the shot, expecting the worst. 'Jim!' she cried, bending over him. Jim was bloody and shellshocked but breathing. *Thank God!* She scanned him from top to bottom, still finding it miraculous that he was alive.

But the blood? Linda then searched for Dan. It was only when she lowered her gaze that she saw Dan lying crumpled on the floor of the truck, a giant hole in his chest. The blood on Jim was actually Dan's.

'Remain seated where you are,' shouted the man who had fired the shot as he saw Linda trying to move closer to Dan. She ignored the gunman's warning and knelt to cradle the head of the man who had followed her halfway across the world. But it was too late to comfort him.

Suddenly, the truck's rear area was flooded with light as an SUV with fog-lamps mounted on roof bars stopped immediately behind it. The black keffiyeh fighters immediately stood to attention.

Meanwhile, Abbasi dismounted from the driver's cabin and approached. The driver of the SUV too got down and shook hands with Abbasi. The latter then walked over to the SUV and took the driver's seat. He honked—a signal for Jim and Linda to get into the same vehicle. The black keffiyeh fighters got into the truck and drove it out of the way. Then they pulled away the corpses of Wasiq's driver and soldiers to make way for the SUV to pass.

'But what about Dan?' asked Linda as they got into the SUV. 'We can't leave him here like this!'

'Let me tell you about your dear late friend Dan Cohen,' said Abbasi acidly, as he turned on the ignition of the SUV.

He then used a phone that one of the attackers had given him. 'Hello?' he said. 'Is that Kam?'

108

PESTONJI UNWALLA REACHED Diu, a windswept island near the south coast of the Gujarat peninsula, in the afternoon. Spread over an area of close to forty square kilometres, most of the island was barren, except for a few residential areas around St Paul's Church and Diu Fort. But even during working hours, Diu looked somnolent. The silence would sometimes by disturbed by the occasional motorbike or autorickshaw, but for the most part Diu was serene, its streets deserted. Having been a Portuguese colony right up to 1961, Diu moved, if at all, at the same slow pace and *saudade* of old.

Diu was where the Zoroastrian refugees from Iran had first landed in the eighth century, well before the Portuguese ever set foot there. They had stayed in Diu for nineteen years before moving on to Sanjan.

Unwalla was not interested in the Diu Fort from where the Portuguese ruled the roost from 1537. Neither was he interested in popular hubs such as the St Paul's Church, Nagoa Beach, or Panikota prison. His focus was entirely on an area that was now being developed by UNESCO-Parzor as a tourist attraction. It was the very first Parsi settlement in India.

What survived of this settlement were only two dakhmas—towers of silence—and a fire temple currently protected by the Archaeological Survey of India. Unlike other Parsi holy sites that could only be entered if one was a member of the faith, the sites at Diu had been deconsecrated because there were no Parsis left in Diu. This meant that ordinary visitors could visit and peek around to their fill.

Unwalla ascended the gradually inclined ramp to the tower of silence and walked in. He entered through a door on the east side—the only way in or out—and found himself on the inside of a vast basin, with a huge sunken ossuary pit in the middle. Bodies would have been laid out on flat stone slabs arranged like the rays of the sun around the circular pit, with men in an outer ring, female corpses in the middle, and children in the innermost circle. Once their flesh had been consumed by vultures, and the bones picked clean and dried by the sun, the remnants would have been collected in the pit, where they would have been allowed to gradually disintegrate into fine white powder. Unwalla wondered if the Hamzaa Dura ... he shuddered and didn't finish the thought.

This practice of sky burials was conducted by Zoroastrians to prevent polluting the most sacred agents in their rituals—fire, water, even earth. Alas, vulture populations had declined owing to the presence of toxic medications such as diclofenac, a common anti-inflammatory drug, in the corpses of humans and cattle. In operating dakhmas, Parsis were now installing solar concentrators so as to speed up decomposition of corpses. Ironically, a large solar park had come up along the periphery of the Diu plot, although the project was completely unrelated to the towers.

The sun was not so kind this day, as Unwalla stood on the stones of the dakhma heated by its rays. He took off his Parsi topi and used his hanky to wipe the beads of sweat off his head. He then ran his fingers through his white beard and carefully replaced the cap. He began examining the blocks of stone along the circumference, hoping to retrieve an inscription that could help connect the dots, just like his find at the Navsari library. Using his phone, he also began taking pictures. For a man in his eighties, he had unbounded energy.

He did not notice that he was not alone. A stranger who had been lurking outside Dastoor House was now making his way up the ramp that led to the east entrance. Unwalla turned around as soon as he heard the man's footsteps. The area was deathly quiet, and the slightest sound could be heard long distances away. He took in the torn jeans, white cotton tee and black sunglasses on the man, who did not look like a local. And there was hardly any tourist business at this spot. It was the rare tourist who visited the dakhmas anymore. Unwalla kept staring at the man, hoping that he was that rare tourist. But when the man came towards him with rapid strides, Unwalla knew that this was no curious sightseer.

The man approached Unwalla and looked directly into his face. 'You know something about Jim Dastoor's whereabouts,' he said. 'I can make it worth your while to share whatever information you have.' Unwalla smelled nicotine on the man's breath. He was terrified to be at this spot, alone and unprotected in the company of this stranger. His wife had advised him against the trip, but he had persisted. He opened his mouth to speak, but no words came out. The stranger put a hand on Unwalla's shoulder. 'I won't hurt you,' he said. 'Just level with me and you'll be fine.'

'Er … I … I … p-p-promise you I have no idea,' stammered Unwalla. 'I ha-have been engaged in a project researching an ancient Zoroastrian relic. That's all. My research has nothing to do with Jim Dastoor.'

'I know you visited Avan Dastoor's office several times,' said the stranger, his grip on Unwalla's shoulder tightening.

'Sh-she's a benefactor,' explained Unwalla. 'I depend on her for financial resources. I promise you; I have no idea where Jim Dastoor is. Why don't you ask his wife?'

The grip on Unwalla's shoulder was now getting painful. The stranger pushed Unwalla backwards. It required very little effort to topple the old man. He fell on the slab, his vision blurred by the harsh sunlight from above. He felt dizzy with fear as he imagined the rasping cry of approaching vultures and the brittle flapping of their wings overhead. He knew that the place he was in hadn't been used in decades, yet he could smell the stench of death. He visualised his own body laid out to rot in the open, as flies, maggots and birds with curved beaks put an end to his earthly presence. 'P-please, please!' he begged as he lay on the baking-hot stone with his head facing the pit.

The stranger pushed Unwalla by his feet towards the central pit. 'No!' screamed Unwalla. 'Please, no!' Once Unwalla's head was dangling above the pit, his assailant stepped over him and straddled his chest, careful not to place his weight on the man.

'One … last … chance,' he hissed, spacing out the words ominously as he grasped the old man's neck.

'Believe me,' Unwalla gasped, 'I am simply trying to find the Athravan Star.' The term brought an instant gleam of recognition to the attacker's eyes. It had been mentioned by Huang to Parker, by Parker to Miller, and by Miller to him.

'Know where it is?' asked the stranger, his grip around Unwalla's neck tightening.

'No,' the man managed the one word. The last, as it turned out. The stranger sighed resignedly, stood up, held Unwalla's legs like the handles of a wheelbarrow and pushed him into the pit. Unwalla shrieked as he hit the floor of the ossuary. He landed on his back and heard the cracking of his bones. The agony prevented him from moving. Winded, he couldn't call for delayed mercy.

From above, he could hear the stranger's voice. 'It's not too late,' he said. 'I can pull you out and get you medical attention. But if you do not tell me what I need, you are going to die in this pit. Just another few hours of heat and dehydration will do the trick.'

The pit was entirely dry, but Unwalla was imagining the mix of old blood and other body fluids, tissue and bones that would have leaked into the pit over the years. Looking up dimly at the undersides of the blocks laid out like the rays of the sun, he saw, instead the outspread wings of vultures. And he suddenly knew what that symbol represented.

109

THEY ARRIVED AT Bagram all right, but the very purpose of their getting there was lost. The gate to the airbase lay wide open with no Americans in sight. The place was almost deserted, a mere vestige of America's stint in Afghanistan. Rows of unused vehicles, equipment and supplies were the last indicators of the US presence at Bagram; where more than 100,000 troops had passed through its gates over its twenty-year life. 'What's going on?' asked Jim. 'Why is this place like a ghost town?'

'The Americans pulled out last night,' replied Abbasi. 'We arrived here just a tad too late. I heard about it only from the guys who intercepted us in Malkhan. The Americans left in a single night, without even informing the Afghan soldiers guarding the perimeter. My sources say they have left behind some 3.5 million items, including bottles of water, energy drinks and military ready-made meals. This is in addition to thousands of civilian vehicles, hundreds of armoured vehicles, arms and ammunition. These Americans are crazy.'

Within half an hour of the Americans' departure, the electricity to Bagram had been cut off, and the base lay in utter darkness. Jim, Linda and Abbasi found themselves driving through deserted alleyways with only their headlights as illumination. A few stray Afghan guards were in sight, but looters had already had a free run over the past twenty-four hours. They had broken through the barriers and ransacked the vacated buildings. Abandoned items from the base had expectedly ended up in nearby markets. Luckily, the Americans had blown up some of the ammunition dumps before leaving, else that too would have reached Taliban hands. The remaining Afghan forces at Bagram seemed utterly disorganised, demotivated and disinterested. Bagram was like an orphan whose abandonment raised no questions from those with the power to rescue it.

'I have visited this place in its heyday,' said Abbasi. 'At the peak of its population, this airbase housed tens of thousands of troops. It grew from an ordinary Afghan air base to an American mini city. Swimming pools, cinemas, spas and foreign fast-food outlets such as Burger King and Pizza Hut were in common sight. Sad to see it now.'

'Why have we come here if there is no one here?' asked Jim. 'We were relying on the Americans to get us back home.'

'Because although the Americans have run away, I am still here to support and help you,' said Abbasi. 'You need my help to protect you.' He did not mention Dan Cohen, but Jim and Linda knew what he meant. The couple were still reeling from the shock of Dan's death.

It had taken Abbasi an hour of their drive to Bagram to explain the situation. 'Dan was being blackmailed,' revealed Abbasi. 'The blackmailer was a man who calls himself Luke Miller and works for Ryan Parker and Asclepius.'

'How can you be sure of that?' asked Jim. 'Dan was my friend and partner. We studied together in Stanford. In later years, he helped me build Gemini from the ground up.'

'I want to jog your memory,' said Abbasi. 'When the American drone attack happened at Wasiq's camp, all of us rushed inside the underground bomb shelter, right?'

'Right,' replied Jim.

'But think carefully, Jim. Dan was not with us. During that time, he made a call from a Thuraya satellite phone to Luke Miller. It was to tip off Miller that we were heading to Bagram.'

'How could Miller have pulled off anything in the boondocks of Afghanistan?'

'One of the main investors in Asclepius is a Chinese government-controlled entity fronted by a billionaire called Huang,' Abbasi told them for the first time. 'The Chinese put in a word to their friends in the Pakistani ISI to ambush us. But none of them knew that the Israeli SIGINT National Unit had been listening in.'

'How did you come to know?' asked Linda.

'Since Mossad had no way to contact me directly,' Abbasi recounted, 'Camp Moshe Dayan requested R&AW in Delhi to find me. They, in turn, put their man, Subramaniam, on the job. Before we left Wasiq's camp, Subramaniam told me about Dan Cohen's call and that Wasiq's driver had been contracted by the Pakistan-based ISI to ambush us shortly before we reached Bagram, at Malkhan.'

There was silence in the vehicle. It was simply too much to absorb at once. 'I could not delay our reaching Bagram, knowing that the Americans were preparing to leave,' continued Abbasi. 'So I requested Subramaniam to ask Delhi to organise an earlier ambush, with the help of a local warlord.'

Jim's eyes were moist. Not with hurt at Dan's revealed treachery, but because of memories of the friend he'd once been. It was true that Dan had not been the same after his wife, Susan, left, leaving Dan to immerse himself in work to compensate for his loss. And now this ...

'What on earth was he was being blackmailed with?' asked Jim.

Abbasi looked at Jim. *How much should I tell him?* he wondered. *Anything to be gained by completely demolishing Dan's image?* Abbasi shrugged. 'It was something to do with the Kettering Prize. And the reason he jumped at the chance to accompany you to Iran—I'm sorry to tell you, Linda—was because he needed to first find, then keep an eye on, Jim and his Hamzaa Dura,' Abbasi thought it wise to tell them. 'You are really lucky that a network of intelligence agencies—including the FBI, NSA, Mossad and R&AW—have been watching your backs for you. Else Jim would be dead by now, instead of Dan.'

'We are most grateful—in particular to you, my friend. But now what? We are at a deserted airbase with no help in sight.'

'Patience,' said Abbasi, as he pulled the SUV towards the edge of the airstrip. 'We just need to wait here for a few minutes.' Jim opened his mouth to speak but Abbasi gestured for him to be quiet. He listened intently and looked relieved. 'Listen carefully ... the rotors of a helicopter in the distance,' he said softly.

They waited inside the SUV as the chopper landed some distance away. The guards from the Afghan army shone their flashlights on the machine to determine whether it was friend or foe. Then they saw the orange sphere with a blue bird in abstract within. It was the logo of Afghanistan's civilian airline, Kam Air. Abbasi quickly started up the SUV and drove towards the chopper. It was a Mil Mi-8 chopper used by Kam Air to provide private charter services. The stairway had already been lowered for them. 'Where are we going?' asked Jim as they stepped up. But Abbasi did not hear him over the whirr and clack of the rotor.

Once they were inside, Linda asked, 'What now?'

'We're going to Hamid Karzai Airport in Kabul,' said Abbasi as the chopper lifted off. 'Kam Air runs a daily nonstop flight from Kabul to Delhi. Kabul is still under control of the Afghanistan government, so we should be safe. Arrangements have been made by R&AW for us to fly to New Delhi.'

110

THE FLIGHT FROM Kabul to New Delhi was uneventful. Kam Air turned out to be surprisingly good. In fact, in spite of the troubles in Afghanistan, the airline now had routes not only to New Delhi, but also to Islamabad, Kuwait, Jeddah, Istanbul, Ankara, Sharjah and Tehran. This was in addition to the thirteen domestic cities that it connected. The airline had a fleet of thirteen aircraft, including Airbus A340s and Boeing B737s. The cabin crew were smartly turned out and courteous. How long all this would last was anybody's guess. The Taliban were poised to take over Afghanistan completely.

Jim, Linda and Abbasi occupied a row of seats in the business class section. When the steward brought trays of hot food, the three of them wolfed it down as though they hadn't eaten in days. 'Stress release,' Abbasi joked.

The flight was on time and landed two hours and fifteen minutes later. They emerged at Indira Gandhi International Airport where a team of officials awaited them at the airbridge. It was impossible to tell which agencies they were from. An electric buggy quickly carried them to immigration where they were whisked through despite not having Indian visas. They had no luggage, so they directly made their way to the exit where a black Mercedes-Benz van awaited them. They got in and made their way to the Lodhi Hotel, Jim clutching his satchel as always. Their accommodation had been organised for them.

Upon their arrival, they were led to a meeting room. Awaiting them was Subramaniam, whom they recognised from their stint in Balkh. He shook hands warmly with them. 'I was pulled out a few hours after you left,' he explained. 'The Indian government decided to pull out everyone except for a few key officials at the Indian Embassy at Kabul.'

Standing next to him was a very tall, bespectacled, bald man. 'I'm B. K. Singh,' he introduced himself, 'National Security Advisor. But you may call me BK.' He cast a friendly look at Abbasi.

Before his appointment as NSA, BK had occupied one of the most critical positions in the country's intelligence apparatus. On the very same road as Lodhi Hotel sat India's external intelligence agency, the Research & Analysis Wing, usually known by the acronym R&AW. The chief of R&AW was known by a low-key title: Secretary-R. The 'R' in the designation simply meant 'Research' and every chief of R&AW had held that odd and rather modest title since the founding of the agency in 1968. BK had been the longest-serving Secretary-R before his further elevation to the rank of India's chief spook.

Unknown to the public, R&AW had a secret relationship with Mossad since its earliest days. Many R&AW operatives had completed an additional training stint in Tel Aviv. As had BK. 'Your colleague Abbasi and I go back a long way,' said

BK to Jim and Linda. 'We have known each other since my training days at Camp Moshe Dayan.'

'We're grateful to all of you for your help,' said Jim.

'Luckily we still had Subramaniam at Wasiq's place,' said BK, waving away his thanks. 'When Fred Smith asked for help, we could actually *do* something. Another couple of days and we would have been helpless.'

Jim smiled at BK. 'India is my home,' he said. 'I may have chosen the US to pursue my research, but India is the land where my ancestors landed thirteen centuries ago. This land did not hesitate in welcoming us then and you have not hesitated in helping us now.'

'Glad to be of service,' replied BK lightly. 'I would suggest that you get some much-needed rest in this city. Rooms have been booked for you here. You can then decide when and how you wish to get back to the US. I understand your sister, Ms Avan Dastoor, is on her way here from Mumbai to meet you.'

'That's wonderful news!' exclaimed Jim. 'In that case, I'll hang around for a few days if you don't mind.'

'Delighted to hear that,' said BK. 'And what about you, Abbasi? What are your plans?'

'My cover in Iran is completely blown,' replied the Mossad man. 'I guess I'll be heading back to Tel Aviv soon.'

'Had it not been for you, Abbasi, we wouldn't be here,' said Linda. 'I don't know how to thank you.'

'Just doing my job,' said Abbasi, self-effacingly.

'When do you plan on returning to Tel Aviv?' asked BK.

'After I've emptied a bottle of whisky at the bar,' replied Abbasi, adding, 'Actually, I'm thinking of staying on until Jim and Linda leave.'

'You've already gone way beyond the call of duty,' said Linda. 'Please don't let us delay you. You must be so tired of handholding us.'

From the minivan at Isfahan to the rescue of Jim at Shahid Daru; from the shipping container at Pardis to the village at Farmanabad; from the qanat exit at Herat to the Haqqani Taliban camp; from the Cessna crash at Balkh to the drone attack at Cheshm-e-Shafa; from the ambush at Malkhan to the chopper at Bagram; Abbasi had been their one constant companion and saviour. Linda found herself getting emotional as memories of the ordeal came flooding back.

Abbasi stepped over and hugged her. 'Glad to have been of help,' he said, pulling away. 'And I plan to stick by your side until you are safely on your way home.'

111

JIM AND LINDA went up to their room and took extra-long hot showers. Fresh clothes had been provided for them. Feeling practically rejuvenated, they headed downstairs to the poolside café of the hotel, Jim not letting go of his satchel for a second. 'I'm not going to make the same mistake twice,' he said, ruefully. They took a table by the edge of the pool and ordered their food.

A few tables away, and hidden from the Dastoors' line of vision, Abbasi was seated with a stranger—a tall and fair-skinned man with a receding hairline and a hooked nose. Dressed in a crisp kurta-pyjama, he wore soft leather Gucci loafers. On the bridge of his prominent nose sat a pair of Bulgari spectacles; on his wrist was a gold Rolex; in his kurta pocket was a Meisterstuck platinum-coated Montblanc pen. This was transparently a man who enjoyed the finer things of life.

'I told you that I would deliver results,' said Abbasi softly to Bhargava. 'I spent over an hour at your house in Srinagar explaining precisely how.'

The eighty-four-year-old Kashmiri nodded. 'I know that you have brought them here to Delhi,' he said. 'But I do not understand why I do not have the Athravan Star yet.'

'This is the final step,' answered Abbasi. 'It has been so difficult to get all the other competition out of the way. That bastard Dan Cohen wanted the prize for the pharmaceutical giant Asclepius. And Soroushpur wanted it for his romantic— though foolish—notion of a glorious Sassanian Empire.'

'What about Tariq Heydari?' asked Bhargava.

'He was hanged by the Iranians,' replied Abbasi. 'But he had no ulterior motive. Maybe if he had stayed on with us, he might have still been alive today.'

'And Mazaar Askani?' asked Bhargava.

'Blew himself up for the Baloch cause,' replied Abbasi, chewing a delectable morsel of tandoori chicken.

'Do your employers at Mossad know that you were not only saving Jim and Linda, but also working for me?' asked Bhargava. He took a sip of his iced lemon tea appreciatively.

'No,' replied Abbasi. 'My trip to Srinagar to meet you was completely off the books. And if you think about it, I did exactly what the agencies wanted—deliver Jim and Linda to safety.'

Bhargava chortled—a vaguely sinister sound to emerge from such an old man. Among all his stints—as Cabinet minister, Lok Sabha MP, governor, university chancellor and diplomat—Bhargava's most challenging assignment had been his four years in Iran as the Indian ambassador. It was during that particular assignment that he and Abbasi had become acquainted. By then the cooperation between Israel and India had already blossomed in areas of defence and intelligence-sharing. The two men had helped each other in areas of mutual interest.

But many years later, 26/11 happened. In November 2008, ten members of Lashkar-e-Taiba, an Islamist terrorist outfit from Pakistan, carried out several synchronised shooting and bombing attacks spread over four days across Mumbai, India's commercial capital. Death count: 174. Wounded: 300 plus.

One of the attacks was on Chabad House, a Jewish centre in Colaba. Abbasi got to know that one of the hostages inside was his maternal aunt, his mother's sister of Jewish ancestry. She was the one person who had always showered affection on him. After his identity change from Bahram Amini to Kaveh Abbasi, he had cut off all contact with anyone and everyone who had known him by his earlier identity. She did not know if her beloved nephew still remembered her—wherever he was.

Abbasi had immediately called up Bhargava, who had many contacts within the National Security Guard—the NSG. Bhargava had managed to convince the NSG commandos to rappel down from helicopters onto the roof and storm the house, covered by snipers positioned in nearby buildings.

Nine hostages were rescued, Abbasi's aunt among them. Some of the others died.

Abbasi was forever grateful and knew henceforth he would have to return Bhargava's favour. Retrieving the Athravan Star for him would be the settlement of an outstanding debt. Although there was nothing to prove that the Hamzaa Dura in Jim's possession was actually the Athravan Star.

Bhargava's own conscience was clear. The material belonged to his family—Jim Dastoor just happened to have it on him. Bhargava knew how wrongful ownership felt to the dispossessed. As a Kashmiri Pandit, he had seen many of his friends' homes illegally occupied by Muslim families. *Just because someone squats in your home, does that make it theirs?* he would rant to himself. *And how could Baba Malik lay any claim to it? Thief!* Bhargava conveniently forgot his own alliances in those moments of raving. 'All right, all right, so you've brought them here. But how do you plan on getting me what I want? And when? How much more time must I wait?' Bhargava asked Abbasi.

'Not much longer,' replied Abbasi. 'See that waiter serving them? The one with the slicked-back hair? He is an ace at pilferage. I have used him before—when we needed some papers stolen from a Saudi diplomat in Mumbai. I have already paid him for the task ahead. During the course of their meal, he will acquire the goods for us without causing any kind of fuss.'

Bhargava and Abbasi discreetly watched as the waiter served Jim and Linda their drinks and starters. Someone had joined them at their table. Bhargava took another sip of his iced tea and licked his lips. Things had been finally set in motion.

112

JIM AND LINDA were delighted to be sharing a meal with Avan. Jim's sister had not only taken over the reins of the Dastoor empire after their father's demise eleven years ago but had also managed to keep the Parsi elders off Jim's back. The relief in her eyes on seeing Jim was evident. She was unable to hold back her tears as she hugged him tightly, allowing her crisp cotton saree to get crushed in the process. 'I've been worried sick about you, Jimmy,' she said. She was among the few who called him by that variant of his name, instead of Jamshed or Jim.

'I know I've worried you,' said Jim contritely, squeezing her hand, 'but I hope you understood the stakes involved. They had even abducted Linda! And it's been impossible for days to tell friend from foe.'

'Rustom Dastoor was right,' said Avan, smiling. 'Our grandfather picked up on that rebellious streak in you a long time ago. That's why he left you that important little box. Little did he know you would rebel even in its usage.' Jim and Linda were enjoying their first taste of relaxed conversation in ages.

'Grandfather too was a rebel,' said Jim. 'Taking up art at the Sorbonne and marrying a Catholic Frenchwoman was nothing short of rebellion—God bless Cecile!'

'True,' replied Avan, taking a sip of her Evian. 'But his uncle, Homi, was no better. Running off to Vienna in pursuit of music!'

'Blood, it runs in the blood!' crowed Jim. 'Our great-great-grandfather, Shapoor, also rebelled by ditching his priestly duties and running away from Udvada to Mumbai.'

Avan nodded. 'Truth be told, had it not been for that attitude, the first 18,000 Zoroastrian refugees would not have set sail from Iran and arrived on Indian shores. And the prototypical nonconformist approach was there in none less than Zarathustra himself, taking on the wrath of the establishment as he did.'

'I'll drink to that,' said Jim, raising his glass. 'But I still can't understand why Iran's Zoroastrians and India's Parsis should unite to see me as the enemy. I am shocked to hear that Unwalla went to see you to complain about me, Avan! Don't they understand anything?'

'The thing is, they *do* understand the tradition of the box passing on to the most independent thinker of the next generation. What they can't get their heads around is your breaking with tradition in the interest of science. It's truly ironic! There are hardly any Parsis left in the world, but we still hang on to our traditions for dear life. What else can explain the collaboration between Unwalla and Soroushpur? You better hang on to that stuff you call Hamzaa Dura!'

'I think what Jim is doing is marvellous,' broke in Linda loyally. 'Every succeeding generation should find ways to work for all of humanity, not just a narrow group.'

'You remind me of Cecile. Are you sure you're not related to her?' joked Avan.

The waiter cleared away their starter plates and placed fresh plates for their entrees. Pan-seared salmon for Avan, fish and chips for Jim and couscous with baby potatoes for Linda. He poured the wine that Jim had ordered for all three, then backed away to leave them to their privacy.

Jim had just dipped a piece of fish on his fork into the tartar sauce when his eyes darted to the little side table that the waiter had placed near them to accommodate their personal belongings. *Where is my satchel?*

Linda spotted his worried expression instantly and guessed the cause: his bag was missing. 'That waiter,' she said, looking around the restaurant for their server. She found that he was in the furthest corner, near the kitchen. 'Stop!' she shouted. Diners at other tables were startled by the noise. Another few minutes and the waiter would have been completely out of sight.

Jim got up from his chair, knocking it over as he ran after the waiter who had discarded the satchel and was directly holding the earthen box of Hamzaa Dura in his hand. Linda followed Jim in hot pursuit. By now the entire restaurant was staring at them and wondering what the ruckus was all about. The waiter made his way through the kitchen and down the main corridor, hoping to use the service entrance to make his getaway. 'Stop him,' roared Jim as he burst into the kitchen, cannonading past other waiters with loaded trays. The thief was now within grabbing distance and Jim lunged after him, hoping to catch hold of his coattails. The waiter slipped on a spill of grease and crashed almost comically to the floor. The box flew out his hands, and in a futile attempt to catch it, the waiter sent it spinning further in the air.

Jim froze as he saw his life's work fly out of the waiter's hands. His mouth was agape as he saw it arc high before it fell into the massive tandoor, used to turn out their famous frontier roasts. 'No!' yelled Jim as he ran towards the oven—if he could, he would have jumped in himself to save the box. The head chef held him back. 'The temperature inside is 480° Celsius,' the rotund man warned him. 'Whatever it was has already been consumed by the heat.' Unspoken was the chef's irritation that he would have to clean the entire tandoor out thoroughly, before it could be used again.

The offender lay on the floor grasping his twisted ankle in agony. The restaurant manager had called security, who were helping him up to his feet before he was handed over to the police. Jim recalled everything frame by frame, in extra slow motion. He was still heaving at the thought of what he had lost, as Linda attempted to calm him down.

What has it all been worth? Jim's expression said it all. *It's all over.*

113

JIM SAT IN the lobby of the Lodhi Hotel, his face in his hands. The waiter had been taken into custody, but it was evident that he was a mere pawn in a much larger game. He would have been thrown a few crumbs for his nifty performance of sleight-of-hand.

Linda tried consoling Jim but knew that he would have to find his own way of coming to terms with the loss. 'What has it been worth?' said Jim again, this time aloud. 'The man whom I considered my dearest friend, Dan, was willing to betray me and died for it. Soroushpur—who helped you out of the clutches of the IRGC-Quds—was on his own quest, that involved stealing from me.'

'It's not been all bad,' crooned Linda.

'How hasn't it?' demanded Jim. 'Firooz Jamshidi—that good man who helped you cross over to the mainland from Kish Island—is probably in custody somewhere. Mazaar Askani—the man who aided us in getting to Afghanistan by introducing us to Al-Baluchi—allowed himself to be blown up in the Baloch cause. Tariq Heydari was publicly hanged to death by the Iranian regime. So many lives lost or ruined. And now the Hamzaa Dura—everyone's Holy Grail—is lost too.' Jim was for all purposes inconsolable.

Just then, the lobby manager approached. 'Sir, there is a call for you from the United States,' he said courteously. 'Are you up to taking it?'

Jim looked up and asked, 'Any idea who's calling?'

'The caller said his name was Greg Walters, deputy chief of the Seattle Police Department.' Jim stood up. Greg seemed like a world away. To think that it had all started with the abduction of Linda in Seattle—and Greg Walters being dragged in to help.

Linda accompanied Jim to the telephone at the reception desk, imperceptibly touching his elbow. 'Hello?' said Jim, putting the phone on speaker so that Linda could hear the conversation.

'Jim! It's good to hear your voice, buddy,' said Greg. 'I have Fred Smith from the Feds here with me. Both of us have been keeping track of you and Linda. What a helluva ride it's been for you!'

'Thanks, Greg,' replied Jim. 'Had it not been for you guys getting all those agencies into the job, I'm not sure I'd be sitting here, or even alive.'

'You owe me a racquetball win, one in which I royally whip your ass,' said Greg. 'But that's not the reason I called.'

'Tell me,' said Jim.

'As you may recall, my father is American, but my mother is Yazidi,' said Greg. 'She moved to America from Turkey in the 1960s.' Jim continued listening, wondering why he was being reminded of the fact.

'I got a call from this guy, Nasr Tamoyan,' said Greg. 'He is a Yazidi scholar and academic in Iran. He sought me out through the Yazidi alumni network. Tamoyan has been trying to reach you. He says that he has information that could help you in your most recent project.'

'It's of no use, Greg,' said Jim. 'We lost the Hamzaa Dura to a sort of fire a short while ago.'

'I'm sorry to hear that, Jim,' said Greg. 'But you may still wish to talk to Tamoyan. Apparently, he was working alongside another person called Behrad Soroushpur.'

Jim's ears perked up. 'Are you sure he said that?' he asked. 'He specifically mentioned Soroushpur's name?'

'He did,' said Greg. 'I haven't told him you're in New Delhi. I wasn't sure you wanted to be found at all!'

'The only one interested in finding me would be Ryan Parker,' said Jim. 'And now, even if he does, I will be of little value to him without the Hamzaa Dura.'

'Stop worrying about Parker,' said Greg. 'He's too busy dealing with his own problem.'

'What problem?' asked Jim.

'An item in the Wall Street Journal,' said Greg. 'It's emerged that the Chinese investor in Asclepius is controlled by a proxy of the Chinese MSS,' replied Greg. 'Stocks have tanked since the past few days. Parker is running for cover at the present moment. He is unlikely to go after you.'

Jim absorbed the new information. He recalled how Parker and his sidekick Luke Miller had been able to activate the Pakistani ISI for Dan. That had been achieved leveraging the Chinese connection.

'This Tamoyan guy seems like an excitable sort,' said Greg. 'I kept trying to calm him down so that I would be able to understand what he was saying. If you're interested, I could find a way of patching him through to you.'

Jim looked at Linda who had heard the entire exchange. *What do you think I should do?* he seemed to be asking. She nodded her head vigorously. 'Fix up the conference,' she whispered. 'You never know what awaits on the other side of the door.'

114

JIM AND LINDA were in a conference room within the business centre of the Lodhi Hotel. Greg Walters had arranged for a video conference with Nasr Tamoyan using Skype—an application that was still not banned by Iranian authorities.

Tamoyan had wondered whether he should speak to Jim Dastoor or not. But after he heard the news that Soroushpur had died at the hands of the Taliban, he felt no conflict. A quick internet search on his part had revealed that Jim was usually based in Seattle. Another few queries on LinkedIn, Facebook and a Yazidi WhatsApp group had thrown up the name of Greg Walters as being of Yazidi heritage and based in Seattle. Tamoyan had known that it was a long shot but had taken the chance.

Tamoyan was himself a Yazidi. The Yazidis spoke a distinct language called Kurmanji and lived in the Kurdish regions of Iraq, Iran, Syria and Turkey. Some scholars considered Yazidis to be a subgroup of the Kurds, but Tamoyan knew that the idea was utter nonsense. Yazidis practised a religion that was distinct from Islam, Christianity, Judaism or Zoroastrianism. For generations, his people had faced persecution because Islamic clerics believed that the Yazidis followed a heretical devil-worshipping faith.

Anti-Yazidi violence could be traced back to the Ottoman Empire. In fact, Yazidis had borne the brunt of seventy-two genocidal attempts that nearly wiped them out. In more recent times, the Islamic State had carried out a ruthless campaign in which five thousand Yazidi civilians were killed. Those who survived the attacks were forcibly converted to Islam and thousands of Yazidi women and girls were captured as sex slaves in Syria.

Jim was surprised to be receiving a call from Tamoyan, because the man made no secret of the fact that he had been working for Soroushpur. 'I know that you have been working on research relating to the properties of Hamzaa Dura,' said

Tamoyan. 'Soroushpur was interested in it because he thought it was connected in some way to the Athravan Star.'

'But why are you sharing any information with me?' asked Jim. 'Soroushpur was working against me.'

'He was only trying to retrieve what he thought belonged to the repressed Zoroastrian community at large,' replied Tamoyan. 'I know what it feels like to be persecuted. My community has been at the receiving end over centuries.'

There was a pause in the conversation. 'You were born in India,' said Tamoyan. 'You may not be aware that we Yazidis bear significant similarities to Hindus. And so do you Zoroastrians. That makes us almost related.' He laughed nervously.

'Really?' asked Jim. 'How?'

'In ancient times, we Yazidis were nomadic and had migrated to India,' replied Tamoyan. 'We eventually returned to Central Asia and the Middle East but after imbibing a great deal of Hindu culture. For example, if you see one of our places of worship—what we call a "lalish"—you will find that it architecturally resembles a Hindu temple.'

'Interesting!' commented Linda, ever curious.

'And the *sanjaka*s, our oil lamps, are similar to the *diya*s used by Hindus during *aarti* prayers,' continued Tamoyan. 'The Yazidi deity known as Tawsi Melek is a peacock, much like the mount of the Hindu Kartikey or Karthikeyan.'

Linda was listening with rapt attention to Tamoyan's words. 'We too anoint our foreheads with the "third eye", like Hindus do,' said Tamoyan. 'We have a caste hierarchy like the Hindus, and we believe in reincarnation, like them. The connections between India and many countries of what used to be the Mesopotamian region are very old.'

'This is altogether fascinating knowledge, and we must discuss it further in depth. But right now, I can't think beyond a problem of some immediacy. My Hamzaa Dura is lost, and I have no way of synthesising it,' said Jim. 'Neither do I have any clue to finding the original source,' he added miserably.

'You have been looking at this with the eyes of a scientist,' replied Tamoyan. 'Now let your wife look at it as a historian would.' Then he added, sententiously, 'The packaging is more important than the contents.'

'What do you mean?' Jim reared back, mystified.

'You will find the source if you focus on the container that you had in your possession,' replied Tamoyan. 'Did it have a faravahar—a winged male figure holding a ring?'

'No,' replied Jim.

'That's good news,' said Tamoyan. 'If it had the faravahar on it, it would have not been as ancient as we thought it to be. What was the symbol that it actually had?'

'It was like a pilot's badge,' said Jim. 'I have a photograph of the lid on my Dropbox account. Let me log in from here and show you.' Jim quickly accessed the photograph he was looking for and shared it with Tamoyan.

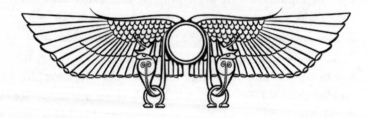

'Exactly what I thought,' said Tamoyan. 'People don't know that the winged sun is one of the most ancient symbols in the world. It appears in architecture, art and cylinder seals from Babylonia, Egypt, Assyria, Sumer, Judah, and elsewhere. It was simply the sun flanked on either side by a *uraeus*.'

'What's that?' asked Jim.

'Uraeus—the cobra—a symbol of sovereignty and divine authority,' replied Tamoyan. 'In ancient Egypt, this symbol represented Horus.'

'What, the box I've been carrying around is *Egyptian*?' asked Jim with astonishment.

'No,' replied Tamoyan. 'The winged disk symbol was adapted by the Assyrians to represent the deity Ashur. But his representation was now as an archer within the winged disk. Hold on a moment, I will find the image for you myself.'

Fifteen seconds later, Jim and Linda saw what Tamoyan was talking about. The winged disk had now become more elaborate with the figure of a bearded archer embossed in the centre.

Jim recalled his conversation with Linda many years ago. 'So the Islamic observance of "Ashura", the Mesopotamian city of "Assur", the Assyrian deity "Ashur", the Rigvedic "asura", and the Avestan "ahura" are all connected?'

And by Achaemenid times, Ashur was being given all the attributes of Marduk so that worshippers of Marduk would effectively be worshipping Ashur.

'Now let's go even further,' said Tamoyan. 'By the time of Darius, a further modification was made to the symbol. The archer was replaced by an elderly male figure, also winged, holding a ring. Sharing the pic with you now.'

'The Zoroastrians adapted the Ashur symbol,' said Tamoyan. 'The faravahar, as it is depicted since Achaemenid times, is an elderly male, generally assumed to represent the human soul. His aged appearance indicates wisdom. One hand points upward, thus reminding followers to strive for improvement. His other hand holds a ring, which represents a covenant. The circle from which the male figure emerges symbolises immortality of the soul. The two wings are made up of three rows of feathers, representing the Zoroastrian maxim of good thoughts, good words and good deeds.'

Jim knew all that. The symbol was ubiquitous among Parsis—on his father's car as a sticker, on Parsi fire temples, as wall paintings inside homes, even on cufflinks and pendants. 'I still don't get where you are going with this,' said Jim a little tiredly. The shock he'd received that day had taken a bigger toll on him than the events of the previous week.

'If the faravahar were to be seen on your earthen box, it would have been an indicator of the box being from during or after Achaemenid times,' said Tamoyan. 'But during Zarathustra's times this would have still been in its earlier evolving form. That is your best proof that your earthen box is of very ancient provenance.'

Linda thought Tamoyan was making sense. 'Any ideas about the origin of the box itself?' she asked.

'I still believe that the answer will emerge from Gundeshapur,' he said. 'I suggest that you focus on the India–Iran connection, in particular the return of the Persian physician, Borzuya, to the Academy of Gundeshapur.'

'Tell me a little more about it,' requested Jim.

'Borzuya was a Persian physician who travelled from Kusrow's court to Kashmir in search of an elixir that could revive the dead,' said Tamoyan. 'Upon reaching Kashmir, he failed in his quest. It was then that he was directed to a sage. The sage asked Borzuya, "When the ignorant can be made wise, of what use is it to bring the dead to life?" He gave a book in Sanskrit called the *Five Treatises* to Borzuya. Borzuya returned to Persia and translated the book into Pahlavi. This would have happened in the sixth century. Unfortunately, Borzuya's Pahlavi version is lost. But I think it holds the answer to your question.'

Jim and Linda continued their animated discussions with Tamoyan. They did not know that a thin and pale man with mousy red hair and dressed in a wrinkled grey business suit had checked into the room next to theirs for one final assignment.

115

JIM SAT PROPPED up in bed, in his room in the Lodhi Hotel. He was still dazed by the happenings that day. On a nearby coffee table lay a copy of the hotel's house magazine. Jim flipped through it absentmindedly while waiting for Linda to emerge from the bathroom. Something caught his eye. It was the kids' section of the magazine that showed a comic strip inspired by the *Panchatantra*. 'Linda,' he called out. She was unable to hear him over the drone of her hair dryer. He opened the bathroom door and placed the magazine on the counter, pointing to the comic strip.

Linda switched off the dryer and looked at the strip. 'The *Panchatantra*?' she asked looking up at him. The she realised what Jim was alluding to. They said it almost together: 'The *Five Treatises*!' Soroushpur had unwittingly mentioned it to them and so had Tamoyan. Outside in the bedroom, there was a faint clicking sound as the lock on the door to the adjoining room was picked.

Jim and Linda went back and sat on the bed. The *Panchatantra* had been written sometime between 200 BCE and 300 CE but was based on a much earlier oral tradition. It was a collection of fables around animal characters. The authorship was attributed to either someone called Vasubhaga, or Vishnu Sharma—possibly even the same Vishnu Sharma who had authored the *Arthashastra*.

'Based on the geographical features and animals described in the *Panchatantra*, Kashmir is considered to be its setting,' said Linda. 'Undoubtedly it is the most translated Hindu work ever. There are 200 versions of it in more than fifty languages around the world.'

'Why did it feature in both Soroushpur's and Tamoyan's conversation? How is the *Panchatantra* related to the Hamzaa Dura?'

'From what I recall, there is a story about a king in Kashmir who was worried about his three spoilt sons,' replied Linda. 'The monarch was terrified about handing over the reins of the kingdom to any of these princes who has refused to learn anything. The *Panchatantra*—or the *Five Treatises*—was authored to teach them good values through the medium of entertaining fables. Apparently, it did wonders for their education.'

'I still don't get it,' said Jim. 'How does a collection of animal stories connect to ancient Persia?'

'Let's take this step by step,' suggested Linda. 'The Sassanian king Kusrow I, a monarch who ruled for five decades of the sixth century, supported the Academy of Gundeshapur. This became one of the most important centres of learning in the world. It was Kusrow who sent the Persian physician, Borzuya, to Kashmir. He was searching for that fabled elixir that could revive the dead.'

'So far, so good,' said Jim.

'Now let's imagine that your Hamzaa Dura was that elixir,' said Linda. 'That would indicate its origin in Kashmir. Now

Borzuya searched for the elixir but was unsuccessful. This would seem to indicate that the elixir had already been taken somewhere else. Then Borzuya was directed to a sage who shared the *Panchatantra* with him. According to legend, it wasn't easy for Borzuya to lay his hands on the work. Some say that the sage only allowed Borzuya to read a small portion of the work each day and the Persian secretly memorised it on each occasion. Other stories say that Borzuya had to offer a bribe of forty camels to get the book.'

'I'm with you so far,' said Jim. Neither Jim nor Linda noticed the handle of the interconnecting door turning ever so gently.

'What if the version of the *Panchatantra* shared with Borzuya contained a reference to the so-called elixir?' asked Linda. 'What if the substance was no longer in Kashmir but references to it were?'

'Borzuya would have carried that information back to Gundeshapur,' said Jim. 'But that was in the sixth century. Wouldn't the reference to such a substance have already been in Persia? That's assuming it was something passed down from Zarathustra's times?'

'But Alexander burnt down Persepolis in 330 BCE,' said Linda. 'It's possible that this was one of the secrets that was lost in that inferno. So while the box and its contents were with the magi, the reference to its origin was now only in ancient Indian texts like the *Panchatantra*.'

'And that came back to Persia through Borzuya!' exclaimed Jim.

'Well, let's consider the fact that Kusrow came to be known as "anushiravan" or "the immortal",' said Linda. 'On the one hand it could mean that the immortal wisdom of the *Panchatantra* had been absorbed by him via Borzuya's Pahlavi translation of the work. Alternatively, it could mean that some great secret related to longevity had been passed on to him. This was centuries ago, Jim. Many secrets lose to time.'

'But we do not have the Pahlavi translation of the *Panchatantra* that Borzuya undertook,' pointed out Jim.

'That's true,' conceded Linda. 'This particular work may have been lost when the Arabs invaded Persia in the seventh century and burned down several libraries. Or it may have been shifted for safekeeping to a location from where it could be easily shifted out of Persia.'

'What would be a likely location?'

'The port of Hormuz,' said Linda without hesitation. 'The Zoroastrians who arrived in Diu had left from Hormuz. It is possible that a copy of the Borzuya work was left behind there. So the Parsis arriving in Sanjan would have had the box but not the written text that explained its origin.'

'But if the Borzuya text is lost, there is nothing we can do,' Jim came full circle.

'Three centuries later, a Persian convert to Islam, Abdullah ibn al-Muqaffa, translated Borzuya's work into Arabic in a style that is often considered to be a prime example of outstanding Arabic prose. The book was called *Kalila wa Dimna*, named after two jackals who are the primary characters in the stories.'

'I wonder why a Persian-Muslim convert would translate a Hindu work?' asked Jim.

'Oh, there are countless examples of such cross-cultural sharing,' replied Linda. 'Brahmagupta's text on mathematical astronomy, the *Brahmasiddhanta*, was translated by Alfazari into an Arabic work called *Sindhind*. Without that translation, Hindu numerals would not have become the world standard they did. Manka, an Indian physician at the court of Harun al-Rashid, translated the *Sushruta Samhita*, the Sanskrit text on medicine into Persian. *Kalila wa Dimna* was primarily targeted at the bureaucracy, but it was so entertaining that it found its way from the Arabs to Spain, where it was translated in the thirteenth century. It was one of the first books to appear in Italy after the invention of the printing press. The rest is history.'

'So the Zoroastrian magi in Persia would have read this?' asked Jim.

'By the eighth century, most Persians would have learned Arabic,' said Linda. 'It's possible that the magi now realised that they needed to convey this information to their brethren in India.'

'I remember my father telling me to memorise the first and only secret rivayat. According to him it was the only one that I needed to remember. I was asked to memorise it and then destroy the note. My father said it came to us secretly via a book that the Zoroastrians left behind in Persia and that many attempts were made to convey it to us.'

The deep carpeting on the floor of the room they were in muffled the sound of the interconnecting door opening. Jim and Linda were so caught up in their discussion that they noticed nothing.

'That fits in with the hypothesis,' Linda had resumed. 'Hormuz would have been a busy port. The magi of Persia could not send a message directly to their Indian cousins because that would have meant revealing the secret to an intermediary. So they could have jotted it down in Pazend into the pages of *Kalila wa Dimna* and asked someone like the traveller Marco Polo to take it to India for them.'

'Only to have it intercepted by Kublai Khan,' said Jim.

'Luckily for them, Changashah decided to send Nariman Hoshang to gather the rivayats in the fifteenth century,' said Linda. 'At this time another copy of the book with the jottings could have come back to the Parsis. And now, in order to take no chances, they decided that future transmission would only be done orally.'

And that's when the figure in the doorway caught Jim and Linda by surprise.

116

It was the second time in my life that I came close to dying. The figure in the doorway may have come as a shock, but not for the reasons you would think. Just as he was raising his gun towards me, he slumped to the floor, his head exploding like a melon over the same carpet that had hushed his entrance.

As it would later emerge, Luke Miller had been sent to New Delhi by Ryan Parker to eliminate me. Parker and his Chinese investors were bent on preventing me from reengineering or synthesising the Hamzaa Dura. This would enable them to protect their vital place in the global pharmaceutical market. Miller had managed to book the room next to ours and was on the verge of shooting me when something else happened. A shot—fired through a silencer—put an end to Miller before he could do the same to me. The act was clinical, precise and, most importantly, silent.

As Linda and I stared in horror at Miller's shattered remains, we also saw another figure at the interconnecting door—now wide open—to Miller's room. It was Abbasi. It took us a couple of minutes to recover from it all, but Abbasi was quick to pull us out of our confusion. He bent to check Miller's pulse, a reflex but unnecessary action, since his brains had escaped his cranium.

Abbasi looked up. 'I was tipped off by BK that Fred Smith had been in touch,' he told us. 'Luke Miller had been spotted leaving the US for India. I did not realise who Miller was until I saw the photograph BK showed me.'

'He was Ryan Parker's enforcer,' I said. 'But you knew that already, didn't you?'

'Yes, but I had no idea what he looked like,' replied Abbasi. 'When I saw the pic, I realised that it was the same person who had screwed up Operation Stanza for me. As a result of his leak, my colleague had been shot down in Frankfurt, even though we eventually succeeded in hampering Iran's nuclear efforts. When I realised that he was on his way to eliminate you, I decided to stay on and take care of this one last assignment.'

'You were leaving?' I asked. 'Without saying goodbye?'

'You will soon realise that all is not what it seems, Jim,' replied Abbasi. 'It's true that I pulled you out of Iran and Afghanistan. It's also true that I saved your life. But I had my own agenda for doing so.'

'Were you also after the Hamzaa Dura?' I asked. I was beginning to wonder if the tandoor incident had anything to do with Abbasi.

He sidestepped the question. 'I'm asking BK to clear this mess so that none of us gets drawn into police procedurals. Luke Miller is dead, and Ryan Parker is evading the law; Soroushpur is dead; Khademhosseini and Mosaffa are gone ... you have no one to fear. But Vijay Bhargava ...'

'Now, who on earth is Vijay Bhargava?' I asked. The plot thickens, I thought tiredly and without humour.

'Ask me no questions and I'll tell you no lies,' said Abbasi cryptically. 'Just watch out for him, though. He thinks that your Hamzaa Dura belongs to him. But I guess that is no longer in play.' He paused, then said, 'In the meantime, I suggest you check out from the Lodhi and check in at the Taj Mansingh.'

'Why?' asked Linda, equally fed up with being shunted around.

'Two reasons,' said Abbasi. 'First, why stay in a hotel where you've just experienced a murder?'

'And second?' I asked.

'The bar at the Taj, Ricks, is the best watering-hole in town,' said Abbasi. There was a soft knock on the door. Abbasi opened it to two men in plainclothes. BK's men had arrived to take care of the mess. Linda and I packed up and left. We would never see Abbasi again.

We resettled in a suite at the Taj Mansingh. The crises dogging us through countries and continents had exhausted us, in both mind and body. Over the next few days, we barely left our room, preferring to watch television, drench ourselves under the hot shower and order room service. In the beginning, by some unspoken agreement, we steered clear of discussing our recent ordeal.

'It's a pity that what could have saved mankind is completely destroyed,' I said on our third day of hibernation. 'There is no known source, and we have no way of reverse-engineering the Hamzaa Dura.'

'I am simply grateful that you are alive and well,' said Linda, taking my hand into her own and kissing it. 'I don't know what I would have done if something had happened to you.'

I knew the feeling. I remembered how helpless I had felt when Linda was abducted. I shrugged off the ghastly memory.

117

THREE DAYS OF hiding from the world at the Taj Mansingh revived our energy, and I noticed that I was even walking differently, not shuffling along like a longtime convict. Linda and I went downstairs for dinner to the Taj's best-known restaurant, Machan. After half a bottle of a wonderful Indian Cabernet Sauvignon, I once again mentioned the topic of the Hamzaa Dura—now forever lost.

'You broached the idea that Zarathustra was from Kashmir,' I reminded Linda. 'Is there a way we could pinpoint exactly where? Couldn't our Hamzaa Dura have originated there as well?'

'All we know for certain about Zarathustra's origins is that he was born in a family of sage-kings,' said Linda. 'He has been described as "Narepish Rajish" or the "prince of Rajish", but we don't know where the place called Rajish is—or was.'

'Hasn't anyone tried to figure that out?' I asked, surprised.

'Successive generations of Iranians called the place by various names—Rajish, Raji, Ragha, Ragau and Rae were just some of them. There is a city not far from Tehran called Rhages, and that is also cited by some scholars as a possible choice.'

'And what do you think?' I asked. Linda's face softened gladly at the priority I always gave her views.

'Rajish is described as being near the Jabbar Mountain and the River Daitya,' she said, from her prodigious memory for names of long-forgotten people and places. 'Now consider this. There is a village called Raihan Bag in the Badgam district of Kashmir. It is close to a mountain peak known as the Urni Jabbar. And of course, we know that Rajish was in Airyanemvaeja and this region was defined by the River Daitya—also known as Diti or Jhelum.'

'So, the place could be Raihan Bag?' I asked.

'Possibly,' said Linda. 'There is also a place called Renji in the Sopore district of Kashmir. That could be it. In addition, there are other villages and towns in Kashmir as well as in its neighbouring Jammu that have "rai" in their names. For example, Raipura, Raika Gura, Raika Labanah, Raika Mahuva, Rainawari and Rai'than. But none of them match the geographical markers the way that Raihan Bag does.'

After a moment of thought, Linda remembered something. 'You told me about a certain rivayat your father gave you,' said Linda.

'It was a few lines of text on a single piece of paper. He asked me to memorise them and then destroy the paper they were on.'

'What did they say?' asked Linda. I was supposed to keep the message secret but given that the Hamzaa Dura was gone,

I figured that there was no harm in sharing it with Linda. I recited it from memory.

Across the Jabbar, light dazzles the eyes
As three great fires roar from the skies
Behold, the Athravan in the Daitya prays
And the Anu people to the heavens gaze
They know the fourth that comes from three
Means powerful Yasna for all time to be.

Linda's expression turned serious. 'There were many rivayats that were sent by the Zoroastrians of Iran to their brethren in India,' she recalled. 'Some twenty-six rivayats were received by the Parsis between 1478 and 1773. I have read them all. This was not among them. I wonder if it could be the same passage that was sent as a jotting on a page of Kalila wa Dimna by Abdullah ibn al-Muqaffa? The very passage that may have earlier featured in both the Panchatantra and Borzuya's work?'

'Maybe it was a secret,' I offered. 'Something that was not to be available to the uninitiated. After all, the Vedas and the Gathas were initially only recited, not written. But why don't you tell me whether the words offer us any clues?'

Linda laughed. 'It says many of the things that we've been discussing,' she said. 'It mentions the Jabbar Mountain and the River Daitya. Assuming that these are represented by today's Urni Jabbar mountain and the River Jhelum, my guess at Raihan Bag in the Badgam district of Kashmir would be correct.'

'There is only one way to find out if your theory is right,' I said thoughtfully.

'Aren't you tired?' asked Linda. 'I would have thought you'd be fed up circumnavigating the globe.'

'This is too important,' I replied. 'If there is even the slightest possibility of finding the source of Hamzaa Dura, then we owe it to the world to know.'

Linda drained her glass of wine and appeared all geared up for action. 'Here's an idea,' she said. 'Zarathustra's family members were known as the "spitamas".'

'And …?'

'The original term was "shwetama," not "spitama". Either way, the word means "most white".' I wondered where she was going with that but waited to find out.

'For a moment, let's go back to the west-east divide,' she went on to say. 'The divide between Yama and Manu, the divide between pitrayana and devayana, the divide between asuras and devas, and the divide between Bhrigu and Brihaspati.'

'The great schism across the Sapta Sindhu,' I summed up.

'Quite,' she concurred. 'Zarathustra, of course, was in the Bhrigu camp. Now, another name for Bhrigu was Shukra. What does the word "shukra" mean? White! So, whether we use the term shukra, shwetama or spitama, they all mean the same thing—white.'

'A-a-a-all right,' I said slowly. 'But I can't see where you're going with this.'

'Essentially, the followers of Bhrigu, including Zarathustra, came to be associated with the term,' said Linda. 'Possibly it was connected to the way that they dressed or their uncompromising adherence to purity. Even today, Zoroastrian priests always dress in white. But what if that isn't the reason for the name?'

'If that's not the reason, what is?'

Linda took a breath. 'What if the white powder—what we call Hamzaa Dura—is the reason for using the term "spitama"?' she asked.

118

WE WERE ABLE *to catch a flight from Delhi to Srinagar early next morning. Flying to and from Srinagar was like winning an obstacle course owing to the tedious security checks that were part of the routine. Kashmir is a pawn in the eternal conflict between India and Pakistan, both nuclear powers. The result had prompted American President Bill Clinton to call Kashmir 'the most dangerous place in the world'. But that was before Afghanistan, Pakistan and Syria became far more dangerous.*

Arriving in Srinagar, we hopped into a tourist taxi I had booked in advance. The driver took us along National Highway One towards our destination: the village of Raihan Bag. It lies in the western part of the Indian state of Jammu and Kashmir, or J&K—as it was called before its dramatic division.

The name 'Kashmir' is derived from the Sanskrit name 'Kasmira', one of the many names of the Mother Goddess Parvati. In the first millennium, Kashmir had been an important Vedic centre and subsequently an equally important centre of Buddhist learning. From the fourteenth century onwards, Kashmir came under Muslim rule, including that of the Mughals, until Maharaja Ranjit Singh annexed it to the Sikh empire. Raja Gulab Singh and his descendants then ruled the kingdom until the partition of India in 1947, and the creation of Pakistan. After Partition, Kashmir became a hotbed of Pakistani and Chinese incursions, Islamic insurgency and messy Indian politics.

We were lucky we had arrived in the region during a period of relative calm. At other times there would be violence in J&K, and roadblocks and military curfews would make regular travel impossible. Our driver, a greying man called Farooq, updated us on the political situation as we drove. He reminded me strangely of my dad's chauffeur, Abdul. Like Abdul, Farooq was soft-spoken, respectful and cautious on the road.

It was impossible to ignore the stunning beauty that surrounded us. Cradled in the arms of the lofty Himalayas, Kashmir is picturesque. It is an elaborate coffee-table book in which each page is a verdant valley, babbling brook, flowering meadow, mountain peak, fruit orchard or glistening lake—each natural and almost impossibly perfect. The Mughal emperor Jehangir was known to have said, 'Gar firdaus bar-rue zamin ast, hami asto! Hamin asto! Hamin ast!' Translated, it means, 'If there is a heaven on earth, it is here! It is here! It is here!' Alas, Kashmir alternates between heaven and hell when Islamic insurgency rears its ugly head from time to time.

As we settled into the rhythm of the journey, I remembered the rivayat that my father had made me memorise.

Across the Jabbar, light dazzles the eyes
As three great fires roar from the skies
Behold, the Athravan in the Daitya prays
And the Anu people to the heavens gaze
They know the fourth that comes from three
Means powerful Yasna for all time to be.

It was those words that had pointed us here. I noted that the verse spoke about three great fires and remembered discussing those with Cecile many years ago. I asked Linda if she knew anything about the fires.

'They are considered to be the holiest of the fires,' replied Linda, 'although information about these three fires has been lost down the ages. I know that Zoroastrian records indicate three names: Adur Burzen-Mihr, Adur Farnbag and Adur Gushnasp. But the questions remain: why were there three great fires? And why three? Why not one? Or five? And were these actual locations, or mythological? If they were real, is it possible that the fires had come from somewhere else, much like the Iranshah that was moved from one place to another?'

'And what about the birthplace of Zarathustra?' I asked. 'Could that have been the original source of the fire?'

'Could have been,' ruminated Linda, 'but we don't know for sure.'

'But what about the reference to Athravan?' I asked. 'Behold, the Athravan in the Daitya prays ...'

Linda pulled down a web page on her phone. The mobile network was patchy, but she showed me the partially loaded page.

Avesta 24.94:
Hail to us! for he is born, the Athravan Spitama Zarathustra ...

'What does that signify?' I asked.
'Remember, there were initially three Vedas—the Rigveda, the Yajurveda and the Samaveda,' replied Linda. 'To these three,

was added a fourth, the Atharvaveda. The word "athar" meant fire—the intermediary for offerings to God. So, Athravans were keepers of the fire.'

'Are you saying the Athravans had studied the Atharvaveda?' I asked in amazement.

'Yes,' said Linda. 'In Sanskrit they were called Atharvans, in Avestan they were called Athravans.' Linda paused. 'But have you heard about something called the fifth Veda?' she finally asked.

'You just said that there were four,' I replied. There was no end to the woman's findings.

'It is said that Vyasa, the author of the Mahabharata, taught the four Vedas to his disciples, and a fifth one, in secret, to his son,' said Linda. 'Why would there have been a reference to a fifth Veda if there were truly only four?'

'And the fifth is lost?' I asked Linda.

'Go back a little in time,' prompted Linda. 'The fourth Veda was indeed the Atharvaveda, but by then there was already a split between the pitrayana and devayana groups, the former worshipping the asuras and the latter worshipping the devas. My own research tells me that the Atharvaveda had two separate portions—the Bhrigu portion and the Brihaspati portion.'

'Are you saying what I think you are saying?' I asked incredulously.

'I am,' said Linda. If my wife wasn't such a serious scholar, I'd say she looked positively gleeful at making the revelation. 'The Gathas of Zarathustra constituted the Bhrigu part of the Atharvaveda that India lost. And what is now called the Atharvaveda was the Brihaspati portion that Iran lost. The Atharvaveda was two books, not one!'

A picture in motion was gradually beginning to form in my head. Of an ancient Vedic civilisation in the region of the Sapta Sindhu; a land demarcated by Yama and Manu; the war of ten kings and the resulting schism between the devas and the asuras; the rivalry between Bhrigu and Brihaspati; the emergence of white-robed Atharvan priests chanting from the Atharvaveda; a young priest called Zarathustra fleeing his home because of the unacceptability of his novel ideas; the final split between pitrayana and devayana; the emergence of a new faith.

But there were grey areas too. Could the figure called Jarutha actually have been Zarathustra? Could he have lived in the place that we were now headed to, Raihan Bag? Could the Gathas constitute the fifth Veda? It all seemed just too ... too ... fantastical.

119

FAROOQ POLITELY ADDRESSED the rearview mirror to announce that Raihan Bag was just half an hour away. 'Saheb, you should also consider visiting Bomai in Sopore district,' he suggested shyly. 'There is nothing much to see in Raihan Bag.'

'Why?' I asked. 'What is unique about Bomai?'

'Rock carvings,' replied Farooq. 'Thousands of years old.'

'That's for another time,' I replied. 'At this moment, my priority is Raihan Bag.'

Turning to Linda, I said, 'Realistically, though, what will we do at Raihan Bag? It's just a village of six hundred people. Where would we even start?'

Farooq was looking at me now in the mirror. 'Saheb, in the village there is a wise old man. He is very old and knows a lot. I could take you to him.'

'Who is he?' I asked, hoping I hadn't thrown my lot in with one of those mild-mannered, phoney tour guides who operate in tandem with charlatans.

'One of the oldest residents,' said Farooq. 'No one knows how long he has lived. People call him "sheikh" or "baba" because he is very wise. The name he goes by is Baba Malik.'

We had nothing to lose. This was as good a start as any other area of enquiry. 'All right,' I agreed. 'Let's go see him.'

Some minutes later, we pulled up outside a small house. It had been made from roughly cut stones that had been piled up on each other and coated with mud. The sloping roof had been fashioned from deodar wood, much like most houses in the area.

We walked into the house hesitantly. Inside the main room, a handsome man with very fair skin sat on a carpet. He was dressed entirely in white and on his head was a white cloth draped like a fakir's. Farooq knelt down before the man respectfully and introduced us. Although Farooq had not instructed us on the protocol, both Linda and I folded our hands in a namaste. He returned our greeting with an adaab-salaam, raising the fingers of his right hand towards his face and almost touching his forehead.

I was confused. Farooq had said that Baba Malik was an old man, older than any of the other residents of the village. But I would have taken him at no more than forty years old. There was a youthful glow on his face. Even his physique was robust, more like a wrestler's than that of an ascetic. Next to him was a copper pot from which fragrant vapours of incense wafted up.

The baba smiled. 'I know what you seek,' he said as we sat down cross-legged in front of him. 'It is everywhere around you, but you cannot discern it.'

Linda looked him squarely in the face. 'Farooq said that you are one of the oldest people in Kashmir,' she said almost accusingly, 'and yet you could pass for very early middle age!' Baba seemed amused. 'Age is just a number,' he replied enigmatically. 'But it isn't my age you've come here to find out.'

'Tell us something about yourself, Baba,' I requested him, trying not to let the urgency show. If this lead didn't pan out, there was probably nothing in Raihan Bag that could help us, and we would be forced to return home from our wild goose chase without anything to show for it. Not even to ourselves.

'People call me Baba Malik,' he said obligingly. 'Many generations ago, the Muslim rulers of Kashmir converted my family to Islam. Can't you figure out who I am from my name?'

I was no good there, but Linda was at the top of her game. 'Malik means "lord",' she said on cue. 'It means that your Hindu ancestors would have had a name that meant the same thing.'

The baba laughed aloud this time. 'Very good reasoning,' he said approvingly. 'Do go on.'

'There are many words for lord in Hindu scripture,' continued Linda. 'But one of them stands out.'

'And that is?'

'Bhrigu, meaning "lord of the creatures". Another name for Brahma. And also, the name of the great sage Bhrigu.'

The baba's eyes twinkled. 'Getting closer,' he said.

'The disciples of Bhrigu were called Bhargavas,' continued Linda. 'I'm willing to bet that your family had the Bhargava

surname. They would have adopted the Malik name when they converted to Islam.'

'Remarkable!' said Baba Malik in glee. He looked at me and said, 'Your wife is really sharp.' I nodded humbly. Everyone knows Linda to be brighter than I am.

'Now that you know who I am, why don't you tell me about yourself?' asked Baba Malik reasonably.

I narrated my story to the baba. There was something so persuasive about him, I felt comfortable opening up. I covered all the bases: that I had been born a Parsi; how my family consisted of a line of dasturs; the earthen box that I had been handed for safekeeping; how I had tried to use it to create a formulation that could help mankind; my abduction and escape; the loss of the box and its contents in the fire—I tried providing as much detail as I could.

'And you think that the source of that material is in Raihan Bag?' asked Baba Malik.

I nodded. 'We have tried connecting the dots,' I said. 'And it seems that this place is indeed Rajish, described as being near the Jabbar Mountain. This village is at the foothills of the Urni Jabbar mountain, in which case, it could easily be the birthplace of Zarathustra.'

'Let's assume you are right,' said Baba Malik. 'But does that tell you that the source of the material you call Hamzaa Dura is here, too?'

I shook my head. 'It does not,' I replied, 'but if there is any hope of saving mankind from perishing from many fatal ailments, it lies in Hamzaa Dura'.

Baba Malik nodded. 'In that case we need to go to Bomai,' he said, getting up from the carpet. I knew better than to ask why of this sphinx-like man.

120

WE SAT IN *Farooq's car and drove to Bomai. Baba Malik sat in front, refusing to answer any queries until we got there. That took us around an hour and a half, passing Magam, Pattan and Sopore on the way. It was a lucky break that both Raihan Bag and Bomai fell on the Indian side of the 'Line of Control', which officially separated Indian troops from the Pakistani ones. I pulled my jacket around me tighter. The evening chill was seeping into the car, but Baba Malik seemed immune to it.*

We finally stopped and got out of the car, taking a short break to stretch and take in the air from the chinar trees. Baba Malik beckoned, and we followed him towards the north-west end of a plateau that overlooked India's largest lake, the Wular.

He eventually motioned for us to stop, and we saw he was pointing to something. It was a conspicuous rock carving, around a square metre in size. On the rock surface were engraved a series of concentric circles.

'What are we looking at?' I asked.

'These rock carvings were executed during Upper Palaeolithic times,' replied Baba.

'So, that would be between 6,000 to 20,000 years ago?' queried Linda.

'Yes,' replied Baba. 'And they are not random, as your husband seems to think.'

He had picked up on my expression. All I could see were a bunch of circles scattered across the carved surface and I was confused as to why he had brought us here. I was beginning to think Baba Malik was senile.

'They represent a major astronomical event that would have happened around then,' explained the baba. 'The men who watched that event wanted to make a record of it.'

'And what event was that?' I asked, duly put in my place.

'A single meteor that disintegrated into several fragments as it entered the earth's atmosphere,' replied Baba. Both Linda and I fell silent. I now understood why Baba Malik had brought us here.

'To the untrained eye, a meteor would simply look like a great trail of fire from the sky,' explained the baba. 'But when a meteorite hits earth it fractures the surface. These fractures are often in the form of concentric circles. These carvings depict just that.'

'But there are no known crash sites of meteors in Kashmir,' I argued.

'That's because the pits that they created eventually got filled with water,' replied Baba Malik. 'The lake that you see, Wular, was one of them. The others were Srinagar's Dal Lake as also the Manasbal Lake.'

Baba Malik turned back to the one that had our attention. 'Based on the carvings here,' he proceeded with his lesson, 'we can safely assume that the meteor entered the region from the north-west and fell in a south-easterly direction,' he said. 'There are three circles on this carving that are co-linear, and their sizes vary—indicating that the fragments were of different sizes. But they approximate the lake locations.'

'Three meteor fragments,' I murmured. 'Three lakes ... three great fires!'

Across the Jabbar, light dazzles the eyes
As three great fires roar from the skies
Behold, the Athravan in the Daitya prays
And the Anu people to the heavens gaze
They know the fourth that comes from three
Means powerful Yasna for all time to be.

'So, the Jabbar is the Urni Jabbar mountain,' I breathed the words. 'The three great fires are the meteors that must have fallen many millennia before Zarathustra. The Atharvans were the followers of Bhrigu. The Daitya was the Diti, or Jhelum. But then there is the bit about the Anu people ...'

'Airyanemvaeja is also called "Anu-varshte", meaning "land of the Anu people",' Linda broke in. 'The Anu tribe were often referred to as the Anavas, and they lived in Kashmir. There is a village, Ainu Brai, named after the Anu people, in the Pahalgam area of Kashmir.'

Baba Malik seemed pleased with Linda and me, as a schoolmarm would when she discovered that two of her young charges were brighter than usual. 'I am an Anu,' he revealed to us. 'All Anu people were Atharvans. So, they were not only familiar with the Brihaspati portion of the *Atharvaveda,* but also the Bhrigu portion that became the *Gathas.*'

'And there would have been a reason why Zarathustra chose to travel to Balkh to the court of Vishtaspa and nowhere else,' *said Linda. 'The Anu tribe not only dominated Kashmir but also annexed Bactria.'*

'What about the reference to "they know the fourth that comes from three"?' I asked. 'What does that mean?'

Baba Malik had the answer. 'When the Three Wise Kings of the Orient—the magi—went to bless the baby Jesus, they carried gifts of gold, frankincense and myrrh. Frankincense was an incense and thus symbolised divinity; gold signified kingship; and myrrh—used in funerary rites—symbolised death. But they also secretly carried a fourth gift, one that was never given to anyone else. It was so powerful that it allowed Christ to be resurrected. It allowed Zarathustra to cure Vishtaspa's horse. That fourth gift is the element that you now seek. It resulted in the name "shwetama" or "spitama" being attached to my people because of the white powder that a meteorite had brought us. We worked hard to preserve the secret. Even the great Sassanian king Kusrow tried to get it from us, but didn't succeed.'

'How did he try, in the first place?' I asked.

'Under Kusrow, the Academy of Gundeshapur had become one of the world's most important centres of learning,' replied Baba Malik. 'Kusrow sent the Persian physician, Borzuya, to Kashmir, to search for the substance.'

'And?' asked Linda.

'He met one of my ancestors,' replied Baba Malik. 'A rishi called Bhargava. My forefather explained to Borzuya that bringing the dead to life is futile but living in wisdom brings true immortality. He gave Borzuya a Sanskrit book called the Five Treatises—*or the* Panchatantra, *as you have newly discovered. Borzuya was never able to get his hands on the substance but returned to Persia and translated the book into Pahlavi. The*

version of the Panchatantra *that Bhargava presented Borzuya had a reference to the origin of the substance. It was in that passage of yours,'* he dipped his head with respect.

'Since we now know that the three great fires caused the three lakes, is it possible that the material that we seek could be in those lakes?' I asked.

'There are three great fires in Hindu annals too,' said Baba Malik. 'The term tretagni *means "three fires". They are named Grahapatyagni, Dakshinagni and Ahavaniyagni, representing the father, mother and the teacher. It is not surprising that Zarathustra adopted this tradition into the new faith he was propagating.'*

'But could the material be in the lakes?' I asked again.

'It is,' said Baba Malik, with certitude. 'The funny thing is that the Hindu branch of my lineage and their descendants— including Vijay Bhargava—are searching high and low for it, while it remains right here under their noses. In Srinagar we have a spring known as the Chashme Shahi. People from all over the world come there because of the curative power of the spring's honey-sweet water. Much of that water would have been infused with minerals that had meteoric origin. I recommend the waters of Kashmir routinely as treatment for my patients. To answer your question: if you dig deep down into these lakes, you will be able to find the miraculous cure that you seek. But first you need to dig deep within.'

Linda and I were quiet as we absorbed the significance of his words. Then Linda spoke. 'And so, the Anu people would have incorporated a white powdery substance from those fires into their own yajnas—or yasnas—knowing that the fumes would *have curative properties,' said Linda. 'It probably explains the longevity of Parsis in general.'*

'This material would have been carried to locations such as Adur Burzen-Mihr, Adur Farnbag and Adur Gushnasp, when consecrating the fires there,' I said. 'But a small portion of the original material must have been passed down from generation to generation for the new fires that would need to be consecrated—like the one at Sanjan. And given that Zarathustra was a rebel, he wanted that this material should be in the custody of rebellious individuals such as he. After all, it was the Athravan Star.'

We looked out at the expanse of the Wular Lake guessing at the secrets that lay on its floor. I knew I would be starting from scratch in my quest. But I also knew that I had been given charge of the earthen box precisely because I was the rebel of the family.

Zarathustra must have known that this day would come.

EPILOGUE

THE LIGHT FROM the stained-glass windows had dimmed as the man at the lectern began wrapping up his speech. There had been many moments of spontaneous applause during his lecture. He tuned out the rapturous clapping and stared at his cufflinks, embossed with tiny gold symbols of the Zoroastrian faravahar.

'Indian gurus have said that true wisdom lies in knowing that one knows nothing. I am grateful to the universe for having taught me that. I proudly stand before you today, as the man who knows nothing. And I raise a toast to my friend Jim Dastoor, who is dead. That Jim is long gone and the Jim standing before you is one who has emptied his cup.'

His eyes settled on a lady in the first row. He smiled at her, singling her out from the politicians, businessmen and bureaucrats who made up the general audience. 'Yes, science and philosophy are intertwined. After all, the lady you see sitting before me today—my own philosopher—has always thrown her tiny weight behind me—a humble scientist.'

The Kettering Prize winner waited for the friendly laughter to end. 'You honour me today because of my achievements in the world of science. But, had it not been for my wife, Linda, none of those would have come to fruition,' he continued, looking directly at the attractive woman in the front seat. She was his contemporary, but could have passed for less. Her blue eyes were clear, the dimples in her cheeks endearingly youthful, and the soft blonde hair that fell in waves about her face had not lost its early sheen. She wore, with understated confidence, a hammered satin drape dress that not everyone could have carried off. She looked a little shy now, embarrassed by the number of necks that were craned for a look at her, but did not avoid her husband's steady and admiring gaze. *Today is about you, not me!* she mentally reproved him. *But yes, my darling, we've travelled a great distance together.*

Seated next to her was the handsome special invitee from Raihan Bag, who had replaced his habitual ascetic's garb with that of a somewhat casual college don—a tweed jacket over jeans—and who radiated fitness, like a man who works out every day.

Jim stepped down from the stage and shook hands with several members of the audience. Towards the end of his talk, he had tears in his eyes as he recalled those moments when he had been ready to give up the quest. After some minutes he caught Linda's eye. He wanted a quick exit from the crowd. In turn, Linda nudged the baba.

Jim, Linda and Baba Malik left the grand hall at Oxford and found a table at The Eagle and Child, a pub dating back to 1650. It had been a regular haunt, even in later decades, of the likes of C. S. Lewis and J. R. R. Tolkien. 'Thank you for agreeing to be here,' said Jim to Baba Malik. 'I could not imagine delivering this lecture without your presence and Linda's.'

'I was happy to come,' said Baba Malik. 'But these clothes are uncomfortable. I would much prefer to be in my usual attire back home.' He laughed. A waitress brought them their orders—no alcohol for the baba! He was satisfied with Darjeeling tea.

'I still find it difficult to believe that we were able to find unlimited supplies of Hamzaa Dura in the Wular, Dal and Manasbal lakes,' said Jim. 'How desperately we tried to preserve the contents of that little earthen box! And how we despaired of ever finding the like!'

'It was funny, wasn't it,' reminisced the baba in his turn, 'how Bhargava tried so fiercely to get it back for Kashmir, when it had been right there under his nose all the while!' He added more gravely, 'His family still holds it against my ancestors for having converted to Islam generations ago. But that does not mean I have forgotten my Athravan roots.'

'Where are the two conspirators these days, though?' asked Linda. She was referring to Bhargava and Abbasi.

'It turns out that Bhargava was in cahoots with Islamist separatists in Kashmir,' replied Jim. 'That was the reason he could remain in Srinagar while most other Kashmiri Pandit families had to flee. Our Indian PM has packed him off to a hardship posting in Algeria.'

'And Abbasi?' asked Linda.

'Missing since that day at the Lodhi Hotel,' said Jim. 'The word is that he is somewhere in Russia. He can't go back to Iran, and now he can't go back to Israel either, poor wretch. My sister Avan took the NSA, B. K. Singh, into her confidence. She told him that Abbasi had been working closely with Bhargava.'

'But BK and Abbasi were buddies,' said Linda.

'True,' replied Jim. 'That was probably the reason why Abbasi was allowed to exit India at all. But he's a wanted person and, as I need hardly tell you, the Mossad always get their man. I will remain grateful to him, nevertheless, for having saved our lives on more than one occasion—at the risk of his.'

There was a sobering pause in the conversation. Jim took a gulp of his beer and looked around at the people in the pub. There was joy, very vocally expressed, in the air.

'Laughter,' said Linda, sipping her wine, 'probably *is* the best medicine.'

'And a healthy respect for body, mind and spirit,' said Jim.

'Remember one thing though, son,' said Baba Malik. 'You are not an earthly body having a spiritual experience. Turn that notion on its head—*you are a spiritual being having an earthly experience*. If you want that substance to take effect, you must bring to it a pure body and a pure spirit. As Indian gurus have always said—*dava* and *dua*. The Athravans understood this. That's why they used it in their prayers over the sacred fire.'

'But that's mere ritual,' argued Jim.

'The word "ritual" is also part of the word "spiritual",' came Baba Malik's riposte. 'If you perform a ritual with devotion, it becomes spiritual. Your wife would know—or she would not have arrived at that name for your universal remedy.'

'I don't understand,' said Jim.

Linda looked prettily smug. Baba Malik and she knew something that Jim did not—for the moment, anyway.

'Hamzaa Dura is just an anagram of Ahura Mazda,' said Baba Malik simply. 'For complete healing, you need both—substance and spirit—Hamzaa Dura and Ahura Mazda.'

REFERENCES

THE BOOKS IN the Bharat Series are fiction based on some elements of fact. Readers often ask me, 'How much of your book is fact and how much is fiction? Which parts are fiction and which parts are fact?' To which, I say that my reader should treat the entire novel as pure fiction. But for those who are interested in exploring further, I always provide a comprehensive list of books, papers, journals, videos and websites that I have used while developing my fictional narrative. Some of these sources may even express views that run contrary to the story. The idea of any book within the Bharat Series is to provide a starting point for further exploration. I am hopeful that my readers will use this list of sources for further reading and discovery.

Books

- *Alexander the Great*, Philip Freeman, Simon & Schuster, 2011
- *Gods, Demons and Symbols of Ancient Mesopotamia: An Illustrated Dictionary*, Jeremy Black and Anthony Green, University of Texas Press, 1992
- *In Search of Zarathustra: Across Iran and Central Asia to Find the World's First Prophet*, Paul Kriwaczek, RHUS, 2004

458 *References*

- *Magicians of the Gods: The Forgotten Wisdom of Earth's Lost Civilisation*, Graham Hancock, Coronet, 2016
- *Mysteries of the Ancient Vedic Empire: Recognising Vedic Contributions to Other Cultures Around the World*, Stephen Knapp, CreateSpace Independent, 2015
- *Original Magic: The Rituals and Initiations of the Persian Magi*, Stephen Flowers, Inner Traditions, 2017
- *The History of the Ancient World: From the Earliest Accounts to the Fall of Rome*, Susan Wise Bauer, W. W. Norton & Company, 2007
- *The Tatas, Freddie Mercury & Other Bawas: An Intimate History of the Parsis*, Coomi Kapoor, Westland, 2021
- *The Travels of Marco Polo*, Marco Polo, Peacock Books, 2017
- *The Zoroastrian Flame: Exploring Religion, History and Tradition*, Alan Williams, Almut Hintze, Sarah Stewart, I.B. Tauris, 2016
- *Thus Spoke Zarathustra*, Friedrich Nietzsche, CreateSpace Independent Publishing, 2018
- *Zoroastrians: Their Religious Beliefs and Practices* (The Library of Religious Beliefs and Practices), Mary Boyce, Routledge, 2000

Ebooks

- *Parsis of Ancient India*, Shapurji Kavasji Hodivala, https://www.ebooksread.com/authors-eng/shapurji-kavasji-hodivala/parsis-of-ancient-india-ala.shtml
- *The History of Al-Tabari Vol. XXIV: The Empire in Transition*, State University of New York Press, Translated

by David Stefan Powers, 1989, https://kalamullah.
com/Books/The%20History%20Of%20Tabari/Tabari_
Volume_24.pdf?__cf_chl_jschl_tk__=pmd_f3b68a0a
762514a7d727a1de8908a044ac441bce-1627363727-0-
gqNtZGzNAg2jcnBszQbi

- *The Religious Ceremonies and Customs of the Parsees*,
  Jivanji Jamshedji Modi, Jehangir B. Karani's Sons, 1937,
  https://zoroastrians.net/wp-content/uploads/2009/07/
  religious-ceremonies-jj-modi.pdf
- *Zarathushtra*, Ardeshir Mehta, 1999, https://arshtad.files.
  wordpress.com/2013/03/zarathushtra-ardeshir-mehta.pdf

Research Papers

- 'Early Vedic Schism: Indo-Iranian Split and Rise of
  Zoroastrianism', Bipin Shah, ResearchGate, 2016,
  https://www.researchgate.net/publication/339484332_
  Early_Vedic_Schism-Indo-Iranian_Split_and_Rise_of_
  Zoroastrianism
- 'A Brief History of the Parsi Priesthood', Dastur Firoze M.
  Kotwal, *Indo-Iranian Journal*, 1990, https://www.jstor.org/
  stable/24655249
- 'Annual Report on the Death Penalty in Iran', Ecpm.org,
  https://www.ecpm.org/wp-content/uploads/Rapport-
  iran-2020-gb-070420-WEB.pdf
- 'Comets and Meteoritic Showers in the Rigveda and Their
  Significance', R. N. Iyengar, *Indian Journal of History of
  Science*, 2009, https://fdocuments.in/document/comets-
  and-meteoritic-showers-in-the-rigveda-and-their-
  importance-ijhs-march2010.html

- 'Gandhara and the Formation of the Vedic and Zoroastrian Canons', Michael Witzel, Harvard University, https://dash.harvard.edu/handle/1/9887626

- 'Imagining Hafez: Rabindranath Tagore in Iran in 1932', Afshin Marashi, *Journal of Persianate Studies*, 2010, https://moodle2.sscnet.ucla.edu/pluginfile.php/548018/course/section/10256396/MarashiATagoreInIran2010.pdf

- 'Introduction to Zoroastrianism', Prods Oktor Skjaervo, Harvard Divinity School, http://sites.fas.harvard.edu/~iranian/Zoroastrianism/zorocomplete.pdf

- 'Iran: Political Opposition Groups, Security Forces, Selected Human Rights Issues, Rule of Law', COI Compilation, Austrian Red Cross, 2015

- 'Numerical Methods in Linguistics', Raamesh Gowri Raghavan, *Resonance*, 2005, https://www.researchgate.net/publication/225401386_Numerical_methods_in_linguistics

- 'On Yasna 51:16', Gikyo Ito, Society for Near Eastern Studies in Japan, 1987, https://www.jstage.jst.go.jp/article/orient1960/23/0/23_0_1/_article

- '*Panchatantra*: An Example of Using Narratives in Teaching in Ancient Indian Education', Shirin Kulkarni, Tampere University Press, 2013

- 'Reclaiming the Faravahar', Navid Fozi, Leiden University Press, 2014, https://library.oapen.org/bitstream/id/0249e838-d67e-46bb-bd90-583b8193ddb7/643261.pdf

- 'Religion after the Fall of the Sassanians', Dr Rustom Kevala, 2015, https://zamwi.org/wp-content/uploads/2015/07/Religion-After-the-Fall-of-the-Sassanians.pdf

- 'Some Early Astronomical Sites in the Kashmir Region', N. Iqbal, M. N. Vahia,, T. Masood, and A. Ahmad, *Journal of Astronomical History and Heritage*, http://articles.adsabs. harvard.edu//full/2009JAHH...12...61I/0000062.000.html
- 'The Celestial Trinity of Indo-Iranian Mythology', Abbas Saeedipour, International Journal of Scientific and Research Publications, 2012, http://www.ijsrp.org/ research_paper_may2012/ijsrp-may-2012-20.pdf
- 'The Empires of Persia, Islam's Takeover of Last Sassanian Empire and Flight of Parsee Community to India', Bipin Shah, ResearchGate, 2016, https://www.researchgate.net/ publication/340006091_The_Empires_of_Persia_Islam's_ takeover_of_Last_Sassanian_Empire_and_Flight_of_ Parsee_community_to_India
- 'The History of Zoroastrians after Arab Invasion: Alien in Their Homeland', Dr Daryoush Jahanian, The Circle of Ancient Iranian Studies, https://www.cais-soas.com/ CAIS/History/Post-Sasanian/zoroastrians_after_arab_ invasion.htm
- 'The Origin and Spread of Qanats in the Old World', Paul Ward English, Proceedings of the American Philosophical Society, 1968, https://www.ircwash.org/sites/default/files/ English-1968-Origin.pdf
- 'The Prehistoric Meteor Shower Recorded on a Palaeolithic Rock', Naseer Iqbal, M. N. Vahia, Ajaz Ahmad, Tabassum Masood, *NRIAG Journal of Astronomy & Astrophysics*, 2008, https://www.tifr.res.in/~archaeo/papers/Others/ Prehistoric%20meteor%20shower%20record%20in%20 Kashmir.pdf

- 'Vedic Elements in the Ancient Iranian Religion of Zarathustra', Subhash Kak, Adyar Library Bulletin, http://ikashmir.net/subhashkak/docs/Zarathushtra.pdf

News Articles

- 'Ancient City Uncovered in Afghanistan', Matthew Pennington, NBC News, 2008, https://www.nbcnews.com/id/wbna26095077
- 'Baluchistan's Rising Militancy', Sonia Ghaffari, Middle East Research and Information Project, 2009, https://merip.org/2009/03/baluchistans-rising-militancy/
- 'Gujarat: Udvada, the Heart of Parsi Culture', Bachi Karkaria, *Outlook Traveller*, Bachi Karkaria, https://www.outlookindia.com/outlooktraveller/explore/story/50155/gujarat_udvada_heart_of_parsi_culture
- 'How Iran Persecutes Its Oldest Religion', Jamsheed K. Choksy, CNN, https://edition.cnn.com/2011/11/14/opinion/choksy-iran-zoroastrian/index.html
- 'How the 'Panchatantra' Travelled the World Thanks to Persian and Arabic Narrators', Anu Kumar, Scroll.in, 2015, https://scroll.in/article/758031/how-the-panchatantra-travelled-the-world-thanks-to-persian-and-arabic-narrators
- 'Magi: The Zoroastrian Magicians', Noshir H. Dadrawala, *Parsi Times*, https://parsi-times.com/2019/03/magi-the-zoroastrian-magicians/
- 'Mystery behind Diamond-studded Meteorite that Hit Sudan in 2008 Revealed', *The Indian Express*, https://

indianexpress.com/article/technology/science/meteorite-sudan-2008-giant-asteroid-water-minerals-7122812/

- 'Panchatantra to Kaleela Wa Dimna', Haroon Mirani, Greater Kashmir, 2018, https://www.greaterkashmir.com/news/opinion/panchatantra-to-kaleela-wa-dimna/
- 'The Ancient Persian God That May Be at the Heart of Game of Thrones', Washington Post, Ishaan Tharoor, https://www.washingtonpost.com/news/worldviews/wp/2016/04/24/the-ancient-persian-god-that-may-be-at-the-heart-of-game-of-thrones/
- 'The Art of Longevity: Why Do Parsis Live Longer than Indians', India Today, Nirmala Ravindran, https://www.indiatoday.in/living/story/reasons-why-parsis-live-longer-than-indians-131855-2011-04-09
- 'The Arya in Iran', Devdutt Pattanaik, Mumbai Mirror, , https://mumbaimirror.indiatimes.com/others/sunday-read/the-arya-in-iran/articleshow/71559634.cms
- 'The Last of the Zoroastrians', Shaun Walker, The Guardian, 2020, https://www.theguardian.com/world/2020/aug/06/last-of-the-zoroastrians-parsis-mumbai-india-ancient-religion
- 'The Obscure Religion That Shaped the West', Joobin Bekhrad, BBC Culture, 2017, https://www.bbc.com/culture/article/20170406-this-obscure-religion-shaped-the-west
- 'The Zoroastrian Priestesses of Iran (Whose Father Was an Indian Parsi)', Giulia Bertoluzzi, Scroll.in, 2015, https://scroll.in/article/757156/the-zoroastrian-priestesses-of-iran-whose-father-was-an-indian-parsi

- 'Zoroastrians: Iran's Forgotten Minority', Kourosh Ziabari, *Asia Times*, 2020, https://asiatimes.com/2020/10/zoroastrians-irans-forgotten-minority/

Blog Articles

- 'A Very Interesting Account on Zoroastrians in Kabul-Afghanistan', Zoroastrians.net, https://zoroastrians.net/2013/02/01/a-very-interesting-account-on-zoroastrians-in-kabul-afghanistan-2/
- 'Avesta and Rig Veda', Varnam, Jai Krishan, https://varnam.org/2007/01/avesta_and_rig_veda/
- 'Family of Zoroaster and Hvovi', RootsWeb, https://sites.rootsweb.com/~dearbornboutwell/fam1241.html
- 'How the Essence of Religion Came From Vedic Culture', Stephen Knapp, https://www.stephen-knapp.com/how_the_essence_of_religion_came_from_vedic_culture.htm
- 'The Cousin Cultures of India and Iran, Lokesh Chandra, Esamskriti', 2016, https://www.esamskriti.com/e/History/Indian-Influence-Abroad/The-Cousin-Cultures-of-India-and-Iran-1.aspx
- 'The Forgotten History of How Ancient Zoroastrians Helped Create the Old Silk Route', Anvar Alikhan, Quartz India, https://qz.com/india/987379/the-forgotten-history-of-how-ancient-zoroastrians-helped-create-the-old-silk-route/
- 'The Rig Veda and the Gathas Revisited', Sreenivasa Rao, https://sreenivasaraos.com/2012/08/31/the-rig-veda-and-the-gathas-revisited/

- 'The Vedic Religion in Ancient Iran and Zarathushtra', HareKrsna.com, 2005, https://www.harekrsna.com/sun/editorials/06-20/editorials17949.htm
- 'The Zoroastrian Nexus', Radhe.net, http://www.radhe.net/history/en/zaratustra.php
- 'The Zoroastrian Texts of Ancient Persia & What They Reveal about Advanced Ancient Civilizations', Graham Hancock, Collective Evolution, 2017, https://www.collective-evolution.com/2017/11/02/the-zoroastrian-texts-of-ancient-persia-what-they-reveal-about-advanced-ancient-civilizations/
- 'Varun, Ved and Zoroastrianism', Roots Hunt, https://rootshunt.com/aryans/zoroastrianandaryans/varunvedandzoroastriasm/chapter1.htm
- 'Varuna and His Decline', Sreenivasa Rao, 2012, https://sreenivasaraos.com/2012/10/04/varuna-and-his-decline-part-one/
- 'Vedic Elements in the Ancient Iranian Religion of Zarathushtra', Sanskriti, https://www.sanskritimagazine.com/india/vedic-elements-in-the-ancient-iranian-religion-of-zarathushtra/
- 'Were the Mitanni Aryans Really Indo-Aryans', Giacomo Benedetti, New Indology, 2017, http://new-indology.blogspot.com/2017/05/were-mitanni-really-indo-aryans.html
- 'Yatha Ahu Vairyo: A Brief Look at the History of the Zoroastrian Religion', Ravi Chandar, http://ravichandar.blogspot.com/2017/03/yatha-ahu-vairyo-brief-look-at-history.html

- 'Zoroaster: The First Magus, Historical Blindness', Nathaniel Lloyd, 2020, https://www.historicalblindness. com/blogandpodcast//zoroaster-the-first-magus
- 'Zoroastrian Gatha: An Interim Revelation in Context of Avestan/Vedic and Early Aryans' Religious Blunder', Dr P. R. Palodhi, Mayadanawa, https://mayadanawa.wordpress. com/2012/08/28/zoroastrian-gatha-an-interim-revelation-in-context-of-avestanvedic-and-early-aryans-religious-blunder/
- 'Zoroastrianism and Hinduism', Himanshu Bhatt, Hindupedia, http://www.hindupedia.com/en/ Zoroastrianism_and_Hinduism

Online Reference

- Ashur, Britannica, https://www.britannica.com/place/ Ashur-ancient-city-Iraq
- Ashura, https://en.wikipedia.org/wiki/Ashura
- Assur, Joshua J. Mark, World History Encyclopedia, 2017, https://www.worldhistory.org/assur/
- Battle of the Ten Kings, https://en.wikipedia.org/wiki/ Battle_of_the_Ten_Kings
- Faravahar, World History Encyclopedia, Joshua J. Mark, https://www.worldhistory.org/Faravahar/
- History of Zoroastrianism, History World, http:// historyworld.net/wrldhis/PlainTextHistoriesResponsive. asp?historyid=ab71
- Magi, New World Encyclopedia, https://www. newworldencyclopedia.org/entry/Magi

- Parsi Communities Early History, Encyclopeadia Iranica, https://iranicaonline.org/articles/parsi-communities-i-early-history
- Piruz-e Nahavandi, The Circle of Ancient Iranian Studies, https://www.cais-soas.com/CAIS/History/today_in_ancient_iran/august/23-august.htm
- Ritual Implements: Baresman, its Consecration and Ritual, Avesta.org, http://www.avesta.org/ritual/barsom.htm
- Suras and Asuras, Tibetan Buddhist Encyclopedia, http://tibetanbuddhistencyclopedia.com/en/index.php/Suras_and_Asuras
- The Gathas: The Hymns of Zarathushtra, D. J. Irani, http://avesta.org/dastur/Dinshaw_J_Irani_The_Gathas.pdf
- The Persian Rivayats, Joseph H. Peterson, Avesta.org, http://www.avesta.org/rivayats/rivayat1.htm
- Zarathustra, Livius, https://www.livius.org/articles/person/zarathustra/
- Zarathustra, World History Encyclopedia, Joshua J. Mark, https://www.worldhistory.org/zoroaster/
- Zarathustra: The Rise of Zoroastrianism in Ancient Persia, Brewminate, Cristian Violatti, https://brewminate.com/zarathustra-the-rise-of-zoroastrianism-in-ancient-persia/
- Zoroaster, BBC, https://www.bbc.co.uk/religion/religions/zoroastrian/history/zoroaster_1.shtml
- Zoroastrianism, Britannica, https://www.britannica.com/topic/Zoroastrianism
- Zoroastrianism, History.com, https://www.history.com/topics/religion/zoroastrianism

- Zoroastrianism, Zoroastrian Heritage, K. E. Eduljee, http://www.heritageinstitute.com/zoroastrianism/index.htm

Video Resources

- *On Wings of Fire*, Persepolis Productions Inc. https://www.youtube.com/watch?v=fIUODqdwYuM
- *The Sanskrit Origin of the Word Khuda*, Subhash Kak, YouTube, https://www.youtube.com/watch?v=KH7sYdl-8bg
- *Vedic Root of Western Religious Traditions*, Suhotra Swami, https://www.youtube.com/watch?v=cZONEhQZGXo
- *Vibration Chant of Zorastrian Prayer Yatha Ahu Vairyo*, Meherzad Patel, YouTube, https://www.youtube.com/watch?v=zkA5427vUkg